the
DM
diaries

OTHER TITLES BY TEAGAN HUNTER

SEATTLE SERPENTS SERIES

Contemporary Sports Romantic Comedies

Body Check

Face Off

CAROLINA COMETS SERIES

Contemporary Sports Romantic Comedies

Puck Shy

Blind Pass

One-Timer

Sin Bin

Scoring Chance

Glove Save

Neutral Zone

TEXTING SERIES

Contemporary New Adult Romantic Comedies

Let's Get Textual

I Wanna Text You Up

Can't Text This

Text Me Baby One More Time

Textin' Up My Heart (novella)

SLICE SERIES

Contemporary Romantic Comedies

A Pizza My Heart

I Knead You Tonight

Doughn't Let Me Go

A Slice of Love (novella)

Cheesy on the Eyes

ROOMMATE ROMPS SERIES

Contemporary Romantic Comedies

Loathe Thy Neighbor

Love Thy Neighbor

Crave Thy Neighbor

Tempt Thy Neighbor

STARS SERIES

Contemporary Upper YA Emotional Romances

We Are the Stars

If You Say So

the

DM

diaries

TEAGAN HUNTER

 Montlake

Published by Montlake, Seattle

www.apub.com

Amazon, the Amazon logo, and Montlake are trademarks of Amazon.com, Inc., or its affiliates.

ISBN-13: 9781662519475 (paperback)
ISBN-13: 9781662519468 (digital)

Cover design by Letitia Hasser
Cover photography by Regina Wamba of ReginaWamba.com
Cover image: © kantimar kongjaidee, © Zlatko Guzmic / Shutterstock

Printed in the United States of America

To Aimee,
for being my biggest cheerleader and pushing me out
of my comfort zone. I can't imagine doing this with
anyone else by my side.
Thank you for believing in me.

CHAPTER ONE

Jude

"You're a Rafferty, dammit. You tell them you don't want your dressing room filled with flowers. That's how you fix it."

"It's stupid to complain about flowers, Jasper. I don't want to come off as a diva." *Like you.* "I'm trying to break onto the scene, not burn bridges in it."

I run a hand through my dirty-blond hair, realizing too late that I shouldn't have touched it. It was perfect, and I'm 90 percent sure that if the hair-and-makeup team saw me do that, they'd beat me with their brushes.

Rising from the couch that's giving me a backache, I tuck my phone between my ear and shoulder and rush over to the mirror to ensure I didn't screw up my hair. I feel every bit like the diva I swore I wasn't as I listen to my brother ramble on the other end of the line.

"Trust me, I've made much more demanding . . . well, demands. Like when I had a splitting headache—I made them change all the bulbs in the room to green ones because I read an article that said they reduce photophobia. It isn't bad to ask them not to leave those awful-smelling things out of your room. Nobody will bat an eye."

My older brother is probably right, but I know I am too. I don't want to be the jerk who has the outlandish rider everyone in the industry talks about behind his back. I'm just now starting to make a career that's not clinging to the coattails of my family name, and I don't need that reputation.

I rub my temples, pacing the room's length and counting every step I take.

One, two, three, four, five, six, seven, eight.

I spin on my heel, then do it again in the other direction.

One, two, three, four, five, six, seven, eight.

I haven't even gone on air for the first interview of my new movie's press junket, and I'm already about to vomit.

Fucking hell. Being Jude Rafferty is exhausting.

I guess it comes with the territory of being the son of the one and only Joel Rafferty, a four-time Oscar-winning actor who married two-time Oscar-winning Camilla Owens. With both my grandfathers receiving countless awards and lists of credits that are miles long, my parents' marriage combined two of the most prominent Hollywood families, creating a legacy I now carry around like a ten-thousand-pound weight on my shoulders.

It's safe to say that nearly everything I do is watched and scrutinized, including this interview. I *have* to nail this, or I'm toast.

"Just do it. Nobody is going to think you're a diva," my brother says.

"I highly doubt that. Remember when Hugh Reynolds asked for whiskey in his mug instead of water or coffee, and now nobody wants him on their show? He was branded a diva."

Jasper snorts. "He was branded a liability."

"Fine. A liability *and* a diva."

My brother sighs. "You're being dramatic, Jude."

"I'm being honest, and you know it. You've been in this industry long enough to know what it's like."

"I've also been your brother long enough to know when you're being dramatic—and you're being fucking dramatic."

"I called for moral support. Not whatever this is."

"Honesty?"

"Jasper . . ."

He laughs. "You'll be fine. Look, I have to go. I'm on a date."

Of course he's on a date. All he does is date. I swear he's worse than DiCaprio some days, always with a new woman on his arm or being photographed on boats with bikini-clad ladies. They aren't nearly as young, however. Jasper would never.

How he has time for all that, I'll never know. I'm nowhere near as well known as he is, and my schedule is packed.

"Am I—your favorite younger brother—not more important than some date whose name you won't remember tomorrow?"

"Who said you were my favorite?" he asks, avoiding my dig. It's true, though. He hardly ever remembers the women he dates, and I highly doubt this one is any different.

"Well, I am your *only* brother, so . . ."

"I'm not letting you win by default. The Rafferty family doesn't *let* anyone win anything. You have to *earn* it."

Ah, there it is—the family motto.

While I'm thankful my family isn't one of those Hollywood institutions that leans into nepotism, I think it would sometimes make my life easier. Like maybe I could have landed a leading movie role years ago instead of at twenty-six. I'd hoped that after my tenure on that god-awful tween show was over, I'd be able to make *some* sort of career for myself. But that wasn't the case. I had one big offer after *Lakedale* ended. I thought for sure *Eternity* was going to be the next big hit, but I guess we missed the vampire craze by a few years, because it was canceled after one season.

Even with the failed ventures, I know I'll be happy when I finally accept my Oscar and can say I did it alone. Well, mostly.

"Besides, if I had a favorite sibling, it would be Cait."

"Cait? What the hell for?"

"I'm sorry, but have you tried her peanut butter fudge?"

Of the three Rafferty kids, Cait is the only one who didn't go into acting. Instead, she opened a bakery here in New York City, and business is booming. When I attempted to stop by last week, the line was wrapped around the corner. While I love my sister something fierce, there's no way I'm subjecting myself to a wait like that when I can get free goodies on the holidays.

"I haven't."

"What? You live like ten minutes from the shop!"

"I've been a little busy lately, Jasper."

He scoffs. "I just wrapped filming on not one but *two* movies. Go visit your damn sister, Jude."

"I kind of have a movie to promote right now."

"I'm aware since we're basically on the same schedule. Look, I'll be back in the city next week. We can go together."

"Together?"

All *three* Rafferty siblings in one building? Cait's small bakery would be swarming with paparazzi. No way that'd go over well for any of us.

But, being swarmed by photographers or not, it sure would beat waiting in this tiny room with these awful flowers.

"Yes, together. Just trying to drum up business for my *favorite* sibling."

"First off, fuck you."

"That's right, little brother. Get all your cussing out now so you don't do it on *live* TV."

I groan. "Ugh. Why'd you have to remind me it's live?"

"Because I'm a good brother."

"No, you're not. In fact, you're officially my *least* favorite brother."

"I'm going to wear that badge with pride." I can practically hear him grinning, and I don't doubt it's true. That's Jasper for you. He thrives off being annoying.

"Whatever."

"Goodbye, Jude—and good luck."

"Bye, Jas. Love you."

I get the all-too-familiar grunt back before the line goes dead, leaving me with a smile. That's good because I need it there. I'm five minutes away from walking out onstage for a live *Good Morning, New York* segment. I *hate* live television. It's the part of this gig I despise the most. They always ask the same questions, and I always give the same answers. It's tiresome, and it all feels so . . . fake. Like the interviewer doesn't truly care about what we're discussing. It's painful. If I could act and never have to deal with all the other crap that comes with it—interviews, premieres, or the press—life would be perfect.

But people who do that don't have long careers, and that's what I want. I want to act—and I want the world to know that Jude Rafferty isn't just another Rafferty. He's something special. *I'm* something special.

"I'm special," I mutter, trying to believe the words.

"Um, that's nice and all, but you're also on in five."

I whip my head around to find the door to my dressing room wide open—*When did that happen?*—and an intern or someone staring at me, wearing a grin that tells me this whole moment is going to end up on some gossip site.

Great. Just what I need.

I toss myself back onto the couch, groaning as the woman practically runs away from the dude talking to himself.

My eyes wander around the horribly decorated dressing room. Why they paired an ugly, uncomfortable burnt-orange couch with dark-green walls is beyond me. It reminds me of peas and carrots, a combination I was never fond of growing up. Then they had to go and add a massive bouquet of *chrysanthemums*—a flower I happen to be allergic to—on the coffee table and vanity.

I scratch my nose. It's already feeling itchy from the flowers. Or maybe it's me being "dramatic" again.

I roll my eyes, and the minute I do, I sneeze.

"Crap," I mutter, pushing myself up from the couch and heading for the small vanity in the corner. I tug open the drawer and am unsurprised to find a slew of last-minute necessities, such as breath mints, gum, candies, face wipes, deodorant, aspirin, and some allergy meds.

Another sneeze races through before I can even reach for the travel-size box.

"Thank god," I mutter, pulling it open and plucking free two pink pills. I toss them into my mouth and grab a water bottle from the mini fridge, then douse my hands in sanitizer before sitting back on the couch.

I close my eyes, trying to block out the offensive decor and the throbbing in my head that's already set in, and take a deep breath.

Inhale, exhale.

Inhale, exhale.

I do it over and over, sucking in and blowing out slow, steady breaths to calm the nerves racing through me.

Why in the hell does live television freak me out so much? It's a camera. I'm used to being in front of cameras. Hell, I make a living being in front of them. This shouldn't be any different.

But it's because if I mess this up, I'm screwed. Sure, most shows aren't recorded live, but *Good Morning, New York*? It's *live* live. You can't get any more live than this show. Everyone knows it—meaning if you mess up here, there's no fixing it. No telling them to cut and no editing out all the bad stuff. It's out there, forever, on the internet. If that's not panic inducing, I don't know what is.

It would be so much easier if Jasper were with me like we originally planned, but his damn agent had to move things around at the last minute, so I'm here alone. I don't want to be here alone.

"I'm going to puke."

"Oh, great. You're talking to yourself again."

I sit up, almost too fast, and see the intern is back.

"We're ready for you." She curls her finger, beckoning me to follow her before adjusting her headset.

I rise from the couch, trying my best to ignore how shaky my legs are—*Is this from nerves or the medication?*—and follow her out of the room. She's at least six inches shorter than me, but she's practically running down the hall, going so fast that my six-foot-two frame struggles to keep up. I run a hand down my shirt, ensuring my clothes aren't in too much disarray as I trail behind her. I want to tuck my tail and return to my terrible dressing room. Hell, I want to run out of the building. I'd rather be anywhere other than here.

But I can't be.

I have a movie to promote. Obligations. I have a door I want to knock down, rooms I want to be in, and people I want to rub elbows with. I can handle one live interview. What's the worst that can really happen?

I follow her down a darkened hallway, nodding and smiling at the people running—literally—around the cavernous studio, all of them with headsets and frowns plastered on their faces. I swear I see someone crying. It does nothing to calm the panic racing through me.

A guy with his head down rushes by, slamming into my shoulder as he passes.

"Sorry," I mutter to him, but he either doesn't hear me or doesn't care. He's too busy staring at the clipboard in his hands and yelling at someone in his mic.

If I thought a movie set was full of mayhem, it's nothing compared to this madness. The studio could easily double as a warehouse, especially given its size. The only things saving me from feeling like I'm inside some alternate-universe version of a Costco are the thin walls blocking the audience from seeing the chaos of what's happening. Sure, they make seeing where you're going hard, but who cares when you're about to be on TV, right?

Another sneeze hits me, and I cover my mouth and nose with my arm. The PA comes to an abrupt halt near a small, round bar table situated at the entrance of a short hallway that leads to the main stage. It's tucked away from sight and, luckily, has a box of tissues and bottle of water atop it. I take a few tissues, wipe my nose, and then face the intern with what I know is a shaky smile.

"You good?" she asks, holding her hand up to her headset, I guess talking to someone on the other end.

I stand there with my hands tucked into my pockets, waiting for her to finish so she can give me instructions.

She blinks up at me.

I blink at her.

"Um, hello? Only used to talking to yourself and not someone else?"

Was she . . . "I'm sorry. I thought you were—"

She waves her hand, cutting me off. "It's fine. Here." She brandishes a bottle of sanitizer from out of nowhere. I hold out my hands as she squirts some into my palm, and I rub them together as she sticks the bottle into her belt. Only then do I realize she's wearing a construction worker's tool belt, but it's packed with hand sanitizer, tissues, a hairbrush, mints, and about ten other things I can't make out. "Come on. We're on in fifteen."

"Fifteen seconds?" The words come out as a squeak.

"Now ten. Get ready." She touches my elbow, steering me farther down the hall and closer to the final curtain, which separates me from my impending doom. "And maybe don't vomit on live television, okay?"

She shoves me closer to the curtain, and I trip, barely catching myself before I fall flat on my face.

Oh yeah. This is going to be a disaster for sure.

"Our next guest is none other than Jude Rafferty. You may know him as the star of *Lakedale*, a quirky teen show from several years ago, or . . ."

The unease in my stomach grows as they go over my list of accomplishments.

"Five . . ." the PA whispers.

Oh no.

"Four . . ."

"And soon you'll know him from *Love and Arson*, the upcoming, sure-to-be-a-hit film by world-class action-film producer Larry Brickey . . ."

I'm going to puke. It's going to happen. Do I really want to act this badly?

"Two . . ." she murmurs. Then she points at me and mouths, *"One."*

No, no, no.

"Here goes nothing . . ."

I take a deep breath, then step under the bright lights.

CHAPTER TWO

Olive

"Holy smokes, Olive, these photos are incredible! You look hot!"

"Oh, stop it."

"I'm serious. Your fans are going to flip out."

"They will, huh?" I smile as I scroll through the camera roll, my roommate looking over my shoulder from her spot on the couch next to me, checking out her handiwork.

Annie may be a badass nurse by day—technically night, since that's her usual shift—but she's also an incredible photographer. Our apartment gets the most beautiful lighting at twilight, the kind of golden glow I've come to associate with the city, so more than once, I've enlisted my best friend's help to snap a few photos of me in whatever outfit tickles my fancy that day. I doubt my following would be as big as it is without her help in getting the perfect shot.

"Thank you. *Again.*" I grin at her.

She bumps her shoulder into mine. "Anything for my favorite girl." She crinkles her nose. "Well, second favorite. I guess Daphne is my first favorite."

"Ugh." I toss my head back dramatically. "That kid is always stealing my thunder. I feel like I should challenge her to a fight or something. The winner gets all your affection and attention."

"You can't fight her, Olive. She's four."

"She's four," I mimic as I swipe through the photos, only halfway kidding about Annie's adorable blonde niece stealing all her love and attention. Daphne *is* really cute, so I guess I'll allow it.

"Oh, that one!" Annie points at my phone. "Post that one."

"You think? It's not too . . . bland?"

"Are you kidding me? No! Nothing is boring in this dress." She runs her fingers over the sleeve of the shimmery golden material that's the star of tonight's mini photo shoot—a new piece from my favorite boutique that caters to plus-size women like me. "It's perfect. Plus, that sexy pout of yours is on full display. People will eat it up."

"Yeah, I guess." I pull up the photo Annie loves on my editing app and adjust the lighting to keep my feed's aesthetic cohesive, but that's all I touch. I refuse to do any facial or body changes, like smoothing this or flattening that, because I've worked hard to love my body the way it is.

"Besides, I've seen the comments on your photos," Annie continues. "You could wear a trash bag, and your fans would still flock to see what Olive O'Brien is wearing."

I tested this theory once and posted a photo of me in a beige jumpsuit that I *know* was not the least bit flattering. Two days later, I saw two women on the street wearing the same jumpsuit, heels, and accessories.

I love my followers, but sometimes I question whether they actually like *me* or just the version of me they have in their heads. I'm not one to shy away from being real, but I also don't share everything. I have a certain set of rules in place to try to keep some parts of myself to . . . well, myself.

"And as much as I'd love to take that photo," Annie continues, "I have to run. My shift starts in twenty minutes, and you know how wild the city can get on Fridays. I'm sure we're already fifty people deep in the waiting room, so I may as well get there early to help if I can."

She rolls her big brown eyes, as if she doesn't thrive off the hospital's chaos, then rises to her feet, her adorable blue scrubs hugging her curves. She wants to talk about me being able to wear a trash bag and making it fashionable—she's one to talk. She makes her scrubs look like they belong on a runway.

"Have fun tonight," she says as she tugs her trusty cardigan off the rack near the door. She's always complaining the hospital is cold, and not a day goes by where she doesn't leave the house with that ratty old thing. "And remember, if you drink too much, call Remi. He'll happily—"

"Annie," I interrupt with my own eye roll. "I know. Love you, Mom."

She narrows her eyes playfully at the nickname. "Love you too," she says as she backs out the door.

I laugh when I hear her lock the handle and dead bolt.

She's always looking out for me, even offering up her adorably nerdy boyfriend to meet me wherever I am in the city so I'm never on the subway alone at night. He'd do it too. The man worships the ground she walks on.

She doesn't know that even though she always offers Remi up, I've never once called him. The number of times I go out vastly differs from how often she *thinks* I go out. In fact, most nights, I dress up and take photos, then stay home.

Which is precisely what I'm planning to do tonight.

I rise from the couch, then unzip my dress as I make my way to my bedroom. After putting the dress back in my closet, I cross my tiny room and pull my favorite pair of sweats from my drawer. They say HARVARD down the side, a school I never attended, and there are at least three holes in these things, but I can't let them go. They belonged to my father, who *did* attend the Ivy League school, and remind me of simpler times. Times when I wasn't spending my evenings doing my makeup and dressing in expensive clothes only to snap a photo, take it all off, and curl up on my couch for the rest of the night.

While I love earning money in fashion—an industry I adore— sometimes it's lonely.

Sometimes *I'm* lonely.

I have friends and plenty of things to do, but it's still hard. I wish I had someone to talk to about it. My mother, bless her heart, doesn't understand the industry in the slightest. Whenever I try to explain what I do to her, she gives me a blank look—like I'm speaking some alien language. Talking to Annie about it isn't easy because she's doing actual challenging work, always on her feet, bustling through the hospital halls, saving lives every night. What business do I have complaining about my career when she's a literal hero?

After sliding on an equally hole-filled shirt, I head to the kitchen to pour myself a glass of sweet white wine. I'd much prefer a sweet red, but this is all we have, and going to the store is not an option. I've already taken off my bra. I am officially in for the evening.

With my glass full, I pluck a box of cheese crackers from the cabinet—an extremely healthy dinner, I know—then climb through the window and out onto the fire escape we've turned into our patio. It's not much: a small table, two chairs, and enough room for me and Annie to relax out here after long weeks. But it's ours.

I connect my phone to the Bluetooth speaker, then hit Play on some Taylor Swift. Nothing says sad and lonely like drinking wine and listening to *Red* on a Friday night.

"What a glamorous life I lead," I say before taking a sip of the wine.

With a sigh, I peel open the box of crackers and pop a few into my mouth as I pull up Instagram.

I scroll through my feed as I shovel food into my mouth, pausing only to write out a new generic comment.

Awww, love it! Total babe!

Soooooo cute! x

HOT!

I don't know these people—not really. They're just internet friends, and by *internet friends*, I mean people whose accounts I follow and who have no clue I even exist. Their accounts are sitting pretty over that one-million-follower mark, sometimes even two million. I only wish I had their following or brand deals or the means to visit all the different countries they travel to.

Don't get me wrong—my numbers aren't small, I have some good brand deals, and I do get to travel a little for shoots. But compared to them? I'm a nobody.

And, unfortunately, that's my favorite thing to do: compare myself to them.

Though I know I shouldn't do it, it's hard not to. They're gorgeous, effortlessly so. People flock to their accounts, and I know that whatever they link to in their storefront gets thousands and thousands of clicks. *They* are what I want. I want that support and that reach. But it's hard being a plus-size model in this industry, especially when you want to make a difference by helping women feel good about themselves while helping the planet.

It's taken me too long to love myself to let that happen. As much as I would benefit from a larger audience or support or reach, I'll be damned if I ever give up that feeling because I could make more money by partnering with brands who aren't truly size inclusive or don't push for more sustainable business practices. After fighting tooth and nail for the small space I've eked out in this community, I'm grateful for what I have, even if I am still in an uphill battle to belong.

I do my rounds on all my favorite accounts, then toss my phone to the side, focusing on the brightly lit city around me.

New York is buzzing. It always is—especially in Hell's Kitchen— but it's a Friday, so it's extra noisy. Horns are blaring, people are shouting, and music is thrumming through speakers up and down my block.

It's chaos, and I love it. Hell, I *thrive* on it. It's a far cry from my small hometown, and I couldn't be happier.

I munch on crackers and sip my wine, watching the street below, where someone walks by wearing a dress that could double as a shower curtain. Another person passes in a suit, screaming into a phone attached to their ear. Some young kid skates by on Rollerblades, jumping over a cardboard box.

I grin to myself, loving everything I see.

A couple strolls by, holding hands, smiling at one another like they're in their own little music video or something.

My smile slips.

I want that. I want *all* that—a person to understand me, to accept me, to support me. Sure, Annie does those things, but having a best friend isn't the same as having a partner.

Ugh, I'm so pathetic. Sitting home alone, drinking wine in holey pajamas while staring at my phone, and eating crackers for dinner . . . How sad for me.

"You're a real catch, Olive. It's shocking that you're single," I mumble, then take another sip of my wine. I want to guzzle the glass, but I don't want to drink it all too fast. Not only because of the headache that would surely follow but also because it's the only bottle I have, and I want it to last.

Truthfully, it's not *that* shocking I'm single. I've dated over the years, but nothing serious has stuck. I'm sure that has everything to do with my lack of getting real with someone, but can I really be blamed? It's scary enough putting yourself out there because you don't want to get hurt, but it's even scarier when you've gone through the trauma of losing someone you love tremendously at random. It tends to make you a little wary of getting close to people for fear of losing them.

I grab my phone again and bury my face in my newsfeed, as if that will make me feel better or something.

I scroll through two photos before I'm faced with yet another happy couple.

"Ugh!" I set my phone aside. "Screw it."

I grab my wineglass and toss the last of the alcohol back, then head inside for another pour.

When I crawl back through the window to the fire escape, I settle into my chair once more, throwing my feet up on the rail and closing my eyes as the cool late-August air flows over me. The sounds of the city pull me into a lull. If I'm not careful, I'll fall asleep out here.

I set an alarm on my phone just in case and am surprised when I see a notification waiting for me.

I learned long ago to turn off my notifications if I wanted any real sort of work-life balance, but there are a few I make an exception for, and the one I'm staring at is on that short list.

Jasper Rafferty has posted an image.

I click on it and an image of Jasper on a talk show fills the screen. The caption is the same thing "he" always posts: the place and the date. That's it. It's obvious his account is run by his publicist or someone else on his team of minions, because everything he posts is generic. None of it is real. All cultivated and fake, fake, fake.

It's probably why I feel so comfortable with my own secret little hobby—messaging him.

Well, it's more like using his DMs as my own personal diary, but still.

When I started seeing my therapist, Ingrid, last year after breaking up with a third guy in as many months, she suggested that, to work through the trauma I'm still carrying—largely from my father dying of a sudden heart attack at forty-four—I journal to process my emotions.

I highly doubt she meant using a celebrity's DMs as that journal, but that's what I did.

Jasper, who is too damn talented for his own good, uncharacteristically posted a throwback photo of his family at Disney World, and it instantly brought me back to the time before my dad's company took off and he'd scraped together every penny we had to take us on vacation in Florida. We stayed in an old, musty motel and lived off peanut butter and jelly for the entire week, but damn, did we have fun. It truly was magical, and not only because of where we were.

So I responded to his post, telling him the story.

Of course, he never saw it. How could he? He's Jasper Rafferty. He has no time for peasants like me. His inbox is flooded with thousands of messages daily. Mine was just another added to the pile.

But after I wrote him, it changed something in me. It felt beyond good to let go of memories and feelings I had been holding on to for so long. So I kept going, and before I knew it, his DMs had become my journal.

I zoom in on the image he posted, looking into his bright-green eyes, which have no doubt gotten him cast in multiple roles with their sparkle alone. He's perfect leading-man material—six foot three, with dirty-blond hair and a smirk that could make my panties disappear in 0.2 seconds. Everything about him is flawless, from his straight teeth to his deep, rumbling voice. But he's not only pretty; he's also a phenomenal actor, able to take on all kinds of roles with ease.

In my perusal of his profile, I see a ring around his picture, indicating he's posted a new story, too, so I click on it. The first slide is just a repost of what he's added to his feed, but the second is different.

An emoji of a palm tree, an arrow, and then the Statue of Liberty. *He's on his way to New York.*

I swipe up and my thumbs fly over the keypad.

@OliveMe: The first time I came to New York, I was with my father on one of his business trips. It was my first time visiting a big city like this, and I couldn't wait to explore. On our flight, he fell asleep and snored so loudly that I cried because I was embarrassed. That was the first and only time I got to go with him anywhere for work.

I hit Send, letting the message slip out into the ether like all the others. That's what makes me feel so comfortable spilling all my secrets to him—knowing he'll never, ever read them.

I scroll back through the dozens of other messages I've sent him.

@OliveMe: I woke up today feeling ready to take on the world, but then I saw my dad's old business partner in line at the coffee shop and broke down in the bathroom. It reminded me of a different family trip we took to NYC when I was a senior in high school, and how we went around to all the usual tourist attractions. Meanwhile, I went and fell in love with this place, vowing to live here one day. I do live here now, and I love it. But it's still so hard without him. He wouldn't understand that I'm a model, but he'd be damn proud of me anyway. I miss that safe space he gave me.

@OliveMe: Annie swore today that if Remi doesn't make a big move soon, she's ending things. I think she's being dramatic. It's clear they're in love. It will happen for her. I know it will. Relationships move at different paces. Just because they've been together for a long time and aren't engaged or married, it doesn't mean their relationship isn't going anywhere. They're moving slower, that's all. Or maybe she's watched one too many rom-coms and wants a big, grand gesture of love. Then again, what girl doesn't, right? Plus, Remi is kind of a goof sometimes. I think he wants the same things she does, but he's too dang . . . well, Remi to do anything about it. They both need to stop being too scared to go after what they want and do it.

@OliveMe: I watched Shut Up and Kiss Me last night. You were a total jerk in it but got the girl anyway. Rom-coms are weird.

@OliveMe: My dad used to take me bowling at this tiny run-down place in Iowa. I have no idea if it's still even open or not, but today, when I was going for a walk, I passed by a vendor with a popcorn machine, and it smelled exactly like the stale stuff they used to sell there. It made me think of him. And it made me want stale popcorn.

@OliveMe: I'm a fraud. I pretend to be this fun, city-loving party girl, but the truth is, I prefer the quiet of my own apartment. Do you ever feel like that? Like nobody ever gets to see the real you? I'm tired of pretending. Tired of hiding. But I'm scared the real me isn't enough.

@OliveMe: I booked a big shoot today with Mitch Dirkson!!!! I wish I had someone special (other than Annie) to celebrate with. I don't, so a night in with wine and ice cream will have to do. Glamorous life, huh?

Next to each entry is a "delivered" check mark, but he has not looked at my messages, and I'm glad about that.

With a grin to myself, finding my little secret amusing, I close out of Instagram, then set my phone on the table. I relax into my chair, tip my head back, and close my eyes as the sounds of the city wash over me.

It's a long way from where I was born, a small town in Iowa. But I knew at ten I was destined to live here. After that last trip I took with my parents, I obsessed over it, and when it came time to apply for colleges, NYU was at the top of my list.

I was denied.

In fact, every college I applied to in New York rejected me.

But I was at a point where I *had* to leave Iowa, and I wasn't about to let a few rejection letters stop me. After some thorough searching—and my mother's final approval—I found Annie online, looking for a roommate for her Hell's Kitchen apartment, so I hopped on a plane and moved my entire life here. I haven't regretted it for a second.

It's been seven years since I left the small town and even smaller farm I grew up on, and my mom still isn't exactly happy about the move, but I don't care. I had to do it for myself, because there was no way I could have continued living in a place where everybody knows your business and then some. It was a constant reminder of everything I had lost. I craved something new and exciting, something to re-spark my joy.

I found it here with Annie and within the modeling industry. It's not without its tribulations, but it beats the alternative—working a dead-end job in a small town where I see my father's ghost at every turn.

But that's not what I want to think about tonight.

Tonight, I want wine, my favorite cheesy crackers, and relaxation.

"I spoil myself," I mutter sarcastically, bringing my wineglass to my lips.

"Are you talking to yourself again, dear?"

I jump at the sudden intrusion, spilling wine from my glass and all over my lap.

I glance over to find Mrs. Hammish squinting at me from next door, her head—completely covered in curlers—hanging out of her window.

"Yes, Mrs. Hammish. Sorry if I was bothering you."

"Nonsense." She waves her hand. "You don't bother me. You just make me sad."

I groan inwardly. Great. Even my eighty-something-year-old neighbor thinks I'm pathetic.

"I'm also sad because I lost my damn glasses again."

"Is that why you're squinting at me?"

"Well, obviously, kid," she says in that raspy voice I've come to love over the years. "Help an old lady out, will ya?"

"Sure." I barely hold back my sigh as I push out of my chair.

"Oh Lord. Did you pee yourself, dear? They have diapers for that, you know."

"It's just wine, Mrs. Hammish."

"Well, good. Now, come on already. I ain't got forever. I'm old."

"Coming, Mrs. Hammish."

I crawl through my window, thinking again about how glamorous my life is.

Lucky me, huh?

CHAPTER THREE

Jude

"Come on, Jude. It wasn't *that* bad."

My sister sets a plate of fudge on the table before me, and my mouth waters at the sight of the decadent pieces of my very favorite flavor—Orange-Cream Swirl. I grab a piece, shoving it into my mouth like a starved man.

I refuse to be embarrassed by the moan that leaves me the second it hits my tongue. It's perfect. Pure heaven.

Just like this bakery, Cait's Confectionery. This is a little slice of paradise my sister has carved out for herself. She transformed what was once a Hell's Kitchen pizza shop into a funky little bakery that somehow makes you go *What the hell am I looking at?* and *Wow, this is cool!* all at once. It's full of eclectic art pieces and decor that make zero sense while perfectly working together all at the same time. Add in the fact that this place constantly smells like fresh fudge and coffee, and it's the perfect haven to escape to whenever you need something to cheer you up.

After yesterday, I needed this. Having my brother and sister here, too, is a bonus.

I chew the fudge, swallow, then run the back of my hand across my mouth in a way that would earn me a glare from my mother. "That's easy for you to say, Cait. You weren't the one who cussed twice, walked off the stage at the wrong time, *and* tripped so badly you ripped your pants and showed all of New York your Snoopy underwear. Oh, and then did *finger guns* to the camera as you continued off."

I hold back a groan just thinking about it. Those damn flowers are to blame for all of it. Well, that and the medication I took, which made me loopy as hell. I'm not usually that embarrassing . . . right?

"Okay, that part was hilarious," my sister—younger by a short fifteen months—tells me, barely able to hold back a laugh.

I drop my head to the table and lightly bang it against the wooden top a few times for good measure. "I'm a laughingstock."

"You're not," my brother says, and I can tell he's trying to keep a straight face. "It's not *that* bad. The Snoopy underwear isn't ideal, and I have lots of questions about it—but it could have been worse."

I lift my head. "Well, for you, sure. You're *you*. Everyone loves you, Jas." I toss another piece of fudge into my mouth, convinced it will make me feel better. It does, but only minimally.

He scoffs into the coffee he's just lifted to his lips. He takes a small sip of the steaming-hot liquid before setting it down. "They do not. I get plenty of bad press."

"Not like this, though. It was awful."

"I saw it. You'll be fine."

"You saw it?"

"What? I have the internet." He shrugs like this is no big deal, when really it is. Jasper is never online. It's not his style. He has social media accounts, but he doesn't post on them. His assistants do. For him to have seen the video, it has to be big. "Mom texted it to us."

Oh, hell. My *mother* has seen the video?

"With a laughing emoji," Cait adds.

"She what?" I instantly feel bad for my outburst. Yelling at my sister is bad enough, but yelling at my *pregnant* sister is even worse. If my calculations are correct, she's just hit the fourteen-week mark. She and her longtime boyfriend weren't expecting to get pregnant, but they're taking this curveball in stride with their usual love and excitement. I'm beyond happy for them and cannot wait to spoil my future niece or nephew. It's a major reason I decided to get a place here in the city too. Plus, being close to my parents isn't bad either. They spend more time here now than they do in Los Angeles.

Cait winces. "Was I not supposed to say that?"

"I don't think you should have added the emoji part," Jasper tells her. "But you have to admit, it *was* funny."

They both look like they're seconds away from bursting into laughter just thinking about my complete and total failure.

I *knew* I should have never told my publicist I'd do the interview. I should have put my foot down and told her no.

But I didn't. I said yes because I didn't want to rock the boat or be branded as difficult.

I grumble again, and Jasper's big hand comes down on my shoulder in a comforting pat.

"Don't sweat it too much. It'll all blow over in a day or two."

"A day or two? That's forever in internet time!"

"I've already seen a parody video," Cait stage-whispers. "And a meme."

"You're really not helping," Jasper says, but I can hear the urge to laugh in his voice.

"You're both traitors. My least favorite siblings."

"We're your only siblings. We can't be your least favorite."

"Can and are too."

"Now that's just mean, Jude."

"And laughing at your little brother isn't?" I shake my head. "My career is over."

"It's not. I've done my fair share of stupid shit, and look at me." Jasper waves his hand around. "I'm thriving. Hell, I closed an entire bakery with my presence alone."

"Excuse me, but *I* closed an entire bakery because it's *my* shop. Not to mention, I only did it because you're both too busy for your pregnant sister anymore, and this is the only way I could get you two alone. I need more sibling time before the baby comes."

Cait's words do what she intended—make me feel guilty.

I was surprised to find Jasper standing outside my apartment this morning. Not just because I was shocked my doorman let him up, no questions asked, but because he'd said he was working and wouldn't be in the city until next week. I guess after my misstep on live television, he felt he needed to come in early.

Even if they're giving me shit, I'm glad my siblings are here to help me through this.

I've been replaying yesterday morning in my head for more than twenty-four hours now. I didn't sleep a wink last night. I just kept refreshing my Google Alerts.

The Youngest Rafferty Falls Flat on His Face Twice—At the Box Office and On Live TV.

Jude Rafferty: Is He Why the Rafferty Family Isn't What It Used to Be?

Is Jude Rafferty on Drugs?

That last one made me laugh.

Drugs? Please. I'm this stupid all on my own, thank you very much. The allergy meds were good but not *that* good.

"Do you want me to do something equally embarrassing to take the heat off you?"

"You'd do that for me?"

Jasper laughs. "Fuck no. I don't want that attention."

I narrow my eyes at him. "Asshole."

He blows me a kiss, and I catch it in the air, then crush it between my hands. He reels back in faux offense, and I smile for the first time in more than a day.

It's funny because, to the outside world, the Rafferty clan is Hollywood royalty. We're household names on so many levels.

But to us? We're just that—*us*.

We're not actors. People don't know our names. We're just siblings who argue and have fun like other ordinary people. Moments like these remind me of that and make me forget I'm now an internet sensation for all the wrong reasons.

A sigh escapes me as I remember that I'm the world's latest punch line.

"Stop thinking about it," Jasper says. "It could be worse."

"Yeah, but it could also be better," Cait points out.

"Not helping," Jasper tells her with a glare.

She lifts her hands in innocence. "Sorry. It's true, though. I'm just glad I'm not in the spotlight like you two idiots."

"Hey, you're famous in your own right."

"Yeah, but I don't want to be." She screws up her lips. "All this extra stuff . . . it sounds exhausting."

She has no idea.

Well, maybe she does. Cait tried the whole acting thing when she was younger, determined to go into the "family business" and all, but promptly discovered that being center stage is *not* her thing. She left the industry after a few guest spots on shows, shifted her focus to creating delicious desserts, and never looked back.

Sometimes I think she's the only sane one out of us. She definitely seems the happiest right now. And she should be happy. Her shop is making a killing. It's been featured on two of the city's most prominent food blogs, and people flock here to grab the new fudge flavors she whips up every week. This place is nothing to sneeze at, and I couldn't be prouder of her.

"Thanks for closing the shop for me," I tell her. "I'm sure you're missing out on a big day."

She shrugs. "I am, but you're family, and family comes first. Besides, Jasper offered to cover my lost wages."

"I did?" He raises his brows, clearly surprised by this turn of events.

"Not yet, but you're going to."

"I am?"

"Yep. Because I'm your favorite sister and because I promise not to tell the parents about you breaking the Tiffany vase."

He throws his head back with a groan. "That was like ten years ago."

"Try two."

"And it wasn't my fault," he continues. He points at me. "You shoved me."

"Because *you* called me a dick," I retort.

"Well, you were *being* a dick."

"I don't think it's possible for Jude to be a dick," Cait cuts in with an eye roll. "He's like the nicest guy ever."

"So, so nice," Jasper agrees.

"Just the best."

"The bestest of the best."

They're mocking me. I know they are. They *always* mock me.

I can't say I blame them. I *am* nice. Just yesterday, I didn't want to tell *Good Morning, New York* that I was on the verge of an allergic reaction because I didn't want to rock the boat.

That's nice. *Too* nice.

"He can hear you, you know. And he thinks you're *both* dicks." I cross my arms over my chest, glaring at them.

They burst into laughter, not caring at all.

"Oh, come on, Jude." Cait grins at me. "It's true, but it's not a bad thing to be nice."

"Except for when you strung that poor girl along for *three years*," Jasper adds.

"I didn't want to hurt her."

"Yes, what you did was *so* much better."

"Well, Jas, considering she cheated on me, I'd say so."

"Oh shit." His eyes widen. "I forgot about that."

"I didn't," Cait says. "Sophie was my best friend."

Jasper and I exchange a look. Cait doesn't miss it.

"What? What's that look about?" she asks, glancing between us.

"Nothing," I say with a shrug.

Cait shakes her head. "No, it was definitely something. What was it?"

Jasper sighs. "It's just . . . Do you *really* think she was your best friend?"

"Yes, of course I do."

Another glance at my brother, who is about to break my sister's heart. I should stop him, but maybe it's time she hears it.

"She was using you, Cait."

"To get to us," I agree.

"What? She was not! We . . . We . . ." Her shoulders deflate. "Oh my gosh, she was using me."

I wince. "Sorry, sis."

She exhales heavily. "It's fine. Wouldn't be the first time it happened."

Jasper pats her shoulder. "I'm sorry. It's truly unfair to have such talented and attractive brothers that everyone wants to bone."

She elbows him off her. "Not *everyone* wants to bone you."

"That's not true. I'm totally boneable."

"More like a total bonehead." Cait rolls her eyes.

"You should see the people at the parties I go to. They throw themselves at me left and right."

"They just want to say they took a famous ride," Cait suggests. "They don't really like you because they don't really know you."

That. It's one of my biggest problems being in the entertainment industry. Nothing is real and everything feels fake. Even with my parents' successful marriage proving it's possible for relationships to survive in Hollywood, I still struggle to have faith in anything real.

It sucks because I think something real sounds nice.

Bang! Bang! Bang!

A loud knock on the bakery's front door has Cait nearly jumping out of her chair.

"What the . . ." She rises to her feet, her hand over her chest. "Who is that?"

"It's me! Open up!"

Oh shit.

"It's Dylan," I say. "I forgot she was coming."

"Dylan? Your publicist?"

I nod, pushing to my feet and going over to the door. I fumble with the three latches—a little overkill, for it just being us in here—then slide the door open enough for her to squeeze by.

"You have three cameras pointed at this shop from across the street," she says by way of greeting, tugging off her scarf as she walks farther into Cait's shop. "Everyone knows this is your sister's place." She pulls off her jacket, handing it to me as she continues to ramble on. "They're putting two and two together, Jude, so we need to work fast; then you sneak out the back way before it gets rowdy out there."

When she's finished, she looks up at me with bright hazel eyes and pursed red-painted lips.

I grin down at her. "Hi, Dylan. How are you?"

She narrows her eyes, but it's not scary with the smile that's curving over her lips. "Hi, Jude. I'm fine—much better than you, Mr. Snoopy Drawers."

I wince and she laughs, patting me on the cheek.

"Don't worry. We'll get it figured out," she reassures me. "Now, here's what I'm thinking: I'll get in touch with some of my contacts to get something set up. You need a date. A big name. Someone who's already making headlines for all the right reasons. We get you a spot at the hottest restaurant and get the paparazzi there. Give them something else to focus on while we clean up everything behind the scenes. If they see you out looking and acting normal, they may lay off the druggy headlines. But until I can get that set up, I need you to do damage control. Post on social media. Make jokes about what happened. Get people talking about it, but in a good way." She points at Jasper as she approaches the small table where we've been sitting. "You. Help your brother. Make some posts for him."

"I don't do social media."

"What? Of course you do. You—"

"My assistant handles all that."

Dylan stares at him blankly, clearly unimpressed, something I find funny because Jasper *always* impresses people. "Can you get me the log-in information for your Instagram?"

"Yeah, but—"

"Perfect." She pulls her phone from her back pocket, her long nails making a soft *clack, clack, clack* noise against the screen as she types faster than I ever could. "Send it to me. Your brother can post for you."

Jasper frowns, not seeming to like having my publicist boss him around.

I wouldn't say I like it either.

"Do I get a say in any of this?" I ask.

Dylan laughs loudly. "No. Not at all."

"But—"

"Do you like Italian?" She shakes her head. "Never mind. It doesn't matter. It's not a real date, all for show." She snaps her fingers. "Let's do three dates. That way, it gives us more opportunities to show up in the headlines. Maybe a morning coffee run too." She looks around the shop. "This place won't do—we'll find somewhere else."

I glance over at Cait, who looks like she's about to burst with anger.

"I'm sorry," I mouth to her.

She exhales heavily, giving her head a slight shake.

Oh, I'm totally going to hear about this later.

"Dylan . . ." She barely glances up from her phone when I call her name. "This is a bit much, isn't it?"

That gets her attention.

"'A bit much'?" Her perfectly sculpted brows shoot up. "No, it's not *a bit much*. In fact, it's probably not enough. You're going to be in the headlines for weeks, Jude. We're in full-blown recovery mode. You have weeks left of press junkets, and you fumbled your first interview. There's no way that you won't be under major scrutiny now."

"Won't the internet just laugh it off?" my sister asks.

Jasper, Dylan, and I look at Cait like she's a fool. And she just might be, suggesting something like that.

"Sure." My publicist crosses her arms over her chest. "The kids on TikTok might laugh, poke fun, then move on, but the headlines? Those are going to be singing an entirely different song. I already have *fifty* emails in my inbox asking if Jude has a drug or alcohol problem, plus three more from executives at the studios asking if they need to be worried and threatening to pull the plug on the press junkets. Those are all from the walk from my hotel to here." She laughs sardonically. "The internet making memes and parodies is the least of our worries."

Cait's eyes are wide as she takes in Dylan's words. "That is . . ."

"Absolutely preposterous? I know."

My sister gulps, wringing her hands together. "Scary." Her eyes flit to mine. "How are you going to fix this?"

I look at Dylan, who is giving me her best *trust me* face. I've been working with her for years now, and at any inkling of scandal, she's always been on top of it, getting rid of it before it even has the chance to spread. I *should* trust her. And not just because she genuinely scares me but because she's good at her job.

But these dates . . . they aren't *me*.

I've tried the whole dating-in-the-spotlight thing before. It didn't pan out well. Yeah, that was years ago, after *Lakedale* had ended, but I know it's not for me. If I'm going to date—which I'm not planning to do anytime soon—I want it to be on my terms and, preferably, quietly.

"There's nothing else I could do?" I question my publicist.

"Sure. You could take more drugs and embarrass yourself on television some more. Maybe next time they'll get a shot of you in your Teenage Mutant Ninja Turtles underwear instead of Snoopy."

"He has those," Jasper says, not helping in the least.

"And ruling that out," I say, ignoring my brother completely, "we have no other options than fake dates?"

Dylan sighs. "Jude. We're trying to keep your name in the headlines, but for *good* reasons. We'll find someone worthy to link you to, and all the hubbub of your little allergic reaction will fade away when you're deemed the next *it* couple. Trust me on this, okay? This is the best way to go."

I hate myself for thinking it, but . . . Dylan's right. I can't count the number of times a celebrity has been in the headlines for something like this, then has landed back in them the next week because of who they were dating. It's a distraction tactic.

And much to my chagrin, it's one I know will work.

One I *need* to work.

After auditioning tirelessly for months, I finally scored a callback with Larry Brickey, a legendary producer in the industry known for his big-budget action films. By some miracle—and, yeah, probably some nepotism, if I'm being fully honest—I landed the lead role in *Love and Arson*, and it's expected to be the biggest action film of the year. I spent months training for it, packing on twenty pounds of muscle and working with dialect coaches to get my character's southern accent down perfectly. Hell, I even did most of my own stunts, too scared to give up control and allow anyone to do any harm to all the hard work I had put in.

It's a true labor of love, and I *need* this to do well in theaters. Not just so I can get more leading roles, but because I spent too long working on this for it to flop. There is no way I'm not going to give this my all, even if it means selling my soul to Dylan and going on a stupid publicity date.

"One date," I tell her.

She grits her teeth, her jaw tightening with tension. "Two."

"One."

With a twist of her lips and a wrinkle to her nose, she sighs. "Fine. One date."

"I won!" I fist-pump the air.

"But, Jude?"

"Hmm?"

"*I* pick your date."

A grin slides across her lips as the one I'm sporting falls.

I didn't win. *She* did.

And now I'm totally screwed.

CHAPTER FOUR

Olive

"Can anything today go right?"

The line for my favorite coffee truck is already eight people deep, almost reaching the end of the block and snaking around 9th Avenue. I don't really have the time to stand in it, but there is no way I'm going to a shoot without a drop of caffeine in me, especially not after the night I had.

I slide into the back of the line, irritation growing by the second.

It's nobody's fault but your own, Olive.

I mentally flip my inner voice the middle finger, then step forward when the line moves.

Oh, goody. We're moving. Maybe this won't take forever after all.

"Hey, folks. We're about fifteen minutes out on orders. We appreciate your patience," JT, the truck owner, says as he flashes everyone that same bright-white smile he gives me every morning.

A few customers grumble over the inconvenience, but unfortunately for me, not a single person leaves the line. Not that I blame them. This truck is easily one of the city's best hidden gems. The coffee is delicious and just strong enough, but the sweet treats are on a whole different level of amazing, and I plan to partake in one—a blueberry–cream cheese danish—this morning.

I wait and wait . . . then wait some more, all for a sip of that delicious caffeinated nectar of the gods I desperately need. I'm thankful I wore a dress and a wide-brimmed hat today, because the morning sun beating down on me is no joke. I really don't need to add *sunburn* to the list of issues I'm having.

I was up entirely too late with Mrs. Hammish last night. She had me looking for her glasses until midnight; then I couldn't fall asleep until nearly 2:00 a.m. because my brain wouldn't stop spinning. I missed the first alarm on my phone, which went off at seven, then managed to sleep *two more hours*, effectively making me run late for the huge shoot I have today—the same one I'm supposed to be at in half an hour. With the way this line is moving, I'm barely going to make it in time.

We finally begin to move at a consistent speed, and I can see the end in sight.

"Just two more customers, then that sweet, sweet caffeine is all mine," I mutter.

The person in front of me turns around, giving me an odd look for talking out loud to myself, but I ignore him. Must be new to New York if he's concerned with someone having a conversation with themself.

Another one goes, then it's just the two of us left standing.

He steps up to the counter and places his order—and finally, it's my turn.

"Morning, Liv. Give me just a minute."

"Take your time," I tell JT as he turns to fulfill orders. I check my phone for the twentieth time since getting in line.

Fifteen minutes.

That's all the time I have to get to this shoot, which is still another ten-minute walk away. And that doesn't account for extra foot traffic or any mishaps along the way. I am so going to be late. I'm—

"What can I get for you?"

I look up, mouth open and ready to order, but it's pointless. JT isn't talking to me. He's talking to someone else.

Someone in front of me.

"Hey!" I call out to the line cutter, wanting desperately to knock the hat he's wearing right off his head. "I was here first."

The intruder turns on his heel, and I stumble backward, tipping my head back to glare up at him.

All kinds of things, like *Get lost* and *Back of the line, jerk*, sit on the tip of my tongue, but they disappear in a flash.

This man—whoever the hell he is—is gorgeous. Like movie-star-level handsome, with the kind of cheekbones that would make Henry Cavill jealous.

And he's peering down right at me.

Not like I can see his eyes, since they're hidden behind a pair of aviators that do nothing but reflect my own oversize sunglasses, but I can certainly *feel* them boring into me.

I let my covered eyes trail over him, noting the most perfectly cut jawline I've ever seen. It's covered in stubble, but not the kind that's from going a day or two without shaving. No. This is the intentional kind of stubble. The *hot* kind.

The kind that makes your panties just a little wet at the sight.

No. No wet panties. Not for this guy and his damn lickable jaw.

"I'm just getting a drip coffee," he explains, as if that should be reason enough for me not to be upset that he just cut the line.

Spoiler alert: it's not.

"Then get in the back of the line like everyone else." I hitch my thumb over my shoulder, just in case he's unaware of where the line begins, which most certainly isn't in front of me.

"Why? So you can stand here playing on your phone, holding everyone up? Some people have important things to do today, ya know."

I glower at him through my sunglasses, not appreciating his remark. As if, somehow, he's so much more important than me. "*I'm* not holding anyone up. That would be you, line-jumping like some entitled asshat."

His brows peek out from over the top of his sunglasses, and the corner of his full lips twitches. "Asshat, huh?"

His voice is deep and rumbly and full of amusement, but I don't find any of this funny. Not even a little.

"Yep," I tell him without hesitation. I don't care who this guy is—an asshat is precisely *what* he is.

The twitch transforms into a full-blown smile, perfectly straight white teeth on full display.

Holy . . .

Don't react to the perfect smile, Olive. Do. Not. React.

When I don't bite at his charming smile—which I'm sure has gotten him out of many similar situations over the years—it slips, but only a little.

Instead of continuing to argue with me or going to the back of the line like he should, he turns back to JT.

"Can I get—"

"Hey! No!"

"—drip coffee?" he finishes, completely ignoring me.

"Ass!" I shout at his back, and his shoulders shake.

His shoulders shake.

He's laughing.

Even worse, he's laughing at me.

I growl, stomping my foot because that's what this has turned into—me being so damn annoyed that I'm acting like a kid.

He must hear the growl and stomp because his broad black-T-shirt-covered shoulders shake again.

"You . . . You . . . ass!"

He points at me with his thumb. "And whatever Little Miss Sunshine wants."

"Little Miss Sunshine"? Is this guy for real?

"I can buy my own coffee, thank you very much."

He looks at me over his shoulder. "I'm sure you can, but how about we just call this my treat for cutting?"

"Ha!" I point a single finger at him. "You admit it! You cut the line!"

He shrugs, then gestures for me to step up to the truck, like *I'm* holding *him* up. I don't move. Screw this guy. I'm not letting him feel like some hero for paying for my coffee when he's the one out of line—literally.

Instead, I stare at him, waiting for him to back down. But he doesn't. He stands there with his arm out, waiting on me.

What this asshat doesn't know is that I'm stubborn as hell when I want to be, and right now, I *really* want to be.

He deserves it.

I stare and stare, and the longer I do it, the more I realize that something about him seems familiar, but I can't place just what it is. Is it his voice? His smile? I'm also positive that I'd remember if I'd met this man before, so it's probably just my caffeine-deprived brain making me see things.

Besides, how could he look familiar with sunglasses and a hat covering most of his face? That's absurd.

The person behind me grouses, but I still don't move. It's not happening. Over my dead body.

Asshat lifts his brows again in a way that says, *Well, are you going to order?*

I lift mine back, telling him, *Get bent.*

"I got it," JT says after a few moments of silence, punching the kiosk screen, looking every bit amused by our standoff.

"No!" I protest, but it's totally pointless.

JT's partner, Ric, is already stuffing my favorite blueberry–cream cheese danish into a bag. He then grabs a clear plastic cup and fills it three-quarters of the way with cold brew before adding almond milk, two packets of sugar, and a squirt of caramel sauce on top. He does it so automatically and fast that it's ready before I realize it.

I guess that's expected when you've been patronizing the same coffee truck almost every day for the last three years.

Asshat hands over a shiny black card and drops a twenty into the tip jar.

What kind of guy goes around cutting in line like he's the most important person in the world, then does something like buying a stranger coffee *and* tipping well?

It's so . . . so . . . *Ugh.*

I hate it on principle, but I can't help but feel as if he's redeemed himself.

But only a little. Like the most minuscule amount ever.

He grabs my coffee and danish from the counter and holds them both out to me. I look at them, then back at him, hating how badly my hands itch to accept his generosity.

But then again, my petty is out to play today.

I fold my arms over my chest, waiting for him to give up.

He doesn't.

"Just take them," the annoyed person behind me grumbles. "This little pissing match between you two was cute for about two seconds, but now I'm bored and need coffee. Move."

Pissing match? Cute? Please, this guy is a prick. There's nothing cute about him or what's happening right now.

But the Midwesterner in me has me stepping out of the way by habit, and Asshat follows, my treats still in his outstretched hands.

He shakes the coffee and pastry. "Come on. You know you want them."

Just the simple act of shaking the bag has the delicious scent of danish hitting me, and my stomach growls at the idea of food.

The crackers I had for dinner last night didn't cut it in the least.

He laughs again, and *that's* what snaps me from my stupor.

I snatch the bag and coffee from his hands just to make him go away—and I try not to react when our fingers brush together. Try not to think about how soft his skin feels. Or how much I like the fact that his damn smile is back.

He turns, grabs his drink from the counter, and sips.

"Ah. Refreshing." Another smile. "Have a good day."

He tips his head at me, then breezes past like the last five minutes didn't just happen, leaving me standing there like a fool with the scent of pine and coffee and something all *him* permeating my senses.

"Hey, Sunshine!"

I turn.

I don't know *why* I turn, but I do.

Because I know. I *just know* it's him.

"You're welcome for the coffee."

He lifts his cup, nodding at me once, then turns and disappears into the crowded New York streets.

All I can do is stare after him, thinking, *What the hell just happened?*

◆ ◆ ◆

"You're late, Olive."

I pause midstride and squeeze my eyes shut. Maybe she won't see me if I can't see her.

"Again, I might add."

Crap. She totally sees me.

I tried my hardest to sneak into the photo shoot without letting my manager catch me first, but I should have known it would be impossible—Uma sees all.

I shouldn't be surprised. It's been like this since day one, when she signed me after I hounded her for months with my portfolio. She swore she'd make my life better and worse all at the same time—I laughed it off then, but she wasn't kidding. She's perceptive and smart and one of the best damn managers in the industry, but she's also a total hard-ass when she needs to be and not afraid to hurt feelings.

Which is why, when I peel my eyes open, the disappointment I see in her hazel eyes has my heart hammering in my chest. I *really* don't like a pissed-off Uma.

Pasting on my best smile, I rush into a *very* believable story.

"Some asshat jumped the line at the coffee truck; then, when I was just half a block down the street, I spilled that stupid coffee on myself, so I popped into Cuties & Curves. By the way, if you haven't checked them out yet, you should. Amazing stuff there *and* it's all sustainable, so totally on brand and one of my favorite shops with great people working there. Anyway, when I found something fast and went to pay, their card machines were down. But since those ladies are amazing, they gave me the dress for free, and here I am!"

I end my speech by throwing my hands in the air, then waving them over the bright-purple maxi dress—a far cry from the lemon-colored sundress I was wearing earlier this morning. I even throw in a little twirl, hoping Uma will let me have this one after my disastrous morning.

After what feels like hours of her staring at me with hard eyes, she twists her lips, and a slow smile finally breaks out.

She shakes her head. "Only you, Olive. Only you."

She'd be right. I swear, I have a day like this at least once a week. Well, minus Asshat at the coffee truck.

I'm still annoyed over the whole thing and his stupid smug smirk when he called me *Sunshine*. Like *I* should thank *him* for being a jerk.

"Come," Uma tells me, giving me her back. "Let's get you into hair and makeup. We'll have to settle for a simpler look since we're short on time now, but I think it will all work out."

I follow her to the other side of the set, sending a small wave to the other model currently in front of the camera, striking all the different poses for our photographer, Mitch.

Mitch Dirkson is one of the most respected photographers in the fashion industry. He's done photo shoots for almost every prominent magazine, so being in front of his camera today for the campaign I'm shooting—an organic energy drink that gives ten cents for every can sold to a charity that provides greenhouses to communities in need—is a complete and total pinch-me moment. I've worked with him in a group shoot but never one-on-one like this.

"Think he'll be mad?" I whisper to Uma as I trail behind her.

"Please." She waves her hand dismissively. "Mitch won't even notice. Now, had you come in looking like hell on toast, we'd be having a different conversation." She looks down at my dress. "Send me the info for the store because I *need* that dress in orange."

That's Uma's thing. She *loves* orange. Orange jewelry, orange shoes, orange clothes, orange nails, orange cat . . . Everything is orange with her.

"Curls. Big ones we can play around with," Uma tells the stylist before hurrying off in the opposite direction. She's always on the go, that one. Constantly barking out orders and moving on. She may seem abrasive to some, but that's just who she is. She doesn't mean a thing by it. She's a busy woman with little time.

My butt barely hits the seat before two hands are shoved into my long chestnut locks.

"Ugh, I just *love* your hair, Olive," Bliss, a hairstylist I've worked with many times over the years, says as she drags her hands through my tresses. "I swear, if you ever cut this, I'm quitting."

She lets out a loud laugh, one I've grown to love, and then sets to work sectioning off my hair for curling.

"Olive, so good to have you back in my chair," the makeup artist, Frannie, says, popping up out of nowhere. "Just moisturizer and sunscreen, right?"

I nod. "Of course. This isn't my first rodeo, Frannie."

"I love models who know what to do." She claps her hands twice before turning around and grabbing a palette off the vanity.

They set to work on my hair and makeup, prattling on and on about dates and parties and every other fun thing they do in their lives.

I let them gab, grabbing my phone and angling it away from them the best I can while I check Instagram. I respond to a few comments and messages before scrolling through my feed.

I'm just three swipes into it before I stop.

"Ugh. Jasper," Bliss says from behind me, and I know she can see what I'm looking at by her words alone. "I swear, Fate was a cruel creature the day Joel Rafferty and Camilla Owens got together. It's completely unfair to the rest of the world that those two made the most beautiful humans to exist."

"I just hope they own stock in a few underwear companies because their offspring are melting panties everywhere," Frannie adds.

I let out a snort. She's not wrong.

Jasper is a whole different level of gorgeous, so I'm currently zoomed in on his picture, looking into his perfect lime-green eyes.

"Who is that next to Jasper?" Bliss leans in closer, bringing her curling iron dangerously close to my head, if the sudden heat I feel is any indication.

"Let me see." Frannie sticks her face in front of my phone's screen. "Click on the tag," she instructs. I do, and she gasps. "No way! That's little Jude Rafferty!"

"Shut up!" Bliss hisses. "That's impossible. Isn't he still in college? I thought he left Hollywood after they canceled that vampire thing he did."

"No, no. He's older now. Maybe twenty-five?" Frannie taps her perfectly manicured finger against her chin. "Or is he only twenty-four? I can't remember—but I swear I saw him in something else recently." She snaps her fingers. "It was one of those cop dramas! He played the bad guy for a few episodes but got killed off." She juts out her bottom lip. "A shame, too, because he's not bad to look at."

I shift my eyes from the oldest Rafferty to the younger one. Jasper has his arm thrown around his brother's shoulder; they're both grinning at the camera, a clear view of the New York skyline behind them. Frannie is right. Even with his face partially hidden by the shadows being thrown off from whatever party they're at, Jude isn't bad to look at by any means. He has the same dirty-blond hair as his brother, but his eyes are different. They're green, too, but darker than Jasper's. Not as bright, but still so captivating. Like he's hiding secrets behind them. Like the crinkles at the corners tell so many stories.

There's something about him that looks a little familiar, but I shake my head. *Of course* he looks familiar—he's a Rafferty. They all have those green eyes and blond hair.

"You totally saved that pic, didn't you?" Bliss teases, sending me a wink in the vanity mirror when I tuck my phone into my lap.

I laugh. "Of course."

I didn't. I didn't even "heart" it. I never do. It's silly, considering I have zero problems sliding into his inbox and spilling my heart out to him, but he doesn't see those messages and never will. A like or a comment, though? That feels different.

Bliss and Frannie doll me up; then it's my turn in front of the camera.

"She's perfect," Mitch comments in that velvety English accent of his. He rakes his eyes over me. "Where did you get this dress? Don't change—it's perfect for the aesthetic of the shoot. Look." He picks up a can of the energy drink we're promoting, pointing directly at the purple blended into the background. "The color complements it well, and I *have* to shoot it. Get them on the phone about a deal."

"I'll call the store now," Uma tells him, pulling her cell from her pocket.

Mitch grabs pieces of my hair, pushing them out of the way and reframing them around my face to his liking. "There. Better. Now come."

The next half hour flies by in a blur of fake laughs and smiles and poses that make my body ache in places I didn't know possible.

"Next outfit!" Mitch calls out, finally giving me a break.

I let my body relax as I head for the wardrobe closet. I massage my face on the way, my cheeks hurting from smiling so much. As much as I love my job and being in front of the camera, sometimes I forget how exhausting it is to be *on* like this for a shoot. I'm typically sitting on my couch, posting photos and writing about fashion, without a stitch of makeup and wearing ratty clothes I've had for years. This is nothing like that, and I'm already tired after just thirty minutes in front of the camera.

From behind the curtain, I unzip my new dress—which I really hope makes it into the final campaign—and let it pool around my feet. I reach for my next outfit: a fun lavender jumpsuit that includes a cropped T-shirt to wear under it.

I let my fingers run over the soft, buttery material, remembering the days when I would never be caught dead in a bright color like this. I was too ashamed of my body to ever try to wear something that would *show* people I'm not a size zero, as if it's not already obvious.

But now? I hardly ever want to wear dark colors. I hate how they make me feel, like I need to hide in the shadows and never show off my body—the same body that's taken me places I never dreamed I'd go.

I've been mean to this body, calling it every horrible name imaginable. I've hidden it with ugly, baggy clothes. I've abused and *neglected* it by starving it or overexercising it.

But that's not who I am anymore. Now I thank this body I have. I showcase it. Cherish it. I love it—curves and dips and rolls and stretch marks and all.

"Back in ten!" Mitch calls from across the room. He gestures to Uma that he's going for a cigarette break, and I'm thankful for the reprieve.

I quickly change, sliding on a pair of white sneakers to complete the lavender-and-yellow ensemble, then enjoy a few minutes alone. I pull my phone from my pocket and am surprised by another notification from Jasper Rafferty. Posting twice in one day is completely unlike him. He's a once-a-week kind of guy—if we're all that lucky, that is.

His story loads, and I let out a soft laugh just from the look on his face alone.

"Bite me," he says grumpily into the camera trained on him, then flips his middle finger up with a scowl. Someone laughs in the background, and the camera is turned around. I glimpse a smiling Jude

Rafferty before the screen jumps to someone else's slide. I immediately swipe backward, dying to watch it again. But this time, it's not just Jasper's sullen expression that makes me smile—it's Jude's laugh and the sparkle in his eyes.

For all I know about Jasper, I know next to nothing about his younger brother. Truthfully, I never paid much attention to him, especially not with that ridiculous tween drama he starred in for years. It was so cringe and awful, and I have no clue how he could stand to act in it. After it ended, he disappeared and went off to college. I thought he was done with Hollywood, but according to Bliss and Frannie, he's back.

I wonder for a moment how that must feel—going off and living a normal life, doing a normal thing like going to school, then being thrust back into the limelight.

It has to be hard to navigate, that's for sure.

"Set!" Mitch's voice booms around the room, and I know he's calling for me.

I don't waste a second, stuffing my phone away and dashing into the studio. The last thing I want to do is upset one of the most respected photographers in the industry.

I don't need this day to get any worse.

CHAPTER FIVE

Jude

"Come on, man. Stop looking at the headlines. Just put your phone down. You're being a buzzkill, and we're here to have fun."

Here is a bar I didn't want to go out to. But thanks to Dylan and her scheme to get me back on the good side of the press, here I am—sitting in Diablo, the latest hot spot for celebs in New York, with my brother, having a few drinks and making sure I'm in perfect view of the paparazzi lined up outside with their cameras. From our spot at the bar near the window, we're giving them a glimpse into our evening together. I hate every second of it, but at least I have my brother here to keep me company in this god-awful place, which is packed wall to wall with people. Everyone is shouting at one another even though they're sitting just a few feet apart, because the music is too damn loud for such a small space.

After I managed to shirk them this morning and grab a coffee without a single camera pointed my way, Dylan was insistent that I show up tonight so they could get some shots. I was in no mood to argue with her, especially not after my run-in with Little Miss Sunshine.

She'd folded her arms over her chest and called me an *asshat* . . . It was the last thing I was expecting. I'm a Rafferty. Nobody has ever talked to me like that, but I liked that she wasn't afraid to call me out on my shit. Sure, I shouldn't have cut in front of her, but I felt feisty this morning, especially after having to sneak down the fire escape of my own damn building just to avoid cameras being shoved in my face.

"I'm not looking at headlines," I shout—the only way to be heard above the music—at my already buzzed brother while looking down at my phone, doing exactly that.

I know better—better than most—that I shouldn't be doing this, but I can't help it. I *have* to know what they're saying about me.

I just wish they were saying better things. I've seen articles declaring everything from my new movie that's not even out yet already being a flop to me checking into rehab.

But I think the worst of all? The "nepo baby" headlines.

Those headlines sting.

If they only knew all the grueling, long hours I put into my craft. All the time I've spent at auditions when I could have easily just called up any director and put a bug in their ear that I wanted a particular role and gotten it quicker than anyone would believe. I know my last name opens doors, sure, but I work hard at what I do, and I do it because I love it—not because I have to fulfill some family tradition.

I love being on set. I love slipping away into another world, where I don't have all these asinine expectations heaped on me because of who my parents and grandparents are. A world where I'm just Jude. Not Jude Rafferty.

Just Jude.

A hand closes over my phone, tugging it away from me.

"Hey!" I yank the phone out of Jasper's grasp. Lucky for me, his reflexes are shit thanks to the number of drinks he's had, so I wrestle the device back without much of a fight.

He slumps in defeat, his bottom lip jutted out in a look I haven't seen from him in . . . well, a long damn time.

Maybe he's a little more drunk than I thought.

I quickly snap a photo of him still pouting, then switch to Instagram and make another post to his account so Dylan sees I've fulfilled my promise. I turn the camera to myself and snap a pic, then upload that one, too, making sure to tag my profile in the photo before swapping back to the article I was reading.

It all feels so damn dumb, but I know this is the game Dylan wants me to play. She wants it to appear like I'm not affected by what's happening in the media. Like I'm hanging out with my older and much more famous brother and nothing is off with me, even though it couldn't be further from the truth. Because right now? I'm kind of freaking out.

I know my public mishap will create more buzz for my upcoming movie, which could be a good thing, but it also means that I will be bombarded with endless questions and stalked for photos for proof of all my alleged issues. I don't want that. I just want to act and be left alone. Is that too much to ask?

"I'm telling you," Jasper rambles on, "everyone will forget about it soon. Besides, that sassy little publicist of yours seems to have a good plan cooked up. Just sit back and let her do her thing and handle this one for you." He shrugs, lifting his bourbon to his lips and knocking back the rest of the glass.

I should probably tell him to cool it on the booze, but Jasper's a big boy. He knows when he's at his limit.

I'm guessing he's not. At least, not yet, with his gaze now on the blonde bartender who's leaning her forearms against the bar in a way that showcases her cleavage.

I pull my attention back down to my phone. I'm still logged in as Jasper; he's already at more than five thousand likes on the photos I posted moments ago, his notifications increasing by the hundreds every few seconds. My brother's career is massive compared to mine, and I know that's why Dylan wants him to feature me on his social media. He has reach that I don't, thanks to the several years I took off for college. As much as I hate to admit it, I need Jasper's help navigating all this insanity now that I'm being thrust back into it.

The bubble at the top of his profile keeps popping up, so I click on it, hoping it'll go away, but instead, it just pulls up the hundreds of messages that are flooding in. It's wild how many people are responding to the posts or dying for just a little bit of his attention.

I remember when I wanted that kind of fame and admiration, back when I was on *Lakedale*. I wanted to be everyone's favorite celebrity. But the older I got, the less I wanted it. And now I just want to make good movies and enjoy a quiet life. No fanfare. No attention. Just to live.

But . . . I can still live a little through Jasper. I scroll through the messages, curious about what people are saying. They're all pretty much the same thing.

> Ur so hot!!!! x

> I swear I'd let u do N E THING 2 me, Jasper. N E THING.

> I'd love to be in that sandwich.

> BRO! Where was my invite?!

> LOL Fun!

> Remember our night in Paris? Call me. Xo

The messages blur as I flick my thumb over the screen repeatedly. Each one is just another variation—all drivel and superficial, and a few that make me blush. I wonder if he's ever thought about setting it so only people he follows can message him, but then I remember this is Jasper I'm talking about—he's completely social media inept.

So I keep scrolling and scrolling. So many messages, so much begging for money or attention with inappropriate offers.

> I have a big photo shoot tomorrow. I'm nervous because . . .

I slam my thumb onto the screen, stopping the maddening scroll, then navigate back to the message that caught my eye.

It's so . . . boring. *Normal.* Different from all the other messages coming in, that's for sure.

But that's not all that sticks out. This person—whoever the hell they are—is talking to Jasper like they know him. Like they're friendly with him.

Curious, I click on the message.

"Holy shit," I mutter, my eyes widening as I take in what's before me.

Messages. Hundreds of them. So many that no matter how fast I scroll, I'm still not at the beginning.

They go back a long time.

One month.

Two months.

Six months.

A year.

A whole damn year. That's how long this person's been sliding into Jasper's DMs.

I let my eyes wander over the one-sided conversations this person has been having for so long, immediately recognizing what's happening.

It's a diary.

They've been using Jasper's inbox as a digital diary, probably assuming nobody would ever read it.

Until now.

Until *me.*

I'm sitting here scrolling through the messages like an asshole, completely invading their privacy.

But that's not exactly true, is it? They wrote these messages for someone to see. Maybe not me, but it's not stopping me from reading more about them.

I click on the profile, surprised to see it's not private. It's public. *Very* public.

In fact, *she's* very public, with half a million followers watching her every move.

A quick look at her bio tells me she's Olive O'Brien, a plus-size model—and apparently a damn good one, based on the company she has tagged. I've been in entertainment long enough to know that Uma Danford doesn't work with just anyone.

"Who are you, Olive O'Brien?" I murmur.

"What?"

I practically throw my phone onto the counter so Jasper can't see me snooping around his inbox, then peer over at him.

His brows are lifted high, and he looks at me like *I'm* the drunk one. "You good, man?"

"Yep." I swallow, nodding a few times. "Yep. All gravy."

Jasper scrunches his face like he's in pain, groaning. "Ugh, Jude. *This* is why you can't get a date that your publicist hasn't set up for you. You say weird shit like *all gravy*." He lowers his voice, mimicking me. Funny, because his natural voice is already deeper than my own.

I shrug off his comment. I'm not looking to date, so his words don't bother me. I'm too focused on bringing back my career to care about getting laid.

Besides, dating hasn't really panned out for me before. Nobody is interested in the real me. They just want Jude Rafferty, not *Jude*. I'll pass on being used again, thanks.

"Fuck." My brother shakes his head. "Now I want gravy. Let's split and get some chicken tenders and gravy. There's gotta be a diner around here."

As amazing as that sounds . . . "We can't go yet. I promised Dylan I'd stay until nine."

"Boo." Jasper pouts. "Can we at least order some food? I'm starving."

"You good with a pretzel?"

He grunts, and I take his answer as a yes. I call over the bartender and order a pretzel to split while Jasper asks for another refill.

"Why'd Dylan have you come here?" my brother asks after the bartender scampers off. "This place isn't your usual scene. I'd figured you'd rather be at a poetry reading than at some bar that's too damn loud and crowded."

"Poetry reading? I don't even like poetry." Though he does have a point about this place being too crowded.

"Then what do you call those things in your diary?"

Just the word *diary* has me feeling guilty for looking at the messages from Olive. I used to write all my thoughts down too—and I was mortified when Jasper discovered my journal and read aloud from it, back when we were teens.

I really, really shouldn't be intruding on her like this. It's wrong. *So* wrong.

But it doesn't stop the pull I feel to keep reading . . .

"You're daydreaming about your diary, aren't you?"

I stare daggers at my brother. "First of all, it was a journal, not a diary. Second, no. I'm not."

"Journal. Diary. Same damn thing."

"A journal is much more personal, which is why you're a total dick for reading it."

He shrugs, then nods toward the guy who has just dropped off a fresh drink for him. "Shouldn't have left it out in the open, then."

"I didn't!"

"Under your mattress is totally out in the open. That's where you're supposed to hide porno mags, not your diary. You lock that shit up tight."

"Journal," I reiterate.

He rolls his eyes. "If you didn't want me to read it, you should have moved it."

"I did move it. Several times. You just always snooped and found it anyway."

"That's your fault for being such a good storyteller. Are you sure you don't want to be a writer instead of an actor? You wouldn't have to deal with all this bullshit." He waves his hand around the bar. "You could be at home right now, safely tucked away in your office, plugging away on Hollywood's next big hit."

I've thought about what he's suggesting too many times over the years. I love writing in my journal—it's something I do to this day—but writing a screenplay? That's an entirely different beast. Besides, I like being in front of the camera too much. I could never give this up, no matter how much I hate all the other crap that comes with it.

"Nah. Not for me."

He lifts his now half-empty glass to his lips. "Suit yourself," he mutters before throwing back the rest of the booze.

How he's comfortable drinking like this in public is beyond me. I never let myself have more than two drinks outside the house. I don't like losing control in general, but I like it even less when cameras are constantly pointed at me—like they have been since we walked into this bar.

With the way Dylan talked about this place, I assumed it would be crawling with celebrities. But so far, it's just me and Jasper here, surrounded by crowds of regular twentysomethings looking to blow off steam. I wonder if my publicist has anything to do with that. Keep the attention solely on us.

"One pretzel with hot honey mustard." A plate slides across the bar in front of me, bearing a huge and delicious-looking pretzel covered in garlic butter sans salt, as requested. "Anything else I can get you?"

I shake my head at the bartender. "Nah, man. I'm good. Thanks."

"No problem," he says before hurrying off.

"Thank god. I'm starving." My brother rips off more than half the pretzel before I can even protest, and I really want to protest. I haven't eaten anything since this morning. I'm running on coffee, anxiety, and pure fucking adrenaline at this point. I need this more than he and his grubby little hands do.

He dunks the pretzel into the mustard, then shoves a huge bite into his mouth, smiling at me in a way that would have Mom pissed if she were here—all his food is showing.

"You're an ass," I tell him, taking a piece for myself.

"Your point?"

He sounds so unbothered as he helps himself to more of our snack, and I'm sure he is. Jasper's always been like that—completely indifferent to what others think of him. It's a trait I've always been jealous of because I care what people think. Probably a little too much, even.

"I don't know who you heard about these from, but whoever they are, I want to kiss them. Like a big, wet sloppy kind of kiss. This is fucking amazing." Jasper sticks his fingers into his mouth one by one, licking off all the pretzel's buttery goodness.

He looks like a damn caveman, but I get it—this thing is incredible, and we finish it off in record time. Before I can ask for another, Jasper orders one.

Oh yeah. He's creeping closer and closer to drunk. He always gets hungry when he's had too much.

"So Jude . . ." He starts, and I know I won't like whatever he's about to say next.

"So Jasper . . ." I mimic, resting my elbows on the bar top, wishing I didn't have that damn two-drink rule right about now.

"Think I could get Dylan's number?"

A burst of laughter flies out of me. That is not what I was expecting, making his question ten times funnier.

"Good one, Jas." I pat his shoulder, relaxing in my high-backed chair. "Good one."

He settles back, too, crossing his arms over his chest and glowering at me. "'Good one,' what?"

"Your joke. Asking for Dylan's number. It was funny."

His eyes narrow further. "It wasn't a joke."

"Yes, it was."

"No, it wasn't," he snaps.

That's when it hits me: he's being serious.

It's not a joke. He wants my publicist's number.

I mirror his pose. "You're thinking of changing publicists, then?"

He shakes his head. "Hell no. Kyle would have my balls if I ditched him, and I'd rather keep those intact for obvious reasons."

Kyle, his best friend—since childhood—turned publicist, totally *would* castrate him if Jasper left. Not that Jas wouldn't deserve it, but still.

Which only means . . .

I sit up straighter. "You want to date her."

He curls his lips. "Ew. Gross. No."

I relax at his words. Good. That's good. I don't want Jasper and Dylan dating. That's a bad idea for so many reasons.

"I just want one night, is all."

I snap my head toward him. "Are you serious? She'll eat you alive."

He grins. "I fucking hope so."

I shake my head with a laugh. "No. No way in hell. I am not giving her number to you. Ask her yourself."

"But she scares me."

I laugh again because, truthfully, she scares me too. "Then that's just something you'll have to get over, because you're not getting her info from me."

"I gave you full access to my Instagram."

"As if you ever go on it yourself anyway."

"It's still my page."

"Then kick me out of it."

He can't. I know he can't. He has no damn clue how the app works. He's never been a big social media guy, and I know he's "on" the platform reluctantly as it is.

"How's that going, by the way?"

"Fine?" I run a hand through my hair. "I don't know. I have no clue what I'm even supposed to be doing."

"Show everyone you're unaffected by the headlines. Be normal. That kind of thing."

"Normal?" I scoff. "I'm a Rafferty. Nothing about my life is normal."

He huffs out a laugh. "Ain't that the damn truth."

We don't talk much about what it means to be part of this family. We don't have to. We both feel the burden of it daily, Jasper even more so—I don't think he's taken a day off since he got his first role at eight.

Before we can dive headfirst into a way-too-deep-for-the-venue conversation about our family drama, a woman slides up next to Jasper. They flirt back and forth, and he offers to buy her a drink, which naturally sweeps her off her feet. Before I know it, Jasper's ditching me for the girl and her friends.

I don't mind. I'd much rather be left alone, anyway.

"Don't wait up, little brother." He gives a suggestive smile.

"Wear protection, big brother," I counter.

He flips me off, and I laugh as he trots off with his flavor of the night like he didn't just beg me for my publicist's number.

Fucking Jasper.

I shake my head, then pick up my phone off the counter.

"Just thirty more minutes, and you can bail, Jude," I tell myself. If I look foolish, who cares? I'm already in the headlines for much worse.

I could leave early, especially now that Jasper's ditched me, but I promised Dylan I wouldn't, and I'm a man of my word.

I pull up Instagram again just as Jasper's now-forgotten pretzel appears on the bar top. With one hand full of stolen food, I tap my phone's screen twice, and Olive's page roars back to life.

With all Jasper's antics, I almost forgot I was about to cyberstalk some random woman on his profile.

And now that I'm looking at her, I'm forgetting why I shouldn't.

From her long brown hair to her summer-blue eyes to her full figure—her hips are hypnotically round, and her belly has a bit of squish to it—to the way she carries herself . . . it's all there.

She's gorgeous, and it's no wonder she has a modeling contract with one of the top management agencies in the world.

Something about her seems familiar, though I can't figure out just what it is. Have I seen her in a campaign somewhere?

I shrug it off, continuing to stalk her through her feed. In her latest post, her brown hair is styled in big curls. She stands on a Manhattan rooftop, gazing directly into the camera, a pouty look on her face as she angles her body to show off the curves beneath a golden dress shimmering against the soft sunset in the background.

The next one is of her in a Barbie-pink jumpsuit, a pair of white sunglasses tugged down her nose, and she's looking over her shoulder, calling attention to her bright baby-blue eyes.

The photos go on and on. So many of them. Some are themed, and some aren't. But she looks gorgeous in each one.

It makes me curious about the person behind the photos. I swipe back over to the messages and begin scrolling back.

Some of them are about funny, random things, like the time she was on the way to a photo shoot and got pooped on by a pigeon. But some of it's serious. Too serious. Like so serious that my heart begins to race because I *really* shouldn't be reading this stuff.

And yet I can't look away.

The more I read, the more interested I become. She seems . . . normal. Which sounds stupid, but after growing up in the world I did, normalcy is a good thing. Olive is lucky she has it.

I crave normalcy as much as I crave being in front of the camera. It's . . . confusing.

"Damn, man. You ate that fast."

I startle at the sudden intrusion, looking up from my phone and at the bartender for the first time in I don't even know how long. I take in the empty plate before me, the pretzel long gone. I was too engrossed in scrolling through Olive's photos and personal thoughts like some creep.

"Oh, um, I guess it's just that good, huh?" I send him my best *on* smile.

True to my other interactions with him, he doesn't smile back. He grabs the plate and walks away, and I turn back to the messages I shouldn't be reading.

@OliveMe: I have a big photo shoot tomorrow. I'm nervous because it's with a photographer who could skyrocket me to a new level of modeling. I want that. I think. Is it weird to be excited and grateful but also completely and utterly terrified? That's what I'm feeling right now, but maybe it's just the wine talking.

My fingers hover over the keyboard, itching to know how the shoot went, which is ridiculous since I've never met this woman.

But if she's brave enough to do this, maybe I *should* know her.

Don't do it, Jude. Just click out of it. Pretend you saw nothing and move on.

This is Jasper's account. It would be wrong to pretend to be him. I shouldn't.

But . . . I'm curious about her. I want to know more.

No. I *need* to know more.

So, for the first time, I do something reckless.

I hit "Accept" on her messages, and I type.

@JasperRafferty: How'd the shoot go?

I set my phone down with a shaky breath.

Then I lift my hand to the bartender and break another rule tonight. "I'll take that third drink now."

CHAPTER SIX

Olive

My day got worse.

It got *majorly* worse.

The shoot was long and exhausting. Mitch is an incredible photographer, but damn, he's demanding. I discovered this little trait of his when he went through the images on one of his smoke breaks, hated every single one, and insisted I switch outfits for the umpteenth time *and* get my hair pulled into a dreadful high ponytail. It lasted two hours longer than I was scheduled for, which made me late for a meeting with a plus-size shop interested in partnering with me. They were kind enough to be understanding, but it still made me feel like crap, being late for the second time today.

Then, thanks to a group of high schoolers thinking the subway was a fun place to party, my train home was shut down for more than an hour. It was hot and muggy and awful being trapped in the car, so not one or two or even three fights broke out—it was four.

Not even my noise-canceling headphones could drown out all the madness.

I deserved some damn pizza after all that, which is why I'm just now getting home at nearly nine o'clock, with a fresh and steaming-hot pie.

"I come bearing pizza!" I yell to Annie as I walk through the door, letting it slam behind me.

"Coming!" she calls back, which I know is Annie speak for *I need at least five more minutes.*

I drop my things at the door and toe off my shoes before padding across the small apartment to the kitchen counter. My phone vibrates against my ass as I peel open the box of cheesy goodness, and I pluck it free.

The screen blazes to life, a photo of my smiling father looking back at me, and I give him a wink before pulling down my notifications bar. There's a whole mess of new messages flooding in, probably due to my latest post about my shit day. I don't typically post about my bad moments, as I try to keep my profile positive, but sometimes they get the best of me, and I feel like I have to say something for the sake of authenticity. Today's post about being kind to strangers and taking into account the fact you never know what someone else is going through felt warranted, especially after the whole coffee incident this morning.

I swipe them all away as I grab a slice of pizza, skipping the plate—saving water by not doing dishes, right?—and taking a bite as I settle onto my favorite stool. I shimmy my shoulders back and forth, my own little happy food dance, before I take another nibble, my phone still vibrating with new notifications. I click on my Instagram app and am met with at least thirty messages waiting for me.

I want to ignore them so badly, but I don't have that luxury. I am full-blown into this social media game, which I know means that the first hour of posting is the most crucial. The faster I respond to messages, the better my stats are.

So that's what I do. I start going through them one by one, sometimes sending generic responses, sometimes more thoughtful ones. I'm moving through them robotically, picking up another slice of pizza, when one catches my eye.

I pause.

Dragging my phone closer to my face, I squint, carefully reading the bolded name.

Jasper Rafferty.

No. It's a joke. A total *ha ha, got you* joke.

But the profile picture is the same—I message him often enough that I would know.

With a thick swallow, I click on the unread message.

The loudest, most high-pitched sound hits my ears, and it takes me only a second to realize it's *me* making that noise.

I slap my hands over my mouth, but it's too late.

Annie barrels down the hall. "What? What happened? What's wrong?" She charges at me, her eyes wide with panic and worry.

I have no clue what she's worried about. It's *me* who is having a complete meltdown right now.

"What happened, Olive?"

I open my mouth to tell her, but no sounds come out. I can't speak. I'm in shock.

"Olive, what's wrong? You're scaring me." She steps in front of me and begins running her hands over my arms, taking my wrist, and checking my pulse. "Are you hurt? Where is it? What happened?"

Leave it to Annie to go into full nurse mode.

But it's enough to snap me out of my stupor. I swat at her, trying to get her to stop feeling me up.

"Knock it off," I demand. "I'm fine."

"That was *not* an *I'm fine* kind of scream." She narrows her eyes. "I swear, if you did all that screaming over another damn spider, I'm going to tit punch you."

Even though there was no spider, I cover my chest anyway. Her tit punches hurt.

"It wasn't a spider," I tell her, noting how *she* also covers her tits.

"Then . . ." She looks around the kitchen. Her eyes land on the pizza, then the greasy mess on the countertop, then down, down, down, all the way to the floor, where the slice of goodness has slid off my lap and is now lying face down, creating a nasty mess I am not looking forward to cleaning up.

"Did you just throw perfectly good pizza on the floor?"

"Yes."

"Why? Was there something on it?" More eye narrowing. "Was it a pineapple again?"

"I'll have you know that finding a chunk of pineapple on my pizza is a perfectly good reason to scream."

"It's delicious, and you're delusional if you think otherwise."

"I'm starting to think otherwise about our friendship," I tell her.

She crosses her arms over her chest, ignoring my threat. "What happened?"

I blow out a steadying breath, finally releasing my tits, feeling safe from any punches.

I slide off the stool, careful not to step in the pizza mess, and grab my phone.

I let out a relieved sigh when I see the screen isn't cracked, but that might be the least of my worries. Something is still definitely wrong with it. The whole thing is just shaking back and forth, like a mini earthquake only the phone can feel.

Annie closes her hand around mine, and I realize it's not my phone shaking. It's *me*.

"Olive . . . I need you to tell me what happened."

How do I tell her what happened when even *I* don't understand it myself?

Because how?

How is it possible that *the* Jasper Rafferty messaged me?

Does that mean he . . .

I shake my head.

"No?" Annie questions. "You're not going to tell me?"

"No. Wait. Yes. I'm going to tell you. I'm shaking my head because . . ." I trail off, swallowing the lump forming in my throat. "He messaged me."

"Who?"

"Jasper."

Annie tips her head to the side. Her midnight-black hair, which is usually pulled into a high bun, hangs loose, and I watch as it falls over her shoulder with the movement. "What about Jasper?"

I pull my gaze from her hair and back to her stare. There's a crinkle between her brows, and her lips are pulled together tightly. She looks mildly annoyed with me, and I don't blame her. I'd be annoyed too. I'm not giving her any details. Hell, I'm barely speaking in complete sentences.

But how can I?

Jasper Rafferty messaged me. Which likely means he's *read* my messages. All of them. *Hundreds* of them. All the ones I've sent over the last year.

I'm stupid. So, so, *so* incredibly stupid. Why? Why did I think it was a good idea to turn his inbox into my very own digital diary?

Ah, right. Because I thought what I was doing was harmless since my messages were going to his *Requests* folder, where all the other messages from people he doesn't follow go. Safety in numbers, right?

Wrong.

"I'm firing my therapist."

Annie jerks her head back. "What? Why? You love Ingrid."

"Yes, but I'm in this predicament because of her."

"What predicament?" Annie throws her hands in the air, completely over my shit.

I sigh, press my thumb against my phone's screen, then hand it over to her.

She takes the phone hesitantly, her eyes not leaving me as she pulls it from my fingers.

"What am I doing with this?" she asks.

"Look."

Her brows pull together, but she heeds my directions, dropping her eyes to the screen.

"What am I looking at here? It's your inbox. It's . . ." Her mouth drops open, and now *her* hands are trembling. "That's . . . That's . . ." She shakes her head, still staring in complete disbelief.

I don't blame her. I'm not sure I even believe it myself.

Why would he message me back? Out of all the people who are undoubtedly sliding into his DMs, why me? It doesn't make sense.

"Are you going to open it?"

"No! Absolutely not. I don't—"

I don't even have the chance to finish my protest before she presses her thumb to the screen.

It's a done deal.

I've *seen* it. He'll see that I've seen it.

This just opened a whole new assortment of problems.

"Oops?" She scrunches her nose as she pulls up her shoulders. "My bad."

But she doesn't sound sorry at all.

I love Annie, but never have I ever wanted to strangle her so badly before.

"Uh-oh." She winces. "You look mad. Why do you look mad? This is a good thing. Right?"

"No. No. It's not a good thing at all, Annie," I tell her through gritted teeth, shaking my head. "In fact, this is the *worst* thing ever."

"But . . . how? This is your in! Look at you, making friends with the celebrities, Little Miss Badass Model." She winks at me, her grin wide and happy.

But I'm not smiling back. There's no way Jasper has any clue who I am. He doesn't know me or my modeling. This is just a fluke. Some random, awful, and embarrassing fluke. Emphasis on *embarrassing*.

"Earth to Olive . . ." Annie waves a hand in front of my face. "Why is this a bad thing?"

"My messages!" I snap.

I regret it immediately. I shouldn't be mad at her. It's not her fault. It's Ingrid's. She's the one who suggested I start a journal. When I told her I hated writing with pen and paper, she suggested I do a digital one.

Sure, Ingrid might not have meant *this* style of journaling, but still. It's all her fault.

Or at least, that's what I'm telling myself to feel better about this whole situation.

Annie tips her head, silently mouthing, *"Messages?"* as she stares at me with confusion in her eyes.

That's when I see it—the second she realizes what she's just done.

"Oh no." She covers her mouth with her hand. "No. No, no, no, no," she chants, the words muffled, but I can still hear them. "Your messages."

"My messages."

After a night of too much wine—something that happens rarely, because I usually handle myself just fine, thank you very much—I confided in Annie about my online diary. She thought it was a horrible idea, naturally, but encouraged me to keep writing to him if it made me feel better.

Now I'm betting she regrets those words as much as I regret following her advice.

She drops her hand, shaking her head. "I didn't . . . I'm so sorry, Olive. I didn't think about those. Not at all."

"I didn't either. Not at first. But now . . ."

She squeezes her eyes closed, then takes a steadying breath before looking at me again. "Maybe he didn't read them?"

I laugh derisively as I bend to pick up the fallen slice of pizza. I carry it to the trash can, then move to the sink to clean the grease off my hands. "Right. He only read this latest one, and that's it."

"Maybe?" She grimaces and hops up onto the stool I abandoned, grabbing a slice of pizza for herself. "Can't you just delete the thread or something?"

"Deleting it will only delete the messages from *my* inbox, not his," I explain to her as she takes a big bite of the pie that I want nothing to do with. It's tainted now. Or maybe I've just completely lost my appetite.

"Block him, then." She shrugs like it's the most obvious answer, and maybe it is. I mean, I don't *have* to follow him. Right?

But that would mean I would lose *all* my messages to him. And some of those contain memories I want to keep.

Not going to lie, the old-fashioned pen-and-paper method is looking really nice right about now.

"Or . . ." She draws the word out, and I glance over at her. "Just respond to him."

"That's not happening." Shaking my head, I push past her to grab a few paper towels from the roll on the counter and a bottle of cleaning spray before making my way back to my mess. I wipe everything up, the kitchen now smelling like fresh orange rather than pizza grease, then discard the paper towels, leaving no evidence of my faux pas. If only every mess were that easy to clean.

"Come on," Annie says as I grab a bottle of wine from the fridge and twist it open. I wasn't planning on drinking tonight since I had a bit too much last night, but after this, it's safe to say I could really use something to calm my nerves. Thank god Annie restocked us or I'd be bumming right now. "It's not the most awful idea ever. What's the worst that could happen?"

I grab a glass from the cabinet and set it on the counter. "Well, for starters, he could respond again."

"So?" She shrugs once more. "We're operating on the belief he's already read everything you've sent him. Which means whatever you sent him didn't scare him away. Would it really be so terrible if he responded?"

"Yes!" I exclaim, a bit of wine splashing from the cup with my outburst.

"Why?"

"What if this is all just some elaborate *She's All That* type of prank? I am not cut out for that shit."

I can tell she wants to roll her eyes at me, but she refrains. "That's not what this is. This is just two people in adjacent industries befriending one another."

"Adjacent? *Adjacent?*" I set the wine bottle down, then hold my hands out flat, my fingertips pointing toward one another. "You're assuming we're both *here*, on this level. But the truth is, I'm here"—I move my right hand down—"and Jasper is here." I raise my left hand up as high as I can possibly reach. "We aren't adjacent. We're on two different planets, Annie."

She waves this away. "You're not, but keep telling yourself that."

"You don't follow celebrity gossip. Hell, you don't even watch movies. You're not caught up in this world. I'm telling you, we're not even in the same atmosphere. Jasper Rafferty is a god, and I'm a peon. End of story."

She huffs. "You're selling yourself short again, Liv."

"I'm being realistic, *Bananie*," I say, using the nickname I know she hates. It earns me a glare, and I don't even care. She deserved that one after opening the message. "There is not a single place in this entire universe where Jasper and I are in the same circles. This is a prank. It has to be."

"One, I'm getting super confused about the solar system. Planets, atmospheres, and universes. I'm going to need a fourth-grade science refresher. And two, what if it's not a prank? What if this is real?"

"It's not real," I promise her, recapping the wine because we're a very fancy screw-top-wine-bottle household. "Which is why I am *not* going to message him again. I'm going to block him, and I'm going to pretend this never, ever happened. Hopefully, he'll do the same. I'm sure he's already forgotten all about the weirdo who spilled all her secrets to him like a psychopath."

Annie opens her mouth but snaps it shut again the second I look at her with hard eyes, silently telling her that if she tries to argue with me again, I might just go to prison for murder tonight.

So she says nothing—at least, nothing about Jasper.

Jasper, the man I am desperately trying to forget exists.

Jasper, the man I am going to pretend didn't see those messages.

Jasper, the man who is . . . so, so handsome and *so* far out of my league.

Damn you, Ingrid.

And damn me too. Because really? Did I honestly think I could get away with this?

Yes.

Because, come on, what are the chances? He has to get thousands of messages a day. How is it that out of all the ones he receives, he looks at mine?

I shake away the thought, bringing my wineglass to my lips and emptying half of it in one go.

"How was the shoot?" Annie asks.

"Mixed bag," I tell her, taking another drink. "Started rocky because I was late."

"Late? Why?"

When I tell her about my extra-shitty morning, she laughs, completely unsurprised. "But after that, it was good?"

I shrug. "Mostly. Mitch—who I am so thankful to work with again—is great. But also exhausting, you know? I'm hoping it'll all be worth it, though."

"It will," she says, sounding confident. "You're so going to get new deals out of this. I just know it. Once people see those shots, they're going to want you in their clothes. And who knows? Maybe something good will come out of you popping into that boutique."

"Hmm. Maybe. How was your day?"

"A lot less eventful than yours, that's for sure."

We spend the next two hours catching up and eating pizza. Annie's not usually one to drink more than one glass of wine, but even she has by the time we're both ready to turn in.

It's not until I'm snuggled up comfortably in my bed, warm and cozy beneath my sheets, that I allow myself to think about Jasper again.

"Why me?" I mutter, grabbing my phone off the bedside table.

The screen illuminates my face as I navigate to Instagram, ignoring the new messages in my inbox in favor of Jasper's.

He hasn't sent anything else. And why would he? It was just a fluke.

But it doesn't stop me from repeatedly reading the four words he sent me.

@JasperRafferty: How'd the shoot go?

I need to block him so I can block this whole messy, awful thing out of my mind.

I click on his name to do that, but it jumps on the screen.

Why did it jump? What's . . .

"Oh no," I gasp, sitting up in one easy motion like all those overly fit hot guys do in the movies. "He's typing."

Three dots dance along the bottom of the screen, and I watch them like they're the most exciting thing I've ever seen. And right now, they are.

What in the world is he saying? What *could* he say?

Whatever it is, he must have changed his mind, because suddenly, the dots stop.

"Thank fuck," I whisper, exhaling heavily.

My relief is short lived, because those damn dots appear once more.

"Crap, crap, crap," I chant as the dots bounce.

They disappear, only to reappear.

I watch the screen for five minutes—I time it and everything—until finally, the dots stop for a full minute, the longest yet.

"It's over," I murmur, still talking to myself. "See? Just a fluke, Olive. Nothing to worry about."

I click off my screen and put my phone away. Resting my eyes, I settle back into my bed, ready to fall into the slumber I desperately need.

Buzz.

My eyes spring open as my phone rattles against my table. I reach for the device.

@JasperRafferty has sent you a message.

CHAPTER SEVEN

Jude

I don't know what the hell I'm doing.

Half an hour ago, I got back from that too-loud and too-crowded bar, and it was as big of a nightmare as I imagined it would be. I had no fewer than fifteen cameras on me as I tried to get into the back of the car Dylan had waiting for me.

"Are you on drugs, Jude?"

"Will you be entering rehab, Jude?"

"This was supposed to be your comeback movie, but critics predict a flop. How do you feel about that, Jude?"

"Do your parents know you're an addict, Jude?"

The questions were as outrageous as they were irritating. I can't tell if my head is throbbing because of the asinine shit I had to deal with or the camera flashes. Probably a bit of both.

Either way, it has me lying in bed before midnight on a Saturday with my phone in my hand, scrolling through messages from some random stranger on the internet, contemplating whether I should write her more.

She knows I've seen the messages. She knows because she's seen *my* message.

Well, that's not true. She knows *Jasper* has seen the messages, and she's seen *Jasper's* reply.

Not mine. None of this is *mine*.

@OliveMe: My favorite part of living in New York is the people. They're assholes half the time, but when they're good, they're really good. Good people make me happy.

Her words from three months ago are like a punch to the gut, given that I'm not currently being a very good person.

"Reading someone's diary is wrong. You're just as bad as Jasper," I say out loud. Maybe if I acknowledge the problem, it will convince me to put my phone down and stop.

But it doesn't. I keep scrolling because I'm an asshole like that.

@OliveMe: I have a small confession to make. I totally believe in aliens. I think they're just scared of humans, and frankly, they have every right to be. This world is a scary place.

@OliveMe: Butterflies are evil. That's it. That's the entry for the day.

@OliveMe: Sometimes I think about quitting modeling and social media and getting one of those boring 9-5 office jobs. It sounds a hell of a lot easier than giving away so many pieces of myself.

She didn't write for a few days after that confession, and I wish more than anything I could reach through the screen and tell her that what she's feeling is entirely valid.

I relate to it more than she could ever know. It's exactly how I feel about acting. I love it, but at what point will it be too much?

@OliveMe: I have a big photo shoot tomorrow. I'm nervous because it's with a photographer who could skyrocket me to a new level of modeling. I want that. I think. Is it weird to be excited and grateful but also completely and utterly terrified? That's what I'm feeling right now, but maybe it's just the wine talking.

It was from yesterday.

That was the last message she sent before I so stupidly responded to her.

I have no business reading these, and even less business striking up a conversation with the woman.

So I let her know just that.

@JasperRafferty: You don't have to answer that. Sorry for intruding.

I stare at the message for several minutes, typing, deleting, and retyping before I finally hit Send.

Then I stare some more.

I don't know why I can't take my eyes off the screen, but I can't. It's like I'm trying to *will* her to respond. To look at the message, at the least. To be okay with me being a total sleazeball.

But nothing happens.

No response. No indication that she's seen the message.

Nada. Zip. *Zilch.*

Just as I rest my phone on my chest, it shakes against me, and I spring up to a sitting position, gripping it tightly with two hands like a man obsessed.

And maybe I am, which sounds absurd.

But it doesn't stop me from clicking on the notification. Or diving back into Jasper's inbox. Or reading a message that's not really for me.

@OliveMe: To be fair, I'm the one who intruded first, using your inbox as my diary. But if you're messaging me back, that means you don't think I'm completely crazy.

@JasperRafferty: Not completely.

@OliveMe: Oh, so you DO think I'm crazy, just not completely?

I laugh, loving that she's unafraid to call me out on my crap. That's the second time it's happened today, and it makes me as happy as it did this morning.

Huh. Guess we're both crazy, then.

@JasperRafferty: I mean, sliding into my DMs is pretty crazy, right?

@OliveMe: Crazy . . . completely stupid and mortifying. Same thing, yeah?

@JasperRafferty: Nothing to be embarrassed by. You're not the first person.

@OliveMe: Probably not, but I really don't think this is what my therapist meant by finding an outlet for my feelings.

@OliveMe: Annnnd now I've just admitted I'm in therapy. Yep. I'm totally crazy.

@JasperRafferty: Two things . . .

@JasperRafferty: Therapy doesn't equal crazy. In fact, I think going to therapy is one of the bravest things a person can do.

@JasperRafferty: I think the digital journal thing is kind of cool. I mean, maybe not the smartest execution if you didn't want anyone else reading all your innermost private thoughts, but still cool. I'm an old-school man myself. Pen and paper for me.

@OliveMe: Wait . . . you keep a diary?

@JasperRafferty: A journal.

@OliveMe: Same thing.

@OliveMe: And don't argue that it's not. We both know it is.

If she really wants to get to the nitty-gritty of it, then fine. I guess they're the same. But there's no way in hell I'm admitting that to Jasper.

@JasperRafferty: You win. This time.

@OliveMe: You'll come to know that I always win. 😉

I wince. Not because I don't find her bold attempt at flirting with me endearing, but because she's implying what can never be—that this conversation will extend beyond tonight.

It won't.

I *can't*.

Because I'm not Jasper.

@OliveMe: Sorry. That came out sounding a little weirder than I intended.

@JasperRafferty: How about we stop apologizing to each other tonight, huh?

@OliveMe: Sorry.

@OliveMe: OMG

@OliveMe: That was totally unintentional! Guess it's my inner Midwesterner coming out.

@JasperRafferty: You're from the Midwest?

@OliveMe: Yep. Born and raised. I lived there until I finally escaped to New York.

@JasperRafferty: I've lived in NYC my entire life. Well, NYC and LA.

@JasperRafferty: But you probably knew that already, didn't you?

@OliveMe: Nah. Who are you again?

I grin. I like her humor.

Even more, I like that she's treating me like I'm not a Rafferty. Like I'm just some random guy she met on the street.

@JasperRafferty: You never did tell me about the shoot.

@OliveMe: Oh. That.

@OliveMe: It was good. I think. I HOPE.

@JasperRafferty: You're not sure?

@OliveMe: I mean, I gave it my all, but that doesn't always mean something in this industry.

@OliveMe: LOL at me for trying to provide Jasper Rafferty industry insight. As if you don't already know.

@JasperRafferty: I don't know about modeling.

@OliveMe: Did you block out your early years as a model that well?

Early years as a model? I never modeled. It was never my thing. It was—

Oh crap.

It was Jasper's thing, and *I'm* Jasper.

@JasperRafferty: Guilty as charged.

@OliveMe: Oh, come on. It's not all that bad.

@OliveMe: Wait. You've read my diary. You know it is.

@JasperRafferty: I didn't read your entire diary, you know . . .

@OliveMe: Thank you. I think.

@JasperRafferty: You're welcome. I think.

@OliveMe: I would understand if you did, though. I mean, I'd deserve it, using your DMs and all.

@JasperRafferty: That was a little . . .

@OliveMe: Bizarre?

@JasperRafferty: I was going to say unorthodox.

@OliveMe: Oooh. I'm totally going to bust that out in therapy when I tell Ingrid all about this.

I want to tell her not to tell *anyone* about this, but that wouldn't be fair, since I plan to share it with Shane, *my* therapist.

He's going to love this.

And by *love*, I mean *completely call into question my sanity*, just like I'm doing myself.

@OliveMe: I'm only kidding. I won't go blabbing Jasper Rafferty's secrets to the world.

There it is again. The reminder that it's not *me* talking to Olive.

I need to stop. Now.

@OliveMe: If you want to block me, this weirdo sliding into your DMs all the time, you can. I'll totally understand.

I should. I really, really should. Block her and delete the messages and pretend she never existed.

Hell, I even hover my finger over the button, aimed and ready to make this all just a bad dream.

But no matter how long I let my finger linger there, I can't seem to make myself press down and do the deed.

Why? Why can't I do this?

Because she makes you feel normal, you idiot.

Ah. Right. *That.*

@JasperRafferty: No blocking necessary.

@OliveMe: And here I was, worried you'd think I'm a complete and total creeper.

@JasperRafferty: Well . . .

@OliveMe: GASP!

@JasperRafferty: Kidding. 😉

Olive doesn't message anything else, and neither do I.

Mostly because I don't know what to say to her. I don't know how to keep the conversation going, let alone end it, which is exactly what I *should* do.

So instead, after several minutes of silence from both of us, I send her one last message for the night.

@JasperRafferty: I believe in aliens too.

Then I get reckless for the third time tonight—I turn off my phone and slip into sleep.

◆ ◆ ◆

As it turns out, shutting off your phone for a peaceful night of sleep is a bad idea when your name is all over the press.

"I swear, Jude . . ." Dylan pinches the bridge of her nose, shaking her head at me, her wild red hair flying all over the computer screen. I figured the fastest and easiest way to give her proof of life was to video chat her. I'm still lying in bed, and I have no doubt she's already been up for six hours. "You are going to be the death of me—heart palpitations like this shouldn't be a thing at twenty-nine."

I wince even though I know she's just being dramatic. She's not having palpitations. She's just annoyed.

Really, *really* annoyed. Likely more annoyed than I've ever seen her.

"I'm sorry," I tell her, shoving the glasses that have fallen down my nose back up. I hate wearing them, but I'm also too lazy to get out of bed for my contacts. "I shouldn't have turned my phone off."

"You're right. You shouldn't have. We could have had a crisis on our hands. Not to mention that I totally thought you were kidnapped and being held for ransom since I couldn't get in touch with you, Mr. Sleep until Ten in the Morning."

"*Jude* will do just fine."

She glowers at me, not appreciating my sarcasm.

I can't entirely say I blame her. She's not the only person who believed something was wrong.

When I turned my phone back on ten minutes after ten, I was instantly bombarded with messages and voicemails from my mother, sister, Dylan, and even Jasper. He was worried about me slipping away on my own last night. Funny, since he's the one who should be worried, slinking home with random women. His untamed sex drive is so going to be his downfall one day.

After I called my mom and sister back, I sent Jasper a single emoji—the middle finger—then tackled calling Dylan, all while ignoring the obvious and glaring notification sitting on my phone:

@OliveMe has sent you a message.

"How can I make it up to you?" I ask Dylan, brushing a hand through my bed head and flashing her the most charming smile I can muster with no caffeine in my system.

I honestly can't remember the last time I slept so late, and if I weren't so scared that Dylan would break into my apartment and go all *Misery* on me, I'd shut my phone off more often.

True to herself, her glare doesn't lessen at all.

"You can start by promising me you'll never, ever scare me like that again."

"Yes, ma'am," I answer with a salute, earning myself an even scarier stare.

Man, I'm on a roll this morning.

"Secondly, you can tell me *why* you shut your phone off."

Because I wanted to hold on to that bit of normal I felt with Olive.

But I can't tell her that. Telling her that would open a box I'm not ready to tackle just yet.

After confessing to Olive how I felt about aliens, I spent half the night plagued by dreams of little green creatures trying to get me to board their flying saucer.

I wasn't entirely surprised I had Olive on my mind when I woke up. Or that reaching for my phone to message her was my first instinct.

But thanks to this morning's slap of reality, I haven't done anything that foolish just yet.

Just leave her be, Jude. Pretend it never happened.

"Hello! Earth to Jude!"

I snap my attention back to the angry redhead. "I'm listening. Keep going."

One of her perfectly shaped brows lifts. "I asked *you* a question."

"Oh." Heat steals over my cheeks. "Can you repeat it?"

Dylan exhales heavily. "You know, you're not making these drug- and alcohol-misuse accusations any easier to dodge. Not with the way you're acting."

She's right. I know she is. "I'm just . . . distracted, is all."

"By?"

"My lack of proper sleep over the last few months?" I shrug. "It's been a whole whirlwind of shit. My parents' anniversary party, the ten different events I 'had' to attend, and then hitting the road for this press tour. I'm out of practice with all this."

It's not a complete lie. I *am* out of practice with how demanding this job can be. Most people believe it's all glitz and glam and constant parties. While that might be true, there's also a lot of work involved. And if you're like me—a person who'd rather be at home than out at one of those parties—it's even tougher to have to push through sometimes.

Sometimes I wish I'd never taken that time off for college, but another part of me knows that without it, I probably wouldn't still love acting like I do. I grew up in this industry. Those years off were neces- sary if I wanted to avoid the kind of nervous breakdown I've seen far too many of my fellow child actors go through, even if they do sometimes make me feel like I'm behind where I "should" be. Sure, I did a few guest appearances here and there, but my name hasn't been first on the call sheet since *Eternity: Forever and Always* failed, which could have had something to do with that god-awful redundant title, I'm sure.

Now here I am, being thrown back into it at full force, thanks to *Love and Arson*.

I'm totally out of touch.

This time when Dylan sighs, it's more resigned. She mashes her lips together, then sits forward, her serious face coming out to play. "We'll scale back on the social events. They really are helpful and can open so many new doors, but I get they aren't your thing. We can cut a few."

A wave of relief washes over me. It's short lived when my publicist opens her mouth again.

"Besides, you're going to need more time for the dates I have lined up for you."

"*Dates*? As in, plural? We agreed on one."

She gives me a wicked grin. "You owe me now for turning your phone off."

"No. One date only. That's it. I am not budging on this."

She narrows her eyes, looking every bit like she wants to argue. To my surprise, she doesn't. "Fine," she bites out. "One date. But I still get to pick it."

I groan. As much as I'm not looking forward to the date, I think I'm even less excited about the idea of Dylan picking it. "You know you're killing me with this, don't you?"

"You're being dramatic, Jude." She cackles—yes, *cackles*—just like a witch. "Besides, you could have fun, you know. Maybe even fall in love."

"Love? You don't even believe in love," I accuse.

She lifts a shoulder. "Not for myself but maybe for you."

I squint at her. "I could fire you, you know."

She grins sweetly. "But you won't. You love me."

"Not at this moment, I don't."

Appearing unbothered by my statement, she moves on to the next task at hand: discussing the interview I need to be at shortly.

She's been like this since I met her when she was working as an assistant to Jasper's publicist—business, business, business. It's why I've been with her for so long. She's professional but not afraid to call me out when she needs to. I was lucky as hell I found her after *Lakedale* ended. I was lost in my career, unsure of what I wanted to do, and along came Dylan, waltzing up to me with all the answers.

She's the one who encouraged me to take time off and figure out who I wanted to be. She's the whole reason I went to college. So when I graduated and realized that acting *is* what I want, she was the first person I called and offered the job as my publicist. I was her first client, the one who gave her a leg to stand on. She's been my ride or die since, and I've not regretted it yet. I don't think she has either.

We run through the rest of my day, one that's packed with me running from interview to interview, then making an appearance at some new Broadway show. I don't have to stay the entire time—thank fuck, because musicals aren't my thing—but I do have to stay until intermission, at least. After that, I'm free for the night.

It's absurd to have my day mapped out like this, to make an appearance here or to show up there, but I get it—it's a necessary evil. It's especially necessary with a new movie coming out. Buzz is good. Headlines, no matter how awful and untrue, are a good thing. It keeps my name in the spotlight, which means more people interested, which means more exposure, which means more moviegoers.

It's one big game . . . one I'm already sick of playing.

I want to go back to how I felt last night messaging with Olive. Go back to that feeling of just being some guy talking to some girl. I'm over the pressure of being Jude Rafferty, the guy trying to make a comeback and not be seen as the kid from *Lakedale* or the failed vampire show.

I just want to be *me*, which means I need to stay away from Jasper's inbox, even if Olive's diary is calling to me.

I need to block her. Delete our messages. Move on.

But no matter how much conviction is behind my thoughts, it's pointless. The second I get off the video call with Dylan, I'm on my phone and navigating to Instagram to see what Olive has sent.

I shouldn't. I know that. But . . . I can't help it. She's too good a distraction from all the chaos and worry that's been slowly creeping in since we started hitting hard on the promo for the film.

I've been working on this movie for years, it seems like, and now it's finally coming out and I'm finally getting my shot at being something more than the kid from the cheesy TV show or "the Rafferty who went to college." The stress of it all . . . it's slowly starting to consume me, which I know is going to lead to more blunders like the Snoopy-underwear incident, and I can't afford those for so many reasons.

Even though I know I shouldn't be talking to Olive, I want to anyway. It makes me feel grounded. Normal. *Real.*

Well, as real as I can be while pretending to be my brother.

But that's a problem for another time.

@OliveMe: Aliens invaded my dreams last night. Big, tall blue ones with rippling muscles and huge . . . bulges. They were kind of hot.

I bark out a laugh, the sound bouncing off the walls of my mostly empty apartment. I moved in only two months ago, and since I've been constantly on the go, I haven't had the time to decorate anything. Not that I'm any good at that, but still. I'm sure my mom will want me to unpack and do something with it, especially since she's not acting as much these days and has entirely too much time on her hands. I'm still planning to split my time between here and LA, but I wanted to be near family too. Now that Cait has a baby on the way and Jasper is spending so much time here, too, it makes sense to put down roots in earnest as well.

@JasperRafferty: I dreamed of aliens too. They were green, though.

@OliveMe: And their . . . bulges?

@JasperRafferty: You know, it never occurred to me to check them out.

@OliveMe: Uh-huh. Likely story.

@OliveMe: I'm kind of surprised you messaged me back . . .

@JasperRafferty: Did you not want me to?

@OliveMe: Honestly, I'm not sure.

@OliveMe: I still don't even know what to make of the fact that you responded yesterday. Or that you've read my diary. I'm still in shock.

I'm in shock too.

Shocked I opened her messages. Shocked I messaged her back. Shocked I'm *still* messaging her. Shocked I'm pretending to be my brother because, apparently, I'm that damn desperate to feel normal.

@JasperRafferty: We can pretend this never happened. Just say the word and you can go back to your diary. The ball is in your court, Olive.

An alarm chimes from my discarded laptop, and I know it's a reminder from Dylan that I need to get moving so I'm not late for what's sure to be another torturous interview.

When I glance back at my phone, I see that Olive's not seen my message yet.

Good. I'd rather not know her response. At least, not now.

Because truthfully . . . *selfishly* . . . I don't want to pretend it never happened.

I want to hang on to normal for a little bit longer.

CHAPTER EIGHT

Olive

Starting my morning off by messaging Jasper Rafferty was not on my bingo card for this summer, but that's exactly what happened.

And of all things to talk about, it was aliens.

"What even is my life?"

"Chaotic," Annie says, and I whip my head up, surprised to find her standing in the doorway to my room.

I'm still in bed, looking every bit like a wreck, and she's already dressed in her formfitting scrubs, appearing refreshed and ready to tackle the emergency room.

"Why are you dressed for work? It's daylight."

She shoves off the frame and saunters into the room, hopping up onto the end of my bed like she's done a thousand times before. "Switched shifts with someone. Remi wants to take me out for dinner tonight. Some fancy place where they have cloth napkins."

She pulls a face, though I'm not surprised. Annie hates anything fancy. She's the practical one of the two of us.

I, on the hand, would be ecstatic to go someplace fancy. Hell, I'd settle for a date at the McDonald's or the Olive Garden in Times Square.

Wow. I sound desperate. But I suppose I am. I can't remember the last time I went on an actual date, and here Annie is, complaining about an elegant dinner with her dreamboat boyfriend.

"Think it's one of *those* dinners?"

"Ugh, I hope not. I'm not ready for *that*." She flicks her eyes to mine, and I see it clearly—she *does* want it to be one of those dinners. The serious kind. The one that's life changing.

Annie's been going back and forth for months about whether she wants to keep seeing her long-term boyfriend, but if you ask me, it's obvious what she truly wants—commitment.

They've been together for four years and still live separately. It bothers my best friend more than she lets on. Even though they're opposites, she loves Remi more than anything. She wants a future with him, no matter how much she pretends she doesn't. I just hope Remi doesn't mess up the best thing that's ever happened to him and does something soon.

"Enough about me . . ." She picks at the pilled pieces on the comforter I've had for way too many years. "How was the rest of your night?"

Translation: *What happened with the message?*

"It was . . . interesting."

"Interesting *how*?" she questions.

How do I explain to her that I spent an hour last night messaging with one of the most famous actors in the world? Or that this morning, I told him I dreamed of blue aliens with huge penises? Or that he offered to stop responding so I can resume my diary entries?

Oddly enough, I trust him not to read them anymore. I don't know why, especially since I don't even know the guy, but I believe him. All I have to say is *stop*, and he will.

"You talked to him, didn't you?" Annie guesses.

I nod, unable to say it out loud because . . . *what*?

I'm still in disbelief over it. In fact, I'm not sure I want to believe it at all. It's not real. It *can't* be real . . . can it?

"And you think it's really him?" my roommate asks, putting a voice to the worry that's been rattling around in my mind since last night.

"I'm . . . not sure."

She nods. "And you're afraid to hope it is." She sighs, continuing to pick at the blanket. "I get it, mixing fear and hope. Trust me."

Her last words are whispered, like she's frightened to put them out into the universe.

She has no reason to be scared. Not when it comes to Remi.

"He loves you, you know."

A grin pulls at her lips. "I know. I love him too. I just . . ."

I reach out, wrapping my hand around hers, stilling her movements. "He *loves* you. The forever kind of love."

Her stare is filled with trepidation, and I don't know why she's so nervous. She doesn't have any reason to be. She has someone who is completely head over heels in love and would do anything for her. She's lucky, and she doesn't even realize it. I wish I had a love half as amazing as hers.

She clears her throat, shoving her shoulders back. "So, about Jasper . . ."

But that's all she says. All she offers.

She's waiting for me to say something, but I don't *know* what to say.

"Are you going to keep messaging him?"

I shrug. "I'm not sure. I haven't thought about it."

And it's true. I haven't. I've done just about everything else. I don't *want* to think about it. Thinking about it means going down a path that could end with the discovery that this is all fake. Annie has a point—it could just be some elaborate hoax. A big *screw you* from the universe.

"Do you want me to ask Remi to investigate it? He could find out if it's really him, you know. He's a computer genius."

Remi is terrifyingly smart when it comes to computers. Like the kind of smart that has the government concerned, which I'm sure has to do with his getting arrested at fifteen for hacking into the White House database.

"I . . . Maybe?" I shake my head, laughing lightly. "How am I sitting here having a casual conversation with you about your boyfriend cyberstalking Jasper Rafferty for me?"

"Because you're a badass, Liv. That's how." She winks at me, which only makes me laugh more. She rises off the bed, clapping her hands together twice. "All right. I'm off to go pull things out of people they had no business sticking inside of themselves."

I cringe. "String of butt-stuff patients?"

"String of butt-stuff patients. Always happens during the summer. I swear, that's when people get extra freaky." She waggles her brows. "I'm going to dinner right after and I'll be home late, so don't wait up for me."

"Have fun!" I call after her as she pads out of my room and down the hall. "And say yes!"

There's no mistaking her heavy sigh just as the front door falls shut behind her. The dead bolt clicks into place; then it's just me, my thoughts, and a waiting message from Jasper.

◆ ◆ ◆

I spend the day doing something I should have done a long time ago: cleaning out my closet.

And I don't even mean metaphorically. I mean literally. There are piles and piles of clothes I know I'll never wear and shoes and bags that are collecting dust. It's time to purge this mess once and for all.

Besides, it gives me something to do instead of worrying over Jasper's message.

I still haven't responded, but I feel like I should, like I owe it to him.

With two giant garbage bags full of clothes, I tromp down the steps of my building and enter the bustling city sidewalks. Hell's Kitchen, with its bagel shops, diners, and funky stores, is packed—which isn't surprising, summer is peak tourist season, after all—and I do my best to navigate where I'm going carrying way more than I should have brought with me. Two bags were a bit much.

I make my way to Cuties & Curves and haul my garments inside, trying to ignore the sweat that's beading across the back of my neck. I knew I should have worn my hair up today, but nope. Since I've been using nothing but dry shampoo for three days, I opted for a hat, which required me to wear my hair down because I've never quite mastered a cute low-ponytail-and-hat combo that doesn't make me look like one of the Founding Fathers.

"Olive!" the woman behind the counter shouts when I walk through the door and into the bright store.

"Hey, Lacey," I greet her, trudging along and wishing like hell I had a free hand to wipe the sweat from my brow.

"Puh-*lease* say you're here to tell me you *finally* snagged a deal with Good Jeans," she says when I stop at the counter, finally letting the bags fall and giving my arms a rest.

I try not to let my dejection show and muster up a half smile for her as I tug off my sunglasses and drop them into my purse. "Not yet."

I say *yet* because I'm trying to be positive it *will* happen someday. It has to. Good Jeans not only caters to plus-size women, but their jeans are also made with recycled material. They are everything I want my brand to represent. We *have* to work together, and Uma's doing everything in her power to make it happen.

"But I do have lots of clothes to off-load." I lift one of the bags as high as I can to show off the goodies I'm bringing her.

"Yay!" she squeals, clapping her hands together as she races out from behind the counter, forgetting all about Good Jeans for now and grabbing one of the bags. I'm grateful for the help since I can barely feel my left arm from the walk over.

How many clothes are too many? It might be time to admit I have a problem.

"Let's get these over to Mac. She can sort through things while you fill me in on how your shoot with Mitch went," she says. Lacey is the one who saved me yesterday, helping me find the purple maxi dress.

We deposit the clothes at their intake station. I say a quick hello to Mac, Lacey's sister and the shop owner, then head back to the register with Lacey.

She leans against the glass, her eyes wide with wonder and excitement. "Tell me everything."

So I do. I fill her in on everything, from me waking up late to the asshat who jumped me in line.

"Seriously?" She shakes her head in disgust. "I hate entitled assholes like that. It's the one downfall of this city—all the rich pricks who think they're better than everyone."

"How do you know he's rich?"

"Was he wearing a watch? And I don't mean an Apple Watch or Fitbit or whatever. I mean, like a *real* honest-to-god watch?"

Come to think of it, I did see something shiny and silver glinting off his wrist when he was taunting me with the coffee and danish.

"I think so."

"Ha!" She slaps the counter. "He's rich. Only rich assholes wear watches."

I laugh. "I don't think he was rich. Just an asshole."

Lacey holds up her hands. "Maybe. Maybe not. But fancy watch equals fancy man nine times out of ten."

I'm no fashion dummy, and there was nothing about his outfit that screamed *look at how much money I make*. If anything, it said the opposite, with a plain T-shirt, faded jeans, and a ballcap that looked like it had seen some shit.

"Who knows." I shrug. "I'm sure I'll never run across him again, so it's whatever."

"You're nicer than me. I'd have dumped his coffee all over him."

"It's true," Mac says, waltzing up with a slip in her hand. "One time in middle school, some kid cut in front of her on chicken-nugget day, and she poured chocolate milk all over him right in front of the entire cafeteria."

"Then I stole his nuggets." Lacey grins, clearly proud of herself.

"You're exhausting, Lace," Mac says, shaking her head at her sister. "Here." She holds out the piece of paper. "This is your total if we sell everything, which I have no doubt we will. There were some good pieces in there."

I sweep my eyes over the paper.

$1,200.

Not too bad for two bags of clothes. I try not to think what the other four bags I have sitting in my room could net me. Hauling those down here is a problem for future me. I'm too wiped today.

"You know . . ." Lacey starts, and I have a feeling I'm not going to like where this is going. "We do have some new stuff in . . ."

Don't do it, Olive. You just got rid of stuff. Do. Not. Do. It.

But then again, it *is* my job, and my brand does encourage sustainable clothing. There's nothing more sustainable than secondhand shopping, right?

"Show me what you got."

And that's how I end up with a bagful of new-to-me clothes and a few pieces from Mac herself, who, in her spare time, makes amazing dresses like the one I wore at the shoot yesterday. I might have an eye for fashion, but Mac has a talent for it.

"The wine-colored dress is perfect for fall. It'll pair so well with tights and my booties," I say to Mac. "You're the best."

"*I'm* the best? Um, *you're* the best! Thanks to you, I'm part of a shoot with *the* Mitch Dirkson. That's huge!"

I grin, then shoot her a wink. "It's all you, baby."

She rolls her eyes in an attempt to brush off the compliment, but she knows she deserves it.

"Thanks, ladies," I tell them as I walk out of the shop, promising myself this is the last time I let them talk me into spending so much money.

I check my phone as I step outside, ignoring the texts from friends asking if I want to get together for drinks tonight and heading straight for my Instagram.

I have plenty of new comments and a few DMs, but nothing from the person I want to hear from.

I try not to be disappointed, but I am. I'm not exactly sure why. He did say the ball was in my court, which means he's waiting for me to message back. It doesn't mean I wasn't hoping he would break our apparent standoff and say something first.

I tuck the device into my purse, then pull my sunglasses from my bag and slide them into place before heading back toward my apartment.

As I round the corner of my street, I stop in my tracks.

It's him.

Not even thirty feet away, wearing dark jeans and a white T-shirt under a light flannel, standing in line for coffee at JT's truck, is the Asshat.

My eyes narrow as I watch him stand *in the back of the line* just like he should have yesterday.

Freaking jerk.

I decide at that moment that I'm going to give him a taste of his own medicine.

I stomp toward him, sliding myself right between him and the guy he's standing behind.

"Hey! I was here first."

I spin on my heel, hoping like hell my long hair smacks him in the face, and sneer up at him. "Oh, I'm sorry. Was there a line?"

His eyes are covered by those same aviators, so I can't *see* if he recognizes me, but by the way his lips twist up into a smirk, I'd say he does.

"Sunshine."

That damn low, gravelly voice of his hits me in places I don't even want to think about.

"Asshat," I counter, giving him my own version of a smirk.

The nickname only causes his smile to grow, and I hate that I love it so much.

I'm smacked with that same wave of familiarity from yesterday, but I brush it aside as quickly as it comes.

"I take it you're still mad I bought you coffee and a pastry?"

Ugh. I want to wipe the smugness right off his face, but I'd rather not go to jail for assault today. So instead, I settle for crossing my arms over my chest, enjoying it a little too much when my bag from Cuties & Curves smacks against him.

"It was the worst coffee and danish I've ever had."

That's a damn lie. If anything, I'd wager that my coffee tasted exceptionally better yesterday, and the danish was damn near orgasm inducing.

I'm willing to bet it had everything to do with it costing me exactly zero dollars.

Again, I think, *Freaking jerk.*

"So bad you're here again today?"

"I live close by."

I regret my words almost instantly. How stupid can I be, telling this stranger I live near here?

"Me too," he says, almost like he can sense my instant unease and he's trying to make me feel better.

It only annoys me more. "Did you get off to your uber-important better-than-everyone-else meeting okay?"

"I did. And did you get that stick out of your ass all right? Don't want it jammed up there for too long."

I glare harder—not that he can see, but it makes me feel better anyway.

"Why are you here?"

"Same reason as you." He leans closer, that same pine scent from yesterday hitting me. "Coffee."

As a reflex, I inhale sharply, and immediately wish I hadn't.

That damn smirk of his reappears, this time somehow even more disarming. "Did you just sniff me?"

"Allergies," I mumble, turning around to hide the redness I know is creeping into my cheeks.

Why the hell did I just sniff him? And moreover, why the hell does he smell so damn good? It makes me want to go climb a mountain . . . or him.

I shake away the intrusive thought, then step forward when the person in front of me does.

"Here," Asshat says, and a familiar-looking scarf appears in front of me. "You dropped this."

But I'm not looking at the scarf I just bought from Lacey and Mac. I'm too busy looking at the shiny watch on his wrist that's glinting in the afternoon sun.

Lacey was right. This guy is totally rich.

"Thanks," I mutter, snatching it out of his hand, hating how much I enjoy the laugh that rumbles out of him.

Who is this guy? And why is he here all of a sudden?

I turn to ask him just that, but suddenly, he's pulling his phone from his pocket and pressing it to his ear.

"Yes?"

In an instant, his playful smirk disappears. Instead, his lips are pressed into a thin line as he listens to whatever the person on the other end is saying.

"No, Dylan. I'm— No. She's— Ugh. Are you serious?" He scratches at the stubble—which appears to be a little longer today—along that perfectly cut jaw of his as his lips set into an even firmer line.

I have no clue what's going on, but it's clearly something he's not happy with.

He sighs defeatedly. "Why do I let you talk me into this shit? I—"

He's cut off again, the Dylan person talking over him. His shoulders slump, and he nods as he continues to listen.

"Mm-hmm. Mm-hmm. Yeah. I know. I *know*. I said I know, Dylan."

He lifts his hand, that damn watch catching the sun again, then squeezes the back of his neck like he's massaging out the tension growing there.

We move up two more customers before I hear him start to get off the phone.

"I'll be there. Yes, I promise. Swear it on my mother." He laughs. "Yeah. Yeah. All right, bye."

I don't dare turn back around. His business is not my business. I need to be a good New Yorker and just ignore him.

And that's exactly what I do—ignore him until I finally make it up to the counter.

"Your usual, Liv?" Ric asks, already grabbing the clear plastic cup.

"Just the coffee," I tell him. Then, without reading too much into it, I toss my thumb over my shoulder. "And a drip coffee for this guy."

"Wait. What?" I hear him splutter behind me. "No. I don't need you to buy my coffee. I—"

I turn around, throwing my hand up before he can protest any more.

"Let's get one thing straight: This isn't *for* you. It's for me. To make me feel better about accepting your apology coffee yesterday and enjoying it. I shouldn't have. I should have thrown it right in your fancy-man face and walked away. But I didn't. I was the bigger person. A lot better than you were, cutting in front of me like that. I was already having a bad morning, and you made it worse. But you're not ruining my day today. It's not happening. So this"—I grab the coffee Ric has placed onto the counter and hand it over to Asshat—"is for me. Not you. We're even."

I toss a twenty onto the counter, then grab my own iced drink.

"Keep the change, Ric," I tell him. I spin on my heel and waltz away, my head held high, trying to ignore the way my hands are shaking around the coffee I'm gulping back like I haven't had anything to drink in days.

I make it at least fifteen steps before I hear him.

"Sunshine! Wait!"

I don't wait. I walk faster.

But damn my little legs, because he catches up just as quickly.

"Sunshine," he says again, and I hate that I'm starting to kind of like the nickname, no matter how ridiculous it is. "Stop."

His hand lands on my shoulder, and I stop.

I stop because his hand isn't just on my shoulder—it's everywhere.

Or at least, that's what it feels like as it burns its way into my skin.

As if he feels it, too, he yanks his hand away, glancing down at it, then back at me. He shakes his head, and I barely see his brows crush together over his sunglasses as he dips his head toward me.

"I'm sorry," he murmurs. "For yesterday. I . . . I wasn't myself. That's not an excuse, but it's the truth. I . . ." He sighs. "I'm just sorry."

Maybe I'm just too damn gullible, but I believe him. I believe every word of it.

More than that, I understand it. I'm not myself right now either. I'm not this bold person who cuts the line and yells at strangers. I guess we're both a little off-kilter.

"Okay," I say, after blowing out a breath. "Apology accepted."

"Yeah?" he says, and I nod, making that smile of his return in full force. "Good." He lifts his coffee, then takes a delicate sip. "I, uh, I'll see you around, Sunshine."

He sidesteps me, taking his smile and his charm and that delicious scent of pine right along with him.

It's not until he's halfway down the block in the opposite direction that I move again.

"Hey, Asshat!"

He turns slowly, almost like he was expecting it, and I can see his grin from here.

"You're welcome for the coffee."

I don't wait for a response. I just turn and walk away, listening to the sound of his laughter ring through the streets.

Feeling bold and brave from the encounter, I dig my phone from my purse and pull up Instagram, my fingers flying over the keyboard in an instant.

@OliveMe: Don't pretend it didn't happen. Tell me more about this alien dream of yours.

CHAPTER NINE

Jude

The message from Olive is exactly what I need as I climb the stairs to my apartment.

It's been a long day already, and it's not even over yet. I still have that damn Broadway show.

Why the hell did I let Dylan talk me into this again?

Oh, that's right. Because my big comeback is already failing, thanks to all the headlines about my alleged drug use. I'm the laughingstock of Hollywood *and* the internet.

My Instagram comments prove it.

> Dude is washed up. They should have gotten someone else to be the lead.

> Snoopy underwear? Grow up!

> He's totally on drugs. You can tell in the trailers.

> There's no way he didn't use steroids to bulk up like that! DRUG ABUSER!

> Yeah, I'm not watching this trash.

@JasperRafferty: They made me dance with them. Like a full-blown disco party kind of dance. I was doing Greased Lightnin' and everything, complete with the gelled-up hair and cuffed jeans.

I press my phone against my front door to unlock it, then shove inside. My footfalls echo against the pristine marble floor in the foyer of my immaculate apartment. Just off Columbus Circle, the huge floor-to-ceiling windows let in almost too much daylight, giving me the kind of view of Central Park that most New Yorkers would kill for.

I make a mental note to have Dylan block off some time for me to meet with a decorator in a few weeks, then kick off my shoes and pad farther inside, setting my fresh coffee on the counter, grinning down at the cup stamped with JT's COFFEE & SNACKS.

I was shocked as hell when someone slid in front of me in the line, and I was even more surprised when she spun around to face me.

Sunshine.

I don't know why I've taken to calling her that. Maybe it had to do with her outfit yesterday, a bright-yellow dress and hat that looked more like they belonged on the beach than a New York sidewalk. Or maybe it's her not-so-sunny disposition toward me. It was obvious I got under her skin, but I don't think I realized until today just how big of a dick move it was cutting in front of her. Sure, it made for some fun banter—something I never get enough of—but I was out of line.

Since it appears that we'll be crossing paths at the coffee truck often, I'm glad we were able to clear the air today. The last thing I need is for it to get out that I'm an asshole in the coffee line. The press would have just too much fun with that.

My phone pulsates against my leg as I plop down onto my couch. I pull it from my pocket, surprised to see that Olive has messaged back so quickly.

@OliveMe: I can't believe your aliens made you dance. I'd pay good money to see you on the hood of a car looking like Danny Zuko.

@JasperRafferty: That'll never happen. I hate musicals.

@OliveMe: Again, right? Because you did one a few years ago, didn't you? Lease on Love, right?

Crap. Crap, crap, *fuck*.

For just a moment, I forgot exactly who I was. Forgot that she still thinks I'm Jasper. That she knows my—or *his*—extensive credits list.

@OliveMe: I only know because Annie is obsessed with musicals and forced me to the theater to see Lease on Love about five times, back when you were doing your Broadway run.

@JasperRafferty: See? I hated it so much that I blocked it from my mind completely.

@OliveMe: LOL! That's fair.

@OliveMe: I love musicals. They're always so ridiculous and over the top. I live for the drama.

@OliveMe: I even went to an off-Broadway one once where everyone was dressed up as chickens.

@JasperRafferty: Chickens? Like the farm animal?

@OliveMe: Yep. Even audience members joined in on it, showing up in chicken costumes too and throwing rubber ones onto the stage. I *may* have stolen one and kept it.

@OliveMe: I kind of have a chicken thing.

@JasperRafferty: All right. You have my attention now. What's with the chickens?

@OliveMe: It's nothing exciting. I used to have baby chickens.

@JasperRafferty: You had chickens? In your apartment???

@OliveMe: HAHAHA! No! I grew up on a farm in Iowa.

@JasperRafferty: Like a real farm? With horses and cowboys and everything?

@OliveMe: LOL! Not cowboys, but we did have horses.

@OliveMe: It was a small farm, really. More of a hobby my mom had to keep her busy while my dad traveled for work. We had two horses, three goats, and about eight chickens at any given time. So nothing too out of control.

@JasperRafferty: Can you ride a horse?

@OliveMe: Why? Need lessons? 😉

@JasperRafferty: I don't know . . . Now I'm kind of itching to see what this cowboy business is all about.

@OliveMe: It's not as glamorous as it sounds, trust me.

@JasperRafferty: Maybe not to you, but it sounds fun compared to how I grew up.

@OliveMe: Ah, yes. It must have been just devastating having your very own butler.

@JasperRafferty: We didn't have a butler.

@OliveMe: *lifts brow*

@JasperRafferty: Well, he wasn't a butler. Lyle was a friend.

@OliveMe: And a butler.

I grimace, thinking about how different our lives must be.

She grew up working hard, and I grew up with a silver spoon in my mouth. It's not my fault my parents are who they are, but it doesn't make me any less privileged.

@JasperRafferty: Tell me more about this farm. Did you name the chickens?

@OliveMe: Of course I did. We had Tender, Thigh, Finger Lickin', Kentucky, Colonel Feathers, Nugget, Secret Recipe, and Toby.

@JasperRafferty: Toby?

@OliveMe: That's the name that got your attention?

@JasperRafferty: Well, yeah. All the others just make sense for a chicken.

@OliveMe: I knew I liked you.

Her words smack me in the face.

She doesn't like *me*. She likes Jasper.

@OliveMe: I take all the credit. I named every chicken myself.

@JasperRafferty: Did you . . . eat the chickens?

@OliveMe: CHICKENS ARE FRIENDS, NOT FOOD!

@JasperRafferty: Duly noted.

@OliveMe: It took me all of two days of owning them to declare myself a vegetarian.

@JasperRafferty: Are you still one?

@OliveMe: Yep.

@OliveMe: Except for when I go to a steakhouse. Or eat chicken Alfredo. Or a cheeseburger.

@JasperRafferty: All valid exceptions.

@OliveMe: The chickens (and I guess the farm as a whole) are a big reason why I love promoting sustainability in my brand. It kind of takes me back to my roots, you know? When I used to have these wonderful animals surrounding me and this great garden giving me fresh food.

@JasperRafferty: I like that. It's very . . .

@OliveMe: Midwestern in the Big City of me? LOL

@JasperRafferty: Now that you mention it . . . yes.

@JasperRafferty: But if it makes you feel better, I'm the exact opposite. We didn't have any of that growing up, and it makes me a little jealous. Hell, I've never even owned a pet.

@OliveMe: Never ever?

@JasperRafferty: Not even a goldfish.

@OliveMe: That might be the saddest thing I've ever heard.

@OliveMe: Every kid should have at least one pet. I feel like you missed out on something magical.

She may be right, but since I spent most of my childhood on set, it didn't make sense to have a pet. I booked my first major role when I was ten. There was no time for normal kid stuff. We had careers to cultivate.

Fuck, that sounds so sad. I've been working my ass off since I was ten. It's no wonder I don't feel at home anywhere besides a movie set. I have a place in LA, but I'd much rather be in New York, where my family is. At least here, I have a better chance of blending into the crowd. Like yesterday and today. Nobody knew who I was at the coffee truck. Sure, I had to wear a hat and sunglasses, but still. I liked being anonymous. This has to be what Tony Hawk feels like all the time—never getting recognized, even when people are staring right at him, asking if his name is "Tony Hawk, like the pro skateboarder."

Hating that I have to get ready for yet another event, I rise off my couch with a sigh and head for the shower.

"Just a few more weeks of this," I say to myself as I shuck my clothes and step under the spray. I'm counting down the days until this press tour is over—and until I get to head to Vancouver to film a small part in a drama slated to release late next year. The role isn't as big as *Love and Arson*, but it's a whole ensemble cast, which could give me some great connections for down the road. I'll definitely need those if this action film does poorly.

As much as I want to, I don't let myself linger, knowing I'll have to get going soon. I'm not sure what I'm dreading more: the show or the fact that I have to put on formal wear.

Reluctantly, I step out of my expansive shower—honestly, my favorite part of the apartment—just in time to hear something no naked person who lives alone wants to hear.

Footsteps.

There is someone in my apartment.

I reach for my phone to call 911, but . . .

"Dammit," I murmur.

I left my phone on the couch so I could have a few minutes alone without Dylan bothering me, which I know she's done about ten times now to make sure I'll attend this damn show.

Man, she's going to be so pissed if I get murdered.

I grab my towel and wrap it around me, then softly pad out of the bathroom and into my dark bedroom, trying my damnedest not to make any noise. I probably should have turned a light on before I got into the shower, but now I'm a little thankful for the darkness—it's easier for me to sneak around.

The intruder moves through the living room, then the kitchen, rummaging through god knows what. I stand just inside my bedroom with the door ajar, staring out, hoping whoever it is, they get what they came for and leave.

I catch a glimpse of movement and shove myself against the wall, pressing my back to it and holding my breath as I listen to their footfalls growing closer and closer by the second.

I'm screwed. Totally screwed. I have no phone and no weapons. Nothing to defend myself with except the minuscule amount of karate I had to take for a role.

I can use that. It's just like riding a bike, right?

The trespasser stalks nearer, and I try not to think about my racing heart or sweaty palms or my utter lack of confidence in my ability to detain this person as I count down from ten, ready to pounce.

Ten. Nine. Eight.

Breathe in, breathe out.

Seven. Six. Five.

Do I even remember how to high-kick someone?

Four. Three. Two.

I should aim for the throat, right?

One.

The door is shoved open, and I attack, falling out into the hall with the big body that's blocking the only exit this apartment has.

"*Rargh!*" I squeeze my eyes shut, going directly for the throat as promised.

I kick and punch and yell, landing a few blows but not taking my assailant down.

Who the hell is this person?

"What the fuck are you doing?" they shout. "Knock it off!"

They push back at me, but I refuse to go down without a fight, kicking at them again.

"Why are you naked?"

I stop moving.

I know that voice.

I spin around—how I got to this position, I'll never know—and cover my nether regions, which are every bit on display.

"Cait."

"Hello, big brother." She rocks back on her heels, looking completely fine, like she didn't just get into a fight with me.

If she wasn't fighting me . . .

I turn back around to see my asshole big brother lying on the floor.

I spring back into my bedroom, barely dodging a now doubled-over Jasper. He's laughing so hard he's not even making a sound at this point as I snatch my towel off the floor and secure it around my waist.

I glower at him, folding my arms over my chest, waiting for his laughter to die down.

"Did you . . ." He lets out another hoot, which turns into a nasty cough as he works to get air into his lungs.

Good. Serves him right.

When he's finally righted himself, he stands with his hands on his hips, smirking down at me. "Did you just attack me with your dick flopping around?"

"Did you just sneak into my house while I was in the shower?" I counter, not at all finding this as funny as he is.

I mean, sure, if I were on the other end of it, I might see the humor, but right now, I'm annoyed. Thoroughly.

"What the hell are you even doing here?" I ask as I yank open my dresser drawer and pull a pair of underwear free. I head into the bathroom and tug them on, depositing my towel into the hamper before marching back out to my room.

"We're going to the show with you," my brother answers from where he rests against my doorjamb, typing away on his phone, probably already telling everyone he knows he just kicked my ass in a fight, even if it's not true.

"What? Since when?"

"Since Dylan called in reinforcements," Cait explains, still out in the hallway, likely hoping she doesn't get another glimpse of my naked ass.

I grit my teeth together as I begin ransacking my drawer for my socks. Of course she did. She doesn't trust me to show up on my own. Which means that I'm going to be stuck there all night now because

Cait *loves* musicals, and I don't want to be the asshole who bails when his sister is having the time of her life.

Yay me.

"So you just let yourselves in?" I shoot an accusatory look in Jasper's direction because I just *know* he's the one who decided that was a good idea.

"I told him not to," Cait says, reading my mind.

I look at Jasper, who just shrugs. "Don't give me a key if you don't want me to use it."

"I didn't give you a key," I remind him.

"No, but Dylan gave me your passcode." He reaches up and rubs near his eyes. "You nailed me pretty good. Better hope it doesn't bruise."

"Does it hurt?"

He presses on it, wincing at the touch. "Like a bitch."

"Good," I counter as I pluck free my favorite pair of dress socks—and by *favorite*, I mean the pair I hate the least, because honestly, I hate them all—and slide them on. I head for my closet next, grabbing a pair of slacks and a dress shirt.

"'Good'? And how do you think that sexy little publicist of yours is going to feel about your brother having a black eye?" Jasper asks, leaning against the door, an overly smug grin on his lips.

"Considering it will likely take some heat off me, she'll be thrilled."

He makes a sour face, like he never considered that, then goes back to fingering his already darkening eye.

I hope it does bruise. That's what he gets for breaking into my apartment.

I pull on my pants and my shirt, buttoning it up as I make my way back to my bathroom. Jasper follows, watching in the mirror as I comb and shape my hair, then spritz on some cologne.

"Aw, don't you look fucking cute?" He sends me a toothy grin, and I want nothing more than to punch his other eye so that he'll match.

Instead, I settle for glaring at him as I brush by and out of my bedroom.

He trudges along behind me as I make my way to the living room, where my dear sister ran off to give me privacy like the good sibling she is.

She's sitting on the couch, and it's only then that I notice she's wearing the same thing I am—all black. Jasper bounces into the room, also wearing black.

He notices. "The Three Musketeers called, and they want our unplanned matching outfits back."

Cait ignores him, her focus on her phone.

Wait. No.

That's *my* phone.

I yank it from her hands, and she looks up at me sheepishly.

"Sorry. It was going off incessantly, though."

"It's probably just Dylan," I mutter, checking my notifications.

"Or a girl. Who's @OliveMe?"

"You're talking to a girl?" Jasper asks, jumping over the back of the couch like he has no manners and plopping down next to Cait.

She looks as annoyed as I am when she uses him to shove herself up from her seat.

"Oof." He grabs at where her hand just was. "That was rude."

"Not as rude as you forcing me to break into Jude's apartment, making me see his very naked and very pale ass."

Jasper laughs. "Please. It's not like it's the first time. Remember when he spent that entire summer mooning everyone who walked in the house?"

"I was four!" I argue, but it's to no avail. They're already discussing all the other horrible nudity habits I had as a kid, including how I used to get completely naked to poop. Thank fuck I outgrew that one.

I let them have their fun, turning my attention to the waiting messages.

@OliveMe: TAP TO SEE PHOTO

I click on each photo—all ten of them—and laughter bubbles out of me as they fill my screen.

It's her chickens. Each one has its own headshot; then there's a group photo, and finally they're all lined up and sitting pretty with who I presume is a young Olive in the middle.

@OliveMe: I'm like 99% certain these don't qualify as dick pics.

@JasperRafferty: I don't know. You did just send me ten pictures of nothing but cocks . . .

@OliveMe: Hey! All of those chickens were lady chickens!

@JasperRafferty: Semantics.

@OliveMe: Now do you think I'm crazy?

@JasperRafferty: Nah. If anything, I think I like you more.

@OliveMe: Lucky me. 😉

"Is that the girl?"

I snap my head up, effectively pulling myself from the spell Olive seems to have me under, to find my brother and sister staring at me with wide eyes.

"Huh?" I ask.

Cait nods toward my phone. "Is that @OliveMe?"

"And more importantly"—Jasper holds up a single finger—"who the fuck *is* @OliveMe, and when did this start?"

When I snooped around your inbox.

For obvious reasons, I don't tell him that. I can't. It would be admitting to entirely too much, and getting into a fight—another one, that is—isn't high on my list of things to do tonight.

I just want to get through this thing, then come home and forget it with a nice glass of whiskey. Only then will I consider telling Jasper I snuck into his messages and made a new friend.

"We should get going," I tell them, dodging their inquiries and grabbing my wallet from the coffee table.

They exchange a glance—one I really, *really* don't like—but don't say anything as they follow me from the apartment.

I'm thankful for it.

So thankful, in fact, I decide to pay Dylan back for sending them over here in the first place.

"Phone," I command Jasper as we step into the elevator.

"What for?" he asks but hands his device over anyway.

"You wanted Dylan's number, right?"

"Jude!" Cait admonishes, shaking her head.

"What? Apparently, giving out personal information is totally on the table."

It's not. But I'd much rather face Dylan's wrath than have my siblings grill me on who Olive is.

Lesser of two evils and all that, right?

The elevator hits the lobby, and we pile out, Cait leading the way. We're halfway to the revolving door when Jasper's hand lands on my shoulder, slowing me down.

We come to a stop, and I glance down at where his hand is digging into me. He doesn't relent. Instead, he steps closer, towering over me like he has our entire lives.

I lift a brow at him. "Yes?"

"She might be willing to drop it . . ." He nods toward our sister. "But I have questions, little brother."

"Questions that you're not getting answers to."

"Oh, come on." He smirks. "You tell me everything eventually, Jude. I'm sure this will be no exception."

I want to argue with him. Want to tell him he's wrong and to butt out of it.

But he's right. I *do* tell him everything. I'm sure I'll come clean about this eventually, and he'll convince me of what I already know: it's all a bad idea.

But I'm not ready to get into that yet. I want to hold on to it just a little bit longer.

I nod once, and he claps me on the shoulder.

"Good." He taps the side of my face twice. "Now come on. We don't want to be late for the show. I have an early flight to LA in the morning, so let's get this over with."

I groan, then follow him from the building, wondering for the millionth time how I let Dylan rope me into this.

I love acting. I love acting. I love acting.

Maybe if I repeat it enough, I'll forget all the reasons I hate it too.

CHAPTER TEN

Olive

The warm August sun wakes me from sleep, but it's my phone rattling across the bedside table that has me peeling my eyes open and reaching over.

A smile spreads across my face when I see the notification waiting for me.

@JasperRafferty: In case you're wondering . . . That musical was just as awful as I thought it would be.

Who thought I'd wake up not one but two days in a row with a message from one of the biggest leading actors in the world?

@OliveMe: I'll bet ten bucks you tapped your toes at least twice.

@JasperRafferty: Then you'll be out ten bucks.

@OliveMe: Nothing? Not even a little head bob?

@JasperRafferty: I guess technically, my head bobbed forward when I fell asleep. Does that count?

@OliveMe: If it nets me ten bucks, then yes.

@JasperRafferty: That feels like cheating.

@OliveMe: Who? Me? *bats lashes*

@OliveMe: For real, I'm sorry it was just as terrible as you were expecting. But if you didn't want to go, why did you?

@JasperRafferty: Well, you're a model, so I'm assuming you understand the obnoxious nuisances of living a life in the public eye.

@OliveMe: Ah. You were forced.

@JasperRafferty: I really love my publicist, but she drives me batty sometimes.

@OliveMe: It's the beast of the business sometimes. We have to do things we really don't want to do in hopes of it paying off nicely one day.

@JasperRafferty: Ain't that the truth.

@OliveMe: You totally hate all the hubbub that goes with being a star, don't you?

@JasperRafferty: That obvious?

@OliveMe: Honestly? No. You look like you enjoy it. But talking to you now, it doesn't seem like you do at all.

@JasperRafferty: Trust me, the media doesn't always portray the truth.

I think back to all the times I've seen articles about Jasper out partying or having a different woman on his arm every month or two. It would seem like he enjoys this life just fine, but I know I shouldn't be so quick to judge. I bet from my photos that it looks like I'm having the time of my life, too, even though there are many nights I lie awake wishing for bigger things.

@OliveMe: You're right. I shouldn't have assumed.

@JasperRafferty: I used to think my parents had the greatest lives ever. Hell, a part of me still does. Then I have a camera shoved in my face a time too many, and I start to rethink all my decisions leading up to this point.

@OliveMe: Do you ever regret following in your family's footsteps and going into acting?

@JasperRafferty: Sometimes.

@JasperRafferty: I know that probably makes me sound like a privileged asshat, but it's true.

@OliveMe: A Rafferty or not, it doesn't make you any less human. You're allowed to be unhappy.

@JasperRafferty: I . . . I don't think anyone's ever told me that.

My heart squeezes at his confession. I can't imagine the pressure he feels being from one of the most prominent Hollywood families. That must come with a lot of baggage.

@JasperRafferty: Well, that got a lot deeper than I anticipated.

@OliveMe: That's what she said.

@JasperRafferty: I walked right into that one, didn't I?

@OliveMe: Face-first and everything.

@JasperRafferty: Wish me luck. I'm heading to another live interview. Fingers crossed this one isn't as awful as the last.

Did he have a bad one lately? I can't recall. Then again, I don't watch much live TV. I just wait for the recap on social media, and I haven't seen anything on him.

Either he's just being dramatic or something happened and I missed it.

Curious, I type his name into the search engine and wait for the results to load. It's mostly him being spotted in New York, promoting an upcoming action movie.

Speaking of his brother . . .

He made a total fool of himself, and the headlines prove it. I cringe as I read some of them, feeling awful for the guy. Speculations of drug and alcohol misuse are running rampant, along with accusations he had his dad call in a favor to get the role in his latest movie—it's all a total disaster.

There's a recent snapshot of him coming out of the Broadway show from the night before. I had no clue Jasper was with his family last night. He left that part out. But at least this means he wasn't lying about going out last night. So maybe that means he's not lying about who he is either.

A new notification pops up.

Jasper Rafferty has posted an image.

Already? That's . . . odd.

I click on it, and I know immediately something is off.

It's a picture of Jasper, but it's the caption that really catches my interest.

On set for Lunch with Kelly and AJ in LA today.

It's from today. It's from today and in LA.

Which means . . .

"Annie?" I call out, hoping like hell my roommate is here.

"Fire escape!" she yells back.

I fly out of my bed, not bothering to stop and put on pants as I make my way to the fire escape.

I poke my head out the window to find Annie with her legs resting on the railing and a fantasy novel in her hands.

"What's up?" she asks, twisting her neck to get a look at me.

"I cha—" She shifts and that's when I see it—something shiny glinting off her finger.

My eyes narrow at her new accessory. "Did you have something to tell me?"

A slow smile forms on her lips, and she lifts her shoulder. "We got engaged."

"You got engaged?!"

"Pipe down over there!" Mrs. Hammish shouts from her kitchen, where I just know she's sitting with her window open so she can hear the neighborhood gossip.

I snicker, then turn back to my supposed best friend. "You got engaged and didn't tell me?"

Another casual shrug, as if this isn't the biggest news of her life. "You were sleeping by the time I got home."

"So? Wake me up! This is huge!"

"Not as huge as your mouth!" Mrs. Hammish hollers.

I flip the old lady the bird, and Annie giggles.

"You better not be making faces at me, little girl!"

We both grin, ignoring our neighbor.

"Well, how did it happen?" I ask Annie. "Oh! Hold that thought. We need celebration wine."

"It's nine in the morning, Liv."

"So?" I shrug. "Time is a construct, especially when it comes to vacations and special occasions. *This* is a special occasion."

I duck back into the apartment before she can argue any further and head for the fridge, then pull out a fresh bottle of sweet red. I am so glad I made stopping for booze an item on my to-do list yesterday.

When I crawl back out onto the fire escape with the bottle of wine and two mugs, I find that Annie has abandoned her novel and is now sitting up.

I unscrew the booze and fill the coffee cups.

"What's with the mugs?" Annie asks, grabbing one for herself.

"It's morning. We can pretend it's breakfast booze."

She laughs, shaking her head and taking a sip. She makes a face. "Wine and toothpaste are not a stellar combination."

"Good thing I haven't brushed my teeth yet, then." I grin over at her, then take a healthy sip of my own wine. "So, tell me everything."

"Well . . ." she starts, drawing out the word and gazing out at the city, our street just starting to come to life with commuters. Early morning is one of my favorite times to sit out on the fire escape. Seeing the sun sparkle against all the different buildings and cars, the people rushing to work . . . There's nothing like it in the world. "It was amazing."

"That's it? Just 'amazing'? No details?"

"I'm getting there, I'm getting there." She takes another sip of her wine, then sighs, resting back in her chair. "He had a bouquet of flowers when he picked me up."

I gasp. I don't know why I do. Maybe I'm just that desperate for any slice of romance, even if it's not happening directly to me. "What kind of flowers?"

"Carnations." She laughs. "But he gets points for trying."

I shake my head with a smile. Carnations are *so* Remi.

While my best friend is all fire and go, go, go, her fiancé is her opposite. He's laid-back and chill and totally content staying holed up in his apartment working on . . . well, whatever he works on. They remind me of my parents. My mom is the one who lives in her own little world, and my dad was always the one wanting adventure. Somehow, they made it work, and I know Annie and Remi will too.

"Anyway, he had flowers, then escorted me—my hand on his arm and everything—to *Dolce*, where he promptly ordered a bottle of their finest, and cheapest, house wine."

I press my lips together, trying not to laugh. It's cute because it's them, and I absolutely *love* the glow on Annie as she recounts what happened next—Remi fumbling his way through dinner, knocking over his water, then dropping the ring not once or twice but *three* times before someone else finally picked it up and helped slide it onto Annie's finger.

By the time she's done, I have tears pricking my eyes, and I want to do nothing but throw my arms around her and hug her.

So I do.

"I'm so happy for you," I tell her.

"Thank you." She squeezes me back just as tightly. "I'm happy too."

I wipe my eyes when we part, and don't miss when Annie does the same. "So, what's next? You're moving out, right?"

Panic shoots through me because *what about rent?*

I instantly feel bad. This isn't the time to be worried about me. This is about Annie.

"Maybe? I don't know. We'll see." She shrugs, and I let out a relieved breath. "I'm not in any rush. Clearly." She laughs, then tips her head toward me. "What'd you need?"

"Hmm?" I ask over the rim of my coffee cup.

"When you came out here. You looked panicked. What's going on?"

"Oh. That."

With all the excitement of Annie's engagement, I'd almost forgotten about my Jasper drama.

"Is it Jasper?" she guesses, and I nod. "Uh-oh. What happened?"

"Nothing. Yet. At least, I don't *think* yet." I dig my phone out from my pocket, then navigate back to what I found on Instagram. "He's in LA."

She grabs my phone, looking at the photo for several moments before saying, "Okay. Is that a bad thing?"

"Well, he was in New York last night."

"And he's a gazillionaire." She hands my phone back to me. "He probably has his own private jet and flew out early this morning. Or maybe it was his assistant that posted it. You never know."

Leave it to Annie to be practical about this . . .

"True," I acquiesce. "But this morning when we were messaging, we—"

"You're still messaging him?" She sounds surprised by this, and I nod.

"I am. It's nothing earth shattering, but it's . . . fun. Easy, you know?"

"If it's easy, then why are you worried about him being in LA?"

"That's the thing, Annie. It's easy. *Too* easy. We get along well and it's just . . . Well, it's . . ."

"Too good to be true?" she finishes for me, knowing I can't bring myself to give a voice to my doubts.

"Yeah," I whisper. "That."

She smiles softly. "But maybe it's *not* too good to be true. Maybe it *is* true. Did you ever think about that?"

Of course I did. I thought about that way too much over the last two days. But just because I've thought about it doesn't make it any more possible.

But it doesn't make it any *less* possible, either, I guess. Crazier things have happened. I've heard of people meeting their celebrity crush and falling in love with them. Heck, I just saw an article recently about a hockey player from North Carolina falling for his now fiancée after he started training her daughter, who was a mega fan of his. It could happen.

Besides, if Annie isn't worried about him being in LA this morning when he was just in New York last night, then I shouldn't be either.

"You're probably right," I say, clicking off my phone and setting it down, exchanging it for my morning wine. "I'm sure it's nothing."

"I'm sure too," Annie says, kicking her feet back up on the railing with her own wine mug in her hands. "But if you need Remi . . ."

I shoot her a grin. "I know, I know."

"Good." She closes her eyes, letting the morning sun wash over her.

That's how we sit for the next five minutes, both of us soaking in the rays and enjoying our breakfast of champions, her probably reeling over the fact that she's now engaged and me trying hard not to think about how wrong this thing with Jasper could go.

But the more I try not to think about it, the more frustrated I get.

Why do I always have to assume the worst? Why can't I just be happy that something good is happening to me? Why do I always—

"I can hear you thinking, Liv," Annie says.

I grimace. "Sorry."

She laughs, then sits up and empties the rest of her cup. Her brown eyes bore into me, a mischievous grin pulling at the corner of her lips.

"Want to go look at wedding dresses with me?"

And just like that, all thoughts of Jasper are gone.

Who needs boy drama when there's a wedding to plan?

◆ ◆ ◆

"You know, you don't have to find the right dress today. We're just supposed to be having fun and doing some *pre*-shopping shopping."

"I know! But I think I found the one!"

I huff, tapping my foot and flipping my phone in my hand as I sit on a couch in the eighth—or is it ninth?—dress shop we've been in today.

"You've been saying that for hours," I mutter.

"I heard that!" Annie calls from the dressing room. "Seriously, this one is perfect. Just wait."

I *have* been waiting . . . all damn day.

But I won't say that out loud. She's having entirely too much fun running from shop to shop, trying on all the different dresses, sipping complimentary champagne while we browse. She's been glowing since this morning, and I don't want to rain on her parade.

Who cares if all this has done is remind me of the fact that I'm single and lonely? This day is about her. Not me.

My phone vibrates in my hand, startling me enough that I drop it.

"What'd you break?" Annie asks.

"Nothing!" I call back, hoping I'm not lying as I pick my phone up off the bridal-shop floor.

Phew. No cracks.

I click on the screen and am surprised to find a waiting notification.

@JasperRafferty has sent you a message.

I waste no time clicking on it, eager to see what he has to say.

I'd like to say that I haven't thought about him or my doubts surrounding him at all today, but that wouldn't be true. There have been too many instances where I think of something funny or something I want to remember for later and go to write it in my journal, only to remember that I can't do that anymore—at least, not like I used to.

@JasperRafferty: How many interviews are too many interviews in one single day? I'm all interviewed out, I think.

He's doing interviews all day? I guess Annie was right, then. It is possible for him to be in LA this morning after being in New York just last night—he's busy promoting his upcoming movie. I've been seeing promos for it, a rom-com coming out in the early fall that looks hilarious. He's going to be flying all over the world, I'm sure.

Guess I worried for nothing.

@OliveMe: Well, that was a lot of interviews just right there. I think you are, indeed, interviewed out.

@OliveMe: Honestly, I don't know how you do it. I'm tapped out for days after a photo shoot. Jumping from interview to interview, where they likely ask the same questions, has to be tiring.

@JasperRafferty: I repeat myself all. Damn. Day.

@OliveMe: Sorry, could you repeat that?

@JasperRafferty: You're kind of a brat, you know that?

@OliveMe: Oh, I'm aware. I'm just glad you are too. ☺

@OliveMe: If it makes you feel better, I've been repeating myself all day too.

@JasperRafferty: Sorry, could you repeat that?

@OliveMe: Ha! Very funny, mister.

@JasperRafferty: I'm a natural comedian.

@OliveMe: Clearly.

@JasperRafferty: Why have you been repeating yourself all day?

@OliveMe: I'm wedding dress shopping, so it's a lot of "This is what we're looking for" and even more "No, next."

@JasperRafferty: . . . you're getting married? I think we might have skipped over some information.

@OliveMe: What? No! It's for Annie.

@JasperRafferty: The roommate?

@OliveMe: The one and only.

@JasperRafferty: I thought she was breaking up with the boyfriend?

@OliveMe: She was bluffing. She always does. He proposed last night.

@JasperRafferty: And you're already wedding dress shopping?

@OliveMe: PRE wedding dress shopping. Allegedly.

@OliveMe: But we've been in so many stores today that I've honestly lost track, so I'm not certain it's "PRE" anything anymore.

@JasperRafferty: That sounds like a big nope for me.

@OliveMe: Good thing you weren't invited, then. 😀

@OliveMe: You did give good advice in Always the Bridesmaid, though. Maybe we could use your help after all . . .

@JasperRafferty: Um, what?

@OliveMe: You know, the movie with all those wedding dresses. You played the best friend to the girl who was always the bridesmaid and never the bride until your character finally realized what was right in front of him the whole time?

@OliveMe: It starred you and Lucy Newsome?

@OliveMe: Did you block that out too?

@JasperRafferty: Must have.

@JasperRafferty: I remember it now.

"Why are you staring at your phone like that?"

I startle, nearly dropping said phone again, and whip my head up to see Annie. All thoughts of Jasper fly from my mind. She's standing before me in a floor-length mermaid-style dress that hugs all her curves, creating the perfect silhouette. It's a beautiful cream color, with a heart-shaped cutout right under her breasts, and it's stunning on her.

I slide my eyes to the saleswoman—she's looking at Annie with the same knowing look in her eyes.

This is the dress.

"You look perfect," I tell her, still unable to take my eyes off the little beaded details. "This is the one."

She chews on her bottom lip, her brows pulled in together. "Do you think so?"

"I *know* so," I assure her. "You look . . . Wow. Remi is going to be as speechless as me."

"You don't think it's too soon? We've hardly even looked. This could be a fluke. We could find something better down the line."

I shake my head. "No. This is the one. I have a feeling."

"But—"

"How many dresses have you tried on today?"

"Probably twenty or so."

I know she's aiming low with her guess. It's more. It has to be. She grabbed at least five dresses at each shop, which means we're definitely inching closer to the fifty mark, if not more.

"And how does this dress make you feel?"

"Like a queen."

Her answer is automatic. No hesitation.

It's a telling answer.

Annie grins. "This is the one."

I nod. "It is."

She looks over at the saleswoman. "This is the one."

"And you're certain?"

"I am."

"Good." The saleswoman grins brightly. "Because I think your friend is right. This is the perfect dress for you. I'll grab the champagne."

Annie claps her hands, bouncing back and forth. "I can't believe it. I . . . I'm getting married!"

Her excitement is palpable, and suddenly I'm on my feet, clapping and jumping right along with her, my phone and the message from Jasper long forgotten.

After celebrating with a glass of champagne—I've lost count of which number we're on of those too—I help Annie unzip her dress, then flop down onto the couch and fish my phone out of the cushions as she heads back into the dressing room.

"Who is that you're talking to?" she asks from behind the curtain, the saleswoman long gone with the dress in hand. "Is it *him*?"

"It's him."

"And why'd your face look so . . . scrunchy when I came out? You were staring at your phone looking super confused."

"Because I *am* confused. I told him we were dress shopping; then I made a joke about one of his movies, and he didn't get the reference. He did that before, too, when I was talking to him about musicals. He said he hates them, but he's done one before, and I know he has because you made me watch *Lease on Love* about ten billion times."

"Oh."

That's all Annie says, and I'm not exactly sure what to make of it. Just like I'm not sure what to make of the fact that this is the second time now that Jasper hasn't been able to remember one of his roles. Is his assistant running his account? Or is it just an actor thing? You do a role and then totally brain-dump it?

I don't know, but I *do* know that it doesn't entirely sit right with me. Something just feels . . . off.

Am I being paranoid?

"Possibly," Annie answers, and it's only then I realize I voiced the question out loud. "But maybe not. That is really weird he's done it twice now. Once, sure. He's been in a lot of things. But to not remember two projects like that? I don't know. My fishy meter is starting to spike."

"You told me earlier it was all in my head."

"No." She pokes her face through the curtains, and I try not to laugh at how ridiculous she looks—a floating head in the middle of a bridal shop. "I told you there was possibly a logical explanation for him being in New York and then LA the next morning. You didn't mention this other stuff."

She disappears again, but not before giving me a pointed look.

Because at first, *I* didn't think it was a big deal. But after the LA thing and now this . . .

Well, my fishy meter is spiking too.

Annie shoves open the curtain as the saleswoman comes flouncing back into the room where we've been tucked away for the last hour.

"Did you need help with shoes? Perhaps a tiara for the queen?" she offers Annie.

"I think I'm all shopped out today. We'll save all that for another time. Besides, we're still a *really* long time away from walking down the aisle."

She says it like she's so sure of it, but I have a feeling that Annie will be saying "I Do" sooner than she thinks.

"Totally understand. You ladies take your time. I'll be out at the register whenever you're ready."

The saleswoman scurries from the back room, leaving us alone.

My best friend throws herself onto the couch next to me with a heavy sigh.

"I'm exhausted," she says. "And hungry. Do you want to grab something for lunch? What about burgers and milkshakes?"

I laugh. "Whatever the bride wants."

"*Bride.* I still can't believe it." She nudges her knee against mine. "Maybe you'll be next. Maybe even with *you know who.*" She waggles her brows up and down a few times. "You know, after you figure out why he can't remember his own movies."

I force a laugh. "Yeah, maybe."

But I don't share her optimism.

If anything, it makes the alarm bells in my head ring even louder just thinking about him. Or his assistant. Or publicist.

"Are you okay?" she asks, staring down at me, worry filling her brown eyes.

"No," I say honestly, then swallow the lump that seems to have formed in my throat. "I . . . I think I need to call Remi."

Her eyes widen. "Are you sure?"

I nod. "I'm sure. I want your fiancé to cyberstalk Jasper Rafferty for me."

CHAPTER ELEVEN

Jude

@JasperRafferty: You never did tell me how the dress shopping went yesterday . . .

@OliveMe: She said yes to the dress. We got drunk on champagne. It was a magical afternoon.

@JasperRafferty: Wow. Well, congrats to Annie.

@OliveMe: I'm happy for her. She deserves this.

@JasperRafferty: Everyone deserves to be happy.

@OliveMe: Yeah, well, not all of us get that.

@JasperRafferty: Rough day?

@OliveMe: Not sure yet.

@Jasper Rafferty: Well, if you ever want to talk, I'm here.

I watch the screen, waiting for her to respond, but after several minutes pass, I know she's not going to.

I push off the wall of the building I was leaning against and make my way to the coffee line I can't seem to stay out of, trying not to read too much into Olive's short answers.

She's probably just having a rough day. I'm sure that's it.

Maybe I should send her something to cheer her up?

I step up behind some guy, then pull my phone back out.

@JasperRafferty: How do chickens bake cakes? From scratch!

@JasperRafferty: Who takes care of chickens? Chicken tenders!

@JasperRafferty: What did the rooster say to the chicken? You're impeck-able.

@JasperRafferty: What do you call a haunting chicken? A poultry-geist.

@JasperRafferty: Okay, that's all the chicken jokes I know.

@JasperRafferty: Hope they cheer you up.

"Next!"

I step forward as the person in front of me inches toward the counter.

After two podcast sessions this morning and a Zoom chat with a studio executive about the Vancouver shoot in a couple of weeks, I'm in dire need of an afternoon pick-me-up.

"You've got to be kidding me . . ."

An automatic grin pulls at my lips at the voice that's now become familiar.

I do a half turn, peeking over my shoulder at the woman standing behind me.

"Afternoon, Sunshine."

"Asshat," she says, crossing her arms over her chest in her usual defensive move, but her words are missing their usual bite. I think we've finally come to an understanding, she and I. "Stalk much?"

"You're behind me, so who is stalking whom?"

"That means nothing. You know I come here. Maybe this is your fourth time here today just so you can stalk me. I mean, your outfit is giving total stalker vibes, so it's possible."

"Has anyone ever told you that you think a little too highly of yourself?"

"Has anyone ever told you that you're an asshat?"

"You know, come to think of it . . ." I tap my finger against my chin, then snap them, pointing at her. "You did."

She grins spitefully. "And I meant it."

I laugh. "At least you say what you mean."

"I'm nothing if not honest, unlike some people."

Her words smash a hole right into my stomach and fall deep down into a pit of unease, that same pit that's been there for days.

Guilt.

Over Olive. Over lying to her. Over impersonating my brother.

It's eating at me, and it's why I think I want to make her feel better, even if it is just by sending her silly chicken jokes.

"Sorry," Sunshine says. "That wasn't pointed at you. Other drama."

"I can't imagine you having drama with someone."

I'd bet good money that she just rolled her eyes. I wish I could confirm, but once again, she's hiding behind those massive sunglasses. Not that I have any room to talk, but at least I'm hiding for a good reason.

"So, am I going to see you here every day now?" she asks.

"I don't know. Are you going to stalk me every day?"

I'm only being a little serious. I'm not getting any bad vibes from her, but that doesn't mean it hasn't crossed my mind. I doubt it, though.

"You got me. I'm super obsessed with you. I'm just swooning into a puddle of lust with each tic of your sexy jawline."

"You think my jawline's sexy?"

Her face falls. "N-No. I didn't . . ." She scowls, tightening her arms over her chest. "That's not what I meant."

Oh, but it is.

However, I'm going to let it slide.

Instead, I focus on her ridiculous shirt. There are about six different types of eggs on it. One is doing "egg-cercise" while another is clearly a *devil*ed egg, horns and all. They keep going, from smiling to frowning, and one is even bent over in a pair of shorts, saying, *Is my crack showing?*

It's silly, and I absolutely love it.

"That's an *egg*-cellent shirt you're wearing."

I watch in wonder as she tips her head back, her entire body shaking as she lets out a loud, attention-pulling laugh.

I've not seen her laugh before—at least, not like this. Most of her laughs are derisive, but this one is the exact opposite. It's genuine.

I like it. A lot.

That same feeling of familiarity claws at me again, but I shake it away, too entranced by what I'm witnessing.

"Thank you," she says when she finally regains her composure. "It's one of my favorites. I've had it a long time, if that's not obvious by the fading."

"It suits you."

She tips her head to the side. "Suits me?"

"Yep. Especially the *sunny*-side-up one."

"Ah." She nods. "Sunshine."

"Yep. It just radiates off you."

It's funny because it's so not true. Not once in the three times that I've run into her now has she been anything other than thoroughly annoyed with me. I mean, I've always deserved it, but still.

"You know, it's funny because I actually am a nice girl. But there's just something about you that brings out the worst in me."

"Is it my sexy jawline?"

"You caught me. I'm just all kinds of riled up by your jaw."

But once again, her words are missing that usual bite of hatred. They almost seem . . . real.

Huh. Interesting.

I go to take a step toward her, just to see if I can get a rise out of her, but I'm summoned by the guy behind the counter before I can.

"Next!"

I turn, ready to place my order, but I'm beaten to it.

"Black drip?"

I chuckle. "That predictable?"

He shrugs. "Most drip people don't stray far from their usual."

He grabs a cup, scribbles something on the side, then sets it next to the group of other cups waiting to be filled by his partner.

"Usual, Liv?" he asks, grabbing another cup, already scribbling what I assume is her name on it. "Danish too?"

"Please, Ric."

"You got it, sweetheart." He shuts off the nozzle and slides my coffee my way. "Two dollars and fifty cents."

"Hers too," I tell him, pulling my black Amex from my wallet. "And another danish for me."

"No, no, no," Sunshine says to him. "I can get my own."

I ignore her, shoving my card into Ric's hand.

"Don't you dare take that card, Ric," she seethes. "I swear, I'll . . ."

"What?" I ask her. "Stop coming here? Then who will you stalk?"

Ric laughs, but it's cut off by the huff she sends his way. He turns his attention to the register, then hands my card back to me and begins to make her drink.

"I can buy my own coffee," she tells me.

"That's a long-winded way of saying *Thank you.*"

She grits her teeth but manages to mutter a pained, "Thank you . . . Asshat."

I laugh, then grab my danish off the counter. "It was good seeing you, Sunshine."

"Hmm," is her response. When Ric hands her the coffee, she grabs her treats and marches down the street in the opposite direction without another word.

It's not until I'm halfway to my apartment that I realize what's written on the side of my cup.

Asshat.

◆ ◆ ◆

"You've been sitting here for two hours, you know," my sister says with a smile as she checks on me for the fourth time since I sat down.

To anyone else, it might seem like she's grinning down at the average customer.

But as someone who has known her for more than twenty-five years, I know that the smile plastered on her face is fake and she's dying to reach out and smack the back of my head.

She wants me gone, and I don't blame her. I've been sitting here taking up a table for two hours. It's frustrating for her, especially with how busy this place is, customers constantly coming and going. She doesn't need me here wasting space like I am. She's trying to run a business.

Problem is, I can't leave.

There are currently four paparazzi loitering out front, and I have zero interest in taking their bait.

I'm waiting them out. The last thing I need is for them to regularly park themselves outside my sister's bakery and cause problems for her.

Until they leave, I'm staying.

"You look like a total tool wearing those sunglasses in here. At least take them off."

"Fine." I tug them from my face but pull my hat down lower. This disguise has done a decent job of keeping the paparazzi off my back over the last week, but based on the circus outside, they've caught on to my tricks.

"You could sneak out the back," Cait murmurs.

"And miss this delicious free fudge?"

"It is *not* free," she practically growls at me. "I have a baby on the way that I have to support."

"Not even for your favorite brother?"

"Right now, I like Jasper more than I like you."

I feign hurt. "That's a low blow, Cait."

"It's the truth, *Jude*."

"You're my least favorite sister now, *Cait*."

"I don't care. Leave, *Jude*."

"You know," I tell her, stretching back into my chair, "these chairs are super comfortable. I think maybe I'll stick around for a bit longer. Could I get a few more pieces of fudge?"

Her eyes tighten on me, and I just *know* I'm going to hear about this later when she can properly yell at me.

"Sure thing, Mr. Rafferty."

She says that last part a little too loudly, and a few heads turn my way.

I grin at the people who've looked over at us with curiosity, then turn that grin toward my little sister. "You're off my Christmas list."

She gives me an equally fake saccharine grin. "Your presents suck anyway."

That earns a real gasp from me. "I took you to Vail!"

"So?" She shrugs. "Mom and Dad took me there first."

"You know, I was considering asking you to be my date for my movie premiere, but I think I'll take someone else now."

"Oh no. And miss a Hollywood event I didn't even want to go to? How will I ever survive?" She rolls her eyes. "I'll grab that fudge for you."

"S'mores!" I call out to her retreating back.

She waves me off, and I laugh.

It feels good to laugh, to banter with my sister and relax for just a moment. I've been so *on* these last few days, hopping from interview to interview—even throwing in a few photo shoots—at Dylan's insistence.

This small moment of normal with my sister is just what I needed.

Especially since I haven't been able to get my "normal" fix from Olive lately. She finally responded to my chicken jokes with a simple "lol," but I haven't heard from her since.

I know it's for the best, given the circumstances, but I can't help it—I miss her.

I liked talking with her about mundane things, like how her day was going or the little updates about her and Annie. It's been nice to not have to be *on* with her. She's never treated me like anything other than ordinary.

I want that.

"Here." Cait sets a fresh plate of fudge in front of me, and I know right away it isn't the flavor I asked for.

"I wanted s'mores."

"Well, tough damn tits. I sold the last piece to a *paying* customer."

"Is that what gets me the fudge I ordered? Money?" I pull my wallet from my back pocket and pluck free a crisp hundred-dollar bill. I slam it on the table. "S'mores now, please."

"We're out." She snatches the money off the table. "But I'll gladly take this."

"Hey!" I call out, but she's already walking away.

I take it back. I don't like this moment of normal. Now I'm out a hundred bucks *and* I don't get the fudge I wanted.

Siblings are the worst.

I pick up my fork and stab at the pile of sugary goodness on my plate, then shove a bite into my mouth.

Caramel flavor explodes over my tongue, followed by a hint of salt, and I grin.

Salted caramel. One of my favorites.

"She loves me," I mutter to myself before I shovel in another piece.

I chew, swallow, then wash it down with my coffee. Cait hasn't yelled at me for bringing JT's coffee into her shop. Probably because she knows just how delicious it is.

I keep my eye on the group of idiots outside while I enjoy the fudge and the coffee, which is how I'm able to spot the woman angrily heading for the shop.

Her head is down, but there is no mistaking that this woman is mad. It's clear in her stiff shoulders, in the way she's moving so fast that the long mustard-yellow dress clinging to her curves flows behind her as she blazes her way into the shop.

She pushes the door open so hard it slams against the wall, and everyone inside freezes, me included.

I pause, the fork halfway to my mouth, as she scans the customers. Thanks to the sunglasses covering her face, I only know this because of her head slowly swiveling around.

I know this woman. How do I know this woman?

She continues her perusal, her shoulders somehow growing tighter and tighter as she looks around. She takes a step forward, approaching a table for only a moment before retreating without saying a word. Another table draws her attention, but she moves on quickly.

People are staring at her as she stares back at them, looking hard at every person. Clearly looking for something.

For *someone.*

Then her eyes land on me, and I only know it because I can *feel* her heated gaze through her sunglasses.

Her back straightens. Her body goes rigid. Then her hands clench into fists at her sides as she marches across the shop, not at all caring about the attention she's drawing.

She halts in front of my table.

She tips her head to the side, studying me from behind her glasses. It's eerie. Not because of what she's doing, but because there's just something about her . . .

Her head drops and it's obvious she's looking at the cup on the table, the one I got from the coffee truck this morning.

The one that says ASSHAT across the side.

Her mouth drops open on a gasp. "It's you."

That voice. I know that voice. It's so familiar. So—

Holy shit.

She pushes her sunglasses to the top of her head, and my entire world tilts. So many things begin clicking into place, and yet so many questions arise at the same time.

It's Olive.

It's Sunshine.

Sunshine *is* Olive.

The woman whom I cut off in line—then let cut *me* off—is the same one I've been messaging with for the last few days.

I . . . I know all her secrets. All her hopes and dreams and every little fear.

This is bad. This is really fucking bad.

Her lips curl in disgust. "I . . . I don't even have the words."

Her blue eyes—how is it even possible for eyes to be that blue?—bounce between my green ones, and I see the second it all clicks into place for her.

She knows.

I'm Jasper.

I'm Asshat.

I'm Jude.

And suddenly, I'm all caught up in the web of lies I've been weaving.

"No." Her long brown hair swishes as she shakes her head. "No, no, no."

"I . . ."

"H-How? How could you, you . . . you . . . asshat!"

A smile tugs at the corner of my lips, and I know immediately it's the wrong reaction to have to this situation.

The same eyes I've gotten lost in so many times over the week—as I've continued to scroll through Olive's Instagram—light with fire, and I know I'm about to get scorched.

"Um, hi," I say, sliding my gaze around the bakery. We have the full attention of every patron. People are turned around in their chairs and staring at us, fully invested in the show that's playing out before them.

I might love acting and performing, but not like this.

I stand, stepping closer to her, but she stumbles backward and away from me.

"'Hi'? *Hi?* That's all you're going to say to me?"

"Sunshine, I—"

"Don't call me that!"

I swallow thickly. "Okay, Liv."

She holds her hand up. "Don't call me that either. In fact, don't call me *anything*, ever. This"—she wags her finger between the two of us—"whatever sick game you were playing, it's over. Delete the messages and delete me from your life."

She huffs in disgust, then turns on her heel and stalks out of the bakery just as quickly as she stormed in, leaving nothing but chaos in her wake.

The paparazzi outside go wild, snapping photo after photo, their flashing bulbs illuminating the bakery and me.

Cait, the amazing sister that she is, rushes to close the door, blocking me from view. I'm still standing in the middle of the shop with my mouth dropped open, looking like the absolute jackass I am.

Did that just really happen?

My sister inches through the bakery, sending her customers soft, reassuring smiles.

"Jude," she says as she approaches, that sweet smile not wavering, "what just happened?"

"It was nothing," I lie.

"Was that . . . Was that the Instagram model Olive O'Brien?"

Her words shock me. "You know her?"

"No. I mean, sort of. I just started following her after I saw her name on your phone." She shrugs. "I was curious." Cait steps closer, whispering, "Are you dating her?"

"No. I . . ." I'm not dating her. That's not what this is. But it's also not *nothing*. Is it? "I need to talk to her. I need to fix it."

"But the cameras . . ."

"I don't have any other option, Cait. I have to go."

The same green eyes I have—a family trait—study me for several seconds until she finally nods.

"Okay. All right. Just . . . go out the back, will you? This is my place of business, Jude. I don't care if you're my brother. If you bring any more drama in here, I *will* ban you."

And I have no doubt she means it.

"Noted, little sister."

No matter how badly she wants to be annoyed with me right now, her lips twitch as she shakes her head at me. "You're exhausting."

"And you love me." I send her a wink, then turn toward the captivated audience. With my best, most charming Rafferty grin, I announce, "Treats are on me today!"

"Jude!" Cait admonishes, but it's pointless—people are already cheering and lining up at the counter to collect. I slide my card over to her, and she stares at it for several seconds before reluctantly taking it with a glare pointed my way. Then she rushes away to the counter, where she's desperately needed.

While she's distracted, I make my escape, flying right out the front door and into the fray because I need to find Olive. I need to fix this.

Paparazzi be damned.

CHAPTER TWELVE

Olive

I knew it. I freaking knew it!

"Stupid, obnoxious, conniving . . . asshat!" I yell, not caring how I look as I march down the bustling sidewalk, weaving through the crowds.

I push my legs harder and faster, putting as much distance between me and that damn bakery as possible.

Jasper is Jude.

Jude is Asshat.

I was duped.

Not once, but *twice*.

I bet he knew the entire time. He had to have, right? There's no way he could have stood in front of me so many times and *not* known it was me.

I mean, sure, I didn't know it was him, but still.

He knew. I'm positive he did.

God, I can't believe I was right. Can't believe I allowed myself to get swept up in this idea that I could possibly have a romance with Jasper Rafferty. I'm a fool. A total laughingstock.

After I asked Annie to have Remi cyberstalk "Jasper," even more evidence that he wasn't who he claimed to be popped up, namely the fact that all the messages were coming from the same place, and it was right here in New York.

It took Remi only a few hours to dig up dirt and find a steady signal. When he texted and said that the signal was stagnant at a bakery in Hell's Kitchen, I *knew* I had to go.

Annie tried to talk me out of it, and I promised I wouldn't go, but the second she walked out the door for her shift, I bolted. I couldn't just sit around knowing he was so close by. I had to confront my catfisher.

But the last thing I expected was to burst into that shop and come face-to-face with the younger Rafferty brother. I was even more surprised to find out the guy hiding behind the sunglasses and ratty hat was him too.

I *knew* something about him was familiar from the start, but I ignored it. Chalked it all up to him being gorgeous, then let myself become distracted by his quick wit and ability to completely disarm me with a smirk.

I should have listened more to my gut instincts. Now look where I am, storming down the sidewalk, ready to rage.

"Sunshine!"

My steps falter. *Did I just hear my name?*

"Sunshine! Wait!"

I sneak a peek behind me, then regain speed.

Jude is following me, arm raised in the air, jogging after me like a madman.

"Sunshine!" he calls, and it fuels me even more.

I push harder, faster. I don't want to be near him right now. I don't want to hear his excuses. I don't want to hear his explanation. None of it.

I want *nothing* to do with Jude Rafferty.

"Please," he begs, gaining ground with those stupid long legs of his. "Wait!"

I don't want to wait. I don't—

"Watch out!"

But the warning comes a fraction of a second too late.

The piano suspended above me comes crashing down, crushing my skull and killing me.

The End.

Or at least, that's what I wish would have happened.

Instead, I'm lying on the disgusting sidewalk, sprawled out with a throbbing head and knee.

"Miss, are you all right?"

I gawk up at the man in a red jumpsuit and matching red hat. His dark mustache is thick, his brows even thicker. His face is pulled into a concerned expression as his eyes rake over me.

"You look like Super Mario," I tell him.

"What was that?" he asks, bending closer.

Panic races through me. Super Mario is inching closer to me and it's weird because, well, Mario isn't real.

What the hell is happening?

"Sunshine! Move! Move!"

Then, suddenly, Mario is gone, and in his place is a prince. Or at least, he looks like one, with the most beautiful green eyes I've ever seen, blond hair you could run your fingers through, and a sharp jawline to match his perfectly straight nose.

Oh, he's definitely a prince. Maybe even *the* prince.

Prince Charming, here to rescue me.

Ha. Yeah, right.

"Are you okay?" Prince Charming asks, sliding his hands over my face. His touch is gentle but still painful, especially when he brushes his fingers over my forehead.

"Ouch. That hurts."

He grimaces. "That's going to leave a nasty bruise."

"You're a nasty bruise."

He laughs, and something about it seems so familiar. I hate it. I hate that laugh.

I hate *him*.

His hands are still tracing over my face. Gentle. Loving. I smack at them. "Get away."

"Don't be like that, Sunshine. Let me help you."

Sunshine.

It all hits me at once.

He's not Prince Charming.

He's Asshat.

"Stop touching me," I growl, attempting to sit up.

"Hey, whoa. Easy now." He reaches out for me again, but when I cut a glare at him, he backs off, hands in the air. "Easy."

I can't tell whether he's saying it because he wants me to go slower or he wants me to be nicer.

Neither option is happening.

I don't want to be nice, and I certainly don't want to be around him. Not right now, and not ever.

I try to sit up again, and a wave of nausea rolls over me. I lie back down, grabbing my stomach and feeling like I'm about to lose its contents any second, but nothing happens. Not even a heave. It just . . . hurts. Like my head and my knees.

Why do my knees hurt?

"Because you ran right into some guys moving a piano," he tells me.

Did I say that out loud?

"I knew I saw a piano."

"You doubled over and smacked your head against it," he continues, "then fell to the ground. You're concussed."

"I'm not. I'm fine."

He laughs lightly. "You're not. You're hurt. We need to get you to a hospital. The paramedics will be here any moment."

"I'm not going anywhere with you," I say through gritted teeth as I try once again to get up.

"Hey, hey. No. Don't move."

"But I want to," I argue.

"Too bad, Sunshine."

I glower up at him, faintly hearing sirens approaching from some-where. *Where are we, even?*

"Stop calling me Sunshine," I demand. "You don't get to do that. Not anymore."

His lips tighten at my words, like they've actually pained him, but he nods. "Fair enough," he mutters. "I just need you to stay here. The paramedics are pulling up now. You need to get checked out."

"I'm not letting you check me out!"

He grins, and it's a good grin. The kind that makes you swoon just a little. "I'm not checking you out. Not unless you ask." He winks, and I want to hate it. "I was thinking a doctor could do the honors this time."

"I told you, I'm not—"

Suddenly, he's there, right in my face, as he hovers over me, so damn close that the green in his eyes is all I can see. It's an endless sea of emerald and jade swirls. So beautiful. So intoxicating.

It has to be the reason I stop trying to fight him and listen.

"There are about ten cameras trained on us right now, and we're drawing a crowd. I know who you are, and you know who I am. Please, if you ever enjoyed any of our late-night chats, then please do me a favor and let the medics do their job without a fight. For both our sakes." His eyes bounce between mine. "*Please*, Olive."

It's the first time he's said my name, and he does it with such famil-iarity and warmth. Like he's said it to me a thousand times before. Like we're old friends. Like we're more.

We'll never be friends and we'll never be more, but I know that what he's telling me is true—I need a doctor, and he needs to get me out of here without causing even more of a scene.

"Okay," I tell him quietly. "Okay."

"Yeah? Good. Now, I'm going to let these nice people step in; then we'll go to the hospital. Sound good?"

I glare at him, but he either doesn't care or chooses to ignore it, stepping away instead and whispering to a man in uniform as another one bends down next to me.

The next few minutes are a blur of hands coasting over me and people asking me basic questions.

What's your name, miss? Olive O'Brien.

What's your birthday, miss? October 13.

Do you know where you are, miss? The sidewalk.

What happened, miss? I ran into a piano that Super Mario was carrying; then Prince Charming tried to rescue me, and I realized he wasn't Prince Charming, just an asshat with a pretty smile.

They laugh at that one, then carefully load me into the ambulance.

"Are you riding or staying?" one man asks Jude, who is taking in the scene with worried eyes.

He looks to me, waiting for me to fight him on it.

I don't. I don't have it in me. I'm suddenly too tired to fight him. My eyelids are heavy, and I really just want to close them and take a good, long nap.

"Sir?" the medic presses.

Jude drags his eyes from me, then to the medic. "Riding."

◆ ◆ ◆

"What the hell happened?" Annie barrels into the room, the inky-black hair that I know she pulled into a neat bun before leaving for her shift now a wreck. All thanks to the full waiting room we passed by, I'm sure. It's why she's here working a double shift today. "What did you do?"

Her brown eyes are trained on Jude, who sits in the corner of the private room, and she looks murderous, like she's ready to hop over my bed and attack him herself.

Truthfully, I wouldn't put it past her. She's mean when she wants to be.

Jude, who hasn't said a word since we were ushered in here—after suspiciously waiting only five minutes—holds up his hands. "It wasn't me."

"Technically, it was." It's the first thing we've said to each other since I was lying on the sidewalk. "I mean, I was running away from you, so . . ."

He pulls his lips tight, shifting around in his chair, but doesn't say anything.

"What happened?" Annie asks me again.

"Would you believe if I said it was a piano?"

"A what?"

I laugh at the shocked expression on her face. Being an ER nurse, she hears it all, so this is a small victory.

"I ran into a piano."

She tips her head, studying me with sharp eyes. Then she cuts a look Jude's way. "She's concussed, isn't she?"

Jude chuckles. "Oh, definitely. But also, she's not lying. It was a piano."

"How?"

So we tell Annie the story. Or at least, Jude does. He leaves out the parts about Super Mario and me mistaking him for Prince Charming, but once Annie is all caught up, she nods, swiveling her head back to me.

"Are you all right?"

"I'm tired," I tell her honestly. "And sore. My head hurts, but so does my knee."

It's all bruised and ugly, and I have a horrible gash from where I fell onto the sidewalk. Coupled with the bump front and center on my forehead, there's no way I'm going to be able to attend the shoot I have booked for tomorrow. I won't be able to post anything on Instagram either.

The panic of what the hell I'm going to do to pay bills begins to set in, evident by the way the heart monitor I'm hooked up to starts to spike.

Jude's out of his chair in a flash, rushing to my bedside, but Annie recognized what's happening before he did and beats him there.

"Easy, Liv," she says soothingly. "Take it easy. We'll figure it out."

That's Annie speak for *I got you.*

I hate that I understand this, because it means she's had to spot me on the rent more than once. Sure, it's been a long time—several years—but it doesn't mean that the fear of failure isn't always lurking in the back of my mind. All it takes is one lean month or one failed ad or a bad set experience and I'm done for.

There's no doubt in my mind I could ask my mom for help and she'd send money in a heartbeat, but I'm too stubborn to do it. I can't bear admitting to her that I've failed, even if it's not my fault this time.

My eyes drift to Jude, who is lingering nearby, his forest-green eyes trained on my every move. His lips are pinched together, and if his brows inch any closer, he'll have a unibrow.

I bet he'd totally still look hot with it.

Wrapped up in my anger at the bakery, I didn't really get a chance to look at the younger Rafferty brother, the one I've apparently been messaging with.

He's just as attractive as Jasper, if not more.

Where Jasper gives off all-American quarterback vibes, Jude is different. He's just as handsome as his brother in that regard, but there's something else lurking beneath his eyes that gives him an edge his brother doesn't have. He just seems so much . . . more. More intense. More soulful. More . . . real.

Funny, given the circumstances under which we met.

"That's it," Annie says, still attempting to soothe me, her eyes on the screen displaying my vitals. "Just relax."

I tear my gaze away from Jude and look at my best friend.

"I'm good now, Mom."

Annie gives me a sharp look, dropping her hands away from me. "Good to see that concussion hasn't messed with your sense of humor." She holds up the tablet she came in with, tapping on the screen for several seconds before looking back up at me. "I'll be back in a bit to check on you. Just rest, okay?"

"You got it," I promise her.

She gives me a sad smile, then squeezes my hand before turning to Jude. "Hallway. Now."

His brows lift with surprise, likely at the way she's talking to him, because, I mean, he *is* Jude Rafferty—but he follows her anyway.

They slip out of the room, and I strain to hear what's going on.

". . . real prick, you know that?"

It's all I can make out before the door closes, and I grin.

Oh, Annie is *so* giving him an earful right now.

Good. He deserves it.

It's several moments before Jude comes padding back into the room, his shoulders slumped and head hanging low, confirming he just got a good tongue-lashing.

He takes his place in the chair once more, folding his hands over his stomach, his gaze swinging back to me.

I look away the second our eyes connect. He laughs.

I grab my pillow out from under my head, then chuck it at him.

He laughs harder, tucking the pillow under his own arms as I lie back, already missing the extra cushion.

Dick.

It's quiet in the room for several minutes. Too quiet. So damn quiet you can even hear the *tick, tick, tick* of the clock on the wall over the machines beeping.

Jude clears his throat like he's about to say something, and I cut him a glare.

He holds up his hands, kicking his feet out and relaxing back into his chair.

Tick, tick, tick.

Jude uncrosses his ankles, then crosses them again.

Tick, tick, tick.

He sighs.

Tick, tick, tick.

His mouth pops open again, then slams shut just as quickly.

Tick, tick—

"This is ridiculous," he mutters.

I can't help the bubble of laughter that bursts out of me. "I'm sorry, but *you* think *this* is ridiculous?" I scoff. "You're kidding, right?"

"I'm not kidding. If you'd have just talked to me instead of running away, then we wouldn't be in this situation, now would we?"

I sit up in the uncomfortable bed. "Let me get this straight, *Jude.*" I say his name like a curse. "You think we're in this *situation* because of *me*?"

"I just wanted to talk."

I snort out a laugh. "That's funny. You've had plenty of opportunity to talk. To tell me the truth. But you never took it. Not once. You just let me keep believing you were . . . you were . . ."

"My brother?" He sighs, raking his hands through his already disheveled hair. "I know, all right? I know I fucked up. I know I had the chance to make this right from the get-go but never did. I just . . ."

"What? You couldn't just message and say, *'Hey, funny story. I'm actually Jude, not Jasper. Lol.'* You couldn't do that?"

"Would you have believed me?"

"Not a chance."

He chuckles. "Then you see my predicament."

"You could have fixed it at any moment in line at JT's." I gasp. "Did you . . . Did you stalk me there on purpose? Was that some sick game for you?"

"I thought we established *you* were the stalker, not me."

"Don't try cute banter with me, Jude. Not right now."

"So now I'm just Jude?"

"Oh, I'm sorry. I meant to use your government name: *Asshat.*"

His lips twitch, but the humor fades from his face as quickly as it appeared. "I didn't know it was you. At the coffee truck, I mean. I had no clue. I mean, we met before we even started messaging. How could I know?"

"How could you not? After you saw my profile, how did you not recognize me?"

"Did you recognize me? In line?"

"No. You were wearing that stupid hat and sun . . ." Oh god. We were both so covered up by our hats and our sunglasses that there was no way we could have recognized each other. ". . . glasses," I finish.

He throws his arms wide in a *see what I mean* kind of gesture. "There you go. You didn't recognize me, and I didn't recognize you. How could I have told you anything at the truck?"

I cross my arms over my chest. "Still. You could have said something over chat."

He scoffs, shaking his head. "Yeah. Maybe."

Lightning quick, he rises from his chair and begins pacing the length of the room. Back and forth and back again.

I count his steps.

One, two, three, four, five, six, seven, eight.

He pivots and walks the other way.

One, two, three, four, five, six, seven, eight.

He does it two more times before finally coming to a natural stop. He turns, eyes on me and nothing else.

"I liked talking to you, Sunshine."

I narrow my eyes at the nickname. "Don't."

He ignores my protest, crossing the room, not stopping until he's at my bedside. He places his hands on the bed, bending until we're at eye level, so damn close that his familiar pine scent fills the small space between us.

I feel like I *should* be scared. That I should be worried he's so close. In fact, I wait for the machine to start beeping wildly again. It never happens. I just feel . . . calm.

"I didn't know," he says softly. Hoarsely.

I swallow thickly. "Which part didn't you know?"

"All of it. I didn't know it was you at the coffee truck, and I didn't know that I was going to like talking to you so much. By the time I figured it out, it felt like it was too late. I was in too deep. But I couldn't give it up, you know? I . . . You . . ." He exhales heavily, closing his eyes momentarily before turning them on me again. "You made me feel *normal*, and I haven't felt normal in a really, really long time. So, no matter what happens from here, thank you for that, Olive."

I expect him to move away from the bed. To step back. To put distance between us. Maybe even walk out the door.

But he doesn't.

He doesn't, and I'm *glad*.

How could I be glad? After everything?

I stare into his eyes, those same green pools that hold so much emotion. That are begging me to give him any indication that I heard him. That I might feel the same.

But truthfully, I don't know what to say to him.

"Olive . . ." he says after a few moments. "Do you want me to leave?"

"No."

The word slips out so effortlessly that, at first, I don't even believe I've said it.

Then palpable relief washes over him, and I know I did.

Worse? I know I meant it.

"Good," he says, then returns to his spot in the chair.

And that's the way we sit for the next several hours—him in his chair and me in this damned hospital bed, trying to figure out what the hell I'm going to do about the fact that no matter how angry I am with Jude, I don't want to lose him either.

CHAPTER THIRTEEN

Jude

If I'd known when I got up this morning that I'd spend the day in the hospital taking care of Olive, I probably wouldn't have gotten out of bed. At least it would have kept her from being where she is right now.

She's pale as she argues with Annie about whether she's good to go home or should stay. She wants to leave, and I don't blame her. It's now after seven, and we've been here for hours. She's just been resting, something she can easily do at home too.

"At least wait until I get off so I can take you," Annie pleads as Olive walks slowly out of her room after finally convincing Annie she'll be okay on her own for a few hours, wincing only a little when she puts pressure on her bruised knee. The gash is bad, but the bruising is even worse. She'll need to ice it for at least a few days.

It's all your fault, Jude. You did this.

I shake away the thoughts, then push off the nurses' station.

"I'll make sure she gets home okay," I tell Annie, going to Olive's side. I try to grab her forearm to help her, but she pulls away.

I don't blame her for that either.

Annie bounces her eyes from Olive to me, worrying her lips between her teeth before finally relenting.

"Fine. But I'll be home in two hours, tops." She looks at me, and I try not to shrink back at the inferno in her gaze. Annie might be little, but she's scary as hell. "Take her straight home. No funny business. I don't care who you are—I'll cut your balls off if anything happens to my best friend."

I look to Olive, expecting her to admonish her friend for her rude behavior, but she just shrugs, pushing past me to the desk to finalize her paperwork.

I fight the urge to slide a hand over my threatened balls and nod. "I'll get her home in one piece. I promise."

"Good." Annie narrows her eyes again before turning to help Olive.

We get everything settled; then, armed with paperwork and a prescription for pain meds, we make our way from the hospital.

By some miracle, there are zero paparazzi waiting for us when we leave.

There's also a cab waiting, courtesy of the nurse at the front desk I sweet-talked into calling one for me.

"Watch your head," I say to Olive as I help her inside.

"I'm not an invalid," she grumbles in return, but she climbs inside gently. She winces only once, and I take that as a good sign.

She's already looking better than she did when we first got here, but she's still clearly in pain.

"Do we need to get this filled?" I hold up the slip of paper.

She shakes her head, then leans it against the cab window. "Nah. I'll be fine."

I don't believe her but let it go, making a mental note to let Annie know. Maybe she can convince Olive to get the prescription filled.

"Where to?" the cab driver asks.

Olive rattles off her address—a place in Hell's Kitchen.

No wonder she's always at JT's. It's parked almost perfectly between us and definitely has the best coffee I've found in the city.

The cab driver keeps the music turned low, and Olive naps beside me while I check my phone.

Dylan: Where are you?

Dylan: JUDE

Dylan: I SWEAR

Dylan: What did you do?!

Dylan: Call me.

Dylan: Now.

Dylan: I AM NOT JOKING, JUDE.

Dylan: Dammit, Jude.

I switch to the other messages waiting for me.

Cait: Did you get everything sorted?

Ha. Not even close, little sister.

Back to my inbox.

Jasper: I talked to Cait. She said you ran out of the bakery. You good?

Jasper: Why is YOUR publicist blowing up MY phone?

Jasper: I just saw TMZ. What the hell happened, man?

Jasper: You'd better at least tell Mom you're okay. She's freaking out.

I groan, checking to see what she has to say.

Mom: JUDE ALLEN RAFFERTY

Mom: When your mother calls, you answer.

Mom: Fine. Then don't answer. Let me worry myself to death over you.

Mom: I'm sorry. I didn't mean that. I love you. Just call me, okay?

And finally, one from my father.

Dad: Call your mother.

Other than the twenty missed calls—ten from Dylan, eight from my mother, and the other two from my siblings—that's it.

It could have been worse, and I'm sure it will be if I dare go on the internet, but I don't want to deal with that—or any of this—now. I can already predict the headlines.

Jude Rafferty: A Hero!

Is Jude Rafferty a Hero or Villain? Eyewitnesses Say She Was Running Scared!

Jude Rafferty Brings Mystery Girl Back from Dead with Hotness

All right, fine. That last one is a bit of a stretch, but still. I'm sure it's already plastered all over the place, and I'd rather not witness being hailed as a hero.

I'm no hero. Especially not to Olive.

Instead of enduring all my worst fears, I tuck my phone back into my pocket and turn my attention to the person who deserves it most, especially after today.

It's wild to me that the woman lying in the hospital bed was Sunshine—yet somehow, being this close to her in the cab and knowing . . . it all just makes so much sense. I couldn't see it before, always too blinded by her oversize sunglasses and colossal attitude, but I can't unsee it.

How did I miss this before? How could I have not noticed her like this?

I let my eyes trace over her soft features, loving that even when she's sleeping, she looks annoyed. Her long lashes cast shadows over her cheeks, and I wish she weren't feeling so awful right now because I'd kill for a glimpse of her eyes again. If she hadn't been wearing those damn sunglasses every time at the coffee truck, they would have been a dead giveaway. They're too unique for me not to notice.

"You're creeping me out."

I chuckle. "Just making sure you're still breathing."

"Scared Annie is going to kill you if I die?"

"No. I'm scared you'll haunt me for the rest of my life."

A smile tugs at her lips. "I will."

She peels her eyes open, then slowly turns her head toward me, finally giving me another look at her baby blues.

They're more clouded than usual, but I guess that's from the grogginess. It doesn't make them any less intoxicating, though.

"What?" she whispers.

"What?"

She lifts a brow. "You're staring."

"I like your eyes."

My confession startles her. It startles me too.

I didn't mean to say it, but now that I have, I don't want to take it back. I mean it too much.

"Thank you," she says quietly, then averts the gaze I can't get enough of. She looks out the window, watching the city pass us by as the cabbie whips in and out of traffic, a seasoned New Yorker.

City lights reflect off her pale skin, making her look like she's a heroine in an indie film experiencing New York for the first time, her eyes wide with wonder.

"I love this city."

"I know," I tell her, still unable to take my eyes off her. "You've talked about it a lot." She casts her eyes over at me, brows drawn together. "In your journal," I clarify.

Gone is the wistful look and back comes the anger.

Her arms go back over her chest—her signature and telling move— and her lips turn down at the corners. "Right. I forgot you invaded my privacy and read that."

"But you were okay with me reading if I was Jasper?"

"No," she snaps, lifting her chin and looking back out the window.

I wonder if that's what this is really about. That she's mad I'm not my brother.

I turn that thought around in my mind for far too long as the buildings pass. By the time we turn onto 9th Avenue, I think we may make it all the way to her apartment before she says another word.

"No," she says again, but softer this time. "I wasn't okay with it. I was mortified by the thought. But I . . . I thought I had maybe met someone who understood."

"Olive."

It takes ten seconds for her to look over at me, and when she does, I see it—unshed tears.

In that moment, I hate myself.

Hate myself for lying to her. For pretending to be someone else. For losing her trust.

"I might not have told you who I was, but everything—and I mean *everything*—else I told you was true. I didn't lie about any of it. It was real. *We* were real."

She just stares at me, her eyes darting between my own as silence fills the cab, my words blanketing us in a moment of understanding.

Then, finally, she says, "Even the aliens?"

I feel the corners of my mouth pull up. "*Especially* the aliens."

She smiles as the cab comes to a halt.

"We're here," the driver announces.

He gives me my total, and I add another fifty bucks, hoping it'll help keep him quiet about who was in his cab.

I crawl out the back, then hold my hand out for Olive. I'm surprised when she accepts it without a fight, placing her soft palm against mine, letting me help her from the car.

She doesn't wince this time, but I still see the tightening of her lips as she puts weight on her messed-up leg.

She allows me to lead her up to her building. She even puts in the code for the door and doesn't protest when I follow her up the stairs, my hand on her lower back and my eyes trained anywhere but her ass I so desperately want to stare at.

In fact, we make it all the way to her door before she finally has a complaint.

"You can't come inside, Jude."

I nod, figuring that's what she'd say. "I know."

"Annie will be home in an hour. I'll be fine until then."

I hate the idea of leaving her alone, but I can't force my way inside her apartment. She doesn't want me here, and I have to respect that.

And I guess I get it. I'm not the guy she was expecting me to be. She wanted Jasper. Not me. The knowledge twists into my gut.

I tuck my hands into my pockets to keep from reaching out to her like I'm itching to. The small touches we've had today weren't enough. "Will you at least let me know you're okay?"

"I won't do that either."

Again, I nod because, again, I expected as much.

It doesn't mean I like it, though.

"I'm sorry," I tell her.

Sorry for lying. Sorry for hurting her. Sorry she *got* hurt because of me. Sorry for it all.

I want to tell her all that, but I have a feeling she already knows.

She nods. "I know you are."

But that's all I get. No forgiveness. No "It's okay." No indication that this isn't going to be the last time I see her.

I hate it, but I know it's what I had coming.

I knew this was never going to end well, but now I realize I didn't want it to end at all.

This sucks.

"Good night, Jude," she says.

"Good night, Olive."

Then, because I can't help myself, I take a step toward.

She doesn't flinch. She doesn't move.

She just inhales sharply, her eyes widening to twice their size as I lean forward and press my lips softly against her cheek.

I pull away and dart back the way I came before I do something really senseless, like kiss her until we're both completely breathless. Or beg her to let me inside.

I don't deserve it. I know that. But I want it all the same.

I'm halfway down the stairs when I finally hear her exhale.

Me too, Olive. Me too.

◆ ◆ ◆

"Well, you're an idiot, but you're being hailed as a hero for it all."

I groan because my exact worst fears have come true.

Those headlines I was dreading so much? I wasn't far off at all. Hell, even a few were *exactly* what I had predicted. The media is so cliché sometimes.

"I'm not a hero."

"*I* never said you were. I said you were an idiot."

I laugh. "Thanks. I can always count on your honesty, Dylan."

"Damn right you can. That tie is awful. Wear a different one."

I grumble but do as she says, heading for my closet to find a better option.

"You know," Dylan says, her voice muffled from the spot on the dresser where I have my phone propped up against a stack of books, our video chat filling the screen, "this is really going to help move things along. People are going to focus on your new superhero status rather than your dumbassery. When I said we should make headlines, I didn't mean like this. But this is a winning situation."

Leave it to Dylan to find the only bright spot.

It's been less than twenty-four hours since I dropped Olive off at her apartment, and according to Dylan, my name has been searched nearly one million times.

To most of the internet, I'm a hero.

But if you ask me, I'm every bit the asshat Olive loves to say I am.

"You forgot about the part where I lied to someone and pretended to be my brother," I say, coming back into the room, two new ties in hand. I hold them up so Dylan can see. "Which one?"

"Hmm. Neither. Go tie-less. And drop a button."

"I might be an idiot, but I'm not a douchebag."

She arches a brow. "Do you *really* want to argue with me right now? After everything?"

I may have skipped out on calling anyone back last night.

After I left Olive at her door, I went for a walk. A long, long walk. I didn't find my way back to my apartment until well after midnight, and by that time, my phone was dead. The first thing I did was plug it in and check Jasper's Instagram for a message from Olive.

There was nothing.

Nada. Not a damn thing.

I was hoping that maybe she'd reach out to let me know she was okay, but she didn't.

I fought the urge to message her first for far too long. Hell, I'm *still* fighting the urge.

I want to know she's okay. I *need* to know.

And it's not even because I'm desperate for her forgiveness—it's more than that.

I want to make things right with us. It may sound ridiculous, but I miss her. I miss her random messages, her life updates, and I miss the way she could make me laugh with something as silly as talking about aliens. Miss the way she could make me light up with just a simple message about her day. Miss the way she could make me feel warm and fuzzy, just like sunshine.

I want that feeling back. I want *her* back. I just wish I knew how to make the first move to fix this.

She hasn't blocked me or Jasper. That has to mean something, doesn't it? Maybe she wants the same thing. Or maybe, in her confusion from the concussion, she just forgot.

Either way, I'm taking it as a sign that perhaps there's still hope. At least, I really, *really* want there to still be hope.

"That's what I thought," Dylan says, bringing me back to the present. "Besides, if her dating history is anything to go by, Keely *loves* douchebags."

Tonight is the night I pay Dylan back for all she's done—one date with a starlet of her choosing. When I agreed to it, I didn't even think about who she might pick, but I should have known who it would be.

My date is none other than Keely Haart, granddaughter of the acting pioneer Henry Haart and the most in-demand actress working right now. She's good in front of the camera, I'll give her that, but that's as far as my praise goes. I've had a few brief interactions with her over the years, and it's safe to say she is not my type. Not by a long shot.

But I owe Dylan. Big-time. This is my repayment, even if it is the last thing I want to be doing tonight, especially after yesterday.

"Remind me then why I'm going on a . . . date with her?" The word *date* sends a shiver down my spine.

"Because she's *the* Keely Haart. She's huge and all over the place. It's basically the equivalent of you dating your brother."

"I'd rather you not phrase it like that."

Dylan throws her hands in the air. "You know what I mean. She's famous on the caliber Jasper is. Being spotted with her is good."

"'Spotted'? You make me sound like I'm on *Gossip Girl* or something."

"Ha. You'd never survive New York's elite, but Keely would. She'll shoot your name to the top of searches for good reasons, instead of Snoopy-underwear reasons. We still really need to talk about that."

I ignore her underwear comment. "I thought my new superhero status did that already?"

Dylan shrugs. "Maybe. But there's no harm in making sure a good thing stays good, right?"

I don't respond because I don't have a response other than I really don't want to fucking do this. I am *only* doing this for her. It sure as hell isn't for me.

Tossing the ties to the side, I heed Dylan's directions and undo the top button of my shirt.

Yep. Douchebag.

"See? You look great!" Dylan claps her hands excitedly. "Now, the florist should be there any minute so you can pick out flowers."

"Florist? Flowers?" My eyes snap to the screen. "You didn't say anything about that."

"It's a *date*, Jude. And we're trying to make you look like a damn gentleman. Flowers are expected. The cameras will go wild over it."

I can read between the lines just fine: *You're bringing her flowers. End of discussion.*

I gnash my teeth together, annoyed that once again, Dylan has the upper hand. "Fine."

Her white teeth stand out brightly against her red-painted lips. "Good. Glad we're on the same page."

She runs over the rest of the evening she has perfectly planned, including a "casual" stroll through Central Park just when the sun begins to set, giving all "candid" photos the perfect glow.

Dylan's a damn maestro, and I'm just an instrument in her symphony.

"And, Jude?" Dylan says. "You'd better kiss her at the end of the night."

There's no way in hell. "I will."

◆ ◆ ◆

"So then she was like, 'I can't work with Keely Haart. She's too beautiful, and I don't want to be second to her.' So she quit, and I got the lead role."

The actress sitting across from me lifts her shoulders, then grabs her wineglass—her fourth of the night—and tosses back the remaining contents. She taps her glass with her gaudy ring several times, lifting her other hand and snapping.

"More wine!" she calls to the waiter, who has been bending over backward all night to keep her satisfied. She looks over at me, her bright-pink lips pulled up in disgust, then shakes her head. "Can you believe this? I shouldn't have to ask."

I shoot her a tight smile, not really interested in engaging with her.

Truth be told, I'm fucking miserable. And it's not just because I find Keely to be the most self-centered and aggravating person I've ever met. There's somewhere else I'd much rather be right now: with Olive.

I check my phone for what feels like the fiftieth time in the last two hours.

Nothing. Again.

"Are you waiting on a call or something?"

I find Keely watching me with shrewd eyes. "Pardon?"

She dips her head toward my phone. "You've checked your phone no less than twenty times since we've sat down." It's more. It has to be. But I'm not about to correct her on it. "I just assumed you're waiting on a call. Maybe from a certain director?"

"Not a director."

"Then who?" she inquires as the waiter appears and refills her drink. She doesn't even acknowledge him, just flicks her long, sleek black hair over her shoulder and waits for my answer.

"Sir?" he asks, holding up the wine bottle.

I've already had two drinks. I should stick to my two-drink limit and say no. But if I'm going to survive the rest of this date, I'll need more booze.

"I'll take a whiskey. On the rocks, please, Daniel."

He looks taken aback when I use his name, and it makes me sad. Is it really such a shock for me to treat him like a human?

"Goody. More wine for me." Keely taps her already half-empty glass, begging for a refill. How the hell did she guzzle that so fast?

Daniel refills my date's glass, then tells me he'll be right back with my whiskey and disappears to the bar.

"So, who are you waiting on a call from if not a director?"

"Just a friend," I tell her, even though I don't owe her an explanation at all. I don't know this woman—not really. She's just a date set up by my publicist. This isn't real, and it never will be.

She narrows her eyes, seemingly annoyed by my answer, but the strained expression quickly transforms into a smile so wide and fake it hurts even me.

"You're mysterious, Jude." She takes a sip of her wine, her eyes sparkling at me over the rim of her glass. "I like mysterious."

Daniel drops off my whiskey, and I sling half of it back in one gulp, relishing the way the liquid burns the back of my throat. It's just what I need to get through this.

Keely might like mysterious, but I like real, which is not at all what she is.

But Olive . . . Olive is real, and I miss her.

How is that even possible? I barely know her, but it doesn't matter. I *want* to know her, and I really want to spend more time with her.

But I've screwed it all up, haven't I? She doesn't want to know me. She doesn't want to spend time with me. How am I going to fix that?

Keely falls into a conversation with herself about some movie she's currently shooting. I'm only halfway listening, my mind in a different place as we wrap up our dinner.

As expected, when we exit, the place is crawling with cameras.

"Keely! Keely! Over here, Keely!"

"Jude, look this way!"

"Are you dating now?"

"How long have you been together?"

"How does your grandfather feel about this union, Keely?"

"What happened yesterday, Jude? Did you really push that woman down?"

I grit my teeth, trying with everything I have to reel in the sudden anger that floods me.

I will not punch the paparazzi. I will not punch the paparazzi. I will not punch the paparazzi.

It's all I can do to keep my cool.

The headlines about yesterday have been mostly positive, but there have been a few blogs trying to drum up drama where there isn't any.

Well, not the drama they're talking about, at least.

I try not to think about it and fight my way through the crowd, following Cliff's lead. I don't usually have a bodyguard following me around, but Dylan felt it was best for tonight, considering my date.

But as big as he is and as much as he pushes through the crowd blocking the narrow Manhattan sidewalk, they shove back. It's a frenzy, and by the time we make it to the car, I'm exhausted, and my shirt is sticking to my back with sweat.

"God, I hate those vultures," Keely complains when we're seated safely in the back seat of the heavily tinted SUV. "They're the worst."

Finally, we agree about something.

"You could say that again," I mutter as our bodyguard slips into the front passenger seat.

He gives the driver our next destination; then we're off for the second portion of our evening: a casual yet not-so-casual walk in the park. It's so staged and so lame.

I will never, ever go on another date set up by Dylan. I don't care how much I owe her. This isn't worth it.

"Do you have any champagne?" Keely asks the driver.

"I'm sorry, miss, I don't."

She crosses her arms, huffing, and for a moment I'm transported back to standing at JT's coffee truck with Olive and her attitude.

Fuck. I even miss the sassy parts of her. If I'd known Sunshine was Olive, I'd have taken more advantage of the time we had together, especially if I had known it was going to be so limited.

It's not long before we're pulling up to one of the park's 5th Avenue entrances, and it makes me wonder why we couldn't have walked, so I voice the question out loud.

Keely screws her face up like it's the dumbest question she's ever heard. "Uh, because I'm wearing heels, and you don't walk in heels like this."

I want to point out that it's exactly what we're about to do—go for a walk. But I'd rather not get into it with her. I can already tell it will be a losing battle, and not the fun kind.

Cliff opens the door. "All clear, Mr. Rafferty," he tells me in a deep voice.

I slide out, giving him a nod, and turn to grab Keely's hand. She looks down at it, then back at me, and her lips curl up into a sneer.

"We need to make this quick. Ten minutes, max. I can't do any more. The last thing I need is for them to snap photos of me sweating." She shudders like she can't possibly imagine showing the media that she's—*gasp*—human.

My brain automatically goes to the alien conversation I had with Olive and how fun and goofy it was, a far cry from how this date is going. I'm not having fun and my date certainly isn't goofy. It's stuffy and forced, and I hate every moment of it.

"Um, hello?" Keely yanks on my hand. "Let's go already."

I snap myself out of my melancholy thoughts, then help her from the car.

We're not even ten feet away from the vehicle when swarms of paparazzi appear out of nowhere. It's like a damn movie, them popping out of the bushes, rolling up in vans, and sliding out like ninjas.

It's all so stupid, I think as we wander around, Keely clinging on to me like none of this is fake and I'm some proper English gentleman who's courting her.

She rambles on about something I have zero interest in, and I take in the scenery. Walking through here is one of my favorite things about the city. From the looming, gorgeous bright-green trees to the hot dog vendors and Frisbee players and families roaming through the park. It's always blown my mind that in a city of concrete, there's this beauty tucked away and preserved. It feels like you're in a different world.

And a different world is exactly where I want to be right now.

Just as I'm about to check my watch, Keely tugs on my arm.

I pause, looking over at her.

She's giving me another forced smile. "I'm ready to leave now, Jude."

It's so creepy she's able to talk without dropping her lips or act. It's like she's a robot or a Barbie doll.

"As you wish," I murmur, then steer us as naturally as I can back toward the car.

When we approach the waiting vehicle, she sinks her nails—talons, really—into my arm.

"Kiss me, Jude."

I ignore her, towing her along.

She sinks her nails in deeper, so deep there's no way she won't leave a mark on my arm.

"Kiss. Me," she instructs again.

I pull us to a stop right in front of the SUV. Keely looks up at me expectantly, her eyes filled with a thinly veiled threat that I had better obey or face her wrath.

I'm not scared of her wrath. Or Dylan's.

But because my mother raised me to be a gentleman, I take a deep breath and slide into the role of a leading man. I slip my hand over her cheek, letting my fingers tangle with her hair as I cup her face, stepping closer and leaving just a speck of distance between us.

Keely inhales sharply, and I grin because it's probably the most genuine she's been this entire evening.

I lean in, my eyes never leaving hers.

Closer . . . closer . . .

Our lips are nearly brushing when I move my head just to the right and place a gentle, chaste kiss against her cheek.

I take a step back, a burst of cool air from the sudden space hitting us both.

It's enough to knock Keely out of whatever trance she was in, and I see it—she's fuming.

We were supposed to kiss. It was part of the deal.

It was going to keep her name in the headlines and make mine climb even higher.

But I can't do it. I won't.

She's not the one I want to kiss.

CHAPTER FOURTEEN

Olive

"Oh, honey. This is going to take a bit of work." Frannie frowns down at me, a giant brush in her hand. "It's just so . . ."

"Ugly?" I finish for her. "I know."

She squeezes my shoulder with her free hand. "Don't worry. We got this. I'll get you looking good as new in no time."

She's full of shit, and we both know it.

As much as I hate the idea of having to have my face edited—it's even in my contracts that I don't allow it—Uma has insisted it's going to be necessary if I want this campaign to run, and I *really* want this campaign to run. I could use a burst of good news, given the circumstances.

It's been four days since the run-in—literally—with the piano, and my forehead looks more like I had a fight with a brick wall.

It's nothing compared to my knees, though. Both are still swollen and sore and purple. It's a damn good thing we're shooting winter clothes today, because there is no way I can let them on camera.

"So," Frannie starts as she digs through her bag of supplies, "is it true that Jude Rafferty came to your rescue and carried you into an ambulance like a hero straight out of a romantic comedy?"

Is that what the media is saying now? I wouldn't know since I've intentionally scrolled by every article even hinting at Jude since reports of his date with Keely Haart broke.

I shouldn't have been surprised, not because of who he is or how he betrayed me—but seeing him with Keely . . . I think that hurt worse than running into the piano.

He has every right to date her. We're nothing.

But it doesn't mean I have to like it.

I *really* don't like it.

I don't want to think about it now. I want to focus on the shoot. I need my focus to be completely on work right now, not on some guy who fooled me. I'm going to have hospital bills to cover. That's important. Not Jude.

"They've definitely exaggerated about him carrying me like some hero, but he was there." I hope it's enough to pacify her.

"So you know him?"

Dammit. It didn't work.

"No. No, I don't know him."

I thought I did—or at least, I thought I knew his brother. But I don't. Not really.

And I'm trying to convince myself I'm okay with that.

She pauses mid-riffle, arching both perfect brows my way. "You're telling me you just happened to have a medical episode right in front of *the* Jude Rafferty?"

No, Frannie. The truth is, Jude was there because he's a horrible, manipulative, lying asshat who was chasing me after I uncovered all his secrets and exposed him for the fraud he is.

"Yep," I tell her. "How was the drag competition with your cousin? Did they win?"

And that's how I get Frannie to ramble for the rest of the session, telling me all about the show she worked on. It's a much-needed break from all the other awful thoughts rolling around in my head.

I block them out, and I keep them out. Since the only thing people want to do is ask about Jude, I'll use the shoot to distract myself.

I've spent the past few years craving recognition, and now I want nothing more than to be anonymous.

My name has been splashed across the internet for days now. At first, nobody was aware who I was, but that changed *very* fast. Overnight, I gained a hundred thousand new followers, and my inbox was suddenly full of reporters from various news outlets asking about Jude and him rescuing me.

I've been all over the internet so much that even my mom called to check in with me. Of course, she didn't quite understand all that was going on, but I appreciated her reaching out anyway. I'm sure it wasn't easy to see me injured in front of the whole world like that.

Between the headlines and fielding my mom's questions, these last few days have been a little too much to handle, and I'm beyond over it.

So I do what I've been doing—tuck it far away in the back of my mind and don't think about it. I'll unpack it in therapy with Ingrid later.

Five hours later, I'm on my way home and feeling a little better. The shoot went off without a hitch, and I didn't google myself or Jude a single time.

Progress, right?

My phone pulses against my hip as I round a corner on my walk home, and I pull it out, surprised to see Annie's name on the screen. Like two rational humans, we call each other only if there's an emergency.

"Hel . . . lo?"

The greeting comes out a broken question. I have no clue what I'm about to hear. Will it even be Annie? Did she get kidnapped? Will it be her captor on the other end? Do they need ransom? Do *I* have ransom?

"Please tell me you're on your way home," Annie—*thank God*—says in my ear as I maneuver through the crowded street toward my trusty coffee truck, in dire need of a pick-me-up.

"I am. Why? What's going on?"

"My brother just dropped Daphne off. Payton is having . . . issues." She whispers this last part, and I assume it's because her niece is right there and she doesn't want to worry her. Daphne may be only four, but she's intuitive as hell and aware that her mother has a new baby growing in her belly. She'll put two and two together. "I have a shift at the hospital in an hour and a half."

Translation: Can you watch Daphne for me?

"I'm stopping for coffee. I'll be home in about twenty, depending on how long the line is."

Annie sighs in relief. "Have I told you lately how much I love you?"

"No, but I'm all ears."

"Well, I love you. So, so much."

"Go on . . ."

She laughs. "Are you going to JT's?"

"Of course."

"Even after . . . ?"

She doesn't say his name, and I appreciate it more than she could ever know.

I've not been by JT's since my run-in with Jude, for obvious reasons. But today feels like it's time.

"I'm not letting him chase me away from my favorite coffee spot," I say, hoping I sound more confident than I am. "Besides, I doubt he'll be there, anyway. I'm sure he's off with Keely Haart, living his best Hollywood-elite life somewhere I could never afford."

"You don't even know if they're dating."

"You saw the pictures, Annie. They're dating."

And why wouldn't they date? Keely is a funny, talented, gorgeous actress. She's famous and rich and from his world. They make perfect sense together. Unlike us. I was a fool to think anything otherwise.

"I don't know. The pictures I saw didn't look romantic at all. If anything, he looked a little pained to be there with her."

She could be wrong and she could be right, but I saw all I needed to see. He was out with her the night after he put me in the hospital. It's clear that whatever we had—if you can even call it anything—is over.

"Are you on his side or mine?"

There's a pause. Too long of one. So long that I pull the phone away from my ear to see if the call is still connected.

It is.

"Annie?" I ask, barely sidestepping some guy on a skateboard.

"I . . ." She clears her throat. "Sorry. Daphne had my attention."

I've known Annie long enough to tell she's lying. Her niece didn't steal her attention. She was just avoiding the question.

"I'm on your side," she finally says.

"Why do I feel as if you're about to come at me with a big *but*?"

"My butt is not that big!"

I laugh, thankful for the joke that breaks the tension between us. Annie and I get along almost always. Any tiffs we have are resolved quickly. I'm glad this isn't going to turn into something big.

"But . . ." I swear I can *hear* her smile as I pass by a store that's been advertising it's going out of business for the past two years. "I do think that maybe you could see where Jude is coming from."

I blow out air, the smile slipping off my face and right into a frown. Mostly because . . . I know she's right.

There is a small—like, absolutely minuscule—part of me that understands why Jude lied. And there's a slightly bigger part that could totally chalk us meeting in the coffee line and him not knowing who I was up to coincidence.

But adding them together . . .

"Just think about it, Liv, okay? I'm not saying you need to forgive him, but maybe just have a conversation with him? He did stay with you at the hospital all day. There's no way he didn't blow off an entire schedule to stick by your side."

She's guilting me, and I hate it.

I hate more that it's working.

Jude *did* take care of me. He was respectful and he was there. Not only that, but the look in his eyes when he poured his heart out and told me he was sorry . . . It was real.

He was real.

I swallow at the thought, then shake my head, almost as if I'm trying to get rid of it, because if I sit and think about it for too long, then I'll forget why I'm mad at him and maybe even miss him.

"I'll think about it," I tell Annie as I round the corner, JT's coming into my line of sight. The delicious smell of fresh coffee hits my nose, and I inhale sharply, already feeling a bit better. "You want coffee?"

"*Please.* A huge one."

"Coffee? I want coffee!" Daphne hollers in the background. "Coffee! Coffee! Coffee!"

"The last thing you need is coffee," Annie mutters, but I'm sure her niece doesn't hear her. She's still chanting about the nectar of the gods. "And I suppose a hot chocolate for the little gremlin."

"One gremlin-sized hot chocolate, coming up. See you soon."

I end the call, then slip my phone into my pocket as I approach. Lucky for me, the line for JT's is only four people deep when I step up to the back.

I shuffle back and forth on my feet as I wait for the line to move. It looks like it's only JT in there today, so it's moving slower than I'd like.

After several minutes, I finally move up one person just as someone slides in behind me, standing so close their body heat wraps around me like an unwanted blanket, making this warm August evening even hotter.

I take a small step forward, trying to run away from it, but they move with me.

Seriously? Hasn't this person ever heard of personal space?

They step closer, and now I can really feel them.

But more than that, I can *smell* them.

And I'd know that scent anywhere.

Pine.

"Hey, Sunshine."

Two words. That's all it takes to widen all the small cracks in my resolve, and they threaten to splinter, to shatter.

I don't turn around or acknowledge he's there.

No.

I squeeze my eyes shut and pretend he's *not* there.

But just like this tactic didn't work with Uma, it doesn't work with Jude either.

He inches closer, the fabric of his clothes brushing against the backs of my arms and sending a shudder through me.

I also pretend *that* didn't happen.

"Can we talk?"

I peel one eye open, then the other, and when the person in front of me moves forward, so do I.

And so does Jude.

"Please."

The word tickles my ear, causing goose bumps to rise along my arms as it slides over me and into those damn cracks that can't seem to stop growing.

Stupid cracks.

Stupid splinters.

Stupid Jude.

He shuffles closer once more, and I can't take it any longer. I whirl around and level him with a heated stare, arms crossed over my chest.

"What?"

To his credit, he doesn't step back. He doesn't even look surprised by my ire.

No.

That *asshat* smirks.

Smirks!

"I missed that look, Sunshine."

And I missed being *Sunshine.*

But I don't admit that out loud.

"You've never seen this look."

He reaches up and lifts his cap, then slides his hand through his ash-blond hair before replacing the cap. Then—and I'm not expecting this at all—he tugs his sunglasses off, securing them safely to the pocket on his overshirt.

His very *wet* overshirt.

"Did you run here?" I ask, taking a step back.

He darts his eyes to the left. "No."

He's lying. The eye shift was a tell.

I lift a single brow.

He chuckles at the challenge, lifting his hand to the back of his neck and squeezing it while giving me a lopsided grin.

I could melt, and not from the sweltering heat.

It's all from Jude.

If I thought he was attractive before, it's nothing compared to now. Seeing his eyes . . . those green and soulful and magnetic eyes . . . Well, I'm a little bummed I've been missing out on this view, but I don't dare voice that. Not to him and not to anyone else. Never, ever.

"Maybe I did run."

I give myself a shake because, oh yeah, we were talking. I forgot, too busy admiring him.

"Why?"

Another eye shift. "No real reason."

"Jude."

His smile slips, and I search my mind for what I've said wrong, especially when he takes two steps toward me, closing the distance I've so carefully put between us.

Suddenly, he's right there. So damn close that gone is the scent of coffee and all I smell is pine and him and everything I can never have because he belongs to someone else.

It's intoxicating and overwhelming and the most amazing thing ever.

"Say that again," he commands.

"What?" I ask, trying with everything inside me not to lose myself in his eyes. They remind me of the sea during a storm—dark yet alluring, and so damn unpredictable. The perfect mixture of green with just a hint of gray.

"My name. Say it again."

"Jude."

It drops from my lips before I can think twice about what he's just asked or *why*.

All I can think about is how his chest is heaving and how tight mine feels. How my throat is closing and how *goddamn hot it is*.

I've said his name before, but only when my voice was full of contempt. This time it's different, and apparently Jude feels that too.

"Next!"

And just like that, the spell he's cast over me is broken, and I stumble out of his warmth, turning toward the coffee truck.

"Liv!" JT says with a grin. "Haven't seen you in a few days. How you been?"

I'm not stupid. JT knows. He *has* to know. How could he not? *Everyone* knows.

JT's eyes shift over to Jude, tightening ever so slightly, and while most people wouldn't notice, I do. I've been coming to this truck for far too long not to see it—Jude isn't welcome here anymore.

"Good, JT. No, scratch that—I'm *great*." I turn and give Jude a look. Not that it does any good. He's staring down at me with a goofy grin. I divert my attention back to my favorite coffee-truck owner. "I'll have my usual, a large iced vanilla oat milk latte, and a small hot chocolate."

He nods, grabbing a cup for each and scribbling on them, then getting to work on my order.

"Having a party?" Jude asks, stepping beside me.

I ignore the way his shoulder brushes against mine.

"Me, Annie, and Daphne."

"Daphne?" he questions, but it seems like it's more to himself than me. "Daphne, Daphne, Daphne . . ." he repeats. He snaps his fingers. "The niece. A total hell-raiser and four going on twenty-four."

He rattles off the information like it's nothing to him, but what I can't wrap my head around is . . . *he knows.*

And there's only one way he could—my diary entries.

He really did read them all. More than that, he read them, and he *remembered* them.

I shouldn't be that impressed, really. He's an actor. It's part of his job to memorize things. But he's getting paid millions to do that.

This is different.

I take another peek at him, and he's still peering down at me.

"Can I confess something to you?" he whispers conspiratorially.

"Sure." I don't mean to say it, but the second it's out there, the urge to know whatever he wants to tell me grows tenfold.

"I knew you'd be here."

"Today?"

"Right now."

"So you *are* stalking me, then."

He snorts out a laugh. "No. Or maybe. I'm not sure."

"You're not sure if you're stalking me? It's usually obvious." I let my eyes rove over him. "Baseball cap, sunglasses, and a basic shirt so you blend into the crowd."

His lips twitch. "'Basic'?"

"I said what I said."

Another twitch. He bends toward me. "I'm not stalking you, Sunshine. Annie told me where you were."

That little conniving, traitorous, hateful, beautiful, perfect, smart best friend of mine.

I love her, but I swear I'm strangling her the second I walk inside our apartment. Why would she send him here? Why is she even in contact with him? And how? Why *any* of this?

"Before you get too mad at her, please know that I was the one who reached out. You didn't want me to contact you after . . ." He trails off, not voicing the very thing that's torn us apart. He clears his throat. "I wanted to check on you after the hospital, but I wanted to respect your wishes."

"So you went behind my back to my best friend?"

"Yep," he says, refusing to be scared off by the very obviously agitated tone in my voice. "And I'd do it again a thousand times over, no matter how much you glare or frown or cross your arms at me, Ollie."

I relax my arms—I hadn't even noticed I'd crossed them over my chest again. Am I really that defensive?

"Ollie?" I question the new nickname.

"You hate Sunshine, and you told me not to call you Olive." He shrugs. "Ollie it is."

"I hate Ollie more."

He grins. "Of course you do."

Of course you do, I mock in a deep voice, which only makes his smile grow and makes me more irritated. At least, I think it's irritation. I almost can't tell anymore.

I should tell him to go away. Should make him leave.

But I don't.

Why don't I?

"Here you are, Liv," JT says, pulling me from my thoughts and back to the present.

Jude turns to JT. "My usual, please."

JT's dark brows shoot up. "Pardon?"

Jude chuckles lightly, but it's an uncomfortable kind of laugh. An awkward one. "Uh, my usual order."

The brows go higher.

Jude clears his throat, then repeats his order once again, this time louder.

"Oh, I heard you," JT tells him as he begins pushing buttons on the register, sounding and looking completely done with the man standing before him. "We're out."

"Of coffee? Drip coffee?"

"Yep. Just ran out."

I try with everything I have to fight the smile that's clawing at my lips, but it's pretty pointless.

Just like it's pretty obvious to everyone except for Jude what's happening right now—JT is refusing to serve him. And it's all because of me. Well, him too. More specifically, him and Keely and their date.

"Oh."

It's all Jude says. He *lets* JT refuse him.

And so do I.

Petty? Maybe. But damn, does it feel good.

JT reads off my total, but he doesn't say it to me. He says it to Jude.

The actor sighs, and then, to my utter surprise, he plucks his card from his wallet and hands it over. When JT does his thing and pushes it back over the counter, I don't miss Jude stepping up and giving him a hefty tip before grabbing Annie's and Daphne's drinks.

The two men exchange a knowing look, each dipping their heads in acknowledgment of what just transpired; then Jude turns to me like nothing's happened.

"After you."

"After me?"

"Well, you have three drinks, and unless you're hiding one somewhere I can't see, you only have two hands. So, after you."

"Jude . . ."

He shakes his head. "After you, Ollie."

I sigh. Jude following me back to my apartment? Nothing good can come of it. I just know it.

So then why—after everything—do I say, "Okay"?

And I let him trail behind me as we make our way back to my apartment.

It's a bad idea. A horrible one.

Yet somehow . . . it feels right.

CHAPTER FIFTEEN

Jude

I'll admit it—following Olive to her apartment probably isn't the smart-est thing I've ever done, but it's pretty clear I'm not in the right state of mind. At least, not when it comes to her.

Hell, I stalked her to her favorite coffee truck, for crying out loud.

Though I do think *stalk* is a harsh word. It wasn't stalking, per se. I just happened to know where she'd be, thanks to Annie.

And yeah, fine, I totally ran there so I wouldn't miss her, but still. Not stalking.

Just . . . noticing.

These are all the things I repeat to myself as I follow behind her. We don't talk the entire time, no matter how many words I want to spew at her. I know better. If I talk, I risk her telling me to leave her alone.

And I really, really don't want her to tell me to leave her alone.

Those few minutes we had back at the coffee truck? Those were the best minutes I've had in days.

I want more minutes like that, and I want them with Olive.

So I keep my mouth shut. All the way down the street, through the door to her building, and up the stairs. I don't speak a word the entire time.

Not even when we reach her apartment—4D—and she digs around in her bag before producing a key and shoving it into the lock.

She pushes the door open, then strolls right in, leaving it open and me standing out in the hallway.

I don't dare walk inside. Not because I'm some vampire who hasn't been invited in—I lived that experience on a TV show already, and no thanks—but because I'm not sure if I'm allowed to come in.

I don't exactly know where we stand right now. It's evident she's still upset with me, but she did let me walk her back to her apartment. That's progress, right?

My phone shakes against my hip, and I ignore it. I ignore it like I have been for the last several days. I'm sure it's Dylan. Just like I'm sure she'll leave another angry voicemail.

It's been the same cycle since my awful date with Keely: Dylan yells at me, and I ignore her until the guilt eats at me, then I answer. She yells again, and the cycle starts over.

But right now, I have more important things to worry about than my publicist being mad at me for not kissing Keely Haart.

I'm standing outside Olive's apartment, and that takes precedence for many reasons.

I let my eyes slide over what I can see from my vantage point. It's small, that's for sure, but it doesn't *feel* small. More . . . cozy. Comfortable. A lot more welcoming than my place, especially with the photos hung on the wall. There are even a couple of funny signs about it being "wine time." There's a little wooden table by the door with a ceramic bowl holding keys, receipts, and sauce packets from random places.

Nothing truly matches, but it somehow makes perfect sense.

Olive disappears around the corner, and the sound of voices floats down the hall to me. I assume she's talking to Annie, and I wish like hell I could make out what they're saying, but they're talking in hushed whispers.

"Who are you?"

I jump, and the hot chocolate—well, now very *lukewarm* chocolate—shakes in one hand and the latte's ice rattles against the cup in the other.

A little girl stands in front of me. She has big, round blue eyes and hair so blonde it could be white. There's a headband holding back her bangs, and she's wearing a school uniform. Did the new year start already?

"Um, hello, mister?" the kid probes. "I asked a question. You're supposed to answer when someone talks to you. My mama said so. She's not here right now, but Auntie says she'll be home soon. She's got a baby in her belly, you know? It's going to be as big as me when it comes out. I think. Momma's belly sure is big, so it definitely looks like the baby is going to be big. I sure hope so. I want someone to play with at home and not just at school. Hey, do you like to play? I brought my Barbies with me."

I stifle a laugh at her rambling. She wants me to answer her, but she's not giving me a second.

"I'm Jude," I finally say, when she pauses to take a breath.

"Jude?" She wrinkles her nose. "That can't be your name. I know Jude, and you're not him."

"You know another Jude?"

"*Another* Jude? There are more than one of you?" Her big eyes are even bigger as this new information sinks in for her. "I didn't know that."

"People share names," I explain to her. "Mine is Jude. Yours is Daphne, just like the redheaded lady from *Scooby-Doo*. Do you watch *Scooby-Doo*?"

She shakes her head, and I try to hide my disappointment. How could this kid not know about the greatest detective gang of all time? "How'd you know my name?"

"Because I told him."

Daphne spins around as Olive comes back down the hallway from wherever she disappeared to. I don't know, as I'm still hanging out in the doorway, waiting to be invited in.

"You did?" the kid questions.

"Yep. He was nice enough to carry your hot chocolate for you."

"Hot chocolate?" She groans, tossing her little head back dramatically. "But I wanted coffee!"

This time, I don't even bother trying to hide my laughter, which earns me a boot-shaking glare from the four-year-old.

"Yeah, and I want you to go to bed at a decent time." Olive sticks her tongue out at the kid. "How about this: we can *pretend* it's coffee, and I'll let you read the newspaper as you drink it. Deal?"

"The *whole* newspaper?"

"Just the comics."

Daphne groans again but nods. "Fine. Deal." She turns back to me with her hand extended. "Coffee me, please."

I hand over the small cup. "Careful. It's still hot," I tell her, playing along with her little game.

"Duh. It's *coffee*." Her words are emphasized with an eye roll as she takes the drink from my hand, then blows on it like I'm sure she's seen adults do over the years. She takes a sip and smacks her lips together, letting out a loud *"Aaah."*

She treks down the hall toward the kitchen, stopping every two feet or so to take a sip and let everyone within earshot know just how good it is with her little exhales.

It's ridiculous and adorable.

"Sorry if she was rude."

I shrug. "Figured she learned it from you."

Olive narrows her eyes, and I laugh.

"She reads the newspaper?"

It's Olive's turn to chuckle. "No. But she likes to pretend she does, just like her dad does every morning at the breakfast table. He slides her the cartoons, and she cackles over them, pretending to understand the jokes, while he looks over the sports section. She's . . ."

"A hell-raiser?"

"Yep." Olive drops her eyes to the coffee I'm still holding, pursing her lips like she's contemplating her next move.

Is she going to invite me in or tell me to get lost?

I truly hope it's not the latter.

But either way, I'm going to let her be the one to make that decision.

I let my eyes wander over Olive as I wait for her to figure it out.

The bump on her forehead has gone down, but there's no mistaking it's still there. I wonder if her knees have healed and want to check, but I can't.

She looks better than she did a few days ago but somehow just as wrecked.

Is that because of me?

I shake away the thought.

Finally, after what feels like hours of me lingering at the threshold, Olive sighs.

"Just come in," she mutters, taking off down the hall again, leaving me to trail behind her for the second time today.

And I do with glee, closing the door behind me before following her deeper into the apartment.

I take it all in—the mismatched furniture; the eclectic collections of vases, candles, and chipped teacups; the distinct smell of cinnamon.

It feels as cozy as it looks, and I decide right then that this is what I want my place to feel like one day.

We round the corner she disappeared around earlier and step into a small kitchen. It's just as mismatched as the rest of the apartment. Appliances litter the counter, but not in an overwhelming way. Everything seems to have its place, and it works. A long counter stretches through most of the space, which is where I find little Daphne sitting, sipping on her "coffee."

"Are you staying for dinner or what?" Daphne asks me the second I walk into her line of sight.

"Kid, you cannot just keep asking rude questions," Olive says.

"It's not rude to invite someone to dinner," Annie's niece argues.

To be fair, she's right. It's not rude. It's just her approach that's rude.

"Are you being rude in here?" Annie asks from behind me. I have no clue where she's come from, but she's dressed in her work scrubs, clearly ready for a long shift at the hospital. Her eyes shift to mine, and they're a lot less heated than they were the first time we met. I think me coming back to the hospital for an update on Olive might have earned me some points with her. "Jude."

"Annie," I counter.

"You know him too?" Daphne questions. "I didn't even know there could be two Judes!"

"You know two girls named Charlotte," Olive points out.

Daphne huffs in a way only a kid can—exasperated and annoyed and yet so damn cute. "So?"

"Well, this is just like that."

She still doesn't look like she believes us, so she looks to her aunt.

"There are probably millions of Judes. There's even a song about one," Annie explains, and Daphne's mouth drops open in shock, her mind probably reeling from this news. "But yes, I know this Jude. Kind of."

"Kind of." Olive snorts. "Does anyone truly know him?" she snarks not so quietly.

"He's going to play Barbies with me." Daphne pushes her shoulders back, tipping her chin high. "I know him."

Olive snorts again, then pulls open a cabinet. She grabs a box of cheese crackers and a bowl from the row of dishes drying on the counter. She dumps a few crackers in, then slides the bowl over to Daphne.

"Eat some crackers. He's not playing Barbies with you. We can play later."

"I will," I offer sincerely. "I'll play Barbies with you, Daphne."

Her eyes light up. "Really?"

"Yes, really. But only if you'll be really, really, *really* good for Olive while your auntie's at work. Deal?"

She nods with enthusiasm. "Deal. I'll go set them up! Olive, help me move the couch!"

Move the couch?

But I guess it's not such an odd request, because Olive does just that—she waltzes right past me, heading into the living room, where she rolls up her sleeves and "helps" Daphne push the couch out of the way.

"I'm glad you got my text," Annie whispers from beside me.

It took a few trips to the hospital, but I finally wore Annie down, and she gave me her number so I wouldn't have to keep coming back. I've been texting her every day in hopes that Olive's changed her mind about seeing me.

She hasn't, but when Annie told me she'd be at JT's coffee truck, I knew there was no way I was going to miss my chance at seeing her, even if just for a minute.

"I'm glad you texted," I say just as quietly. "I'm glad you're giving me another chance to make this right and prove I'm not a total asshat."

"Yeah, well, it's not really me you need to convince, now is it?"

"No, I guess not."

It's Olive I have to convince, and that's what I intend to do.

I want to show her I'm not just some douchebag Hollywood actor. That even though I might have not been upfront about my name, I'm still me. I'm still that guy from the messages. The one who made her laugh. The one she told all her secrets to.

I might not be Jasper like she was hoping, but I could still be everything she was looking for in him—a friend. Much as I may want to, I don't even let myself think of being more than that right now.

Annie sighs. "Just don't make me regret it, okay?"

"I won't," I promise her, and I mean it. She won't regret this second chance she's given me. I'll make sure of it.

"Hmm." It's all she says before stepping into the living room and crouching down. "Hug, kiddo."

Daphne abandons Olive, running to Annie.

"Hey!" Olive complains, but her protest falls on deaf ears as Daphne wraps her arms around her aunt.

"I'll see you in the morning, okay? Make sure Auntie Liv reads you a bedtime story."

"The one about the normal lady and the prince falling in love?"

Annie's eyes dart between me and Olive, and she snorts. "Yeah, that one is fine."

They hug again; then Annie shoves to her feet.

She looks at her best friend. "Be nice. To *everyone*."

I'd be a fool to think the last part isn't pointed right at me.

Olive laughs. "We'll see."

Annie leaves, and I like that she locks the door behind her. It makes me happy to know that Olive has someone looking after her like that.

Then the reality of it all sets in.

I'm in Olive's apartment.

It's just me and her. Together. All alone. No interruptions. Just—

"Which Barbie do you want to be?"

Oh. Right. Daphne.

I sneak a look over at Olive, who is watching us with an amused look. I clear my throat. "I'll let you pick."

"Hmm . . ." Daphne taps her painted nail—really, it's more finger than nail that's painted—against her chin. "This one."

She thrusts a doll with long brown hair into my hands, then plops down onto the floor, peering up at me.

"Well, come on. Let's play!"

I take another glance at Olive, who is very much enjoying this; then I fold myself down to the floor, sitting across from Daphne.

When I woke up this morning, the last thing I thought I'd be doing was playing Barbies with a four-year-old, but here I am.

And honestly, if it made Olive grin at me like she is, I'd do it every damn day.

"We're hungry," Daphne announces, pretending to be her Barbie but not at all hiding the fact she's really talking to Olive as herself. "And we want cheese pizza."

"Cheese pizza, huh?" Olive asks.

"Yep!" Daphne looks over at me. "Is that okay? I don't really like pepperoni, but I'll pick 'em off. Mama makes me do that sometimes because Daddy loves pepperoni."

"I'm not sure if I'm staying for dinner," I tell her.

"What? You have to! Auntie Liv reads the *best* bedtime stories." She pauses. "Don't tell Auntie Annie I said that, okay?"

I laugh. "It'll be our little secret. But I'm still not sure about pizza. That's up to Auntie Liv."

"Can he stay?" the kid asks Olive.

"Yeah, can I stay?" I echo.

Olive looks like she wants to make us both leave, but instead, she nods, letting out a resigned sigh. "He can stay."

She can act annoyed all she wants, but I see the way her lips tip up at the corners. The corners that I desperately want to kiss.

She doesn't hate the idea of me staying, and neither do I.

And that's how I spend my evening, playing Barbies and eating cheese pizza with a four-year-old, all while I try to ignore my burgeoning desire to kiss the woman who hates me.

"You know, I think your description of her was on point," I whisper to Olive as we slip out of Annie's bedroom.

After the story of the "normal lady" and the prince, plus four other books, Daphne is *finally* asleep.

She's a hell-raiser, all right. A total storm. One minute she's bossing everyone around Barbie City, and the next she's eating *five* slices of cheese pizza, just to beg for ice cream and a movie afterward.

I've spent upward of eighteen hours on set before, but never have I been so damn exhausted.

Olive laughs as we step out into the tiny hallway, pulling the door shut behind her. "It was, wasn't it? She really is a firecracker."

She straightens, and it becomes very apparent just how tiny this hallway truly is.

Her back is pressed against the wall and so is mine, yet somehow, we're almost touching.

Her blue eyes flick back and forth between my green ones as the heat between us gets cranked higher and higher, the air growing thinner and thinner.

Now we're alone, and that's becoming abundantly clear by the second.

Just us. In the hall. By ourselves. No kid to interrupt us. No roommate.

I swallow the lump in my throat, and Olive inhales sharply. Our sounds are so damn loud in the otherwise silent apartment. It even seems like the city has turned mute just for this moment, which is absurd. But no sound filters in from the street—not a horn is honked, not a pedestrian yells. Nothing.

Just us.

"I . . ."

But that's all I say because I don't really know what else to say, other than to ask Olive what I'm still doing here.

I didn't need to wait around in the living room while she gave Daphne a bath. I didn't need to stick around for the first story, the second, the third, and definitely not the fifth.

But I am still here, and Olive still hasn't kicked me out.

That has to mean *something*, right? Like maybe we can go back to the way things were before? Or maybe she doesn't hate me as much as she's pretending to?

And fuck me, but I hope that's the case. Because the thought of being cut from her life feels all wrong, and I don't have time for wrong.

Truthfully, I don't even have time for *right*.

I'm trying to rebuild a career for myself. Working to make a name that's all me. One where I don't have to worry whether I'm getting the part just because I'm a Rafferty or if it's because I've earned it on my own. That's supposed to be my focus.

But I can't focus on all that knowing Olive could possibly hate me, and I really, really don't want her to hate me.

I want to be her friend as Jude, not Jasper.

I want to know her, and I want her to know *me*.

I suck in a deep breath, then try again. "I—"

"Does Keely know you're here?"

I rear back, the question and the name coming out of nowhere. "What?"

Olive shrugs. "I saw the photos. I was just wondering if your girlfriend was aware of where you are tonight. Or do you lie to her too?"

My chest stings as if I've been punched in it, and I guess I kind of have been.

And I also guess I kind of deserve it.

"We should probably talk about that."

"There's nothing to talk about. You're free to do whatever you want."

She turns to leave, and before I know what I'm doing, I'm grabbing her wrist and tugging her back to me.

To us.

My hands go to her waist as she lands against my chest with a soft gasp, her eyes snapping to mine. They're even bluer up close, and I realize that, other than when she was lying concussed on the street, this is the closest we've ever been.

I like it. I like it a lot.

"There is something to talk about," I tell her quietly.

Her brows pinch together at my words, and I hear the implication in them too late. She tries to pull free of my hold, but I don't let her, enjoying the way she feels in my arms entirely too much. She's soft in the best places, her hips splaying wider than my hands can hold, but I like it. It feels good. *She* feels good.

"It was a date, but it wasn't a *date*. It was orchestrated by my publicist and hers. We were pawns in a game. That's all. It meant nothing."

"You don't need to explain. I—"

"I *do* need to explain, Sunshine," I interrupt, and she doesn't even react to the nickname like I expect her to. It's almost as if she's resigned to it.

So I test my luck. I move one hand from her waist, ghosting my fingertips over her arm and up, up, up, until I'm caressing her cheek. It's soft, just like the rest of her, and I love the way she feels under my touch. Love how her breaths pick up with each stroke of my thumb. Love how her pupils dilate and her thighs shift back and forth, like this simple touch is doing something to her.

"I need to explain because I need you to know that I never, ever would have gone on that date if I didn't owe it to Dylan. If I didn't *have* to, I wouldn't have. I would have rather it been you sitting on the other side of that table."

Her breath catches, but I don't stop.

"I would have rather it been you in the park," I continue.

Another brush of my thumb. Another stuttered inhale from her.

"I would have rather it been your cheek my lips were pressed against."

Her chest brushes against mine with each labored breath she takes. One breath, one stroke of my thumb.

"Not her. *You*, Sunshine."

Olive's eyes widen, taking in my words—my confession—as she blows out another strangled breath.

She studies me, watching for any tell, any hint of a lie. She won't find one. I never wanted to be there with Keely. I wanted Olive, and I still do.

I don't understand what it is about her, but I can't stay away. I couldn't from the start, and I really can't now. Not after I know how fun it is to rile her up or how loud she laughs or how smug she looks when she's won an argument.

I like Olive, and I think she could like me too.

Then, finally, she swallows and says a single word.

"Okay."

It's the sweetest word I've ever heard.

"Okay?"

"Yes."

"Good." I exhale a relieved breath. "Because I know I messed up, Olive. I know I did. I should have been honest with you, but I wasn't and I'm sorry. I just really, really don't want you to shut me out. I . . . I like you, and I want to get to know you. For real this time, if you'll let me."

"Jude, I—"

"Please," I interrupt. "I'm not afraid to beg."

"Clearly," she muses with a grin. She sighs. "Fine. All right? You win. I'll give you another chance."

"Is there a *but* to that statement?"

"No." She shakes her head. "There should be, but no."

"Good. Because, Olive?"

"Yes?"

"I'm totally going to make you like me too."

She grins but doesn't say anything.

And I have the feeling that maybe she already does.

CHAPTER SIXTEEN

Olive

@TheJudeRafferty: What are you doing today?

I grin at the message on my screen.

After I agreed to give Jude a second chance last night, I ushered him out of the apartment before I did something stupid like kiss him.

And I *really* wanted to kiss him.

I never realized before just how small our hallway is, but with me and Jude stuffed in it? It felt tinier than any other room I've ever been in. It was as suffocating as it was intoxicating. And that was before he even pulled me to his chest. After that, I was a goner. One whiff of that familiar pine was all it took. I wasn't walking away. I couldn't.

I'll admit that I liked being in his arms far more than I should have, for someone I'm supposedly upset with. But can I really be blamed? He's hard in all the perfect places, but not so much that it's uncomfortable. He didn't feel like being in the gym is his life's mission, but he obviously works out. It was . . . nice. *He* was nice.

And don't even get me started on the words that dropped from his lips with so much sincerity it hurt.

His confession wasn't what I was expecting. Am I surprised his publicist would set him up on a date? No. I'm not stupid. I understand how Hollywood works. There are plenty of relationships orchestrated for the media to eat up. It happens probably far more than people real-ize. Those "couple goals" celebs they're rooting for? It's all fake. A sham.

I'm not surprised he did it for the publicity. It makes sense. He needs to create buzz for his upcoming movie, the one that's supposed to be his big comeback and paint him as a leading man whom Hollywood wants to hire, not just that guy known for *Lakedale* or the failed vampire show.

And I get it. I do. I guess I just hoped that maybe . . . maybe Jude wouldn't be that kind of person. And maybe he's not. Maybe I have him all wrong. The only way I'm going to know if he truly is the person I liked talking to so much is by giving him another chance.

Apparently, today is that day.

@OliveMe: I was going to clean out my closet, maybe shoot some content. Why?

@TheJudeRafferty: Want some coffee and company?

I look around my destroyed bedroom.

Instead of sitting around reading the comments on my posts that are blowing up since a photo of me and Jude from outside JT's truck yesterday is making the rounds, all of which have turned into peo-ple debating whether I'm "good enough" for Jude or "hot enough" or whether Keely is "clearly the better choice" for him, I decided it would be a good idea to finish cleaning out my closet. I've been at it for an hour already, and all I've done is manage to create a giant mess that I really, really don't want to clean up right now.

I recognize that all I'm doing is avoiding the comments and the mess, but it's the only thing I can think to do that's not going to send me into a total spiral.

Those comments . . . they shouldn't bother me—I know that. They're just random people with random opinions. They shouldn't mean a thing to me.

But . . . well, I'd be a damn liar if I said they don't start wearing on me after some scrolling.

I should have stuck to the golden rule of the internet: never read the comments.

@OliveMe: I'm sold on the coffee, but my answer is going to depend on the company.

@TheJudeRafferty: He's tall and cute, with green eyes and ashy blond hair. A jawline to die for. Some scruff. Funny and oh so irresistible.

@OliveMe: You know Jasper Rafferty?!

@TheJudeRafferty: Ha. Very funny.

@TheJudeRafferty: Me. I'm your company.

@OliveMe: Hmm . . .

@TheJudeRafferty: Trust me, I'm the better Rafferty brother.

@TheJudeRafferty: Want to meet in our usual spot?

@OliveMe: Our usual spot?

@TheJudeRafferty: JT's?

I grin. I guess that *is* our usual spot, isn't it?

"Oh, good. You're smiling again."

I lift my head to find Annie standing in the doorway. She's got a coffee cup in each hand.

"Are you still mad at me?" she asks, inching into the room with trepidation.

"Yes." It's an honest answer. I wasn't exactly her biggest fan when she got back to the apartment last night, and I'm not her biggest fan right now. I'm still upset with her for going behind my back.

"Too bad." She pushes a cup of coffee my way. "Here. Love me again."

"I already love you," I tell her, taking the peace offering as she settles onto the bed next to me. "I'll always love you. But you shouldn't have set me up like that."

"I know. It's just . . . I have a feeling about him, Liv. He's a good guy. He . . ." She sighs, takes a sip of her coffee, and then turns to face me. "He came to the hospital."

"I know. I was there."

"No." She shakes her head. "Afterward. He showed up the next day."

"He did not."

"Then the next," she continues as if I never spoke. "He came back every day you didn't talk to him to get an update on you. He didn't have any other way to check on you, so he went through me."

"He . . . did?"

"Yes."

Her words send a shock wave through me.

He checked up on me.

I thought he was off with Keely Haart, but he was busy checking up on me the whole time.

That's . . . a lot to process.

"Why didn't you tell me? When I was complaining about him and Keely, why didn't you say anything?"

She arches a brow. "Would you have believed me?"

"No."

And it's true. I wouldn't have. I didn't believe her when she tried to tell me their date was fake either.

But I should have. I should have believed her, just like I believe Jude now. I owe Annie that much.

"Thanks," I tell her, swallowing my pride. "Sorry I got mad."

She bumps her shoulder against mine. "I would have been mad, too, so I get it. I'm just glad you're giving him another shot."

"You know, before you got engaged, you'd have told me to dump his ass."

She wrinkles her nose. "Yeah, probably." She laughs, shrugging. "I think this damn ring has gone to my head. I'm all . . . *mushy.*"

"*So* mushy," I agree, bumping her back. "But seriously, Annie, thank you."

"You don't need to thank me, Liv. Not for looking out for you. I'll always do that."

"You're my best friend."

"You're mine. Just don't tell Daphne I said that. She's getting mean in her old age."

I laugh. "She really is. You should have seen her last night. She looked Jude right in the eyes and told him he was the worst person she's ever played Barbies with. Jude Rafferty!"

Annie tosses her head back, her whole body shaking as she laughs. "Why am I not surprised?"

"She's a hell-raiser."

"Yeah, but she's *my* hell-raiser. I'm just glad Payton's okay. Sucks she's on bed rest for the remainder of the pregnancy, but it could have been so much worse."

"Me too. Because who else is Daphne going to terrorize? I'm tapping out and leaving that to her future younger brother."

Annie snorts. "Poor kid."

My phone shakes again, and now it's Annie who is grinning like a fool.

"Are you going out with him?"

"Yes."

"Tonight?"

"No. Today."

She squeals loudly. "Oh my god, Olive! You're going out with *Jude Rafferty*!"

"Great story, gals! Now keep it down!"

"Sorry, Mrs. Hammish!" we call out in unison before falling into a fit of giggles. Sometimes our super-thin walls are a curse, but sometimes they provide us a good laugh.

I wipe under my eyes, and Annie clutches her stomach as we sober up.

"Oh man. I needed a good laugh like that to get my day started." She shakes her head, taking another sip of her coffee before shoving off the bed. "All right. I'm off to Remi's. He wants to 'compare calendars' today."

"Is that a euphemism?"

"Nope. He actually wants to compare calendars." A slow smile pulls at her lips. "He wants to set a date."

"A date? Already? That's so . . ."

"Soon?"

"Says the girl who bought her wedding dress already."

Another giggle bubbles out of her. "I know."

"I think it's good he wants to set a date."

"You don't think we're rushing things?"

"Annie, you've been together *four years*. You're not rushing a thing."

"But we don't even live together yet . . ."

"So ask him."

She jerks her head back. "What? Ask him to move in here? With us?"

"Yeah?" I shrug. "It's not like he doesn't already spend time here. It wouldn't be that weird. A little cramped in the bathroom department, but we could make that work. He has four roommates. Do you *really* want to go live with five dudes, anyway?"

"Ew. No." She shudders. "That sounds . . . *yuck*." She sighs. "I guess . . . I suppose I could ask him to move in. I never really thought of that. I just thought . . ."

"That you'd stick to the 'traditional gender roles' like a lame-o?" I wag my finger at her. "Don't make me take your feminist card away."

She gasps. "Not the card!"

"I'll let you keep it . . ." I narrow my eyes playfully. "But only if you ask Remi to move in."

"Olive . . ."

"I'm serious, Bananie. This is obviously something that both-ers you. Take it into your own hands. If you ask and he says no, then you'll know he's not truly serious about this whole marriage thing—plus, we're still in the return window for your wedding dress. But if he says yes, then you can stop being so damn worried all the time. Even though you *so* don't have a thing to worry about," I add because it's true.

She groans, kicking her feet a few times. "Fine. I'll do it. But if he does say yes, you *have* to promise you won't get mad when he takes superlong showers or eats your crackers."

"As long as he pees *in* the toilet and keeps his mitts off my wine, we're square."

"Deal."

We hook our pinkies together, shaking them up and down twice.

"Good. Now go," I tell her. "I want to gloat about how right I was."

She rolls her eyes. "Whatever. Just promise . . . I'm taking a risk today, so you have to take one too." She lifts her brows, so I know she's serious.

I huff. "Fine, Mom. I'll take a risk."

"Good." She throws me a wink, then flounces away.

I pick up my phone and decide she's right. I will take a risk today.

@OliveMe: Give me thirty.

@TheJudeRafferty: See you then.

@TheJudeRafferty: Oh, and Olive?

@TheJudeRafferty: Wear socks.

◆ ◆ ◆

"You know, when you said to wear socks, I didn't think *this* is what you had in mind."

"What? Do you have something against bowling?"

"No. It's just . . . well, I guess I just couldn't picture *you* doing it."

"Why not?"

I shoot him a look, and he just smiles, knowing exactly what's going through my mind.

I'm out with Jude Rafferty.

I'm *bowling* with Jude Rafferty.

A multimillionaire—or billionaire? I have no clue what kind of trust fund I'm sure he has—and little old me.

How is this even real life?

"Why bowling, though?"

"Because I read somewhere once how you used to go with your dad, and I figured . . ." He lifts his shoulders.

Now it's my turn to smile.

He took me bowling because he knows how much I used to love going every other Sunday. How my dad would put everything else aside, no matter how busy he was or how pressing his work, just to take me.

He took me bowling because he remembers.

He remembers.

Maybe . . . maybe even though he wasn't truthful about who he was, he was honest about being real with me.

That excites me and terrifies me all at once because I *liked* the guy I was talking to. A lot. Maybe even more than I ever let on, and I'm scared of what that actually means. That maybe this thing—this . . . well, whatever it is we're doing—could be real too.

We step up to the counter.

"Two, please."

"Shoe size?"

"Twelve for me and . . ." Jude glances over to me.

"Eight and a half, please," I tell the guy behind the counter, but my attention isn't on him. It's everywhere else.

This bowling alley is nothing like the place I used to go to with my dad. That one was old and run-down, with more stains on the ceiling than actual bowling balls on racks. Some days, I even wondered if anyone else went there besides us.

Not this place, though. This one is fresh and new, the smell of paint still faint in the air. And it's packed with people. Laughing families. Young kids running around. Cute couples snuggled up next to each other. It's overflowing, nearly every single lane taken up as early 2000s music blasts through the speakers, clashing with the sounds of pins being knocked over.

"Here." The guy slides our shoes across the counter, then starts punching something into the screen in front of him, never once looking up at us. "Lane eight is open. It's all yours."

"Thanks," Jude says, then grabs both our shoes as we head for the lane.

I try to ignore the hand resting on the small of my back as we make our way, just like I try to ignore the eyes I can feel burning into me.

People are staring, and I know it's not because of me. It's all Jude. They recognize him. How could they not? He seems too gorgeous to be real. There's no way people aren't going to stare.

We change our shoes, and I settle behind the monitor.

"Do we want nicknames or real names?"

"Nicknames," Jude tells me from the ball rack, where he's carefully weighing his options. His brows are pinched together, and his lips are pursed as he studies them. It's comical, really, seeing him take this so seriously. "Only weirdos use real names. Nobody wants to say, 'Hey, Brad, it's your turn next.' That's so lame."

"Nicknames it is."

I punch two names into the screen and look up at my handiwork, feeling quite proud, before going off in search of my own ball.

I choose a bright-yellow one, and Jude goes for black. We couldn't be more opposite if we tried.

"Ready to get your butt kicked?" I slide my fingers into the holes and step up to the line. "Because I've had a lot of practice over the years. I'm practically a pro."

"Uh-huh. Whatever you say, Sunshine."

I turn away from him to hide my grin at the nickname I've grown used to over the last few weeks. I check out my target, line up my shot, and fire away.

And just as the ball has done for me too many times before, it starts off well, then slowly veers to the side and right into the gutter.

Jude lets out a loud laugh, drawing entirely too many pairs of eyes our way. He doesn't seem bothered by the attention, so I guess I won't be either.

I send a small wave to our audience as I return to my seat.

"Stop laughing," I hiss at him.

"I'm sorry. Really. But was that you schooling me on bowling?"

"Yes!"

"You do realize gutter balls are not going to win you the game, right?"

"Who says I'm *only* going to get gutter balls?"

I shoot him a glare, then grab my ball and toss it down the lane again.

Unsurprisingly, it curves to the right and rolls straight into the gutter. Again.

"You're right. You could still turn this around. But in the meantime, it's"—he checks the board, a grin forming on his full lips—"Asshat's turn. Watch and learn, Ollie."

He grabs his ball, lines up his shot, then lets it go.

"Yes!" he yells loudly, pumping his fists in the air. "Strike!"

"Beginner's luck."

"Beginner's luck, or am I just better than you?"

"You wish," I grumble.

But it turns out he's right. He *is* better than me. Way better than me. It's really no surprise, though. I might love bowling and talk a good game, but eight out of ten times, I'm going to gutter ball and lose with an embarrassingly low score.

Bowling with my father was never about winning. It was just about spending time with him.

Just like today is about spending time with Jude.

"Are you hungry?" he asks during our second game.

"Why, Jude Rafferty, are you going to spoil me with cheap bowling alley food on our first date?"

"First date, huh?"

I sit up straighter, my cheeks flushing with mortification. Did I just say *first date*? This isn't a date. At least, I don't think it is. Is it? I don't know. We didn't really discuss that, and I don't even know if I even actually *want* it to be one. I just—

"You're spiraling." Jude plops down next to me, nudging my leg with his own, his warmth making me feel ten times hotter than I already do. "Don't."

I risk a peek over at him. He looks cool and calm. Totally unbothered.

"Don't spiral, or don't think this is a first date?"

"Don't spiral." He leans into me. "Because I don't know about you, but I'm totally counting this as our first date."

Relief floods through me, and I release the breath I've been holding. "Oh."

He tilts his head to the side. "Is that . . . okay?"

"Yes."

The word slips out effortlessly, almost automatically.

The craziest part?

I mean it.

I'm not sure when I started thinking of this as a date, but somewhere between Jude's hand on my back, the soft smiles, the teasing, and the inside jokes . . . it became one.

"Yeah?" He grins. "Good. But just so we're clear, I'm still not letting you win."

We spend the next two hours bickering back and forth and splitting a basket of cheap fries while Jude kicks my ass at bowling.

It's hands down the best first date I've ever been on.

Jude takes our shoes and drops them back at the counter, then pays for our time at the lane before coming back over and extending a hand to me.

"What next?" he asks, tugging me up from my seat.

"Arson?"

He chuckles. "I was thinking something along the lines of ice cream."

"Good idea. We'll save arson for our third date."

The bright light stings as we emerge from the bowling alley, and I expect him to pull his sunglasses from his pocket any second, but he never does.

I'm secretly glad too.

I like seeing his eyes. I like seeing *him*.

"So, did you have fun?" he asks as we walk side by side down the sidewalk, cutting through the Upper West Side, the warm end-of-August air teasing our skin as it rolls off the Hudson.

"Getting my ass kicked at bowling? Oh yes, it's every girl's dream first date, especially with a famous actor."

"Is that what little girls dream of? Growing up to date movie stars?"

"Are you calling yourself a movie star?" I tsk playfully. "Someone's full of themselves."

He grimaces. "That did sound kind of douchey, huh?"

"I was teasing. That's what you are, isn't it? A movie star?"

"No. Yes? I don't know." He sighs, shoving his hands into his pockets. "Some days, I'm not sure what I am."

"You're Jude Rafferty."

He snorts. "Right. I'm a Rafferty. How could I forget?"

I realize then that maybe being part of Hollywood's most elite family might not be all it's cracked up to be.

"How *is* that?" I ask. "Being from the famed Rafferty clan?"

"Hard. But also amazing. It's just . . . finding that balance, you know?"

"Honestly? No. I don't know. I grew up in the middle of nowhere, Iowa. I have no idea what it's like to come from Hollywood royalty."

He nods. "You're lucky for that. I mean, don't get me wrong, I'm well aware of the privileged life I've led. We never wanted for anything. We had nannies and drivers, and everything we could ever desire was right at our fingertips—all while our parents showered us with love."

"But?"

He sighs. "But there's a whole other side to it people don't consider. I grew up in front of the world. *Literally.* I had awkward teen years, and instead of leaving them in the past, they're documented for everyone to see. I've made mistakes, and those are out there too. For all the amazing things I've been afforded in my life, privacy has never really been one of them. It's hard being a Rafferty. Not just because I'm constantly in the public eye, but I'm also always being compared to my grandparents or parents. Hell, even my brother gets brought up in all my interviews. While I might be Jude Rafferty, sometimes I wish I could just be Jude. The guy with the nice, private life who doesn't have a legacy to carry on."

The longer he talks, the more my heart aches for him.

I never really thought about that side of things. Sure, I know it's not easy to be in the spotlight—my own Instagram comments prove that—but I can't imagine having to live life on the scale he does.

"Have you considered leaving it all behind?"

"Yes."

I don't know why, but his answer surprises me. I know he disappeared from the limelight during his college years, but I'd never guess he wouldn't want to come back at all.

He chuckles at my bewildered look. "College was the first time I had a break from everything. I'm still a Rafferty, so it's not like I didn't have any attention or cameras pointed my way, but the novelty of me attending college like a regular person wore off for people fast, and they were content to just leave me be. For four whole years, I was just Jude. It was nice."

"Then why'd you come back?"

He smiles. "Because as much as I hate everything else that goes along with it, I truly do love acting. Guess you could say it's in my blood."

I roll my eyes. "That was lame."

"But true." He nods toward an ice-cream cart that's just inside the entrance to Central Park. "Want some?"

"I mean, you *did* already promise me some."

He grabs my hand, dragging me toward the mobile frozen-dessert bar.

We get our treats—a waffle cone with vanilla and sprinkles for him, and swirl with sprinkles for me—then venture farther into the park, our hands still locked together.

Jude runs his thumb over the back of my hand as he licks at his cone. I watch as his tongue delves into the vanilla soft serve, then peeks back out as he runs it over his lips to grab the excess.

Has eating ice cream always been so hot?

I've never really paid attention before, but if someone were to make an hour-long movie of just this, I'd watch it on repeat.

That spot between my legs that's been ignored for far too long tingles, and I try my best to subtly squeeze my thighs together. Anything to relieve the ache that's forming.

But then Jude takes another lick, and it becomes a fruitless effort.

His tongue sneaks out again, and this time, the corners of his mouth flip up with it.

"You're dripping."

How does he know what's happening between my legs?

"Your ice cream, Ollie. It's dripping all over your hand."

"Oh!" I drop our joined hands, instantly missing the feeling, and begin cleaning up the mess I didn't know I'd made.

Was I really so distracted by Jude that I didn't notice the ice cream dripping down my arm, almost to my elbow? What's wrong with me?

"Here." He digs into his jeans pocket, producing a wad of napkins I never saw him take. "Got these just in case."

"Thanks." I wipe up the mess, toss the napkins, then finally take my first taste of my cone. "Mmmm."

"Good?" he asks, but his eyes aren't on mine. They're focused on my mouth, on my tongue moving through the vanilla-chocolate swirl.

I run it around the melting mess once more, watching as his eyes and nostrils flare.

Oh, good. I'm not the only weirdo getting turned on by ice cream.

"Delicious," I tell him, and he finally snaps his eyes to mine.

His cheeks tint red as he clears his throat and looks away with a squint.

"Come on," he mutters, grabbing my hand once more. "Let's go sit over there."

I let him lead the way down a grassy hill, following along as he finds us a spot to sit in the sun. We fold ourselves down on a patch of grass. Jude stretches out his long legs and rests his hand between us so it's touching my own as I relax onto my free palm, my legs crisscrossed in front of me.

We enjoy our cool snacks in silence, letting the bustle of the park fill the space.

People are spread out all around us, some with blankets and some just sitting on the grass. Some are reading and some are talking. There's a couple who look like they're in the middle of a breakup, and another one is kissing. Some guy in a suit sits quietly, staring blankly ahead of him like he's having a midlife crisis in real time. It's a whole mix of people, and it's magnificent. It's the exact reason I love living here.

"The sun feels nice," he murmurs as we finish up our cones.

"It does. I had to do a shoot for winter recently. It's always so strange trying to get into that headspace when it's ninety degrees outside."

"Just like it's weird to shoot a Christmas movie in the middle of July."

"Well, that's less weird. Christmas in July is a real thing."

"A real ridiculous thing."

"Not a Christmas fan?"

"Oh, no. I love Christmas. I just love Christmas at Christmas, you know?"

"My dad used to do Christmas in July."

Jude's face falls, and I laugh. "Gotcha!"

His jaw slackens. "You little . . ." His eyes narrow. "That was mean."

"Maybe. But you should have seen your face. You were all . . ." I pout, giving him my best sad-puppy impression.

"That is not what I look like."

"Sorry, but it is."

"No. *This* is how I look when I'm sad."

Then, right before my eyes, Jude transforms, turning on his actor switch and effortlessly slipping into the look of a man heartbroken.

It's wild to watch in person yet so mesmerizing as tears well in his eyes and a single drop slips down his cheek.

He brushes it away, then shoots me a grin. "See? *That's* what I look like when I'm sad."

"That was . . ."

"Cool?"

"And creepy and amazing and totally weird. Do it again."

He barks out a laugh. "Sad boy again?"

"No. Do something else. Do Matthew McConaughey."

"I'm not good at impressions."

I lift my brows. *All* actors are good at impressions. That's their whole shtick—impersonating human emotion.

"Fine." He lifts his shoulders up, then shimmies them, clearing his throat. He squints just a little, cocks his lips to the side, and says, *"All right, all right, all right."*

Now it's my turn to laugh. "That was terrible."

"See? I told you. I'm horrible at them."

"No. You just need more practice. Do another. Do Keanu Reeves."

"That one's easy." He clears his throat, sitting up straight, and quotes one of the best lines from *John Wick*. He settles back down. "Better?"

"I'm sorry. Who are you again? Because a second ago, I thought I was sitting next to Jude Rafferty, but now I'm pretty sure it's Keanu."

"Which one do you like better?"

"Hmm. Depends. Do another."

"Who?"

I tap my chin, thinking. "Oh! I know! Do Jasper Rafferty. Oh, wait. You've already impersonated him."

He leans into me, eyes narrowed tightly as he whispers, "Brat."

I match his movements. "You like my brattiness."

"Maybe just a little." He pinches his finger and thumb together, leaving only a speck of space between them. "Like that much."

I reach over, pushing his fingers farther apart. "More like that much."

"Nah."

"Uh-huh."

He inches closer. "No way."

"Yes way," I counter, inching in closer too.

We're close. So damn close that all I can smell is pine and all I can feel is his heat.

His gaze darts to my lips, then back to my eyes.

"Can I ask you something?" he whispers.

"Depends. Is it going to ruin the moment?"

He laughs lightly. "I hope not."

"Then ask."

"Do . . ." He inhales, once again pulling his eyes from my lips. "Do you have a thing for my brother? Is that why you were DMing him?"

"No." The answer falls from my lips with no effort, mostly because it's true. "Do I find him attractive? Yes. But that shouldn't be surprising. But do I have 'a thing' for him? No. I don't even know him."

"You thought you did."

"Right. I did think that. But it was you the whole time, right?" He nods. "Then it's not your brother I have a thing for."

It's you.

The words go unsaid, but I don't think we need to hear them anyway.

Jude's eyes dart to the right, over my shoulder, and everything about him tenses—his eyes, his shoulders, his jaw.

"What is it?"

"We're being watched," he says through clenched teeth. "There are some paparazzi not so subtly hiding in the bushes about three hundred feet away."

"Are you sure?"

He laughs. "I said *not so subtly* because their cameras are very, *very* clearly sticking out."

"Oh."

I go to turn, but Jude stops me, placing a hand on my cheek and keeping my attention on him.

"Don't look at them. It's just going to give them more ammo."

Does he . . . not want to be seen with me? Is that what it is? Because I'm not Keely Haart? Because I'm not his usual type? I've seen the few women he's been photographed with over the years. They're all tall and slim and look just like all the women I've seen gracing magazine covers my entire life.

They all fit a certain look, and that look is completely opposite of me.

"It's not you, Sunshine," he says, reading my mind. "No. That's a lie. It *is* you, but not for the reasons you might be thinking. I . . . I want to protect you from all this. I don't want them bothering you."

His words are sweet, but they're pointless. He knows it, and so do I.

Do I really want my life splattered all over celebrity news sites or the pages of gossip magazines? Not at all.

But I'm not really interested in hiding either.

He winces. "I'm sorry. I thought this was going to be a peaceful day. Nobody bothering us."

"No, don't be sorry." I shake my head. "I just think . . ."

"What, Sunshine? What do you think?"

"Well, if they're going to take pictures, let's make it worth their while."

Then I take my second risk of the day—I kiss Jude Rafferty.

I press my lips against his softly, waiting. *Hoping* he'll kiss me back.

And after a few shocked seconds, he does. *Hungrily.*

His hands dive into my hair, tugging me to him as our mouths move in unison. When he slides his tongue along the seam of my lips, I grant him access, and the growl that rumbles through him is almost too much.

But it's nothing compared to when he drags me into his lap.

I don't dare break our kiss, though. Not as I settle onto his lap. Not as I wind my own hands through his blond locks, loving that they're as thick as they look. And not even as I hear shutters in the distance.

His lips are soft and hard and everything I thought they would be. I dance my fingers over his jaw, loving how his rough scruff feels under my touch as he glides his own hands over my hips and just under my shirt, which has ridden up. The pads of his fingers brush against my skin, and I swear I feel it not just at my back but everywhere, right down to my toes, as our mouths continue to tangle together.

I don't stop kissing him for I don't even know how long. Long past appropriate, that's for sure. There's no way I won't feel it in my thighs later, being stretched over his lap like this for such a long period of time.

I don't know who pulls away first, but eventually, we're no longer kissing, our lips just resting together as we try to catch our breath.

Jude plants one last, soft kiss on my lips before pulling back and smiling up at me.

I can't help it—I laugh.

I laugh at his smile, at his messy hair, at the ridiculousness of it all.

I'm sitting in Jude Rafferty's lap in the middle of Central Park.

I would have never, ever predicted this. Not in a million years.

But now that it's here . . . I don't want to let it go.

So we don't.

We sit there long enough to debate which is better, *Legally Blonde* or *Legally Blonde 2: Red, White & Blonde*, and whether you should eat two slices of bagel sandwich style or separately. It's long enough that the paparazzi must have decided they've gotten all they'll get, because they take off as the sun begins to set.

And long enough for me to decide that giving him another chance was the right choice.

"It's getting late," Jude says. "We should probably get you home."

And just like that, my shoulders slump.

He laughs. "It's not goodbye forever. Just for right now. Because, if we're being honest, Sunshine, if you sit on my lap much longer, I'm *really* going to give the media something to talk about." He lands a peck on my nose. "I think I'll save that for date two."

I grin. "Date two, huh?"

"Oh yeah. Date two for sure. Besides, we have to have a date two if we want to get to date three."

"Ah. Arson. How could I forget?"

He laughs, patting my butt, and I rise off him. He stands along with me, wiping the dirt off himself and very, very subtly adjusting the evidence of our make-out session.

"Hey, Jude?"

"Yeah?" He reaches for my hand, threading our fingers together like it's the most natural thing in the world. Like it doesn't make my heart skip a beat.

Like it doesn't make me wonder what it would be like to hold his hand more often.

"This was a really good first date."

"Would this be a really inappropriate time to ask if I'm forgiven now?"

I roll my eyes. Only he would be so bold to ask.

"Ooh. An eye roll. Good or bad?"

"There are good eye rolls?"

"Pfft." He shrugs. "Of course. Eye rolls like that cute one you do when I say something annoying that you secretly find funny."

I roll my eyes again, because . . . well, for that exact reason.

"See? That?"

I shake my head. "You *are* annoying."

"But forgiven?"

Am I still mad that he lied? Yes. Do I understand why he did it? Sort of. But can I keep holding it against him when he's already proven that, yeah, sure, he lied about his name, but he didn't lie about who he *really* is? No, not really.

I blow out a breath. "You're forgiven, Jude."

"It was the kisses, wasn't it?"

It was that and so much more. The way he checked up on me even when I didn't want to talk to him. How when he read my diary, he truly read it. How he helped with Daphne. This whole damn day. It was so many little things that added up into a really big thing that overshadowed him pretending to be Jasper.

And that really big thing? It's Jude.

"And the promise of arson."

He laughs, then slides his arm around my shoulders, tugging me close to him. "Come on. Let's get you home before I change my mind and decide to try out some date-two activities."

CHAPTER SEVENTEEN

Jude

"You really don't think it's a little convenient that she kisses you when the paparazzi are there? That she's just a little too comfortable about all of this?"

"No, Dylan. I don't. But I'm glad to know how you really feel about it."

She sighs, side-eyeing me from her spot on the uncomfortable couch we're both sitting on while we wait backstage for my turn to be interviewed by the ultra-obnoxious Timmy Jeffers, late-night host of *Late! At Night with Timmy.*

Considering my last appearance on television ended with me flashing my underwear to the entire world, it's safe to say I am not looking forward to this interview for many reasons.

I even made sure to wear plain black boxer briefs, just in case.

"I'm just looking at this with a more critical eye than you because clearly you're not paying attention," Dylan says. "She's gained three hundred thousand followers *just* since you've been linked. How do you not think she's using you to gain fame?"

"Because I just know she's not."

Dylan doesn't know her, so she doesn't understand that Olive isn't like that. I know she's not . . . right?

She did kiss me, though. She knew the cameras were right there, pointed at us, and she kissed me. Did she do it on purpose? Did she want to be in the spotlight?

I shake away the thoughts as soon as they slam into me.

No.

She's not like that. Not at all. I've had my fair share of people like that in my life. Olive isn't that kind of person. I can feel it.

And I'm not just saying that because kissing her was the best damn thing in the world. Having her in my lap . . . feeling her mouth on mine . . . my hands on her hips . . . It was fucking perfect. *She* was perfect.

I'm usually careful about public displays of affection. I know how easily they can get blown out of the water, how much the cameras eat them up. But when Olive pressed her lips to mine, none of that mattered anymore. I was all-in with her, and there was no stopping it.

I honestly haven't even looked at the photos, and I'm sure I don't want to. I already know what we were doing was too much in public. I don't need to see the evidence spread before me.

It was reckless, totally senseless—but also so, so good.

And I cannot wait to do it again. Two days is too long to go without her.

"Look," Dylan says, pulling me from my thoughts, and it's probably a good thing. My mind was getting ready to slide down a slippery slope, and now is not the time. I'm already a bundle of nerves. I don't need to add to my anxiety at this moment. "I might be your publicist, but I can't tell you how to run your life. If you trust her, then fine. Just don't be surprised when it crashes and burns, and the truth comes out."

I grunt at her harsh words. "Thanks for believing in me."

Another sigh. "I'm sorry. I'm just . . ." She waves her hands in the air. "It's nothing. Ignore me."

"I always try to, but you never let me."

She laughs, but it sounds forced. So not like the Dylan I know.

"Is everything okay with you?"

"Hmm?" She peeks up at me. "Oh yeah. It's nothing. I'm good. Totally fine."

"Are you sure? You seem a little extra doomy and gloomy."

"I'm good." She clears her throat. "Timmy is going to ask about you two. You know that, right? He's nosy as hell and obnoxious enough to do it."

And just like that, we're back to business. "Yeah, I know."

"Then have an answer ready. For her sake—and yours."

"So you *do* care about her?"

"No. I don't know her. But I do know you, and I'd rather you not make another mess I have to clean up."

"Tell me how you really feel, Dylan."

"You couldn't handle it, sweetie."

I laugh because she's probably right. Dylan can be mean when she wants to be, and I'd bet a thousand dollars that right now, she wants to be *very* mean.

Something's up with her lately, but I'm not going to push it. If she wants to tell me, she will. I just really hope that whatever it is, it doesn't have anything to do with me giving Jasper her number. He's an ass, but there's no way he'd do anything to hurt Dylan and jeopardize my career.

I make a mental note to check in with him about it later, see if I can casually bring it up without giving too much away.

The door creaks open, and I snap my head up to find a PA stealing a quick look into the dressing room.

"Mr. Rafferty? We're ready for you in five."

"We'll be right there," Dylan says, a fake smile plastered on her face before turning back to me. "Just remember . . ."

"Give a good answer, and don't say anything stupid. This movie is my gateway to other leading roles. I know, I know."

She shoots me a wink. "That's my boy."

She steps out of the room, ushering the PA away and giving me a few moments to collect myself.

So that's what I do.

I rise from the couch and begin my usual ritual—pacing.

I count each step.

One, two, three, four, five, six, seven, eight.

I turn, then walk the length of the room again.

I do this four more times, inhaling and exhaling deep breaths in an attempt to get my nerves in check. I even recite the damn alphabet backward to get my mind to focus on literally anything else.

If the way my heart is beating erratically is any indication, it's not working.

I'm a fucking wreck.

My phone begins to pulsate, and I snatch it off the table with shaking hands. I glance at the screen, grinning when I see who it is.

Olive.

And just like that, all my nerves fizzle away.

Sunshine: Break a leg!

Sunshine: Wait. Do non-stage actors say that too? I have no clue.

Sunshine: Good luck!

Sunshine: (Is that better?)

Me: It's much better and very much appreciated it.

Sunshine: I know you get nervous . . .

Me: That obvious?

Sunshine: Not at all, Snoopy.

Me: I'm glaring at you right now.

Sunshine: Ooooh. I'm big scared.

Me: I can't wait to see you tonight.

Sunshine: I can't believe you're cooking me dinner.

Sunshine: Do you even know how to cook?

Me: I guess we'll both find out, won't we?

Sunshine: Just say the word. I'll order a pizza.

Me: I'm so glad you have faith in my abilities.

Sunshine: I have faith in SOME of your abilities. *waggles brows*

Sunshine: Now, stop being a perv and go kick butt at your interview.

Me: You were being the perv!

Sunshine: Who? Me? *blinks innocently*
Me: Brat.
Sunshine: Your point?

"Sir?"

I glance up. The PA is back at the door, waiting on me, looking less patient than she did a few moments ago.

"Sorry," I tell her, pocketing my phone. "I'm ready."

◆ ◆ ◆

"So, Jude, tell me about your new movie in your words."

"Well, Timmy, it's an action movie. I play a guy named James who is kind of this jerk that everyone hates. He works for the FBI, and nobody wants to be his partner. He gets saddled with this new agent, a woman—played by the amazingly talented Kendra Hallstead—who hates him too. They get sent on this big mission to save New York from this bad guy, and—"

"They fall in love, don't they?" he guesses, the wrinkles around his eyes deepening as he grins over at me with raised, bushy, near-white eyebrows. "The usual clichéd stuff."

"They fall in love," I confirm, ignoring his other dig, then smile out at the crowd and instantly wish I hadn't.

I've not done a late-night gig like this in a long time, so I'm already on edge. But seeing an audience *this* huge? It's nerve-racking on a whole new level. This place is filled to the brim with people, not an open seat to be seen in the two stories it takes up.

"That sounds fun, huh? A little cheesy but fun." Timmy laughs and so does the audience. I smile, laughing along, even though I don't find it funny. "Well, based on recent photographs, it's safe to say there's no romance between you and your costar."

"I mean, the fact that she's married should have ruled that out anyway." I force another laugh, enjoying too much how Timmy's eyes narrow at my words.

Yeah, that's right. I can play this game too.

"So, Jude, tell us about this new mystery lady. It looks like you two had a lot of fun in the park the other day." He holds up some cards displaying the photos of us while the crowd whistles and hoots.

I shift in my seat as subtly as I can, trying not to draw attention to the fact that it suddenly feels ten degrees hotter and I have the urge to run far, far away.

Timmy grins at my discomfort and cuts right to the chase. "How long have you been dating social media sensation and plus-size model Olive O'Brien?"

I knew this was coming, but that doesn't make it any less surreal hearing her name roll off his lips, my two worlds colliding.

It's strange. I'm well aware of who I am, and so is Olive. Yet somehow, when I'm with her, I don't *feel* like a movie star. I just feel like me.

Or at least, I did until we made the tabloids.

Now that weird invisible box we've seemed to be existing in over the last few weeks comes crashing down around me.

I've not had to navigate this before. I've had short relationships, but nothing like this. Nothing so in the public eye. I don't understand how Jasper does this all the time, having such high-profile relationships. It's exhausting.

"Um, it's new," I mutter.

"Like last-week kind of new?" He grins, seeming to feel awfully proud of himself for connecting those dots, as if the media didn't already do that. "This is the same girl you saved on the sidewalk last week, isn't it?"

I swallow, nodding tightly. "That's her."

"Wow! You're a real-life movie hero now. You saved the girl *and* you got her. Lucky you!"

Timmy laughs. The audience laughs. And I die inside a little bit.

I'm saved by the cue for a commercial, where Timmy ignores me as they retouch his makeup.

The rest of the interview is quick, focusing only on my upcoming movie, and then I'm ushered off the stage so the next guest can take my place.

I've never been so glad to be out from in front of the camera—and that includes the drugged-up Snoopy interview.

"Well, that was something," Dylan mutters as we walk back to the dressing room. "Told you they'd ask about her."

I grunt in response but don't say anything else as I barrel through the door.

Dylan lingers outside as I grab my things; then I meet her back in the hallway.

"Hey," she says, resting her hand on my arm. "Are you okay?"

"I'm fine." It's a lie. We both know it.

I'm not fine. I'm fucking annoyed.

About the media always trying to link me to my married costar. About reporters asking about Olive. About having to do this damn interview in the first place. I may have grown up in the public eye, but I've never felt so exposed.

"Hmm," Dylan hums, letting me stew in my own anger. "I had those groceries you requested delivered to your apartment."

I feel a smile tug at my lips, remembering that even though the interview sucked, I still have something to look forward to today—Olive.

"The flowers too?"

"Of course. And wine."

"Good. She likes wine."

Dylan lifts a brow but doesn't say anything—though I can tell she wants to.

We leave the building through the stage door, and we're almost instantly bombarded by photographers. I fight the urge to glare at my publicist, knowing good and well she was the one who called them.

I wonder if she sent them to the park too.

When we're tucked safely inside our SUV, I ask just that.

She barks out a laugh. "Ha. No. That wasn't me. That was all your own fault for not wearing your disguise."

"My stalker disguise?"

"What?" Dylan asks, only half listening, her attention already on her phone, which is buzzing incessantly in her hands.

And that's how we spend the rest of the ride—Dylan on her phone and me thinking of all the things I want to do to Olive tonight.

"All right, fine. I'll admit it. You win this round."

"You liked it?"

She gestures to her empty plate. "Clearly."

"Well, I didn't want to assume anything. You could have totally just eaten it to make me feel better."

"Just like I could be telling you that you win this round just to make you feel better." She takes a sip of her wine, her brows arched in a challenge over the rim of her glass.

Dylan had that delivered too. I'm not a wine guy, much preferring whiskey if I'm going to drink, and I didn't have a single wineglass in this place.

I'm sure I could have served it in any cup, but I wanted this date to be special. For Olive.

"I'll let you in on a little secret . . ." I curl my finger, beckoning her closer.

She leans across my kitchen island, where we've just had dinner. "You totally had this delivered, then plated it to look like you made it?"

I shake my head. "Better. I called my mom and FaceTimed with her the entire time I cooked it just to make sure I didn't mess anything up."

"It was macaroni! How could you mess up macaroni?"

"Excuse me. I had to cut *chicken* for that macaroni. I could have easily messed that up. We're both lucky I'm not bleeding out right now."

"Don't worry, I'll sit by your hospital bed."

"You're damn right you would. You owe me."

She grins, taking another sip of her wine. "Can I at least help you clean up?"

"Nah. I've got it."

I pull open a cabinet, expecting it to be the dishwasher, but find only a drawer.

This place has a drawer inside a cabinet? Who designed this loft?

I reach for another one, and this time I find a trash can.

I have a trash can under my sink?

"Jude?"

"Hmm?" I ask, checking another cabinet.

"Do you not know where your dishwasher is?"

The tips of my ears grow warm as I straighten, looking over at Olive, who seems very amused by this. "No. I, um, I'm not even actually sure I have one?"

She lets out a loud laugh, tossing her head back even, then rises from her stool.

"I'll help," she insists. "You wash, I'll dry."

So for the next ten minutes, we work side by side in comfortable silence, washing the dishes like we've done it a thousand times before.

It's comfortable—comfortable in a way I've never experienced before.

I saw someone casually in college and even dated a few women afterward, but nothing ever lasted very long. I've definitely never had someone over at my apartment before. It's always easier to be the one who comes and goes, who keeps their private life out of dating.

But with Olive . . . it just feels right. *Normal.*

I really like normal, and I especially like normal with her.

And I really hate that I'm going to have to leave that feeling behind when I head to Vancouver. For the first time since I got the role, I'm not excited about it. Yeah, this is everything I wanted, but I feel like Olive and I just got to a good place. I don't want the distance to jeopardize anything. Dating someone is hard enough. But dating an actor who travels often? It's even harder. I don't want to screw this up so soon.

When we finish up and Olive stacks the last plate into the cabinet, her short little sundress riding up just enough to drive me wild, I can't help myself.

"Oh!" she gasps when she turns around and I'm right there, her hand even going to her chest.

"Hi," I say, sliding closer.

"Hi back." She giggles, and I love the sound.

"I've been thinking . . ."

"Uh-oh."

"No. It's a good thought. I think."

Her lips twitch. "Very reassuring."

"I've just been thinking, *Why should Ollie get to make the first move and not me?*"

"Because I'm not a chickenshit?"

I pull my head back, smirking. "Did you just call me a chickenshit?"

She lifts a shoulder, pulling my eyes to her soft, exposed skin peppered with freckles. "Maybe."

I shake my head. "Anyway. I was thinking about it. Thinking about how unfair it was to be ambushed like that."

"I don't know. Based on the way you reacted, it didn't seem too unfair to me. I mean, even *I've* seen the photos. You were rather . . . *enthusiastic.*"

"I'll show you 'enthusiastic.'"

"Is that a promise?"

"Maybe." I stalk closer, pressing myself against her until her backside hits the counter and there's nowhere for her to go. She doesn't look too scared, though. If anything, she looks excited, almost like this is where she wanted to end up anyway. "Maybe I'll ambush you when you're least expecting it and give you the most enthusiasm you've ever had in your whole life."

"You can't *tell* me you're going to ambush me. That ruins the surpr—"

I swallow the rest of her words, pressing my lips against hers.

It takes her all of three seconds before she realizes what's happening and kisses me back.

Her hands delve into my hair like they did a few days ago, and she runs her fingernails against my scalp in the most delightful way.

I grip her waist, then move down, down, down until I scoop her into my arms and drop her onto the counter.

"Jude!" she gasps. "What are you—"

But her protest is moot when I take her mouth again, and she moans against me, still clutching my head.

I let my hands wander, getting my feel of her soft-as-sin skin. I float my hands over her arms, down her sides, and around her waist, digging my thumbs into every inch of flesh beneath my touch. She feels so, so good underneath me, and I want to feel more.

No. I *need* to feel more. I need to touch her. *Taste* her.

I just need *her*.

I pull away, loving how she whimpers at the loss of my lips. She's breathing heavily, her mouth is swollen, and her eyes are glazed over. She's fucking gorgeous like this, and I want nothing more than to see her truly fall apart.

"Do you trust me?" I ask.

She nods. "Yes."

"Good."

Slowly, I skim my hands past her waist and down her thighs. She wiggles against my touch but doesn't tell me to stop.

I don't.

I keep going, going, going until I reach her knee. Then I start again, dragging my fingertips featherlight over her until I reach her waist again.

I move an inch inward, then start the trek all over, each pass moving closer and closer to between her legs.

By the time I reach the inside of each thigh, she's squirming against the counter and glaring at me.

"Now who's the brat?"

"Your point?" I counter, like she's done to me.

She smashes her lips together, fighting a smile, but that smile turns to a sigh when I run a single finger over her center.

Even through her panties, still hidden by her dress, I can tell she's wet.

She's enjoying this tease just as much as I am.

"Jude . . ." she pleads, arching her hips toward my touch as I run the back of my finger over her again. Her legs fall wider apart, granting me more access. "Please."

I move my hand from under her dress, gripping her waist again and pulling her to the edge of the counter. In one swift motion, I hook my fingers into the band of her panties and start dragging them down her thighs.

Catching on to what I'm doing, she helps, lifting herself so I can pull them off, letting them drop to the floor at our feet.

Olive crashes her hands back into my hair, pulling my mouth to hers and kissing me until we're both out of breath.

When she lets me go, she says three words that are my undoing.

"Touch me, Jude."

Who am I to say no to that?

I step back, shove her legs wide, and take my first real glance at her.

Gorgeous.

Dark curls cover her mound, and just below it sits the prettiest, pinkest pussy I've ever seen.

A pussy I am *dying* to taste.

I drop to my knees like a man possessed, loving how she sets her legs even wider to accommodate my shoulders.

I love even more the sounds that leave her when I press a kiss to the inside of her thigh, then the other.

I love how she wriggles and shakes when I kiss higher . . . higher . . . right at her center.

"Fuck," she moans.

Oh, Olive, I intend to.

There's no way I won't. Not after knowing she tastes this damn sweet.

I slide my tongue over her again, and another loud mewling sound leaves her. It's not forced or phony—it's all real. This is all real. *She's* all real.

And she proves that to me as I take my time tasting her, sliding my tongue over every inch of her sweet, sweet pussy. Licking and sucking and *feasting* on her.

I can't remember the last time I felt so starved like this. So ravenous. So damn needy.

But she does it to me.

I press my hand against my cock, which is straining against my jeans, trying to give myself some sort of relief.

Olive doesn't miss it.

"Take it out," she tells me. "I want to see."

I don't dare deny her.

Instead, I reach into my jeans and pull myself free, sighing when I wrap my fist around my shaft, returning my attention to her.

She moans, and I groan, and that's all we are—a mess of sounds as I pump myself in time with what my tongue is doing to her center.

When I suck her sensitive clit into my mouth, she lets out a loud cry, falling apart just like I wanted.

I give myself a few more pumps, falling right behind her, making a mess all over my jeans and the kitchen, but not caring a bit.

And how could I? Not when she's staring down at me with glassy eyes and a satisfied grin.

Man, I could get used to this.

"What?" She giggles, sliding her hand through my hair.

"Nothing." I shake my head. "You just look beautiful like that."

"Post–best orgasm ever?"

"Best ever, huh?" I rise to my knees, tucking myself back into my jeans despite her pout. "That's quite the compliment."

"That's quite the tongue you have there."

I laugh, standing back up and stepping between her legs, placing a gentle kiss against her lips. "We should probably get cleaned up."

Her shoulders fall, but she nods anyway, pushing at my chest until I move and then hopping off the counter.

She snatches her underwear off the floor and begins to pad out of the kitchen.

"Olive?" I call to her.

She pauses, peeking back over her shoulder at me. "Hmm?"

"I want to fuck you, just so we're clear. But not tonight. That's third-date material."

She smirks. "After arson?"

"After arson."

CHAPTER EIGHTEEN

Olive

Asshat: Look what I found on my chair waiting for me this morning.

    Asshat: [image]

I laugh at the photo that fills my screen.

Jude left for Vancouver two days ago, and truth be told, I miss him.

Which is silly because it's entirely too soon for me to miss him, but I can't help it.

Lucky for me, he's got lots of downtime and has been sending me all the updates from set.

    Me: You're never going to live that down, you know that, right?

    Asshat: Wear Snoopy underwear one time and now nobody leaves you alone about it . . .

    Asshat: They left this on my chair with a note that said, "Don't worry, you'll grow into them." Quite rude, if you ask me. I thought I fully filled out that Snoopy underwear on Good Morning, New York.

    Me: You're twenty-six, Jude! You shouldn't be wearing Snoopy anything.

    Asshat: So? You're twenty-five. Don't think I didn't see the day of the week stitched across your underwear on my kitchen floor the other night.

    Me: HOW DARE YOU

    Me: Snoopy Drawers

    Asshat: Day of the Week Drawers

Me: I'll block you.

Asshat: Nah. I'm starting to think you might like me.

Me: Do not.

Asshat: Really? Because that's not what it sounded like the other night.

Me: Stop it.

Asshat: You're totally glowering at me right now, aren't you?

Asshat: I bet you have that cute little crinkle between your brows.

Asshat: You may even be crossing your arms.

Asshat: But that's okay. You still like me.

Me: How are you so annoying thousands of miles away?

Asshat: It's a gift.

Me: I hope you kept the receipt.

Asshat: Oooh. She's got jokes today. No JT's yet?

Me: I'm in line right now.

Me: It feels weird not being stalked.

Asshat: I still can't believe he won't serve me.

Me: I can. He likes me more.

Asshat: Clearly. But Ric took pity on me and gave me coffee the morning I left.

Me: GASP! I'm telling JT.

Asshat: You wouldn't dare.

Me: Oh, wouldn't I, though?

Asshat: Sunshine . . .

Me: Asshat . . .

Asshat: Just admit you miss me.

Me: Never.

Asshat: *I miss you, Jude.

Asshat: There. I fixed it for you.

Asshat: Gotta run. They need me to utter three whole lines!

Me: I hope you forget them.

Asshat: GASP! Now who's the annoying one?

I smile, rolling my eyes at the absurdity of him.

But that's just Jude. He's so . . . well, *him.*

He's funny and charming—sure, a little brash sometimes, but still somehow nice and thoughtful and so fun to hang out with.

After the other night in his apartment, when he dropped to his knees in the middle of the kitchen, we spent the next two days together, soaking in all the time we could before he left.

He took me Rollerblading because he knew I'd never been before, then to the top of the Empire State Building just because. He cooked me dinner at his apartment again; then he came over to mine, where Daphne trained him to play Barbies better for three full hours before he finally convinced her to give *Scooby-Doo* a try. She fell asleep singing the theme song, making Jude feel awfully proud of himself.

Having him around has been so easy that sometimes I forget he's Jude Rafferty, big movie star who can be whisked away on a private jet at a moment's notice to go film a movie with other huge movie stars.

It's so strange.

Nothing has really changed, yet everything feels so different at the same time.

My phone rattles in my hand, and I glance down at the growing notification number.

Speaking of different . . .

In the days since the park pictures, my social media has blown up to proportions I can barely even fathom. Uma's been calling almost nonstop to book shoots for me, and I've been trying to keep up with the influx of comments and messages and emails requesting brand deals. It's been a lot, and I know it's because of Jude.

There's an obvious part of me that's grateful for it—I'm finally getting past some of the hurdles I've been stuck at over the last year or so. My audience is increasing, and brands are reaching out now more than ever. My engagement is up across the board too. It's everything I wanted.

But there's another part of me—an admittedly bigger one—that feels guilty I'm benefiting from this at all.

I like Jude, but I don't like Jude for what he does. I like him for who he is, and I kind of wish I could keep those worlds separate.

My phone vibrates again, and this time it's a call.

Uma.

"Hello?"

"Great news," she says without a greeting. "I just booked you with Peter Pierre for a major international campaign."

"Peter Pierre? *The* Peter Pierre?"

"Yes! Isn't it fabulous? It's for Blush Jeans, and it's going to be huge."

I frown. "Blush Jeans? But they're . . ."

"The hottest jean company out there right now? I know. This is a great opportunity."

"Sure, but—"

"No *but*s, Olive. This is fantastic! Good Jeans isn't cooperating like we want. This could be the next best thing."

And that's apparently all it is to her—*fabulous, huge, a great opportunity, fantastic, the next best thing.*

But to me, it's something else—it's selling my soul.

Blush Jeans doesn't align with my personal beliefs of sustainability, *nor* do they cater to a true plus-size audience like Good Jeans does. Blush's biggest size is a sixteen, a size I'll barely even fit into. They don't go beyond that, which means they don't actually care about being there for every *body* and every size. That's not the kind of campaign I want to be part of.

"Right, Uma, but their mission isn't *my* mission."

"No, but it could be."

"How?"

"Well, maybe you could bend your mission just a bit. You have to look at the bigger picture here, Olive. Your mission is great—it truly is—but it's also limited. You've been saying for years now how you want to grow your brand and your opportunities. Well, *this* will do that."

She's right. I know she is.

But it doesn't feel right. It doesn't feel like me.

Worse, I know *why* they want me in their campaign when they've never wanted me before.

Jude.

"Can I think about it?"

"Olive . . ."

"Uma . . ." I say in the same exhausted tone.

She's not happy with me, but right now, I don't care. I refuse to be pressured into anything, including this undeniably huge chance.

"Fine," she concedes. "But I need an answer by Friday."

"Fine," I echo.

She sighs. "Just *really* think about it, Olive. Okay?"

"I will."

But even as I say the words, I know they're a lie.

I already know my answer.

Asshat: I come home tomorrow.

Me: So I've heard.

Asshat: Yeah, but I mean it this time.

Me: Right, right.

Asshat: I MEAN IT mean it.

Me: Sure thing.

Asshat: I'm serious.

Me: I'll think I'll believe it when I see it.

Asshat: Get ready to believe it, then.

I shake my head, tucking my phone back under my pillow.

It's almost midnight, and I've been wide awake for the last two hours.

I can't stop thinking about the offer Uma gave me yesterday or my deadline tomorrow.

She needs an answer, and I have one. I just really, really don't want to give it to her. Mostly because I know she's going to be so disappointed, but I just can't do it. I can't say yes. I can't do that to my fans.

My account has blossomed once again, especially after Jude's interview on *Late! At Night with Timmy* went viral and photos of him in Vancouver without me exploded. I've had no fewer than fifty new calls for a comment on our relationship status.

I wanted to laugh at those—even I don't know what our relationship status is.

Is he my friend with a few benefits? My boyfriend? Are we just hanging out? I don't know. We've not talked about it, and I don't really know how to talk about it.

How do you ask a movie star if you're dating?

My phone buzzes again.

Asshat: What are you even doing up still? Missing me?

Me: Nice try.

Me: You know I'm kind of a night owl.

Asshat: Ollie . . .

Me: Fine. Can't sleep.

Asshat: What's going on?

Me: It's nothing.

Not even two seconds after I hit Send, my phone lights up, this time with a call.

Asshat.

"Hello?" I say, pressing the phone to my ear.

"Talk to me, Sunshine."

"Why are you whispering?"

"Because it's late?" He poses it as a question, almost like he's not even sure why he's whispering. "Now, what's going on?"

I sigh. "It's really nothing."

"That's not a *nothing* kind of sigh. Talk to me. Please."

His plea is my undoing, and I find myself launching into the whole sordid tale with Uma.

When I'm done, he's the one who sighs.

"That's . . . well, that's bullshit."

"What?" I laugh. "What do you mean?"

"I mean, it's bullshit that Uma would even come to you with that opportunity. She's your manager. She knows your mission. She should know better than to even entertain this. It goes against what you believe in and stand for. She's in the wrong for this one. Not you."

This time when I sigh, it's a whole different kind.

"Thank you," I tell him. "Thank you for understanding me and for having my back."

"I'll always have your back, Ollie. And your front. Waggles brows."

A laugh bubbles out of me. "Did you just say *'waggles brows'* out loud?"

"Yes. You can't see me, so I wanted you to know what I was doing."

"You're ridiculous, you know that?"

"I know. Just like I know you miss me."

"I do," I say, not even bothering to try denying it this time. "I really miss you."

"How much? Scale of one to ten. Go."

"A solid four."

"A four? *A four?* That's a low blow, Sunshine—literally. Try again."

"Fine. Maybe a six."

"Moving up two points. Nice. But try again."

"A seven."

"Sunshine . . ."

"An eight . . . and a half."

He laughs. "Keep going. You're getting closer."

"A nine. That's my final offer."

"No, no. See, you're supposed to say ten, and I'm supposed to do this."

"Do what?"

"Shh!"

I clamp my mouth shut, holding my breath and listening closely to what's on the other end of the line.

There's a faint chime.

A *familiar* faint chime.

225

And I realize then it's not coming from the phone. It's coming from the apartment.

I spring up.

"Jude?"

"Hmm?"

"Are you . . ."

"Am I what?" I can *hear* the smile in his voice as I climb out of my bed and pad through my room and into the living room.

"Please tell me that's you at the door and not some stalker."

"I thought I was your stalker."

"You are, you creep."

He laughs. "Why are you whispering?"

"Because someone's at my door."

"Open it."

"No. I'm scared."

"Open it, Sunshine." The command comes out deeper, huskier, and it spurs me on.

I move across the room, taking tentative steps, all while listening to Jude's soft breaths in my ear.

"Please don't let me die. Please don't let me die," I repeat.

He chuckles, and I hear it.

I *hear* it.

I wrench open the door, and my already pounding hearts pumps faster.

Jude.

He's leaning against the wall opposite my door, a grin plastered on his face. He's wearing a pair of faded jeans and a plain black T-shirt, looking a lot like he did the first day I met him.

"I told you I'd see you tomorrow." He winks, and I melt into a puddle right in front of him. "Want to know the best part about being up so late?"

"What's that?"

"No cameras around, so I can do this."

Then he crosses the space, captures my face with his hands, and slants his mouth over mine.

And it feels like coming home.

It's perfect and everything I've been missing for the last few days. I fist my hands into his shirt, tugging him closer, and he laughs into our kiss.

"I knew you missed me," he says against my lips.

"Shut up and kiss me."

He does. He kisses me hard, then soft, then hard again. It's such a push and pull, both of us grasping each other, making out in the middle of the hallway for I don't know how long.

Eventually, we part, Jude placing one last kiss on the tip of my nose.

"Hey, Ollie."

I giggle. "Hey."

"Want to invite me in?"

"What are you? A vampire?" I tease.

He narrows his eyes. "Brat."

"Mm-hmm. Sure am, and I'm proud of it." I step back, already missing his touch the second I'm out of his embrace, then cross the threshold into my apartment. I swing my arm wide dramatically. "You can come in, Mr. Definitely Not a Vampire. That's quite the mouthful of a name."

"I'll show you 'mouthful,'" he says, stepping past me, not looking the least bit sorry for his words.

I like this Jude, the feisty part of him he doesn't let show too often.

I shut the door behind him and follow him into the apartment. I watch as he toes off his shoes, sets his bag down, then pads into the kitchen and pours himself a glass of water, almost like he's done it a hundred times before. He seems so comfortable here. So at ease.

I like that.

"Are you hungry?" I settle onto the stool, trying to hide the fact I'm not wearing a bra the best I can. I wasn't expecting Jude to show up at my front door and suddenly feel wildly underdressed as he stares over at me. I'm just glad Annie isn't here. Now, Remi . . . I have no clue if he's here or not. He's been staying here almost every night since Annie asked him to move in, and I know she mentioned something about him playing cards with friends tonight. "We need to go grocery shopping, but I'm sure I can scrounge up something."

"Oh, I'm hungry." He finishes off his water, then rinses the cup and places it in the dishwasher. I smile to myself, loving that he knows where our dishwasher is but not his own. He turns back to me, folding his arms over his chest as he rests his back against the counter on the opposite side of the kitchen. "Just not for food."

"Not for . . . *Oh.*"

My answer is right there in his eyes as they rake over me, dark and full of desire.

It's me.

I clear my throat, casting my eyes to the side, starting to feel hot under his stare. I want what he's offering so damn badly. But I think we need to clear the air about a few things first.

"I saw your interview from the other day."

"My interview? With Timmy?" He grunts when I nod. "I cannot stand that guy. He's so . . ."

"Fake?"

"*So* fake. He tries to be all buddy-buddy with everyone, but it comes off forced and just so . . . I don't know. I hate it."

"It was . . . interesting."

"I'm sorry he asked about you. Dylan warned me it might happen, but I was hoping he was better than that. People like him live for those gotcha moments."

I wave off his words. "It's okay. I promise. I guess I just wasn't expecting it, is all."

He reaches up with both hands, rubbing at the back of his neck. "I know this is a lot to handle. If at any point it gets to be too much, just tell me. I'll . . . I'll . . ."

"Jude?"

"Hmm?"

"It's not too much to handle."

He snaps his attention back to me. "It's not?"

I shake my head. "No. Not at all. It's just . . . Well, I've been getting phone calls and questions."

"About us?"

"Yes. They want to know what we are."

"Oh." He sucks in a breath, then slides his eyes my way. "Do, uh, do you want to be something?"

"I mean, I kind of thought that's what we were already doing here."

"It is," he says quickly, crossing the small kitchen and rounding the counter, stepping between my legs and cupping my face in his hands. "It is. I just wasn't sure if that's what *you* wanted."

"I kissed you in front of the paparazzi, Jude. If that doesn't say I'm in, then I don't know what will."

"True." He presses a soft kiss to my forehead. "I guess what I'm trying to say is, I didn't know how I should talk to the press about you. I didn't know if you wanted me to ignore the questions entirely or answer them or what. I didn't want to announce to the world that my girlfriend was this hot model without her consent."

One word sticks out to me, making my heart hammer in my chest like the wings of a hummingbird.

Thumpthumpthumpthumpthump.

It's silly. So absurd. I'm twenty-five. Am I really going to get butterflies over being called someone's girlfriend?

Yes.

"Girlfriend, huh?"

He grins. "You caught that." Another kiss, this time on my cheek. "Yes, *girlfriend*. If you're okay with it, of course." A kiss on my other cheek. "Because I don't want to do anything unless you're okay with it."

"I'm okay with it," I assure him as he trails soft fingers down my cheek and my neck, ghosting over my heaving chest. He doesn't stop, trailing them all the way down my sides and to my exposed thighs. My shorts have ridden up high, practically hidden away under my sleep shirt.

"Yeah? Good. But now that we've gotten that out of the way . . ." He kisses my cheek, then my jawline, then my neck, only to trail his mouth back up and start again until I'm practically a panting mess under his lips and his hands, which are still tantalizing my thighs. "There's just one other thing we need to discuss."

"What?" The single word comes out breathy as he kisses his way back to my mouth.

He pulls away just enough to peer into my eyes, his green gaze solemn. "These pajamas are ridiculous."

I bark out a laugh, shaking my head as I glance down at my very non-ridiculous and totally normal unicorn pj's, a gift from Annie last Christmas. "Like you have any room to talk, Snoopy."

"You're right. I don't. But that's all in the past. Right now we're focusing on this monstrosity."

"'Monstrosity'?"

"Horrendous," he says, fingering the edges of my shorts, which are riding up so high he's getting dangerously close to the spot where I want him the most. "The worst offense I've ever seen."

"Is that so?"

"Afraid it is. But the good news is, I have a solution."

"What's that?"

He grins wolfishly. "We take them off."

"Here?"

"Tsk, tsk, Sunshine. You have a roommate. She could come home at any moment, and you're sitting here begging me to ravish you in the kitchen."

"Annie's at work; she's on a double. And I'll have you know I have *two* roommates."

"Two?"

I nod. "Remi moved in yesterday. He brought his computer and two duffel bags. That was it."

"That's . . ." He shakes his head. "I don't want to talk about Remi. I want to talk about this." He tugs on the shorts. "Let's get rid of them, yeah?"

"Jude! We cannot have sex in the kitchen!" I hiss at him.

"Why not? You let me eat your pu—"

I slam my hand over his mouth, feeling him grin beneath it. "You're done."

He pulls my hand away. "Actually, I was just getting started."

"Jude . . ."

"Sunshine . . ." he counters, his eyes sparking with mischief.

Then, without warning, he hooks his hands under my ass and tugs me from the stool.

I let out a loud yelp, and he shushes me.

"Stop it. You have roommates," he admonishes as he carries me through the living room.

"You're so annoying."

"Yeah, but you like it."

"I like *you*."

"I know you do, Sunshine." He winks at me, then brings me to my room, closing the door behind him and flicking on my bedroom light.

"Now, which side of the bed is mine?" he asks as he sets me on the mattress, then grabs the hem of his shirt, pulling it over his head, giving me my first full glimpse of his shirtless torso.

God, no wonder he carried me in here like I weigh nothing. Jude is . . . *wow*.

I was wrong before. It's very clear he spends a lot of time in the gym. He's all corded muscles and defined abs, and utterly hot.

"Ollie?"

I shake my head, swallowing as I force my eyes from his half-naked form to find him smirking at me, probably knowing full well that I was enjoying the show entirely too much.

"Are you staying over?"

"Yep," he says, climbing into the bed next to me. "But don't get any funny ideas about trying to feel me up while I'm snoozing, because I absolutely will allow it."

I laugh as I pull the covers up over us.

"Hey, what are you doing?" he asks.

"Uh, going to sleep?"

"With clothes on?" He reaches under the covers, shuffles around, then produces his jeans, tossing them to the floor. "Get naked, Sunshine."

"You want me to sleep naked next to you?"

"Yes. Who else are you going to sleep naked next to?" His brows slash together. "Actually, don't answer that," he says darkly, almost like he can't stand the thought of me being naked with someone else.

"I've never slept naked before," I admit.

"Really? That's the best way to sleep. That way, if someone breaks into your house, you can attack them. Nobody wants to fight a naked person—trust me."

"*Trust you?* I feel like there's a story there."

His cheeks tinge red, and now I *know* there's a story there. "Just get naked," he mutters.

I want to argue but instead heed his direction, tugging my top over my head. I reach under the blanket like he did, pulling off my shorts and letting them fall to the floor beside me.

I clutch the blanket tighter, pulling it to my chin to hide from him. I feel silly for it, but I've searched Google a hundred times over. Jude doesn't date women who look like me.

I'm not ashamed of my body, but I am very aware that it's different from any body he's seen this close before. I roll onto my side, sucking in a deep, calming breath.

His hand lands on my hip and I tense. Jude tugs at me, pulling me closer and fitting himself against me like it's where he belongs.

And that's how we lie for several quiet moments, Jude holding me and me holding my breath.

"Hey, Olive?" he whispers after a few moments.

"Yeah?"

"Are you going to lie still as a statue the entire night?"

I laugh, relaxing for the first time. "No."

"Good." He presses a soft kiss to my naked shoulder. "You're beautiful, by the way. Just in case I haven't said it yet."

I sigh. "Thank you."

"You're welcome. Good night, girlfriend."

"Good night . . . Asshat."

He chuckles, and that's how we fall asleep—him holding me close and me thinking that maybe . . . just maybe . . . this thing could work.

CHAPTER NINETEEN

Jude

"This is for real, then?"

"He talked about her on TV, Jas. TV!" Cait claps her hands excitedly. "It *has* to be real."

"Yeah, but it could have all been for show. Something Dylan cooked up."

"True, but I don't think so. I think it might be the real thing. His eyes when that Timmy douchebag talked about her . . . He's so smitten."

"He's so sitting right here. You both know that, right?"

My siblings shrug, neither of them caring.

I shake my head, lifting my fresh, hot coffee to my lips and taking a sip.

It burns, but it's necessary, especially after the late flight into New York last night.

When I stepped onto the plane, I had every intention of sleeping in my own bed last night, but the longer I sat there, the more I missed Olive. I knew I had to see her, no matter how late it was.

And it was worth it just to see the look in her eyes when she opened the door.

Sleeping naked next to her was just a bonus.

"He's smiling," Cait whispers to Jasper.

"Has anyone ever told him he has a creepy smile?"

"Has anyone else told either of you that you suck?"

They shrug again.

I roll my eyes, picking up my fork and stabbing at my slice of fudge.

We're sitting in Cait's bakery, just like before, waiting for Dylan to show up. She bombarded me with messages this morning, begging to meet with me, Jasper, and Cait. So here we are.

"What did Dylan want again?" my sister asks, taking a sip of her own coffee. She's wearing her apron, fully intending to open the shop again after we leave.

"Yeah, this is starting to feel all very Mafia of us," Jasper chimes in. "Having secret meetings in the bakery with your grumpy publicist."

"She's not grumpy. She just doesn't like you, Jasper."

He grunts. "Whatever. Her loss."

"But is it?" Cait eyes our brother, and he flips her off.

We are so mature.

A loud knock sounds at the door, a figure pressed against it.

"Password!" Jasper yells as Cait gets up to unlock it.

"It's me, you dick," Dylan hollers back, and I laugh.

"Told you," Cait throws over her shoulder as she pushes open the door just enough to let the redhead in. "Dylan."

"Hey, Cait. Thanks for closing for us again."

"Anything for my big movie-star brothers." Cait follows Dylan back to the table, taking her seat once again and clearing her throat. "So, what's the meeting about? Do I need the bleach?"

"Do I need to count the money?" Jasper quips.

"Should I flip the restaurant around just in case we get raided?" Cait adds.

Jasper snaps his fingers. "I knew I should have worn a suit."

Dylan's eyes bounce between them, then finally land on me. "What the hell are they on about?"

I shrug. "That's for *the family* to know."

Cait and Jasper exchange grins, and Dylan shakes her head, tossing her hands in the air like she's already done with us.

I don't blame her.

"Anyway," my trusty right-hand woman says, "I wanted to get your thoughts on Olive."

I groan, tossing my head back. "We've already been through this. It's my life, and I get to choose who I call my girlfriend. End of story."

"Girlfriend?" Dylan's eyes are twice their normal size. "I didn't realize it has progressed that far."

"It's new," I mumble.

"Super new," Jasper adds.

"Like *last night* new." Cait bounces her brows.

I don't bother correcting them, mostly because I know the point is moot. They know I came straight here from her place, but they don't know the details and they don't *need* to know them.

"Oh. I see." Dylan folds her hands over the table. "So, if it's that serious, then you must have invited her to the premiere." She pulls a tablet from her bag and starts poking at the screen. "I'm going to need her dress size and her information so I can coordinate things with the makeup artist and designer."

I don't answer her because I don't *have* an answer for her.

Dylan doesn't miss it.

She lifts a brow my way. "You *did* invite her to your premiere, right? Because it's in a week and a half, Jude. We need to get to work on this."

"I, uh, haven't."

Cait gasps like the drama queen she is, and Jasper laughs, seeming to enjoy watching me squirm under Dylan's ire. Or at least, he's laughing until she turns her burning stare toward him; then suddenly, he's not laughing anymore at all.

Ha! Take that, big brother.

"Jude?" Dylan asks, bringing my attention back to her. "You're not asking her?"

"I didn't say that. I just said that I haven't. *Yet.* I haven't asked her *yet.*"

"But you're going to, right?"

"Of course," I say quickly, though I'm not certain I actually mean the words.

I want to invite Olive. Of course I do. But I'm also absolutely fucking terrified of dumping her into this world any more than I already have. I grew up in this. She didn't. It's one thing to be photographed wandering the streets, but it's a whole different thing actually walking a red carpet together. Especially when I know I'm going to have to leave the day after to start the international tour.

She said she was all in, but would this be pushing it too far?

"Well, you need to get on it. We don't have much time before the event, and if this is where we're going to be debuting your relationship, we need to make sure she looks red-carpet worthy."

She already does.

That's what I want to scream at her, but I don't. Part of me understands where Dylan is coming from. She wants this to be perfect for us, and I do too.

"I'll ask her," I promise. "Tonight."

It's a lie to get her off my back, but she doesn't need to know that. I'll ask Olive, but it won't be tonight. I'll do it on my own timeline.

"Good." Dylan clears her throat. "Now, on to the next item of business . . . Your parents will be at the premiere, of course. Let's make sure that's not the first time they're meeting Olive, okay? We don't need a meltdown from her in front of cameras."

"Easy, Dylan," Jasper says. "She's not going to melt down. Olive will be fine."

"And how do you know?" She glares over at Jasper. "Have you met her?"

"Well, no." He shifts under her gaze.

"I didn't think so." She smiles, but it doesn't reach her eyes. "You'll fix that, too, right?"

I know Dylan's not trying to be mean. Really, she's being nicer than the media is going to be to Olive—I know that. But I feel like I'm being bombarded with all this at once.

Maybe I shouldn't invite her . . . Maybe this *is* too much for someone not involved in the industry. Maybe . . .

I shake my head.

No.

If Olive said she's in, then she's in. I trust her to know what she can and can't handle. She's a model; this can't be that different.

"We'll be ready for the premiere," I promise Dylan.

I just hope I don't have to break my promise.

"Hey, I— Whoa! Jude!"

I slam the door closed behind Olive after I tug her safely inside my apartment.

I press a quick kiss to her stunned face, then grab her hand once more and lead her farther inside.

"What's going on?" she says, trailing after me. "Why are you in such a rush?"

"Because I have to tell you something that might make you freak out, and we only have a few minutes to get through the initial freak-out."

"Tell me what? What freak-out?" Olive wrenches her hand from mine, stopping. "What is even happening right now, Jude?"

I blow out a breath, hands on my hips. "We . . ." I shake my head. "I have a premiere next week, though I'm sure you're aware of it."

A smile pulls at her lips. "I might have heard a thing or two about it. Is that why you're freaking out?"

"Yes? No? I'm not sure."

"That was very helpful and not at all confusing," she deadpans.

I sputter out a laugh, running a hand through my hair. "I know. I'm sorry. Let me start over."

I cross the distance between us, gently grab her face, and kiss her properly, just as I should have done when I opened the door.

Olive melts against me, gripping my shirt and tugging me closer. I let myself get lost for a moment, loving how soft her long brown hair is between my fingers. Savoring how her body feels pressed against mine, even though I just saw her yesterday. It wasn't enough then, and it's not enough now, but it's all we have time for.

I pull away, putting distance between us so I don't haul her to my bedroom and *finally* have my way with her.

We don't have time for that right now.

"Hi," I say softly.

She grins. "Hi back. What's going on?"

"Well, funny story . . ." I wince. "I sort of invited my entire family over here to meet you because I have a premiere next week, and I want you to be my date, and they're going to be there, and I didn't want that to be the first time you met everyone with all the cameras watching." I suck in a breath. "So, yeah, that's what's happening."

Olive's brows slowly inch upward, her tongue poking out and sliding along her lips. "Did you . . . did you just ask me to be your date to a movie premiere?"

"Well, technically, I think I *told* you that you were *going* to be my date."

"Is that so?"

"Yep." I laugh, not able to keep up the ruse. "No. Not at all."

"So do we want to try that again?"

"Yes." I close the distance between us again, because I must be a masochist, and slide my hands into her hair, tipping her head back so I can look into her almost-too-blue eyes. "Olive O'Brien . . . will you be my date to my movie premiere?"

"Yes."

"Really?" I don't know why I'm surprised, but I am. I wouldn't blame her if she didn't want to fully immerse herself into this world, especially not with how I'm acting right now.

"Really." She nods. "I told you before that I was okay with this all, and I mean it. I'm in, Jude. All in."

All in.

Her words give me a peace I didn't know I needed.

"I'm glad. Because, Olive?"

"Yeah?"

"My parents are already here."

◆ ◆ ◆

I have no clue why I was so worried about Olive meeting my family. If this conversation I'm witnessing bears any meaning, then I had nothing to worry about.

"You're telling me you had several chickens named absurd things like Tender, Thigh, and Nugget—and then you had one lone little chicken named Toby?" My dad throws his ever-graying head back with laughter, slapping his knee, shaking the whole couch with the gesture. "That's amazing."

Olive shrugs from her perch on the armchair, then takes a sip of the wine I bought just for her. She doesn't even look a *little* nervous sitting next to the famous Joel Rafferty. It's like she was meant to be part of this family all along, which is strange. I've dated in the past and had a steady girlfriend in college, but even she didn't fit in with my family like this. She was always nervous around my parents and even worse around Jasper. She would get tongue tied anytime he was in the room. When this continued after nine months together, I knew there was no way we could keep things going. She'd never be ready for what life in the limelight entails.

That seems to be my dating life in a nutshell—either women not prepared for this outlandish world I live in or women entirely *too* excited about it, eager for what they can get from it.

Olive, though . . . It's like she doesn't care about my parents' fame at all. Or Jasper's. And especially not mine.

I've never been happier for it.

"You should hear what I named my horses."

"Oh, I have to hear this."

My dad leans forward as Olive launches into her horse names, all of them just as ridiculous as the chickens'. They keep going back and forth, coming up with new names for new horses that will never exist, both laughing harder the longer the list grows.

"She seems really sweet," my mother says, stepping up beside me where I'm resting against the kitchen counter, watching Olive and my father bond.

Truthfully, she's gotten along with everyone so far. My mother wrapped her into a warm hug the moment we waltzed into the living room. Cait was just excited that another woman other than my mother and Dylan—who is hanging out on the balcony, likely negotiating a new deal over the phone at this very moment—was present. And Jasper was . . . well, Jasper. He said hi, then asked for booze.

I turn to my mother, taking in how she looks a little older since the last time I saw her four months ago. Some fresh lines grace her eyes, and new streaks of gray wind through her hair. But it doesn't matter how old Camilla Rafferty gets—she will always be the kind of beautiful people talk about.

"She is," I tell her. "And funny. Smart too. Gorgeous. All the best things wrapped into one."

My mother grins. "You like her."

"I do." There's no point in denying it. It's true. I like Olive. A lot.

"And this . . ." My mother nods toward Olive. "This is real?"

I know what she's asking.

Can we trust her?

She's worried over the same thing Dylan is—that Olive is using my name and fame to grow her own audience.

But just like Dylan, my mother has nothing to worry about. Olive isn't like that.

"It's real."

My mother smiles. "Good. I'm glad. Because she makes your father laugh, which we both know is next to impossible."

My father is a serious man and has been for as long as I can remember. It's not that he never has fun, because he does; he just also holds himself to high standards and is well aware that he has an image and family to protect. He comes off a little abrasive most of the time, but once you get to know him, you find out he's just a big softy.

Like he's being with Olive right now. He's laughing and relaxed. She's fitting right in, and I couldn't be happier.

"Please tell me we get to keep this one." My sister squeezes herself between us. "She has chickens, Jude. Chickens!"

"Since when do you like chickens?" my mother questions my sister. "I recall you running from them the one time we went to that petting zoo in North Carolina."

"That was forever ago. We've made peace since then."

"Yeah, *Mom*. Get with the program," Jasper says, appearing out of nowhere and grabbing my whiskey from my hand, tossing it back. "Gotta jet, little brother."

"Where are you going?"

Jasper looks over my shoulder as he says, "Hot date."

Dylan huffs, pulling our attention as she saunters back into the room. When she notices our eyes on her, she shrugs, then downs the rest of her wine and reaches for the bottle.

Oh, there is definitely something going on there.

"Jas . . ." I step closer to him. "Please tell me you're not banging my publicist."

"I'm not." He grins wolfishly. "Yet."

"Jasper."

He laughs, then claps me on the shoulder. "It's fine. I promise."

But it doesn't seem fine. Dylan's been extra moody lately, and I have a sinking feeling it has everything to do with Jasper.

He gives my sister a hug, then pecks my mother's cheek before interrupting Olive and Dad to tell them bye.

Then he's gone, and they dive right back into their conversation like he never bothered them.

"I do really like her," Cait comments, still watching as my dad tells Olive the story of when their beloved Tiffany vase was broken. I swear he's only telling it because he thinks one of us will confess to breaking it, but I know Cait is holding on to the real details until it'll benefit her to spill the beans of who the culprit is. "And not only because of the chickens."

"I was just telling him the same thing," Mom agrees. "He seems quite smitten with her."

"He's *very* smitten, apparently," Dylan says, strutting up next to us.

She's been watching Olive all night with shrewd eyes, but I'd bet anything she can't find a single thing not to like about her.

I'd wager the same for me. There isn't a thing about Olive I don't like. Her sense of humor, her smarts, her smile, her beauty, the way she's taking all this in stride . . . I like it all.

As if she can tell I'm thinking of her, she looks my way. Her eyes sparkle from the wine, and there's a smile pulling at her lips. A secret smile just for me.

She's gorgeous, and she's all mine.

"Is she ready for next week?" my mother asks, not missing the moment between us.

"She is," I tell her, and I mean it.

Olive's ready, and so am I.

We might be fools for this, diving headfirst into the spotlight, but for the first time in a long time, I'm okay with being a fool. Excited about it, even.

And I have no doubt it has everything to do with the woman sitting next to my father.

I don't know what I've gotten myself into with Olive, but I've never been so thrilled for the unknown in my life.

Two hours speed by in a blur, and after a lot of ushering on my part, everyone finally files out of my apartment, leaving just me and Olive.

"Finally," I say, pushing off the door I've just locked, then stalking the length of the hallway to the smiling woman at the end of it.

Our lips meet in a frenzy, like we haven't kissed in weeks instead of hours.

It's rushed and sloppy but somehow just as good as it always is.

When we finally part, we're both out of breath.

"Sorry," I say on a laugh. "I just . . . Thank you."

"For what?"

"For putting up with them. I'm sure it was a lot."

"You mean, meeting your very famous; very gorgeous; very, very legendary family members on a moment's notice was a lot?"

I grimace. "Did I mention how sorry I was?"

She laughs. "You did, but I'm sure you'll find a way to make it up to me."

"You know, if you wanted me out of my pants, Sunshine," I say, following her to my bedroom, "all you had to do was ask."

"That's all it takes?" She stands in the middle of the room with her hands on her hips. "Take your pants off, Jude."

I drop my hands to my buckle, tugging at the leather, and she laughs, covering my hands with her own.

"Stop, stop. I was teasing."

"So no sex?"

She shakes her head with a smile. "No sex. I was thinking of taking advantage of that giant tub in the bathroom that's clearly never been used."

"Because baths are lame."

"They are not! I'd kill for a tub like that."

"It's all yours. I'll just be sitting here, *not* having sex."

"No pouting. I didn't say no sex ever. Just not tonight."

I check my watch. "So in like four hours and forty-three minutes?"

"That's oddly specific."

"That's how long we have until tomorrow. If not tonight, then . . ." I lift my shoulders.

"We'll see."

"Four hours and forty-two minutes . . ."

"Jude?"

"Hmm?" I look up from my watch just in time to see her pull her shirt over her head, letting it drop to the floor.

My jaw slackens as I take her in, her honey-gold bra so pretty against her soft skin.

"I said no sex, but that doesn't mean we can't do other things."

"'Other things'? Other things like . . . ?"

She shrugs. "Guess we'll have to find out."

I follow her into the bathroom, then into the tub, where we spend an hour getting dirty before we get clean again, and Olive effectively changes my stance on baths.

CHAPTER TWENTY

Olive

"Is it silly I'm nervous?"

"Um, you're about to fly to LA to walk a *red carpet* on the arm of one of the hottest actors ever, then go off and do a photo shoot for Good Jeans. *The* Good Jeans! The same company you've been trying to get in with for years," Annie says. "I'd think you were a robot if you weren't nervous."

Uma was a little bummed I turned down Blush Jeans, but that didn't last long because just two days later, my dream job came up—Good Jeans wanted me, and they wanted me *fast*.

They're shooting their upcoming winter line, and it just happened to line up perfectly with Jude's movie premiere. We'll walk the red carpet, he'll fly off to do some international promo, and I'll stay behind in LA for a few days to shoot with Good Jeans. Jude's insisting on paying for the hotel for a few extra days; it makes me feel a little uncomfortable having him spend so much money on me, but he's claiming it's a gift for booking the big gig I've always wanted. It's sweet, but I don't want him to think I'm only with him for the luxury of it all.

I laugh. "Thanks, Annie."

"I'm just mildly jealous I can't go with you. Are you sure he didn't say anything about plus-ones for the plus-one?"

"What are you talking about? We invited you."

"Yeah, on a work night!" Annie pouts. "Couldn't there just not be an emergency for one night?"

"In New York? I don't think so."

"Boo." Annie tosses herself down on my bed beside the suitcase I've been packing for the last two hours. She looks inside. "Is this it?"

"Hey! I've been working hard on this!"

The sad part is, I'm not lying. I *have* been working hard, yet somehow it still contains only my sexiest underwear and a few pairs of socks.

Turns out packing for a trip to a Hollywood event is a lot harder than I could have thought. I have no idea what I'm supposed to wear.

"You're overthinking it," Annie says. "Just grab some clothes and stuff them in there."

"Grab some clothes?" I ask her incredulously. "I'm a model, Annie! I can't just *grab some clothes*. That's not how it works."

I knew dating Jude would be a big deal, but I didn't think it would be in the headlines almost daily and that my whole life was going to be put under the microscope. When my relationship with Jude really started getting out there, Uma insisted I scrub my accounts of any personal info, and I am so happy I did. A gossip site somehow found an old photo of me, Annie, and Daphne and took off with the image. It felt like such an invasion of privacy, especially to include a little kid. I had to have Jude step in and get it all taken down. Thank God he was able to pull some strings.

Since then, I've been more careful of the things I post, making sure to leave out any mention of location or any information that could be used against me or the people I care about most.

It's strange to think that all I've wanted in my career is notoriety for doing good things for the planet and being a fat badass bitch while doing it, and now that I'm here, I wish I could scale it back about tenfold.

I guess Jude was right about craving normalcy. I could go for some normal right about now.

Funny, considering I'm about to walk the red carpet with my movie-star boyfriend and have my life on full display.

"Did you tell your mom?"

"I did. Then she promptly asked if I was dating that kid who lived in a hotel and was a secret rock star. I had to explain to her that was two different shows, and I was dating the rock star."

Annie laughs. "Your mom is so out of the loop with . . . well, everything."

"She is," I say, grabbing another pair of underwear, bringing me to ten for a three-day trip. "But she's happy with her little farm in the middle of nowhere, and that's all that matters."

I stopped fighting my mom on being so out of touch a long time ago. She's been through enough after losing my father. She's earned her happily ever after, whatever her version looks like.

"Good for her." Annie reaches in, pulling out two additional panties I've just stuffed in my suitcase. "I think ten is a good number."

"But those are so pretty," I whine when she grabs my lacy lilac pair.

"They are. But I bet Jude wants to see you in something other than your underwear."

I smile, thinking about what happened in the tub, where he spent so much time playing between my legs that our fingers turned into prunes. "I'm not so sure about that."

"Oooh. You're so going to have hot Hollywood sex with him, aren't you?"

"I hope so—minus the cameras, of course."

We've been playing this cat and mouse game, getting each other off multiple times yet never actually going all the way. But I think maybe this trip might change that.

Annie tips her head, wrinkling her nose. "Yeah, I guess Hollywood sex does involve a camera. Though I don't think that would be the worst thing."

"Remi?"

"Yeah?" he calls from his favorite spot on the couch. I have no doubt if I walked out there, he'd have his laptop covering his legs and a can of Mountain Dew beside him.

"Your fiancée wants to film you two having sex!"

"Olive!" Annie yells, throwing a confiscated pair of underwear at me.

"I'm game!" Remi hollers back, seemingly unfazed.

I laugh at Annie's dropped jaw, then shrug. "At least he's adventurous."

"He probably didn't realize what you said. He's all hung up in his code like a dork."

"I prefer the term *geek*, and I totally heard what she said! I'll charge the camera!"

"Can you kids talk about your pornos with the windows shut? I didn't realize moving him in here would make you even bigger sex freaks!"

"Sorry, Mrs. Hammish!" all three of us yell in unison.

Annie and I exchange a look, tucking our lips inward to keep from laughing.

"Did she just call us *sex freaks*?" Annie whispers.

"I think so. Funny, considering it's been over a year since I've been laid, and I've seen at least three gentleman callers leaving her apartment in that time."

"Gross." Annie shudders. "Old-people sex."

"I wonder if she's ever recorded her fun times . . ."

"Ew, ew, ew!" Annie shouts, pushing off the bed, tossing her hands in the air. "I'm done. I'm out. You're packing yourself."

"Good. That's exactly what I wanted."

I turn back to the mess in front of me, picking up a dress just to put it back down again. I grab another, and the result is the same.

Nothing I have looks good. Nothing works.

"You know . . ."

I jump at the intrusion, my hand going to my chest. I turn to find Annie still standing in my doorway. "Yes, Mom?"

"I bet the girls down at Cuties & Curves could help. Just a thought." She shrugs, then disappears into the living room.

Her idea isn't bad. It actually gives me an even better one . . .

I grab my phone off my nightstand and make a call.

◆ ◆ ◆

"Olive! Olive! Over here, Olive!"

"Jude!"

"Olive! Look here!"

"Over your shoulder, Jude. Look here."

Camera after camera clicks, over and over again.

I've stood in front of cameras so many times over the last seven years, but none of that prepared me for this.

"You okay?" Jude asks from out the side of his mouth, his hand squeezing my hip tightly but not tightly enough to hurt. It's just enough to let me know he's there and ready to rescue me if he needs to.

"I'm good," I tell him. It's only a little bit of a lie.

I *am* good. For the most part.

Sure, there are about a hundred photographers here, flashing their cameras all at once. Yes, people are shouting my name and Jude's. And okay, there are so many famous and beautiful people that I feel like I'm walking around looking like a trash goblin.

But I'm good. Totally, totally good.

It's overwhelming, sure, but I'll be fine.

He leans over to me, his lips going to my ear. "You're a damn liar, but I'm going to let it slide because you look fucking stunning in that dress. I can't wait to peel it off you later."

My breath whooshes from my lungs, and goose bumps break out over my arms.

"Jude . . ."

"Sunshine . . ."

He smirks, then looks back out at the cameras as if he didn't just make my knees weak.

We got to LA late last night and went straight to the hotel and crawled into the bath. It wasn't as nice as the one in Jude's apartment, but it was good enough for the night.

We slept in and were treated to a huge brunch buffet—then the storm began.

Dylan burst into the room with a team of makeup artists and stylists carrying rack after rack of dresses. I thought she was going to blow a fuse when I told her I'd brought my own dress, but the moment I slipped it on, I could tell she was on board.

"Just two more spots," Dylan says from my other side. "You're doing great, Olive. Remember, keep your answers short and sweet."

I send her a smile, then move with Jude at my back to the next black X on the carpet, where a reporter is hanging out with a giant microphone.

I take a deep breath, then plaster a smile onto my face.

"Oh my gosh, Jude Rafferty!" the reporter coos. "It's so lovely to see you!"

"You too, Erin," he says, leaning in to press a kiss to her cheek.

"And *the* Olive O'Brien. Wow! You look stunning. Who are you wearing?"

I glance down at my floor-length dress, with cream tulle at the bottom and a satin heart-shaped top with a matching bow tied tight around my waist.

"Thank you. This is a custom piece by designer Mac Mann at Cuties & Curves in New York. It's made from upcycled dresses."

"Beautiful *and* environmentally friendly. We love it. So, Olive, are you excited to see Jude's new film, *Love and Arson*?"

"I can't wait. I'm sure he'll be amazing in it."

"Have you always been a fan of his?"

"I . . ." I glance over to Dylan, who shoots daggers at Erin for her question but nods that it's okay to answer. "I haven't, actually."

Erin gasps, and Jude laughs, knowing it already.

"You've never watched a Jude Rafferty film?"

"Only if Jasper was in it."

Another gasp from Erin.

Jude squeezes my hip again. "That's all right. I forgive her." He presses those same lips he just put on the reporter's cheek to mine, but there's more behind it. More pressure. More care. More . . . everything. "She knows which brother is better now."

"Someone say my name?" Jasper pops up behind us, slinging an arm around his brother's neck, looking perfectly at ease among the flashing cameras. "I heard *better brother*, so I figured you were talking about me."

Jude rolls his eyes, his hand never straying from me as his brother takes over the interview, turning it into a one-man show.

I like Jasper just fine. He's a great actor, and the few times I've met him, he's been kind and charismatic. But I am so glad it was Jude on the other side of those messages and not Jasper. He's definitely the better brother for me.

We're ushered away from the reporter, who has long forgotten about us, then to the next. I let Jude answer the questions this time, and he keeps it brief, moving us forward. We pause for one last group of photos before moving into the theater.

The second the doors close, the deafening sound of clicking cameras is gone, replaced by a soft, melodic song playing over the speakers.

This room is filled with people, but it's a lot less chaotic than it was out there.

Jude shifts his grip to my hand, pulling me deeper into the grand lobby, not bothering to stop even when people call his name. He just keeps pulling me and pulling me and pulling me until we're stuffed inside a small alcove, blocked out from the rest of the world.

"Hi," he says quietly when we're alone.

He has me pressed against the wall, one arm up, boxing me in, that scent of pine wrapping around every inch of me.

"Hey," I breathe back, grinning up at him.

"You all right?" He runs the back of his fingers over my cheek, careful not to press too hard and mess up the makeup the hired crew spent so much time on. "That was kind of a lot."

"I'm good."

"Yeah? Even with Erin's impromptu interview?"

"Even with that. Though I am glad Jasper jumped in at the last minute."

"He's useful sometimes. Just don't tell him I told you that."

I giggle, then press to my tiptoes—because even in heels, Jude still towers over me—and lay my lips against his cheek. "Your secret is safe with me."

"All my secrets?"

"Every last one."

"Well, in that case . . ." He leans forward, running his nose along my neck. "I might still have my old teddy bear I used to sleep with. His name is Mr. Proctor, and he's a very, very distinguished gentleman."

"Mr. Proctor, huh? That's strange. I had a teacher named that."

"You don't say?" He kisses my jaw, then my cheek, making a line right for my mouth. He kisses the corner of it, then retreats like a tease. "Guess it was just fate for us to meet, now wasn't it, Sunshine?"

"Or you're just a creepy stalker."

"No, no. We established this. *You're* stalking *me*, remember?"

I huff out a laugh. "You wish."

"Oh, but I do, Ollie. I do wish." Another kiss at the corner.

If I turned my head just a little . . .

He continues his teasing, kissing my cheeks and my neck and my forehead and my nose and everything other than my lips until I'm a panting mess, *needing* his mouth on mine. I don't care if I spent nearly an hour getting my makeup done and this messes it up. It's worth it all and more.

"Jude . . ." I whine, and he laughs.

"Yes, Sunshine?"

"Kiss me already."

"I want to. I want to so damn bad, but I can't. Because if I do, then I won't stop, and I *have* to stop. I kind of have a premiere . . ."

"People miss their own premieres all the time."

I'm teasing. Totally joking.

But that doesn't stop Jude from pulling away and saying, "You know what? You're right. Let's get out of here."

He grabs my hand, pulling me away from the wall, but I stop him.

"I was kidding! You can't miss this. You've worked too hard on it."

"I can, and I will. Besides, I'm going to be on the road for the next two weeks promoting the film and doing premieres. I can miss one. I want to spend this last night with you and *only* you." He tugs at me again, but I put all my weight back, trying to stop him.

He still drags me forward a few steps.

"Dylan will kill you."

"That's okay. It's a risk I'm willing to take."

"Jude, come on."

"No, *you* come on. Let's live a little, huh?"

"We are. We're at your movie premiere. That's totally living."

"Let's live where there are corn dogs."

"Corn dogs?"

"Yeah, let's go get some corn dogs." Another tug. "Come on."

"Jude!" I stomp my foot. "I did *not* fly all the way to LA for corn dogs and for you to miss your premiere."

He stops pulling, his shoulders slumping. "Fine. Fine. We'll go in."

"Really?"

"No." He gives my hand another yank, and with me so distracted, it works, and then he's pulling me down the hall.

And as much as I want to fight him, I don't.

I just laugh, letting him pull me from the theater, ignoring the shouts from Dylan behind us as we make our escape.

It's the best premiere I've never attended.

◆ ◆ ◆

"You know you're going to have to answer her eventually, right?" I say to my boyfriend as the elevator takes us up, his phone buzzing away in his pocket.

Dylan's called no fewer than twenty times since we ditched the premiere, and I bet she'll call at least another ten before the night is over.

She's upset that Jude bailed, and I can't entirely blame her. This is his career. He *should* be at the premiere. It's what is right. This could change everything for him, and not in a good way. Studios will be pissed, so angry they'd avoid casting him. Nobody will trust him to follow through. This isn't what he should be doing.

But I also understand *not* wanting to be there too. I don't think most people understand just how grueling it can be to have people in your face all day long and having to be *on* like that.

Hopefully, Dylan—and the studios—can understand that.

"I know," Jude says, and there's just the slightest bit of worry in his voice, like he knows this could be bad for him too.

"You could at least text her. Let her know you're alive."

"Well, I'm guessing those photographers who caught us did that just fine."

Just as he promised, we found our way to Santa Monica Pier. We looked silly climbing into the back of an Uber wearing formal clothes, but the driver didn't even bat an eye—just asked us where to, and off we went.

We walked the pier for two hours, weaving through the rides and games and eating our weight in corn dogs.

It's nearing midnight now, and we're finally headed up to our hotel room, my head resting on Jude's shoulder as the elevator takes us higher and higher.

He presses a kiss to my head as we come to a stop on our floor, and the doors slide open.

A weight settles around us the second we step into the hallway.

There's no mistaking what's about to happen.

Jude knows it, and so do I.

We've spent all night giving each other small touches. His hand on my lower back, mine brushing over his arm. Him kissing my neck as we rode the Ferris wheel. Me running my nails along his thigh.

It's been back and forth all evening, and now, as we walk closer to our room, the reality of what's about to happen settles over us.

We always did say after arson, didn't we?

Jude retrieves the room key from his back pocket, but before he slides it into the door, he looks over at me.

"I just want to be clear that if the night ends here and all we do is walk into that room and go to sleep, I'm okay with that, Olive."

Olive.

It's his sign he's being serious.

And while I absolutely love that he's being serious about this, there's no need.

"I want this, Jude."

"You do?"

I nod. "I do. So badly."

"Oh, thank fuck."

Then his mouth is on mine, the key in his hand long forgotten as he pushes me against the wall, taking everything he can in that moment.

His lips are hard and soft and so damn perfect as he nips and sucks on me, pressing his knee between my legs. I sigh when I fall onto his strong thigh, loving the contact that I've been craving since the last time he touched me.

I don't think I'll ever get enough of this. Of him. It's too good. Too perfect.

"You taste so good," he mutters against my mouth. "I can't wait to taste more of you again."

"Then open the door, Jude. Open the door, and you can taste me all you want."

"You mean you don't want to have sex in the hallway?"

I laugh, pushing lightly at his chest.

"Maybe. But not tonight. Tonight, I want it to just be me and you."

"Me and you," he repeats. *"Us."*

"Us."

He nods; then, with shaky hands, he inserts the key.

The door swings open slowly, and we step inside.

The lights we left on earlier cast a soft glow around the room, creating an ethereal feel. I suppose that's fitting since none of this seems real.

I'm standing in a hotel room with Jude Rafferty, about to have sex with him, and I never, ever thought this would happen.

Jude grabs my hand, tugging me gently against his chest.

To steady myself, I grip the lapels of his suit, the same one that somehow makes him even sexier than he already is.

"Trying to undress me already? You move fast, Sunshine."

I laugh, pulling my hand away. But I don't get far.

Jude's hand closes around mine, bringing it right back to where it was on his chest.

I peer up into his gorgeous pools of dark green, loving when one side of his mouth kicks up into a smirk that is so lethal it should be illegal.

"I didn't say I didn't like it," he says softly.

And then his mouth is on mine once more.

This kiss is softer than the last. It's slow and calculated and just as good.

Kissing Jude feels like coming home, and I've never craved the feeling more.

His lips trail from my mouth to my chin and back to my lips, all in the span of seconds. It's like he's trying to commit every inch of me to his memory.

I'm more than willing to allow him to try.

I push at the material still bunched in my hands, and Jude doesn't waste a second, knowing exactly what I want—him.

He wrenches his lips from mine, and I have to swallow back the cry that's begging to leave me at the loss of his touch. Then he begins shrugging out of his suit jacket, and I suddenly don't care about him not kissing me anymore. Not when he's stripping out of the black material like he's . . . well, a movie star stripping in a movie.

I laugh at the thought, and Jude doesn't miss it.

"Are you laughing at me getting naked, Ollie?"

"No." A giggle escapes again. "Maybe."

He tips his head, his fingers falling to the cuff links on his wrists.

"It's just . . . well, I was kind of thinking about how you looked taking that off." I nod toward where he's pulling one arm from the jacket, then the other. He begins slipping button after button through the holes, taking his time undoing his dress shirt like I'm not standing here, salivating over his every move. "It reminded me of all those let's-rip-each-other's-clothes-off-but-look-extra-hot-doing-it scenes in movies. Then I remembered who you are."

He pauses mid-undress, his eyes searching mine with an intensity that has my heart racing.

"And who am I, Olive?" he asks quietly.

"You're . . . Jude. You're just Jude."

One.

Two.

Three.

That's how many seconds pass before Jude moves.

Then suddenly, he's right there, pressing his lips against mine in a rough kiss. Not the kind that hurts physically but the kind that bruises the deepest part of you, marking you for all eternity.

Jude doesn't just kiss my lips. He kisses my soul.

And I'd be a damn liar if I said it doesn't make me want to bare it all to him.

I kiss him back with equal fervor, and gone is the slowness of the evening. Gone are the little jokes and the teasing. It's pure lust and lost inhibitions. Nothing else.

Jude's hands coast over my body, digging into the material of my dress, tugging at it like he wants it off.

"Where the fuck is the zipper?" he mutters against my mouth. "I need you naked."

I laugh. "It's under a slip of fabric, to cover the zip track."

"Fashion is weird," he says, his fingers finding the spot I'm talking about and deftly tugging the metal down its track. The dress loosens against my body, already falling to expose my strapless-bra-covered breasts.

But to Jude, it doesn't matter that I'm still covered. He's looking at me hungrily anyway.

"Off," he instructs, not once taking his eyes from me.

I do as he says, slipping the dress the rest of the way down my hips, letting it fall to the floor where I stand. I go to reach behind me to remove my bra, but Jude puts his hand out.

"Hang on. I want to commit this memory for a moment."

Heat steals up my cheeks, not just from his words but from how he's looking at me standing before him in nothing but a pair of heels, the white bra, and a matching white thong.

I should feel silly being exposed like this, but I can't find it in me. Not when his stare makes me feel like I'm the most beautiful woman he's ever laid his eyes on as he moves his gaze from head to toe, taking in every detail of my body—dips, curves, and even the faint stretch marks I have on my stomach and thighs.

I've been in expensive gowns before. I've had my makeup done by some of the best out there. Had my hair styled to perfection. I've modeled and posed and done so many things that have made me feel sexy and empowered.

But all of them pale in comparison to this moment.

"More," Jude mutters, the single word coming out low and dry. He clears his throat, then raises his eyes to mine. *"More."*

I reach behind me for the hooks on the bra, then unsnap it, letting it fall away from my body.

Jude's eyes darken when my hands fall to my hips, then even more when I push the thin, barely there material down my legs. I step out of the underwear and bend to undo the strap on my heel.

"Leave them."

I peek up at Jude.

"The heels," he says. "Leave them on."

It's the last thing he says before he crosses the small space between us, sweeping me into his arms as he presses his mouth against mine once more, carrying us both over to the bed. He drops me down gently, giving me a soft shove until I fall onto my back.

He steps between my legs, fitting himself there perfectly as he traces a single finger over my naked breasts, brushing the pad of it over my already puckered nipple. He drags that same finger lower, down my stomach, running it against the marks marring my skin. He doesn't stop there. He keeps going, going, going until he's right where I want him.

"Oh god," I cry out when he slides over my already soaked slit.

"Jesus, Olive, you're so fucking wet for me." He slips his finger between my folds, grazing against my clit and sending zings of pleasure through me. "Your pussy is dripping. I can fucking see it."

He runs his tongue over his bottom lip like he just can't help it.

"I want to taste it again," he whispers, then slowly pulls his eyes away from where his finger is playing a perfect rhythm against my clit. "Can I taste you, Olive?"

God, yes, please!

But I don't say that. I can't. Mostly because even sucking air into my lungs feels like work right now.

Instead, I nod, and Jude's eyes light up.

Then he sinks down, down, down, not stopping until he's on his knees.

He picks up my right leg and presses soft kisses from my knee to *just* close enough to where I really want his mouth, then pulls back and sets my legs on his shoulder. He gives my left leg the same treatment, teasing me and enjoying it far too much when I buck my hips toward him.

He laughs, meeting my eyes. "Someone's eager."

"Someone's being an asshat."

He shakes with laughter again. "Testy, testy, testy."

"Asshat, asshat, assh—*ooooh!*"

Jude skims his tongue over me, silencing my insults once and for all.

"Still an asshat?" he questions, and I shake my head eagerly. "Good. Now, be a good girl and put those heels to good use. I just got hungry for dessert."

Then he wears my thighs like earmuffs, his tongue lashing against me in a delicious cadence as I push my heels into his back as instructed.

He licks and sucks and fucks me with his mouth, bringing me to the edge and back time after time. It's torturous yet so, so good.

When he hits a spot that sends a sudden jolt through me, I crash my hands into his dark-blond hair, holding him steady right where I want him as my orgasm barrels through me like a Mack Truck.

I sigh long and loud. "Holy . . . *fuck.*"

Jude laughs against me, sending the tiniest of aftershocks through my body, which makes him laugh even more as he kisses each thigh. He doesn't stop kissing me, either, as he works his way up my body. He kisses my soft belly, paying extra attention to the marks stretched along it. He kisses my tits, sucking each nipple into his mouth, lavishing me with lashes and nibbles that sting just enough. He kisses my collarbone, my throat, and my chin. He kisses all the way up until his lips are pressed against mine and I'm dying for something more.

For him.

And he must be feeling the same, because he's wrenching his mouth from mine and pushing from the bed. He yanks off his shirt, then reaches into his back pocket, pulling an expensive-looking leather wallet free. I barely catch sight of a familiar foil packet before his lips are back on mine. He slips his tongue into my mouth as he slips the condom over his cock, then presses his hips against me, running his hard length against my clit in teasing thrusts.

"I have a confession to make, Sunshine."

"Please tell me you're not a virgin. I mean, I'm honored, and I'll gladly accept this challenge, but wow. Way to wait until the last minute to tell me."

He laughs against me, kissing from my chin to my ear. "No. But it has been . . . a while."

"So? It's been a while for me too."

"So . . . I'm not sure I'm going to last long."

"Me either and I don't care. I just need to feel you inside me."

He groans against me, the vibration tickling me in all the right places.

"Jude, I—"

He grabs my leg, wrapping it around his hip, then slides his cock inside me with a hard thrust, turning my words into a loud sigh.

It's only now that I realize he never finished taking off his pants, and I'm not sure why, but it makes the whole thing hotter. Like he couldn't wait another second to have me.

"Fuck, Sunshine," he groans, burying his face into my neck. "You feel so goddamn good around me. Heaven. Pure fucking heaven."

He's wrong. This isn't pure fucking heaven. It's hell because I *need* him to move.

I dig my heels into his lower back. "More," I command, repeating his plea from earlier.

He doesn't hesitate to fulfill my request, beginning to slowly pump into me, letting me get used to his size.

When I dig my heels in a little more, he takes his cue, then finally gives in to everything he's been holding back, going to his knees and pushing into me with just the right amount of roughness he somehow knows I need.

It's the perfect mixture of pleasure and pain as he slams into me, hitting every spot I need except one.

Like he knows I'm just on the brink, he presses his thumb against my clit, and two short circles later, I fall apart around him.

Jude swallows my moans as my orgasm rattles through me, thrusting into me with abandon until he follows me into the bliss.

Now *this* is pure fucking heaven.

His thrusts slow first, then his kisses, and soon we're just lying with our lips resting together as we work to catch our breaths.

At some point, we move—Jude first, slipping down my body, leaving a trail of kisses along the way.

He stops at my feet, then slowly and methodically peels off my heels, tossing them aside. He shucks his pants, then disposes of the condom before crawling back into the bed, pulling the cover up over us both.

He tugs me to his side until my head is resting against his chest, my legs strewn over his as his fingers tangle in my hair and his lips brush against my forehead.

"I don't know how I'm going to leave tomorrow now," he says into the still darkness.

"Don't."

He laughs, pulling away and peering down at me. "Don't tempt me, Sunshine. Because for you, I'd do it."

I know with everything in me he means it.

And for the next eight hours, he shows me just how much.

CHAPTER
TWENTY-ONE

Jude

The last thing I wanted to do after spending the night between Olive's legs was fly out to London to start a two-week international press tour for *Love and Arson*, but here I fucking am.

"Are you going to glare at me this entire flight?" I ask, looking over at my travel companion for the next few weeks.

We're sitting in first class on a long, boring flight overseas, and Dylan has been burning holes into the side of my head for thirty of the forty-five minutes we've been in the air.

"Are you going to run off on me again and ditch me during *your* movie premiere?" she counters.

I want to tell her no, that I promise I won't, but I can't be certain. Standing in front of all those cameras was painful, and I had to get out of there. Sure, a lot of that leaving had to do with Olive, but I could have still bailed even if she weren't there.

Dylan sighs. "You know you're going to be bombarded with questions about Olive now, don't you? It was very obvious you two slipped off together, and pictures of you fleeing the venue are already going viral."

"All press is good press, right?"

"That's what the studio is saying, but they're still angry. You're going to have to do something major to get back in their good graces—you know that, right?"

I try to hold back a groan. She's right. No matter how worth it leaving was, I know how badly I messed up by doing so. And I know I'm going to have to pay the price for it eventually. "I'm aware."

Her pinched expression tightens. "You need to be prepared. Now more than ever, they are going to be hounding you about her. They'll want details. Like why you were on that sidewalk with her. If you knew her before then. And why she isn't on this trip with you." Dylan scoffs. "I'm curious about that one too."

"She's shooting with Good Jeans, then has another job lined up when she gets back to New York. She works. That's why she's not there." I sigh, scrubbing a hand through my hair, ignoring Dylan when she fusses over me messing it up. "Why don't you like her again?"

"I don't *not* like her. I just don't really know her yet. And when it comes to you and people I don't know, I don't trust them."

"But *I* trust her. That should be all that matters."

"Yes, you also trusted Sophie in high school. And your costar Elizabeth. Or Ruby or—"

"Okay, I get it," I say, interrupting her never-ending list of all the women who have wronged me over the years. They weren't all bad in the same way, but they all wanted the same thing—my name. Who my family is or what I could offer them to help elevate their careers was all that mattered. Not me. Never *me*. "It's not like that with Olive."

"I'm sure it's not. But I do find it awfully convenient she's unable to make this trip because of a photo shoot with Mitch Dirkson. He's one of the most sought-after photographers working now. You're telling me that before her account blew up like it did, she was collaborating with him?"

"Yes."

Dylan's brows raise. "No kidding." She pulls her lips down, impressed. "Well, color me surprised. I wouldn't think she'd have the numbers to be on one of his shoots."

I've trusted Dylan with a lot over the years, and I know deep down that her attitude toward Olive is all to protect me, but I can't help but be annoyed by her flippant attitude. Olive isn't suddenly getting jobs because she's dating me. She's getting jobs because she deserves them.

"She turned down Blush Jeans."

"She did not."

I tip up my chin, feeling proud of my girl. "She did."

"Why on earth would she do that? That company is *everywhere*. It's owned by Diamond Sands, the billionaire heiress to the whole Sands dynasty. That's a *huge* opportunity."

I shrug. "She said the company didn't align with her mission."

"Her mission?" Dylan questions, more to herself than to me. "Huh. That's . . ."

"Impressive?"

"Honestly, yes." Dylan shakes her head. "But—"

"Don't let my guard down? Watch for signs? Make sure I resign myself to a life of worry, and never let anyone in because I'm scared I'll get used?"

She frowns. "I've never said that, Jude."

"No, but you've implied it enough."

"I'm sorry. I just . . . I worry about you."

"And while I appreciate it, I know when my gut is telling me something good. And Olive? She's good, Dylan. The really, *really* good kind of good."

Dylan smirks. "So she's good?"

I narrow my eyes at her. "I will fire you."

"As if." She clears her throat. "Okay, let's go over some stuff."

I repress another groan as she drags out her tablet and begins to inundate me with questions and schedules and everything else I'm sure is super important but that I have no interest in right now.

Not when all I can still think about is a naked Olive.

The same naked Olive I left in that hotel bed this morning, with the early sun poking through the curtains, casting a soft glow over her skin.

The same naked Olive I am dying to get back to.

I have no idea how I'm going to survive these next two weeks.

When Dylan finally gives me a reprieve from her endless lists, she heads off to the front of the plane to talk someone else's ear off—the poor flight attendant—and I pull my phone out.

I grin when I see the message waiting for me.

Sunshine: This is me admitting that I miss you.

Me: Say it again.

Almost immediately, dots begin to dance across the screen, and my smile grows wider.

Sunshine: Nope. That's all you get.

Me: Not even if I promise to do that thing you like again?

Sunshine: What thing?

Me: All of it.

Sunshine: It was really nice.

Me: Nice?

Me: NICE?!

Me: I think we can come up with a better adjective than that.

Sunshine: You're right. We can.

Sunshine: It was . . .

Sunshine: Fine.

Sunshine: Okay.

Sunshine: Decent.

Sunshine: Adequate.

Sunshine: Sufficient.

Sunshine: Amazing.

Sunshine: Fantastic.

Sunshine: Incredible.

Sunshine: Mind-blowing.

Sunshine: Toe-tingling.

Sunshine: Toe-curling.

Sunshine: Toe . . . Well, I'm out of toes.

Sunshine: WAIT! I thought of another one.

Sunshine: TOEtally awesome. (See what I did there?)

Sunshine: Unforgettable (the good kind).

Sunshine: The-hands-down-best-I've-ever-had NICE.

Sunshine: Do any of those work better for you?

Me: There are a few I'm rather fond of.

Me: And since I'm not a ninny, I'll admit that I miss you. LOUD AND PROUD.

Sunshine: Did you just call me a ninny?

Me: Sure did. Ninny.

Sunshine: Oh, just you wait until you get home.

Me: What are you going to do?

Sunshine: Probably kick you.

Me: I think your phone autocorrected that last text. Surely you meant KISS instead of KICK.

Sunshine: Did it, though?

Me: You're so mean to me.

Sunshine: You like it.

Me: I do. Though I'm not entirely sure what that says about me.

Sunshine: That you really, really like me.

Me: You're right.

Me: I do really, really like you.

Sunshine: I knew it.

"Is that her?"

I glance up to find that Dylan's settling back into her seat. "Yep."

"You smile a lot when it comes to her."

"Do I not smile otherwise?"

"You do. But this is just . . . different. Better."

It's the nicest thing Dylan's said about Olive yet, and I'm not about to ruin it by asking follow-up questions or saying something stupid.

So I say nothing at all, turning my attention back to my phone as it vibrates in my hand.

Sunshine: I really, really like you too.

Me: I knew it.

Sunshine: How are you so annoying, so many miles away?

Me: It's a gift.

Sunshine: Hope you kept the receipt.

Me: See? Mean.

Sunshine: See? You like it.

Sunshine: I have to run. Photo shoot time!

Sunshine: Video call later?

Me: Naked and everything.

Sunshine: Tease!

Me: Shhh. Go model, or I'm going to start thinking you miss me or something.

Sunshine: Never.

Me: *Always

◆ ◆ ◆

"You're not naked."

"I never promised I'd be naked. That was all you." Olive smirks into the camera.

From what I can see of the background, she's on the balcony of the room we shared just last night. The sun is shining brightly, casting a soft-orange glow around her like a halo. She's gorgeous, even from thousands of miles away.

"Well, if you'd like to participate, too, I'll gladly wait for you to undress."

"Keep dreaming, Jude."

"Oh, I will—because a naked you is a really, really good dream."

Her cheeks redden, and I love every second of it.

"So." She clears her throat. "How was the flight with Dylan?"

"Long and slightly painful."

"Painful? Why?"

"Have you met her? She gives a mean tongue-lashing when she's angry."

Olive winces. "I take it she wasn't happy about you abandoning her?"

"Oh, her feelings weren't important. It was all about the press."

"Do you ever get tired of that? Of it all being about the press?"

"Of course." It's true. I do get tired of it. "But I can't imagine myself doing anything other than acting. When I took those years off for college, I needed the break, but I always knew I'd come back to this." I shrug. "It's hard, but I deal with it because I love acting."

"Not every actor lives in the spotlight."

"True. But not every actor is the product of two legacy families joining together as one."

"Ah. How could I forget I was talking to *the* Jude Rafferty?" She sticks her tongue out. "My bad."

I laugh, adjusting myself on the hotel bed. Dylan made sure a car was waiting for us when we landed, and the second I got my room key, I booked it upstairs to call Olive. I didn't even bother telling Dylan good night, something I'm sure I'll hear about later.

Can I really be blamed? Especially when Olive is grinning at me like she is?

"So how was your first day on set?" I ask her.

"Amazing and wonderful and long and exhausting."

"Do you ever get tired of that?" I toss her question back at her. "Of fake-smiling for the camera?"

"Of course." She winks. "But like you, I couldn't see myself doing anything else. I love it too much."

"What are you going to do after?"

She tips her head to the side. "After?"

"Yeah. After, you know, the modeling career, uh . . . um . . ."

She bursts out with a laugh. "You mean, after I'm too old to be considered hot anymore—so in like five years, max?"

I scratch at the overgrown stubble lining my chin. "I mean, I was going to word that a little more eloquently, but yes, that."

"I'd like to continue my work to fight for more inclusive and sustainable clothing, maybe even start my own company making just that."

"A clothing company?"

She nods, tucking her hair behind her ear, which somehow makes her look ten times cuter than she already does. She's scrubbed off all her makeup from the shoot, and her hair is up in a messy bun with two strands hanging down to frame her face. She looks relaxed and refreshed as she picks up a glass of wine, taking a sip. "Yes, a clothing company. I think it could be fun. It's a huge pipe dream, though, so . . ."

"Don't do that."

"Do what?"

"Minimize your dreams. You deserve for them to come true, Olive."

Her lips part on a soft gasp. "Is that right?"

"It's very right. You deserve more than anything for them to come true."

A smile transforms her face. "I wish I could kiss you right now."

Fuck. Me too, Olive. Me too.

"I miss you."

Three words.

Three simple words and suddenly, my heart is hammering inside my chest.

They shouldn't affect me. Not really. But they do. They make me want to get right back on a plane and fly across the country to her, just to press my lips to hers.

They make me want things I haven't allowed myself to want in a long, long time. Like a commitment . . . a relationship . . . something real and honest and something so damn good it hurts.

But I don't tell her any of that.

I clear my throat.

"Don't tease." I wink at the camera, trying to play off how much her words have affected me. "Especially not when it's so late."

"Oh god." She sits up, the phone shaking as she jostles around. "I totally forgot about the time difference. You must be exhausted."

"Nah." I totally am. Overseas travel always takes it out of me, especially the first night. "I'm fine."

She narrows her blue eyes. "Liar."

I laugh, loving how she can read me so easily, so soon. "Maybe just a little."

"Go to sleep, Jude. You have a big day tomorrow."

"So do you, Miss Good Jeans Model."

Olive smiles so brightly I swear I can see it from across the sea that separates us. "I am a Good Jeans model, huh?"

"You are, and I'm so proud of you for it."

"Stooooop." She drags out the word, covering her face with her free hand. "You're making me blush."

"You're cute when you blush."

"That doesn't help, Jude," she says from behind her hand. She lets it drop, still beaming with happiness. "You're only being nice because I gave you great sex."

I shrug. "It was nice."

She glares at me, and I laugh.

"Fair is fair," I tell her.

"I take back all the nice things I ever said about you."

"You do not."

"I do too." She lifts her chin in defiance, but it's pointless. A smile is already trying to push through her tough exterior.

"What if I told you how nice it really was?"

She rolls her eyes, but I don't let that stop me.

"Because it was, Olive. It was nice. But it was also amazing and spectacular and stupendous and wonderful and holy-hell-I'm-going-to-have-to-take-*many*-long-cold-showers-while-I'm-gone kind of fan-fucking-tastic.

Especially because all I can think about is how good your pussy tastes and how much I can't wait to sink back inside of you."

"Jude," she chides, but there's no real bite behind her words. Not with how she's squirming in her chair, looking around to make sure no one else can hear. How her eyes are now wide and shining bright with the same thing I'm feeling—lust.

"I miss you."

A slow, soft grin curls at her lips. "I miss you too."

"Good night, Olive."

"Good night, Jude."

I turn off my phone, then do just what I said—take a cold shower, all the while thinking of Olive and how I can't wait to see her again.

◆ ◆ ◆

I've been standing on this red carpet for all of twenty seconds, and my head is already throbbing from the flashing lights.

"Jude! Jude! Over here!"

"Are you alone, Jude?"

"Jude, look here!"

"Just one shot, Jude! Just one shot!"

"Where's Olive, Jude?"

It's the exact same as it was in LA: bright flashing lights, people shouting my name incessantly, and being asked the same questions every stop along the way. Every red-carpet event is the same. It might be a new country and new carpet each time, but nothing ever changes.

I am officially over this and wish I were back in New York.

No. That's not true.

I wish I were with Olive.

Our video chat last night wasn't nearly enough. I want more. I *need* more.

But as much as I wish she were here, there is a small part of me that's glad she's not. No reason for her to have to endure this along with me.

"Keep smiling," Dylan says, pressing me on to the next stop along the arduous walk through the sea of photographers before nodding toward a tall woman with long wavy hair and a microphone. "This is Alexa. She works for *B! News* at their London branch."

B! News, otherwise known as one of the worst "gotcha" media outlets to exist.

"Is there anything I need to know before I walk up?" I ask Dylan out the side of my mouth.

"Nope. You're good. They don't have a thing on you. Though I am sure they'll ask about Olive, so be prepared for that. Best to keep your answers simple with that one."

I nod, completely agreeing, especially seeing the smirk Alexa is wearing as I approach.

This should be fun.

"Jude! It's so lovely to have you here!" She shoves her microphone into my face, waiting on a response.

"Hi, Alexa. It's lovely to be here." I paste on the most charming smile I can muster. "How are you? Having fun?"

"I am, now that you're here," she answers with a flirty grin that makes me uncomfortable, especially when she rakes her gaze down my body.

I laugh politely, trying to catch Dylan's eyes, but she's not paying attention. She's locked in a conversation with someone else.

Awesome. Guess I'm on my own for this torture.

"Have you been doing any other traveling here in London?" she asks conversationally, but I know better than to let my guard down, especially when it comes to her.

"I haven't, actually. All work and no play." Another forced laugh. "But that's life, right?"

"Totally understand. So, tell me, Jude, what are you most excited for with this film? It's incredible! So much action and fun. Audiences are loving it so far. It's your big comeback, right? You've been out of the game for some time. Do you think this will be your push that gets you back to where you were all those years ago on *Lakedale*?"

Of course she had to bring that up.

"Well, I sure hope so," I answer honestly. I want this to be the thing that takes me to the next level, helps me move past being just another nepo baby or a forgotten teen heartthrob. I want to be something else. Want to be something more. Hopefully, this movie and all the positive buzz around it can do that.

"So did you not like your time on *Lakedale*, then?"

Son of a . . .

I shoot Alexa a grin that I really hope covers my annoyance. "No, no. Nothing like that. Look, the show was great. It was fun. I learned a lot from the cast and about myself, but it also feels like it was another lifetime ago. I'm ready to focus on this. To focus on *Love and Arson* and whatever else the world throws at me."

Alexa nods a few times, then pulls the microphone back. "Like a new girlfriend, perhaps?"

Just thinking about her has me smiling and wishing, for the tenth time since I stepped onto this red carpet, that she were here.

"Yeah, I guess you could say that."

"Olive O'Brien, right? Where is she tonight? I think we were all expecting her to be your arm candy for such a big event." Her eyes twinkle, and she clearly feels proud of herself for bringing Olive into this. She stares at me with wide eyes, ready for me to make a mistake and slip, to say something she can use against me.

But that's not happening. Not tonight. I am not about to give her more ammo for her vapid magazine.

"She's off being a badass model, making the most out of her own career. She doesn't need to be my arm candy. She shines all on her own."

Alexa's still smiling at me, but that excited spark in her eye fades a bit. She was ready for me to deny it or to play coy. But I'm not going to. Not for her and not for anyone else.

Her grin grows wider. "And what about Keely Haart? You were recently photographed with her, weren't you? Was there something between you two? Maybe a quick little fling? Or is there something still going on?"

Keely?

Truthfully, it's been weeks since I've even thought about her and that stupid fake date. All my attention has been focused on getting through this premiere and getting back to Olive.

I try to catch Dylan's eye again to see if she has any idea how I should navigate this, but she's still looking elsewhere.

Really? This is when she chooses not to be up my ass?

I turn back to Alexa. "That was simply two friends getting dinner together."

Please drop it. Please drop it. Please drop it.

"It looked like a little more than that to me," she presses, and I have to remind myself there are several cameras trained on me right now. Rolling my eyes would be really, really frowned upon.

"Nah. We're just friends." *Friends.* The word leaves a bad taste in my mouth because I am *not* friends with Keely, and I never plan to be.

"I guess that means you're okay that she and your brother were spotted out together in LA last night?"

Jasper is seeing Keely? Why doesn't that surprise me?

"Totally good with it," I lie to her. I'm not good with it, but not because of our stupid forced date. I'm not good with it because Jasper can do so much better.

Alexa grins. "How amazing would it be to bring together *another* Hollywood family?"

"No idea. I don't really think about that much."

"And Olive? How does she feel about your brother dating your ex-girlfriend?"

It's taking everything in me to not walk away from this absolutely fucked so-called "interview."

Instead, I paste on a smile that's big and wide and shows that I am not going to let Alexa from fucking *B! News* get the better of me.

"I'm sure Olive wouldn't care, since Keely and I are just friends," I reiterate.

Alexa grins. "Even if Olive might have a little interest in more than one Rafferty brother?"

I rear my head back. "Excuse me?"

"Jude, come on." Dylan grabs my arm and tries to pull me away, finally stepping in to rescue me.

But right now, I don't want to be rescued.

I want to know what the hell Alexa is talking about.

"What are you implying?"

She smiles coyly. "Nothing."

But that's not a *nothing* kind of smile. She knows something. Or better yet, she's up to something.

I just don't know what.

"So, Jude, tell me more about Olive and Jasper."

She thrusts that stupid fucking microphone in my face again.

I clear my throat, then force a smile. "I'm—"

"No comment," Dylan says before I can answer, stepping in front of me protectively. "We're done here, Alexa."

My publicist glowers at the *B! News* correspondent, who doesn't even flinch. She's still wearing that slimy smile I can't stand as Dylan pulls me away.

"What the fuck was that?" I whisper to her.

But she doesn't answer.

Instead, she marches us past the rest of the photographers, who are still screaming my name, and all the way behind the makeshift screen I'd normally be standing in front of.

Only then does she stop.

She pulls me right in front of her. Her hazel eyes are hard. Serious.

"If I let you go, are you going to run?"

"What?" I laugh. "Why would I run?"

"You . . ." She sighs, shaking her head twice. "Promise me you won't, okay?"

"I . . . What? Let my arm go."

"Not until you promise."

"You've officially gone off the deep end, haven't you?"

"Jude . . ." She squeezes my arm tighter. "Promise me."

"Damn, all right. I promise."

"Good." She releases my arm. "Good."

"Are you happy now?"

"No." She blows out a shaky breath. "Not even close."

I pull my brows together, letting myself really look at her for the first time.

The hardness in Dylan's gaze has turned to worry, and if the way she's biting her bottom lip and eating away at the red lipstick slathered over it is any indication, I should be worried too.

I straighten my shoulders, dipping my chin low as I take a step closer to her. "What's wrong?"

"It's . . ." Another nibble on her lip. "It's Olive."

Panic shoots through me.

"What? What about Olive? What happened? Is she okay?"

Dylan's mouth drops open; then she snaps it shut, casting her eyes anywhere but at me.

Panic rips through me, and I take another step closer, forcing myself into her line of sight. Forcing her to face me. "Is. She. Okay?"

She pulls her eyes to mine and says one word.

"No."

All my senses rocket into overdrive, and even though we're outside and not in some stuffy room, that's exactly what it feels like as the air leaves my lungs.

"I mean yes, yes. Physically, she's okay."

I gulp in a breath, gasping like I've just run a marathon.

"Oh god. You . . . I almost . . . You scared the shit out of me."

I force a laugh, running a hand through my hair in an effort to quell the shakiness.

But Dylan doesn't look relieved.

Why doesn't she look relieved?

"What?" I question, my eyes shooting back and forth between hers. "What is it?"

Wait . . .

"You said *physically*," I say. "Why did you specify *physically*, Dylan?"

"Because she might be okay physically but not emotionally."

"Why not emotionally, *Dylan*?"

Her name comes out sounding like a curse, and it's justified because I'm getting tired of this game. Why is she stringing me along? What could be so bad?

She clears her throat. "Her diary, Jude."

"Her . . . diary?"

"The messages to Jasper. They were leaked."

"They were . . ."

Dylan nods, her lips pulling down. "Leaked, Jude. Someone leaked them. I don't know who, but I swear to you, I'm trying to find out." She groans. "Ugh. I should have made you delete those messages the second you told me about them. I should have . . ." She trails off, muttering to herself about how awful this is.

I nod, swallowing the lump lodged in my throat. How could this happen? Why did this happen? And . . .

"How bad is it, Dylan?"

She tries to force a smile, but it's pointless. It wobbles and fails so damn fast.

"Tell me," I beg.

"They're all over the internet. She's viral. *You're* viral. Jasper too."

And just like that, my entire world goes dark.

I turn on my heel and do the one thing I promised I wouldn't—I run.

CHAPTER TWENTY-TWO

Olive

"You're doing great, Olive. Keep it up," Juliet, the photographer, says from behind her camera. "Now, over your shoulder."

I turn, looking right down the lens as requested, loving the sound of the camera snapping away.

It's still completely wild to me that I'm working with Good Jeans, and even more wild that I'm on set with them for the second day in a row.

I let my eyes wander around for a moment, taking in the busy background; the stylists and makeup artists flutter about, getting all the models ready for their chance in front of the camera.

This is easily one of the biggest, busiest sets I've ever been on, and I love the energy of it all. I've worked with some high-quality brands and photographers before, but nothing as big as this. Nothing that could give me the chance to be on an actual Hollywood billboard.

"God, this camera loves you," Juliet tells me. "You're going places, Olive. I'm calling it now. If you're not in front of the camera in the next five years, you'll either be behind it or you'll be doing something else to take the industry by storm."

For the first time in a long time, I don't have to force my smile in front of a camera. I'm genuinely happy.

Not only because of Juliet's words. It's everything.

It's this shoot I've worked so hard to get. It's Annie's engagement. It's the whole last month of my life.

It's Jude.

Just thinking of him has me reminiscing about our video chat yesterday. His dirty words echoed in my mind all night, making me wish I weren't half a world away from him. Or that I'd at least thought ahead enough to pack my vibrator.

"I can't tell if you're excited about what I just said or something else; either way, keep it up because this shot is *hot*," Juliet instructs, still clicking away.

I'm not even bothered by the bright lights and the flashing like I normally would be at this point.

I feel good. Beautiful. Happy.

Alive.

Distantly, I hear my ringtone—Taylor Swift's "Lover"—blast through the background noise. It's loud enough to hear over the other music thrumming through the studio, even though I don't recall turning on the volume. I must have accidentally turned it on before it was my turn to shoot.

The song dies down, then starts back up again.

Who the heck is calling me?

I slide my eyes over to Uma, who has been watching with a proud smile.

"Yours?" she mouths in questions, and I nod.

"Ignore it," she instructs.

"Yes! That one!" Juliet says, and I shake my head, turning my attention back to what's happening.

I run my hands over the mustard-yellow crop top I'm wearing, then over my hips, loving how the pair of Good Jeans hugs all my curves in just the right way.

I let myself get lost in the swell of the '90s R and B bumping through the speakers and focus solely on what I'm here to do—my job.

I give it my all, heeding the instructions Juliet gives me, like *Move your arm* or *Relax your shoulders* or *Yes, more*, as the minutes tick by.

I have no idea how many shots she's taken or how much time has passed when she finally calls it good.

"All right. That's good for now. Let's get you in the flare jeans. Head over to Wardrobe." She sends me a wink, then turns to her camera to look over the shots, Uma right at her side, already nixing some of them.

I race across the room to my station, pulling my phone from the mini backpack I brought along with me, eager to see who is blowing it up.

I snatch it up as it rings again.

Annie.

Why is she calling me?

My finger hovers over the green button, ready to answer.

"There you are!" I look up to find Yuli, the wardrobe coordinator, holding up different options for the next session. "Come on," she says, tipping her head to the side. "This way. I think you're going to look amazing in the flannel. It's going to make your eyes pop like never before."

I glance back down at my still-ringing phone, torn between wanting to answer it and knowing that now is not the time. I'm working. Annie knows that.

Which also means Annie wouldn't call unless it was important . . .

"Let's pick up the pace, people," Juliet calls across the room. "We still have two remaining fall looks and all of winter to get through and only two more hours to do it. Hustle, hustle, hustle!"

Everyone begins moving faster, speed-walking from one end of the room to the other, grabbing clothes off the racks at breakneck speed.

I check my phone once again. It's gone silent, and I intend to keep it that way. This shoot is too important, and I can't mess this up.

Besides, I'm sure Annie is just having a meltdown about something with Remi or the wedding.

I silence my phone, then slip it back into the pocket of my mini backpack, pushing away all thoughts of it and anything else.

Today is a good day. A drama-free day. A day where my dreams are coming true.

Nothing is going to put a damper on that.

"Ah, come here. Give me a hug." Uma wraps me into a warm embrace, squeezing her arms around me so tightly my breath stutters. It's alarming, but not for obvious reasons. Mostly because she's hardly ever this affectionate, but I guess the shoot has her in a good mood. "I'm so proud of you," she says, and I can *hear* the smile in her voice.

Warmth spreads through me. *I'm* proud of me too. I've worked hard to get to this point, and these last few days in LA have been everything I've ever dreamed of.

"Thank you." I hug her back just as tightly. "Couldn't do this without you."

She pulls away, beaming at me, her orange lipstick nearly as bright as her smile. "You could, you'd just miss me too much." She shoots me a wink. "Now, get some rest. Tomorrow morning we're going shopping. My treat."

"You're on." I grin, never one to turn down a shopping spree.

Uma waves goodbye, then gets into her Uber, the one that's taking her in the exact opposite direction. She's rented a place down by the beach for a week. I'm going back to my hotel room, which still smells like Jude.

Jude, who I miss so damn much it hurts. He's gone for two weeks, and that's about thirteen days too long.

A white Ford compact rolls up a minute after Uma pulls away, and after verifying it's my ride, I hop in the back.

I'm blessed with a driver who doesn't want to talk, and after watching palm trees pass by for a few minutes, I pull my phone from my small backpack to do some work. LA doesn't hold the same appeal to me that New York does.

Almost as soon as I retrieve my phone, it lights up, Annie's name filling the screen. Again.

I don't even hesitate to answer this time.

"Hello?"

"Finally!"

I pull the phone away from my ear with a wince. It's so loud that even the Uber driver glances up from the road to make sure everything is okay.

I send her a soft smile and a thumbs-up. She doesn't return it, just goes back to weaving in and out of traffic.

"Well, hello to you, too, *Bananie*," I say, cautiously bringing the device closer. "What the hell was that for?"

"Have you been on social media today?"

"Why?"

"Just answer me, Liv."

I pull my brows together, not at all liking the rushed and worried tone of her voice. "No. I've been on set all day. You know that."

"Oh, thank god." She sighs. "Don't go on there."

"What?" I laugh. "You realize that's part of my job, right?"

"I know, but right now, you need to stay off it. Have you talked to Jude?"

"Not since this morning when he texted me. Why? What's going on?"

The silence on the other end of the line has me on the edge of my seat—literally.

Dread settles into my stomach as I lean forward, gripping the headrest in front of me like it's my lifeline.

"Why?" I ask again when she doesn't speak for a full ten seconds. "What happened, Annie?"

"You," she says. "*You* happened."

"Me? What did I do? I've been working nonstop for the last two days. I—"

My phone beeps, and I pull it away from my ear.

Uma.

The dread turns to lead, my whole stomach dropping out from under me. Uma shouldn't be calling. I *just* saw her. There's no reason.

"Hang on," I say loudly enough for Annie to hear. "Uma's calling."

"Liv, I—"

But Annie's words are cut off as I switch over to my manager.

"Hel—"

"You're viral," Uma says, talking over me. "Why didn't you tell me about this? I could have prepared a statement for you. I could have—"

"Hang on, hang on. I'm what?"

"Viral, dear." She laughs humorlessly. "You've officially made it— though I'm not exactly sure *this* is the kind of thing you want to be known for."

I grab my now-pounding head. "Known for what? What is going on? Annie's calling me in a panic, too, asking about Jude, saying things I don't understand. Just tell me what's going on."

Uma's quiet. Too quiet. So damn quiet that it's deafening, blocking out the sounds of the city passing by and even the music that's been quietly playing on the stereo.

The silence is so loud it's all I can hear.

So when it breaks, I jump, my heart racing.

"Your messages to Jasper Rafferty, Olive. They're all over the internet."

Her voice is calm. Collected. Which is the complete opposite of what I'm feeling, because now my heart is racing for a whole different reason.

Did she just . . .

"My messages?" I ask, though I'm not sure why. I heard her clearly.

But there's no way, right? She's not saying what I think she is . . . is she?

285

"All those DMs you sent him. They're all over the place. I would have pulled you aside during the shoot, but I didn't see them until after. Are you okay?" Concern is so clear in her voice, and it's the gentlest I've ever heard Uma be in the years I've known her. It's unsettling, which is unfortunate because this is already an unsettling situation.

"I . . . I don't . . ."

My messages were leaked? How? When? *Why?*

"Tell you what: I'll give you some time to process this and work on a statement—because you're definitely going to want to make one—and I'll call you in about an hour. Sound good?"

"I . . . Sure."

"Talk soon, dear."

The call goes silent, but it doesn't last long. The screen fills with Annie's name and face, but I ignore it, instead going straight to Google, wanting to see for myself.

Uma is wrong. She *has* to be. There is no way what she's saying is possible.

I type my name into the search bar and hold my breath as I wait for the results to load.

Five seconds later, I'm staring down at my absolute worst nightmare.

Uma wasn't lying.

It's all there, splashed across the internet for the entire world to see.

My diary.

My hopes and dreams. All my deepest and darkest confessions. Memories with my father. My . . . life. Everything.

My heart falls right out of my chest and onto the floor of the Ford.

I look down, as if I can see it lying on the carpet next to the stale french fry the driver forgot to clean out from under the seat.

Hi, heart.

I drag my focus back to my phone, navigating over to Instagram like some masochist.

More than five hundred notifications smack me right in the face, like they're saying, *Hey, this isn't fake. It's very, very real. We're the proof.*

I click on them, instantly regretting it.

> Did she really cyberstalk her way into a relationship with a Rafferty?

> Wait. If she's sOoOoOo into Jasper, what's she doing with Jude???

> This is cringe AF!

> Figures. She probably can't get a date, so she has to creep on a guy to get him to notice her.

> Definitely not Rafferty worthy, no matter which brother it is!

> So she's thirsting after one brother and ends up with the other? BIG ICK.

There are more—*so* many more—but I can't stomach another second of scrolling.

I click off the screen and set my phone in my lap. The Uber driver catches my eyes in the rearview mirror. She lifts her brows in a silent question, but I don't have any answers for her. I don't even have any answers for myself.

I squeeze my eyes shut, trying to block out her curious stare, the comments that are on replay in my mind, and the reality of . . . well, everything.

This can't be happening. This can't be happening. This cannot be fucking happening.

My phone buzzes against my hand, and I must answer it, because the next thing I hear is Annie calling my name.

"Liv? Are you there? Liv? Hello?"

I pull the phone to my ear.

"Liv?" she asks again.

My head feels heavy, and my eyes start to burn, tears springing to them, threatening to spill free at any moment.

"Annie . . ."

She sighs. "You're there."

I sniffle, trying my best to hold back the incoming onslaught. "I'm here."

"Oh, Liv."

There's a loud screech from somewhere nearby, so awful and raw it draws the attention of the driver, causing her to jerk the wheel.

"What the hell?" she shrieks, glaring back at me from the rearview mirror.

That's when I realize it—the sound is me.

That terrible, contorted sound is me, and my face is wet, tears streaming from my eyes as the reality of this whole fucked-up situation truly hits me.

"Ma'am, are you okay?" the driver asks, voice softening, but I don't answer. I couldn't even if I wanted to. My voice is caught in my throat.

So I don't even bother trying. I cry.

I cry and cry and cry, clutching my phone to my ear as the miles pass us by, taking me back to the last place I was truly happy. The last place I was with Jude.

Jude, who I miss.

Jude, who I wish I could talk to right now.

Jude, who lied to me. Who pretended to be his brother. Who knew about these messages.

Jude, who could very well be responsible for this.

I feel sick just thinking it, my gut telling me I'm way off. Jude would never. I know that because I know *him*.

But if it's not Jude, then who could it be? Jasper? They were in his inbox, after all.

But just like I can't truly see Jude being the one to do this, I can't see it being Jasper either. I didn't get that vindictive vibe from him. Besides, what would he stand to gain from leaking them—other than making my life a living hell?

"Liv . . ." Annie says cautiously. "Are you okay?"

"No," I answer her.

She sighs on the other end of the line. "It's going to be fine. We'll . . ."

"What?" I snap. "What are we going to do? Deny it all? Say it's fake? It's pretty damn obvious it's real, Annie. Nobody is going to believe me. I'm ruined. Everything I worked so hard for is gone in a flash. I'll never be known as something other than the girl who slid into Jasper Rafferty's DMs."

She doesn't deny it, and how can she? She knows I'm right.

She swallows. "Have you talked to Jude?"

"No," I tell her again. "I . . ."

She exhales heavily. "I know, Liv. I know. I . . . I'm so, so sorry."

Me too.

"Do you need me to come out there? I'm sure I can get someone to cover my shifts. I—"

"No," I interrupt. "No. Don't." I wipe away the errant tears still streaking down my cheek, take a deep breath, then say, "I'm coming home."

◆　◆　◆

"Olive, whatever you do, do not go on social media, okay? I . . . Fuck. I don't know what's happening. I don't have a goddamn clue. I just . . . I'm so sorry, Sunshine." A pause. "I'll fix this. I swear it to you. Just . . . stay off the internet. Stay out of sight. I'll be home soon."

I hit Stop on the message I've played no fewer than fifty times over the last twelve hours, letting my phone fall back to the bed—where I've been lying since I got back to the East Coast.

My Uber driver in LA ended up being completely amazing and sympathetic to the very obvious crisis in her back seat. Once we got back to the hotel, she offered to drive me to the airport, free of charge. I paid her, obviously, but it was still a gesture I desperately needed.

Especially given that once I entered the airport, I could feel it—the stares and the knowing.

No one approached me or said anything directly, but they didn't have to. From the TSA agent's knowing glance to the snickering teens at my terminal, I could tell they knew.

Even the flight attendants kept their distance, whispering behind their hands and not so subtly gesturing toward me.

The flight was easily the longest five and a half hours of my life.

I kept my head down leaving the airport, ignoring the almost-constant stare from the cab driver on the way to my apartment, and didn't speak again until Annie pulled open the door and dragged me into her arms, then right to bed.

That's where I've been since I got back to New York.

I've tried sleeping, but it's pointless. Every time I close my eyes, all I can see are the snippets of my diary plastered all over the place—from gossip sites to TikTok. And all I can hear is the desperation in Jude's voicemail.

That may be the worst of all this.

I like Jude. A lot. Way more than I ever thought possible, given how we met.

But this? The attention? Constantly being thrown into the headlines or photographed or stared at? My damn diary being leaked?

As much as I like Jude, I'm not so sure I'm cut out for this life. I knew dating an actor would be a challenge, but I didn't know it would be this cutthroat. That the headlines could be so nasty. That the comments could be so personal. That all the things I've worked so damn hard for could be stripped away in a moment, like what's happening right now.

It's a hard dose of reality I wasn't aware I needed.

This thing with Jude . . . If I keep it going, I could lose everything. My audience. The brand deals. This little corner of the world I've cut out just for me.

I can't take losing everything. I can't take something I love so much slipping through my fingers and not being able to do a damn thing about it. Not again.

I'm being given a chance to walk away before that happens. I have to take it. There's no way I'll survive it otherwise.

I press my hand over my heart to quell the literal ache I'm feeling. *Easy there, heart. I'll keep you safe.*

"How you holding up?"

I raise my eyes to find Annie standing in the doorway of my bedroom.

Her lips dip into a frown when I don't answer.

"Scoot over," she tells me, padding into the room. I do as she says, moving over a couple of feet to give her space. She settles onto the bed next to me, looking down at me with that same sad smile she's been wearing since I walked in the door in the wee hours of the morning. "You look like shit."

Something resembling a laugh flounders out of me. It's rough and raw, which I suppose is fitting since that's exactly how I feel right now.

"Anything other than the voicemail?"

I shake my head. "No."

"Maybe that means he's on his way here?"

I scoff, rolling onto my back, groaning at the ache in my body. "I doubt that. He's in the middle of a press tour. He's not going to bail on that to come comfort poor, poor me."

"He cares about you, Olive. Don't dismiss that so easily because you're hurt."

"Whose side are you on here?"

It's supposed to be a joke, but Annie doesn't respond to it.

I lift my brows. "Seriously. Whose side *are* you on?"

She throws her hands in the air. "Neither. Because there aren't sides. Jude didn't do this, and neither did you. There's no reason I need to pick."

She's right. I know she is. I'm just feeling bratty right now.

But I guess that's justified when all my deepest, darkest secrets have been spilled to the world and my whole life's been flipped upside down.

"I'm sorry," I tell Annie.

She tips her head to the side. "You're sorry? Why?"

"Because I wrote about you. About Daphne. I wrote about everything. I'm sorry your name is out there too."

She shrugs. "It's not like I'm anyone important. There are millions of Annies out there this could be about. And like half of those are nurses. I'm more worried about *you*."

"I'm fine."

It's a lie, and we both know it. I'm far from fine, and I'm not even sure when I'll be fine again. It won't be for a long time, that's for certain.

"Are you hungry? Remi!" she calls out.

Her tall, raven-haired fiancé comes sprinting into the room, his long locks blown around his head like he's just stepped off the set of a music video.

"What's wrong?" he asks, shoving his hair out of his face, then his black-rimmed glasses higher up his nose. "Something wrong? A spider? Because I'll grab my flip-flop and kill it."

"Those stupid flip-flops . . ." Annie grumbles. "Could you run down to the store for us? We need cheese crackers, two bottles of red wine, and whatever chocolate you can find. A variety of it. Think of it as a period kit."

He nods, completely unfazed by her request. "I can do that." His deep-brown eyes meet mine. "I've been working as hard as I can to find the source of the leak. We'll get to the bottom of this, Liv. You have my word."

He bows at the waist—because that's what Remi does—then promises to be back with supplies soon. Just moments later, the apartment door closes behind him.

I poke Annie's shoulder. "He's weird, but he's a keeper, Bananie."

She wrinkles her nose with a grin. "He is, huh?"

Annie's lucky to have someone like him.

I thought Jude could be my someone, but now . . . now he can't. Not after this.

"Can we at least admit now that Jasper Rafferty's DMs probably wasn't the best place to keep a journal?"

My body shakes with the laugh that bursts out of me, then it's shaking for another reason—tears.

They start to fall, and I can't stop them.

This is all my fault. Why did I think that was a clever idea again? It was bad enough when Jude discovered my messages and pretended to be Jasper, but this? It's a whole different level of bad.

I should have seen this coming, and I'm so mad I didn't.

"Shh," Annie says, brushing my hair out of my face. "It's okay. We'll figure this out."

I nod, even though I've already made up my mind on *how* to figure this out.

Before she can dive into another speech about how this is going to be okay, the doorbell echoes off the apartment halls.

Annie's brows pinch together as she stares out toward the living room.

I glance at the door, then back to Annie. "Who's that?"

She shrugs. "No clue. Maybe Remi forgot his keys. He does that a lot." She propels off the bed. "Be right back."

Her footsteps slap against the hardwood floor as she slips out of the room while I close my eyes, squeezing them shut and wishing I could be anywhere else right now.

No. That's not true.

I wish I were *someone* else right now. Anyone. I don't even care who at this point. Because I'm not sure if I can take another minute of this. It's pure torture. From knowing my diary was leaked to the pity smiles from Annie and Remi. It's all too much, and I want to be done with it already.

"Hey, Liv?" Annie says.

"Hmm?" I don't bother opening my eyes.

"There's, uh, someone here to see you."

"I'm not really in the mood for visitors. Tell them to come back later."

"Even me, Sunshine?"

My eyes pop open, and I sit up with lightning speed. Too fast, if the way I wobble back is any indication.

Jude, ever the gentleman, crosses the room in a flash, reaching out to anchor me in place.

I don't need an anchor. I'm being dragged down enough as it is.

"Easy," he says in that deep, smooth voice of his, which I've missed way more than I care to admit.

The voice I *will* miss.

I try to move away from his touch, and he takes the hint, releasing me, then sits on the edge of the bed where Annie once was.

I look to the doorway for her help getting rid of him, but she's already gone, trying to be a good roommate and giving us our privacy.

I don't want privacy. Not right now and especially not with Jude.

Privacy means we're alone, and I can't be alone with him. If I'm alone with him, I'll be more likely to remember all the reasons I like him and none of the reasons I should stay away.

"Hi," he says softly, lifting his hand like he's about to brush back a strand of my hair, then, thinking better of it, dropping it into his lap. "How are you?"

Anger floods through me.

How am I? Is he serious?

"How do you think I am, Jude?" I snap at him.

He grimaces, squeezing the back of his neck nervously. "Right. Probably a bad question."

"Yeah, probably."

I shuffle around until my back is resting against the headboard. I drag my blanket up higher, too, like it's some sort of shield. It's really the only defense I have at this point. The only thing keeping me from doing something stupid, like leaning over and pressing my lips against his. The ones I know are soft yet hard, and say the sweetest and dirtiest things.

It's all his fault too. How dare he come here, looking so good after such a long flight? His ash-blond hair is disheveled, like he's raked his hands through it a million times over. He's wearing slacks and a simple white dress shirt that's unbuttoned far enough to show off his smattering of chest hair. His eyes are puffy but still as mesmerizing as ever.

He looks like hell and heaven all at once.

"I came as soon as I could. I . . ." He shakes his head, his Adam's apple bobbing roughly as he swallows. "Fuck, Sunshine. I am so damn sorry. I don't know how this happened. I don't even know when this happened. But I swear to you, we will find who did this."

I want to laugh at his promise, the same one so many people have made—Uma, who is working hard on a statement. Annie and Remi too.

So many promises, yet none of them matter.

Who cares who did it? The damage is already done.

When I don't say anything, he dips his head, trying to catch my gaze, which has been focused on the blanket over my lap.

"Ollie . . ." This time when he reaches over, he doesn't stop himself. His finger slips under my chin, and he tips up until I meet his eyes. "Talk to me."

"I can't."

His brows squeeze together. "Of course you can."

"No, Jude. I mean *I can't.*"

He inhales sharply through his nose, my words really hitting him this time. "Can't what, Olive?"

Olive.

Not Sunshine. Not Ollie.

Just Olive.

I hate it and love it at the same time. I don't want to be his Olive, but I need to be if I'm going to get through this.

I blow out a long, slow breath, then meet his green eyes, which seem to be darkening by the second.

"Look, Jude, what we had . . . It was fun."

He shakes his head, dropping open his mouth to stop me, but I don't let him.

"But that's all it was," I continue. "Because I can't do this anymore. This life you have . . . this world of yours . . . It's too much. I was doing fine in my own little corner of fashion, and I can't lose everything I've worked for. I can't let myself be swept up in your world. I . . . I can't, Jude."

His shoulders sink lower and lower with every word that tumbles out of my mouth, and I war between wanting to take them all back and say them over and over until we both fully understand what I'm saying.

We're over.

"Sunshine . . ." he whispers.

"I can't," I repeat, for me and for him.

He stares at me, his eyes bouncing between mine. I don't know how long we sit like that—me pressed against the headboard and him looking like I just broke everything inside him.

It's okay. I broke everything inside me too.

But I had to. I had to because I've spent too much time building something for myself, and I can't let it continue to be torn down because of who I'm dating. It's not an option.

I'm not sure how much time passes before he squeezes his eyes closed, then nods once.

"Okay," he says softly. "Okay. I understand."

When he slides his eyes open once more, there's no mistaking the redness in them.

I want so badly to reach out and touch him one last time, but I'm too scared that if I do, I won't be able to stop.

Slowly, he pushes off the bed, stumbling two steps backward before righting himself.

He takes another deep breath, then pulls his shoulders back, but it doesn't do much. He still looks so . . . defeated.

I hate it. For him. For me. For us.

But I know it's what I need to do.

He turns on his heel, and I look away, unable to watch him leave. Instead, I count the footsteps he takes.

One.

Two.

Three.

Four.

He pauses, but I still don't look.

"For what it's worth, I really am sorry, Sunshine. I . . ." He clears his throat. "Goodbye."

Then he's gone. He's gone and I'm alone, hurting more than I ever thought possible.

This time when the loud wail pierces my ears, I know it's me.

And it's Annie who holds me, ready to help put me back together.

CHAPTER
TWENTY-THREE

Jude

This may be the absolute worst I've ever felt, and that includes the time I had chicken pox *and* a stomach virus all in one week.

It's been a week since I've seen Olive, and I can count on one finger the number of times I've showered.

I stink, I'm tired as hell because I can't sleep for more than three hours a night, and my entire body aches from sitting on my couch for days at a time.

I can't even remember the last time I peed. Have I had anything to drink today? When's the last time I ate?

I glance at the clock on the wall, watching as the seconds tick by. I count them. It's my new favorite game to play.

Well, that and counting how many times I turn my phone off and on to check to see if Olive's called or texted or posted or done anything.

How Many Times I've Looked at My Phone: 567

How Many Times Olive Has Given Me Any Indication She's Alive: 0

I've thought about texting Annie a million times just to check on things, but I haven't.

Olive said she was done, and I want to respect that.

No. That's bullshit. I *don't* want to respect that. Not at all. In fact, I want to run over to her apartment, bust down her door, and tell her to her face that she's a ninny for bailing on me.

But I don't do any of that either.

I look at the clock again.

Only forty-five seconds have passed.

I check my phone again.

I contemplate getting off the couch.

I check my phone again.

I think about showering.

I check the clock.

I roll over back into the crevice that's now perfectly formed to the shape of my body, then close my eyes.

Time for my daily three-hour nap.

◆ ◆ ◆

A loud pounding ricochets off every inch of my head, startling me awake.

When did I fall asleep?

I peel my eyes open slowly, looking around. The sunset bathes the apartment in different golds and oranges, shining in bright from the open curtains.

I really need to close those.

I push myself up from the couch, stumbling backward and falling right onto my ass almost instantly.

What the . . .

Am I . . . drunk?

A glance toward the living room table tells me, yes, that's exactly what I am.

I pick up the empty bottle of whiskey, rolling it around in my hand. Bits and pieces of the day come crawling back to me. After falling asleep around noon, I woke back up at two, then promptly checked my phone. When I didn't see anything from Olive, I finally put the thing to use—I placed a grocery order.

And by *grocery order*, I mean *liquor order*.

I had four bottles of whiskey delivered right to my door, and judging by the bottle I'm holding, I polished one off already.

My head pounds again, and I reach up to rub my temples.

Fuck, man. It hurts bad. Not just hurts—it *throbs*.

Ba-boom.

Ba-boom.

Ba-boom.

"Open the fucking door, Jude!"

Oh, cool. So now my headache can talk. I really am drunk.

"Jude! Come on, man!"

Why does my headache sound like my brother?

"I'm giving you one minute. If you don't open this fucking door, I'm busting it down. And you know I can. I do a lot of my own stunts, man."

I roll my eyes, then immediately regret it.

Even my damn eyeballs hurt.

"Forty-five seconds, little brother."

I groan, shoving off the couch once more. Every inch of my body aches with the movement. Muscles I didn't even know I had are sore. I want nothing more than to sit back down as I slowly make my way across my apartment, but I know Jasper isn't messing around. He's using his big-brother voice, so I know he means business.

"Thirty," he warns when I'm only steps away.

I try to pick up my pace, but I can't. Like literally, physically cannot. My bones are too damn heavy.

I reach out to steady myself on the wall, really regretting that last bit of whiskey I slung back before I passed out.

"I'd give you another warning, but based off that disgusting odor wafting from under the door, I'm guessing you're close."

Odor?

I turn my head to the left, lifting my arm to sniff, but I don't have to. The second I move my arm up, I can smell me too.

It's a mix of pine, whiskey, regret, and absolute fucking heartache.

I grab the dead bolt, turning it over. It's barely even unlatched before Jasper is shoving inside, and I'm getting my first look at an actual human in more than a week.

Now he's the one who's stumbling back, his hand coming up to cover his nose.

"Holy fuck, little brother. You smell like ass. Pure ass."

"Hello to you too," I say, my throat scratchy and sore, before turning away from him and making my way back to the couch at a snail's pace.

Jasper follows behind me, coughing and being dramatic, as usual.

I flop back down on the couch, which has shown me more love in the last week than I've shown myself. "What are you doing here?"

"Seriously?" He scowls, shaking his head as he stands over me with his hands on his hips. "What the fuck do you think I'm doing here? I'm worried about you. We all are."

"Why?"

"Because nobody has heard from you in over a week, Jude."

"That's not true. I texted you back."

"Yes, the middle-finger emoji."

"Proof of life," I mutter, sliding down onto my side and tossing my legs back up on the couch. This is much better, especially since the room is starting to spin. "Why do you care so much?"

"Because you're my brother."

"So?"

"And because you just had the movie you've spent so much time on come out, then proceeded to ditch all promotion for it and act like it means nothing to you. You're throwing away everything you've worked so hard for."

Who cares if I've worked so hard for it? Does it even really matter, if this career is going to do nothing but destroy my life? "So?"

He sighs. "Your mother is worried sick about you."

"Well, my mother is *your* mother, so you can tell her I'm doing just fine."

"You're lucky she's not the one here right now," he continues. He moves the empty pizza box—when did I get that again?—onto the coffee table, setting it next to the near-empty bag of chips and some melted ice cream that smells rancid. "I was barely able to convince her to send me in her place."

"I'm not scared of Mom."

"Well, you fucking should be. You should be scared of her and even Dylan, who has been blowing up my phone too."

"I fired Dylan."

Jasper rolls his eyes. "You did not."

Fine. So I didn't. But I've thought about it. Isn't it her job to make sure I make headlines for all the right reasons? To protect me?

I don't feel very protected right now.

Right now, I feel torn in two, and it's fucking excruciating.

I hate it. I hate it so damn much. I hate that even more, after working so fucking hard on that movie, I couldn't give two shits about it right now. Right now all I can think about is how much this sucks.

About how much I miss Olive.

"Have you talked to her?"

"Dylan? No."

Jasper shakes his head. "No. You know who I mean. *Her.*"

He doesn't say her name. I'm so damn glad he doesn't say her name.

"No." The single word comes out a whisper, like I'm even afraid to say it out loud, and I guess I am.

For the first three days, I had a lot of hope that Olive would realize she was wrong. That what we had was worth fighting for. By day four, that hope had dwindled. And last night, that hope drowned in the bottom of a bottle of whiskey.

Olive and I are done.

"She's miserable, too, you know."

I sit up quickly and regret it even quicker.

"Oh fuck."

I cover my hand with my mouth as nausea rolls through me.

Don't puke, Jude. Don't puke. The only thing worse than being drunk is being a sloppy drunk.

I inhale through my nose and exhale through my mouth a few times, working to quell the urge to make a mess all over the place. When the wave of sickness churns down to nothing but a dull ache, I remove my hand.

I look over at Jasper, who is watching me with lifted eyebrows.

"How do you know she's miserable? Have *you* talked to her?"

"Yes."

"What?" The word bursts out of me so loudly that even I wince. "When? What'd she say?"

"Not much. It was a few days after the news of everything broke, and I finally got curious about it and went to my Instagram, since apparently it was *me* she was messaging with." Jasper's eyes narrow. "Are you a fucking idiot, Jude?"

"Yes," I tell him honestly.

"Pretending to be me?" he continues like I never spoke. "Why in the world would you ever think that was a good idea? Why the fuck would you go and get *me* dragged into all this bullshit?"

I shrug. "She liked you."

"No, she didn't. She liked the idea of me. She didn't know me. And if she did, then she'd know I'm a rake and an asshole, just like the tabloids claim." He smiles like he's proud of it, and I don't doubt he is. That's just who Jasper is, and he's okay with it.

"You really are an asshole."

"Yeah, and you're a dick. Getting me caught up in this mess. Souring my good name. And fuck you very much for not telling me about this and letting me find out this way. If you'd have come to me before, I would have understood. Or helped you. Insisted you delete the messages. I could have been there for you, little brother. Cait too. That's what family is for."

I swallow back the bile that rises in my throat.

He's right. I know he is. If I'd gone to him about this and confessed everything, he would have called me a dumbass, but he would have helped me. He would have never let it get this far.

This is all my fault. The messages getting leaked . . . Olive getting hurt . . . All of it. It's all on me. I should have protected her better than this, and I didn't.

I deserve this hurt right now.

"I'm so confused about why you thought lying to her wasn't going to blow up in your face," Jasper says.

"It did. It blew up in my face big-time."

"How?"

So I tell him about everything. About the night I saw Olive's messages. About her confronting me like a total badass. About me winning her back and getting her to give me a second chance. About what happened while I was in London.

When I'm done, my brother rubs his temples, shaking his head.

"I think this is all my fault," he finally says.

"Your fault?"

"Yeah, I think I might have knocked you out a few times too many when we were kids, because that's the only reason you'd do something so monumentally dumb. Truthfully, I kind of want to knock you around again for it."

He'd have to get in line. I want to knock me around too.

I deserve it, that's for damn sure.

"Seriously, why did you lie to her?"

I shrug. "She was real."

"So you lied?"

My cheeks heat, and not from the whiskey still in my system. I reach up and scratch at the short beard covering my face. "Yeah, it does sound kind of ridiculous, doesn't it."

"Not 'kind of.' Completely."

"I just . . ." I lift my shoulders again. "I liked her. There was something different about her. She seemed so sincere. So honest. I liked it. You of all people should know how that feels, to find something like that. We live in a world of make-believe, Jas. You can't tell me that doesn't get to you sometimes. That all this shit we do—the fake dates and relationships and the perfectly set-up so-called 'candid shots'—it's all a fucking facade. I wanted something honest, and Olive was that something."

For a moment, I worry he might call me stupid again—not that it wouldn't be a justified insult—but he doesn't.

Instead, he nods, sitting back in the armchair and kicking one leg up onto his knee.

"You're right," he says. "Sometimes real sounds nice."

"Sometimes?"

He arches one brow at me that says, *Fine, more than sometimes, but I'm not saying that out loud.*

He sighs. "Really wish you would have told me about this before. So that I could have been a little more prepared."

He cuts a glare my way, and I wince. "Sorry."

He's right. I should have told him about it before. I mean, shit, it was his name I used, after all.

I guess I never thought anyone else would ever know about it.

Boy, was I wrong about that or what?

"Has it been bad?" I ask him.

"Eh. I got my publicist on it. Kyle's doing all the damage control he can and trying to figure out who the hell hacked into my account, but I'm really not the one taking the brunt of all this. She is."

That ache that settled into my chest last week grows.

I don't know how it's possible, considering I already feel like I have a permanent hole in my chest, but it does.

I rub at it, trying to ease some of the pain, but it's pointless.

"Has Kyle had any luck?"

"Nope. I've been with Keely for the last few weeks, and she has her people on it too."

"Keely? As in, Keely Haart?"

Jasper grins wolfishly. "Yep. She's hot, and kind of freaky in bed too. You missed out, little brother."

I'm not really interested in hearing about my brother's bedroom activities. But I guess I'm not surprised he's hanging out with her. They fit together. Even Dylan said that.

Speaking of Dylan . . .

"What happened with my publicist? I thought you two might have had something going on."

"I tried." Jasper shrugs. "Dylan didn't want me, though. Something about not mixing business with pleasure, which is a shame because I could have given her *a lot* of pleasure."

If the alcohol didn't already have my stomach rolling, his words would do the job just fine. I don't love the idea of him and Dylan together *at all*.

"So," my brother says, "what are you going to do?"

"What do you mean?"

"I mean, how are you going to win her back this time?"

Oh. That.

I sigh. "I . . . I don't think I'm going to."

"What? Pfft. Of course you are."

I shake my head. "I'm not. She said we were done. She said this life was too hard for her, and I get that."

"So she runs at the first sign of trouble?"

"To be fair, her entire life was splashed all over the internet."

"Hmm." He nods. "True. But, I mean, 'mine' was, too, and I'm still here. Loved your alien dreams, by the way."

I give him his very own real-life middle-finger emoji, and he laughs.

"Come on. I'm being serious. Tell me how you're going to win her back."

I grit my teeth, hating his question because it *makes* me want to win her back. More than I already want to. But I can't. She's made up her mind. Whatever we had, it's gone, and as much as that sucks, it might be all I have.

"Look at me, Jude."

My brother sits forward in the chair, reaching over and smacking my leg to drag my eyes up to his face. I reluctantly do.

"What?"

"You're Jude motherfucking Rafferty. Are you really not going to fight for the girl you love?"

I sputter out a laugh. "The girl I lo . . ."

But the word dies on the tip of my tongue.

Mostly because I'm scared if I say it, I might realize how right Jasper is.

Do I like Olive? Yes.

But do I love her?

Yes.

The word slams into my mind before I can stop it.

Oh no. No, no, no.

Love? This wasn't supposed to be love. This was supposed to . . . Well, shit. I don't even know anymore. But love? It can't be . . . can it?

But the more I toss the word around in my head, the more I realize how right it feels.

Love.

Me and Olive.

Me and Olive and love.

I . . . I'm in love with Olive.

I swallow at the realization.

When did that even happen? *How* did it even happen?

But that's a dumb question. I know exactly how it happened.

It happened slowly. It happened when she called me *Asshat*. It happened when she told me her hopes and dreams. It happened when she called me on my bullshit. It happened when I pulled her onto my lap and she didn't back away from the paparazzi. When she ran away from my premiere with me. When she called out my name as she fell apart around me.

It happened in all the little moments.

"You didn't know, did you?"

I shake my head. "No."

"And now that you do?"

"I . . ." I snap my mouth shut, my head fighting against my heart. She said she wanted out. I should let her out.

But that was before I realized how badly I wanted her all in.

No. How badly I *needed* her all in.

"I think I'm going to win her back."

The ache in my chest heals a little as I say the words.

I can do this. I can get Olive back.

Jasper grins slowly, nodding. "Good, little brother. Good. But can I give you a little advice, brother to brother?"

"Shoot."

"Take a damn shower, man. You reek."

I laugh, and it's the first real laugh that's left me in more than a week. It hurts and feels good all at the same time.

"I can do that."

"Good. I'll wait for you." He curls his lips at the mess on the coffee table. "We can go grab something to eat that doesn't come out of a cardboard box or the microwave."

I'm about to tell him I don't want to go anywhere that's going to cause a stir, but he beats me to it.

"I know a place that's super low-key. No photogs. We'll be good."

I nod. "Okay."

I shove off the couch, moving a little faster than before, the whiskey having worn off after the sobering realization of me being in love with Olive.

I'm nearing my bedroom when Jasper calls my name.

I peek over my shoulder. "Yeah?"

"How come you didn't ask me if I was the one who leaked the messages? I used to read your diary all the time."

"Because you're my brother, Jasper, and that's the kind of shit brothers do. This is different, and you'd never do that to me or to her."

And he wouldn't. I know it. I never questioned it.

But damn if it doesn't make me even more curious to know who did. I *have* to know who did it. If not for my sake, at least for Olive's. Maybe she thinks we're done, but that doesn't mean I still can't find out and protect her from anything else the monster might do.

Jasper nods. "You're right. I wouldn't."

"You might be an asshole, Jas, but you're not *that* big of one."

He rolls his eyes, muttering, "Whatever."

"And for the record, I wrote in a journal, not a diary."

"Same fucking thing." He waves me on. "Go shower. I'll clean this mess up. You've got a girl to win back."

He's right.

I do have a girl to win back, and I fully intend on making it happen.

CHAPTER
TWENTY-FOUR

Olive

It's been a little over a week since the diary-leak debacle, and things are slowly starting to get back to normal. I've showered every day.

Okay, fine, every other day, but still.

I've been eating. I've been journaling—the old-fashioned pen-and-paper way, thank you very much.

And I've even been working. Kind of.

I've not had the guts to go on social media myself, but Annie's been keeping track of things for me, and today is the first day I have fewer than two hundred notifications when she opens Instagram for me.

"Good news! Your follower count is down!"

I've never been happier to hear those words.

Annie bumps her shoulder against mine. "Look at you, Little Miss Trending Downward."

"What?"

We look over to Mrs. Hammish, who has made herself at home in our apartment over the last week. If Annie is at the hospital, then it's Remi sitting with me, and whenever he gets too swamped with whatever coding thing he does, Mrs. Hammish comes over to sit with me.

I tried telling Annie I was fine alone, but she wasn't having any of it.

I'd never admit it to her, but she was right. I did need the company.

"Nothing!" Annie hollers back at her, logging out of my Instagram so I can't get back in. She's now the only one who knows the password. Not that I want to right now, anyway, but still.

"You don't have to yell. I'm right here," Mrs. Hammish grumbles, going back to the scarf she's been knitting for the last year. I have no idea who it's for or why it's taking her so long, but she's committed to the project.

I can't help but laugh at the entire exchange. Half the time, the old woman hears things we don't want her to, and the other half, she doesn't listen to shit. It's a no-win situation.

"All right." Annie hands my phone back to me. "I've done my best-friend duties. Now it's time to go play nurse." She steeples her hands together. "Please don't let the ER be busy tonight," she says like a prayer.

She's been busy the last few days but has still somehow found the time to sit up with me and make sure I'm okay.

How I got so lucky in the best-friend lottery, I'll never know, but I am so, so grateful to have her.

This week has been hard. The gossip flying around me has been brutal, sure, but thanks to a few extra sessions with Ingrid, I've been working through that okay.

No, the hardest part has been missing Jude.

And I do miss him. So damn much it hurts.

I miss his corny jokes, his smile, his deep chuckle, those green eyes I could get lost in for days. I miss everything about him and then some.

I keep telling myself that no matter how much I miss him, breaking things off is for the best, but with each passing day, I lose more and more certainty about my decision.

I know it's just my heart battling with my head, but damn, the battle is getting ugly.

Annie gets up from the couch—my new home—then grabs her water bottle from the coffee table and heads to the kitchen for a refill.

"Do you need anything? I can have Remi stop by the store on his way back from the coffee shop."

"I'm good, Mom, but thanks for asking."

Annie flips me off, and I laugh lightly.

I haven't done that often over the last week, so it comes out sounding off, but it feels good to get *some* sense of normalcy back, especially since I'm still hiding away in my apartment.

That all changes tomorrow, though.

Uma, who has been a rock during all this, called earlier to remind me of a small shoot I had on my calendar for tomorrow afternoon. As much as I wanted to cancel it because people-ing is not high on my to-do list right now, I can't. My career is already in turmoil. I'm not about to pile "bailing on commitments" onto the dumpster fire.

Annie finishes getting her stuff together, then heads for the door, grabbing her trusty cardigan before turning to me with a soft smile. "You look better today."

"Thanks. I feel better."

Her smile grows, and she blows me a kiss. "See you tonight. BYE, MRS. HAMMISH!" she shouts, just to be a brat.

The old lady either ignores her or doesn't hear her. Who knows.

Annie pulls the door shut, laughing quietly to herself and leaving me alone with our eccentric neighbor.

We sit in silence for a long time. So long that I think maybe she's fallen asleep, if her closed eyes are any indication.

When I run out of the tea I've been sipping on, I rise from the couch, in search of something else to drink and to maybe step out on the fire escape for some much-needed sunlight.

"You lied," Mrs. Hammish says, scaring the crap out of me as I'm pouring water from the pitcher into a glass. It misses my glass by a mile, spilling all over the counter.

"Pardon?" I ask, trying to get my heart to stop racing.

"You lied to her." She nods toward the door. "The dark-haired one," she says, like she doesn't know Annie's name. "You don't feel better. You feel like shit."

I sputter out a laugh, completely caught off guard by her accusation. "I . . . I don't know what you mean."

But even as I say it, Mrs. Hammish's brows go up. She knows I'm lying again.

She's right. I did lie to Annie. I *don't* feel better. Not even a little bit.

"You miss him."

It's not a question, but I nod anyway. "I do."

"Then go to him."

"I . . . I can't. It's not that easy."

"Sure it is. You love him, so go to him."

I laugh lightly, shaking my head as I reach for a towel to clean up the mess I've made. "I don't love him, Mrs. Hammish."

"Hmm. Maybe not yet, but you were falling for him."

The words hit me right in the spot that's been hurting more than anything else—my heart.

Is that why this is so painful? Being away from him? Because there was a real chance I could love him? That I could be falling for him?

That I was already in love with him?

"Is that why you're running from him?"

"I'm not running," I argue. "I'm putting my career first."

"Bah." She clucks her tongue. "That's a crock and you know it. You're running because you're scared of how you feel about him. Scared to face it head-on."

Is that . . . is that why I pushed him away? Because I'm terrified of the way he makes me feel?

No. I broke things off to protect my career. That's what happened. That's *all* that happened.

"My diary was posted all over the internet."

"So? Isn't that the whole point of your little job? To post to the internet and share your life? Is that really any different?"

I scoff. "It's different. Trust me."

But the more I think about what she's said, the more I realize . . . *is* it that different? Sure, I shared stuff in my diary I wouldn't dream of sharing with my followers, but was it really such a departure? I post about my father all the time. I post about my aspirations—and about my insecurities.

Was it truly so different and scary that I had to walk away from Jude?

I swallow back the realization that maybe it's not so different, because that would mean that I lost him for no reason other than my own fear of losing something that means so much to me.

"Well, *trust me*, dear. When a guy like *that* comes along, you don't push him away. You hold him tight and keep him close. Those men are few and far between. And the chance to love that kind of man—*truly* love him—doesn't come along more than once in a lifetime either. If you love him even a little, don't let him slip away yet. And especially not because you're scared. I've watched you parade around this damn city for years now. Sometimes wearing some of the most ludicrous things I've ever seen, I might add. So I know you're brave. Don't chicken out now."

She turns her sharp eyes back to her project, immersing herself in it like she didn't just drop some hard truths I wasn't expecting to face today.

Hard truths I *still* don't want to face.

So I give myself a shake and return to my task.

I refill the water pitcher, then grab my glass and a fresh box of cheese crackers.

"Want to join me on the fire escape?" I ask, shaking the box at Mrs. Hammish.

"You want my old ass to climb out the dang window? As if."

I press my lips together, smothering a laugh. "I'll be out there, then."

"Good. Get out there. You're so pale I should have brought my sunglasses."

I lift my eyes skyward as I push open the window and climb outside.

"Don't forget sunblock!" she yells to me as I sit down.

Which is it: Get a tan or wear sunblock?

The old bird is confusing, always spouting off random stuff, like all the mumbo jumbo about me being brave and running from Jude.

She's wrong. About all of it.

But if she's so wrong . . . why do her words feel so right? Why does what she's saying make so much sense?

Why is my heart beating so much faster at the idea of loving Jude? Because it's such a crazy idea? Or . . . because maybe it's not so crazy after all?

I like Jude. But do I love him? No way.

Yes, I miss him when he's not around. And sure, he's the first person I think of whenever I wake up—and possibly the last before I go to bed. He's the one I want to call with all my good news and even all the bad too. Or, heck, even when I'm bored, with nothing to do. He's annoying as hell, but he also makes me laugh and smile and feel so damn good about myself that it feels as if I'm walking on sunshine. And he—*oh my god*.

"I'm totally in love with Jude," I say to myself.

Then, two seconds later, I hear, "I told you so!"

CHAPTER TWENTY-FIVE

Jude

How I went from having my girlfriend on my arm to walking my sister down the red carpet over the course of a couple of weeks is beyond me.

But that's exactly what I'm doing right now.

"Smile. Turn. Smile," Dylan murmurs from our side.

"She does realize I've done this a hundred times, right?" Cait says from out the side of her mouth, her smile never waning.

I laugh. "She's trying to be helpful."

"Well, please tell your publicist I don't want her help. Just like I don't want to be here."

"Have I mentioned lately how much I love you?"

"No, but please feel free to go into great, specific details about what an amazing sister I am. Then buy my baby everything they'll ever want in their life. Maybe even pay for their college too."

I shake my head, placing my arm around her shoulder, hugging her close and loving how she fusses at me for almost messing up her hair.

Cait scowls up at me, pressing the one little hair that moved back down, then steps away and onto the next marked spot where we need to stop.

After Jasper showed up at my place to pull me out of my funk, I slowly started getting my life together.

First, I called Dylan and apologized not only for bailing on her in London but also for skipping out on the rest of the premiere tour. I even let her chew me out for a solid thirty minutes without a single interjection.

She felt better afterward, and I felt worse.

All was right with us again.

Besides, despite me not showing up for all our scheduled press events, the movie still managed to break all box office records in the last five years, which I'm sure has something to do with her forgiving me so easily, but I'm not about to point that out. Especially when I know that a lot of this success has to do with the press Olive and I received and are *still* receiving.

And because Dylan is Dylan, I had to promise to attend this premiere for some new period piece I have no interest in, but it is worth it to have her talking to me again.

I'm not sure I would ever tell her this, but I kind of missed her bugging me.

Which is probably why I'm not complaining about it too much right now as she presses us on to the next area—the interviews.

"Remember what we practiced: short, vague answers. Smile. Flip the script to them."

I nod. "Got it."

She locks her hazel eyes onto me, narrowing them slightly. "You better. *Love and Arson* is doing great. You've had no fewer than ten scripts offered to you in the last week. You're getting everything you wanted. Don't mess this up now."

Her words hit me square in the chest, and the smile I've had plastered on my face falters.

The movie is doing better than I ever imagined. There have already been talks of turning it into a four-film franchise. And I'm being offered more scripts and roles than I could have anticipated.

But everything I ever wanted? She's wrong about that.

I'm not getting everything I ever wanted.

Because it turns out, Olive is what I wanted all along. She gave me everything I was always missing. She gave me something real.

And without her, all I have is this, and it's not enough anymore. I love acting. I always have and always will. But none of that excitement and sense of achievement I get from it means anything if I can't share it with the one person who makes me feel more alive than I ever have.

So yeah, the film might be a total success, and it might seem like I have it all right now, but I don't.

And until I have her back, I won't.

"Go, go." Dylan shoos us forward.

Cait and I step up to the interviewer—Becky from *Entertainment Access*.

Becky beams over at us, her smile genuine and not at all forced.

"Oh my gosh. I cannot believe I have *the* Caitlin Rafferty right now." Becky bounces back and forth on her heels, letting out a little squeal. "How are you? How amazing is this? Are you having fun?"

Becky points the microphone at my sister, and bless her soul, she takes it all in stride.

Cait breezes through the interview, answering all the questions with a smile. She even plugs her bakery a few times. It's flawless, and before I know it, we're herded along to the next stop.

That's how most of the evening goes.

It turns out Dylan was right. Having Cait here was a clever idea. She's the elusive Rafferty, so almost nobody is worried about me and Olive.

Almost.

"So, Jude," Gigi from *Just Hollywood* says, "how are things with you and Olive O'Brien? We haven't seen anything in about two weeks—not since the diary leak?"

I swallow, then try to remember what I practiced with Dylan.

"We're working through things."

"You're still together, though, right?" Gigi presses, and I have to fight the urge to rip the giant microphone from her hands and snap it in two.

Not just because of the question, but because of the giant hole that's still in my chest. The hole I know only Olive can fill.

The truth is, I still haven't spoken with her.

I've tried, so many times. I pick up my phone to call or text her at least once an hour, but I freeze at the last second.

I love her, but what if she doesn't love me back? What if she pushed me away because she realized she couldn't do this, not because it was hard, but because I wasn't worth it?

The questions are on a never-ending loop in my head.

"Oh my gosh, Gigi! I know where I know you from! Our parents were friends growing up!" Cait says with false enthusiasm.

And I know it's fake. There's no way she didn't remember Gigi right away, seeing as Gigi had a massive crush on Jasper until he told her that her name reminded him of a dog.

Let's just say it didn't go over well, and Jasper still gets queasy at the mention of hot dogs since Gigi filled his locker with them at the private school we all attended between acting gigs.

It was one of the few times I've ever seen Jasper embarrassed, all those sad, floppy links falling out of his locker without any explanation. He tried to play it off, but the poor guy smelled like hot dogs for the next week, the stench clinging to everything.

Cait—who I now owe tremendously—effectively takes the heat off me, turning the conversation to her and reminiscing about our childhood days.

Meanwhile, I pray the rest of the evening doesn't take this same turn, getting bombarded with questions about Olive.

They hurt too much.

"Thanks for your time," I hear Gigi say; then Dylan's hand lands on my arm, tugging me along.

Cait follows closely, and just as we step up to the next reporter, there is no mistaking that someone new has entered the event.

"Jasper! Over here!"

"Jasper! Have you talked to Olive?"

"Can we get a photo of the whole Rafferty clan?"

"Are you and Keely dating?"

"Keely, look here!"

The chaos pulls everyone's attention, all eyes on the good-looking couple as they strut down the red carpet, dressed to the nines—Jasper in an all-black suit and Keely in a bright-pink dress that clings to every inch of her.

They look picture perfect together, like a prom king and queen.

As if he can feel our eyes on him, Jasper looks our way.

His mouth drops open, and he points; then, in total Jasper fashion, he sprints down the carpet right to us, ignoring the lines of shouting photographers.

He scoops Cait up in a hug, laughing when she smacks at him, then wraps his arm around me too.

"Gosh, I can't believe you're both here." He winks because he *can* believe it. We literally just talked to him this morning. He's playing it up for the cameras. "The Three Rafferty-teers, back together again."

He squeezes us in tight, and I fight the urge to punch him in the stomach just because I can.

"Jasper, that's where you ran off to," Keely says, strutting up to us with a smile fixed on her face but fire in her eyes.

She is not impressed by Jasper's antics, which kind of makes me love them a little.

Keely tries to push herself into the group by nudging Cait out of the way, but my sister, the little rebel, doesn't budge, forcing Keely to find a spot at the end.

"Jude, so great to see you again," she says to me.

I nod at her.

"I didn't think you'd be here after the whole leaked-diary thing. Kind of weird your girlfriend has a thing for your brother, isn't it? Especially when he's clearly taken."

She tosses her head back on a laugh, and the reporter laughs along uncomfortably, but she's the only one.

Cait is too busy glaring at her, Jasper's too busy looking everywhere else, and I'm too damn busy being pissed.

In what world does she think that's an okay thing to say? She's been in this industry as long as we have. She knows better than to bait the press like that.

"Jude . . ." Dylan says from behind me, and I turn to find her with a tight smile plastered across her face. "Let's move on, shall we?"

I've never wanted to hug Dylan so badly before.

"Tell *Olive* I said hi!" Keely shoots my way, laughing loudly again.

Maybe I'm wrong but . . . is that bitterness I hear in her voice?

Is Keely mad at me for our fake date? Because I didn't kiss her?

No. That felt like a whole lifetime ago. Besides, none of it was real, and she knew that going in. She's not mad about that. She couldn't be.

I'm sure I'm imagining it.

"Hmm," is all I can muster as a response before I move on with Cait.

We make two more stops, and I'm asked several questions, but I can't recall a single one—nor the answers I give.

All I can think about is the tightness in Keely's eyes and the animosity in her tone.

It's still sitting in the forefront of my mind when we're ushered inside the theater.

Dylan and Cait head for the bathroom while I hurry for the bar.

I could really use a drink right about now.

I order a whiskey on the rocks, then rest my elbows on the counter, tucking my head low between my shoulders in hopes nobody stops to chat, because I am *so* not feeling it right now.

I want to get through this night, then go home and sleep for twelve hours so I can forget all about the questions about Olive I keep getting.

All it does is dredge up memories I'm not sure I'll ever be able to shake.

"I'm telling you, he's totally clueless, Whit."

My ears perk up. I'd know that grating voice anywhere.

Keely.

"Are you sure he doesn't know?"

"No way," Keely says, sounding closer and closer by the minute. "He's so dumb. Pretty, but dumb. He's basically a frat boy, and it's comical. He was clueless when I got into his phone and took those screenshots, sent them to myself, then deleted the whole text thread."

Wait a second. Does she mean . . .

The other woman, Whit, cackles. "God, you're so bad, Keely. That was *mean* to leak someone's diary. I'd be mortified."

No. No, no, no. NO!

It was Keely? Keely leaked Olive's diary? But why?

"Well, she deserved it."

"You're really still mad Jude didn't kiss you?"

"Um, yes! Talk about mortifying. *Ev-ery-one* saw him reject me. And for what? A few headlines that ultimately went nowhere?" Keely huffs. "Clearly, going after his older, dumb brother was what I should have done from the beginning."

"You gotta be fucking kidding me."

I lift my head at the new voice, turning to find my brother *seething*.

He's staring—no, he's *glaring*—right at Keely, whose jaw is sagging, her eyes wide.

The people gathered around the bar are now fully invested in whatever's happening, all their conversations coming to a screeching halt, their eyes trained on Jasper and Keely.

"J-Jasper! Where did you come from?" She looks around, panicked, as she steps toward him, placing her hand on his chest. "Let's go talk, huh?"

"Fuck no!" my brother says loudly, pulling away from her, his lips curled up in disgust. "I don't want to go anywhere with you. How could you do that to Olive? To Jude? To *me*?"

Keely lifts her nose in the air. "I'm not discussing this with you when you're being like this."

My body shakes with pent-up anger, and I'm lucky I have this bar to hold me steady right now. Is that really where she's going with this? Like this is all his fault and not hers?

"You're a real fucking piece of work, you know that?"

"Jasper!" She stomps her foot, crossing her arms over her chest. It's cute when Olive does it, but Keely? She looks like a petulant child right now. Like she can't believe that *he's* upset.

Jasper is right. She *is* a real piece of work.

I push off the bar, drawing my brother's attention.

"Jude, I swear, I didn't—"

I hold my hand up, stopping him. "I know, big brother. I know." I turn to Keely. "You should probably leave."

"E-Excuse me?" She looks around in disbelief. "You're kidding, right?"

"I'm really not."

"Have you forgotten who I am?"

I sneer down at her. "You do know who *I* am, don't you?"

"I . . . I . . ." She sputters out a choked laugh, looking around like she's waiting for someone to jump to her rescue, but it's not happening.

Nobody steps up. Not a single soul.

She scoffs, turning her nose back up. "Fine. Whatever. We're leaving. Come on, Whit."

"A-Actually, my date is over there . . ." Her friend points behind her, slowly backing away.

"Fine," Keely snaps, lifting the hem of her dress and stomping away, but not before sending one last sneer over her shoulder, directed right at me and Jasper. "Fucking Raffertys."

The crowd goes back to their chatter now that the drama is done, and Jasper and I exchange a look . . . then burst into laughter at the same time.

And that's what we do for the next few minutes—laugh. Long and loud. I don't know why. Maybe the absurdity of it all. Maybe because that's all we can do to stop us from ordering an entire bottle of whiskey. Or maybe it's because if I don't laugh, I'll do something else, like run from the building and straight to Olive.

Jasper claps his hand on my shoulder, squeezing it tight as we begin to sober up. It's one of those *We're going to be okay* kind of squeezes. The kind that says, *You're my brother, and I'll always have your back.*

Cait emerges from the crowd. Her eyes bounce between me and Jasper, both of us still grinning like fools.

"Hey, guys. What'd I miss?"

And we fall into a fit of laughter all over again.

For the first time in two weeks, I get the feeling that everything is going to be okay.

CHAPTER TWENTY-SIX

Olive

"I'm coming!"

I drag myself out of bed, glancing at the clock on my bedside table as I stumble my way out of the room.

6:04 a.m.

Who in their right mind is pounding on the door this early, and where do they want to be buried—because I am *so* close to committing murder.

I slept like crap last night, which isn't all that unusual lately, but last night was really one for the books after I had a three-hour-long conversation with my mother that involved a lot of tears. We talked about Jude, my messages getting leaked, and most importantly, Dad. We haven't done that in years, but all my journal entries dredged up some stuff we haven't really sorted through before, and though it was a rough conversation, it was healing at the same time.

I shuffle through the living room, barely registering that Remi is still awake, a pair of noise-canceling headphones over his head as he types away on the laptop that's balanced across his legs. He is so immersed in whatever he's doing that he doesn't even look my way.

Man, I wish I had that kind of concentration.

I check the peephole and am stunned by who I see on the other side.

I unbolt the door, then tug it open.

"Dylan."

She gives me a tight-lipped smile. "Hello, Olive."

"What are you doing here?"

Her left brow ticks up slightly, a small curve to her lips. "I'd like to talk, if you have a minute."

"It's six in the morning, and you want to talk?"

Now *both* brows are up, which I'm guessing means *yes*.

I swing the door open wider, waving my hand. "Come on in. I have a feeling I'm going to need coffee for this."

She brushes past me, stopping just inside the entryway to let me pass and lead her through the tiny apartment.

I head straight to the kitchen, going right for the coffee maker.

I grab a cup and a pod, then pop it in and let it do its thing as Dylan takes a seat at the counter, her back straight as a board as her eyes carefully track the room, taking it all in with her absurdly large purse clutched tightly in her hands.

I'm sure this place is a dump compared to where she lives, but I don't really care what she thinks.

The machine gurgles behind me, filling the cup with coffee, the aroma permeating the room.

I notice from the corner of my eye that *this* is what gets Remi's attention.

He tips up his head when he spies Dylan, then shrugs and turns back to his work.

"What can I do for you?" I ask when she doesn't speak.

"For starters, you can forgive Jude."

I wrinkle my nose. "Forgive Jude? For what? He didn't do anything."

"If you think that, then why haven't you spoken to him in two weeks?"

"Because I . . ." I sigh. "I can't be part of that world. It's too much for me."

She twists her lips to the side, nodding as she finally lets go of her purse, setting it on the empty stool next to her. "I get that. I do. But . . ."

I open my mouth to stop whatever it is she's about to say, but she holds up her hand.

"Let me get this out, okay?"

I don't want to. Not really.

But if I'm honest, I am a little curious what she's going to say, so I motion for her to continue.

She clears her throat, pressing her shoulders back even more. "I can protect you from all this."

I scoff, giving her my back as I retrieve my delicious cup of caffeine. I go to the fridge, pulling out my almond milk. I drop a splash into the mug, then scoop in two teaspoons of sugar before turning back to Dylan.

"I know that sounds improbable, given everything that's already transpired," she says. "But that situation was different. That was completely out of anyone's control."

That's what it seems like. Remi is still trying to figure out the source, but Hollywood is secretive when it wants to be. He hasn't found anything concrete yet but thinks he's close.

"We know who posted your diary, Olive."

Now it's *my* shoulders that go straight. "What?"

"Last night, at an event, Keely Haart confessed to the leak."

My entire world spins.

There's no way she just said . . .

"She was hurt because of that stupid date I set her and Jude up on," she continues. "He didn't kiss her at the end because he was hung up on you, and she felt slighted. So when she and Jasper started seeing one another and she snooped through his phone and found your messages, I guess all that anger came flooding back. She's the one who took the screenshots you've seen plastered all over the internet. She texted

Teagan Hunter

them to herself, covered her tracks, then sold them to the press under a pseudonym."

"You're kidding."

Dylan and I both look up to find Remi standing in the middle of the living room with his hands on his hips.

He shakes his head, his long hair swishing back and forth. "That would explain things. I found a name, but it went nowhere. Not a trace of the person on the whole internet. I had a hunch it was a fake, but I never thought to connect it to Keely Haart."

He looks as pissed as I feel, though I suspect he's more upset he couldn't find the person.

The Keely Haart sabotaged me?

"I know it's a lot to take in, but I need you to believe that Jude had nothing to do with it. And neither did Jasper. It . . . it wasn't expected, and it caught us all off guard. But I promise you, Olive, I can protect you from anything else. I can make sure you're out of the headlines. That you're left alone by paparazzi. That whatever other fears you're harboring, I can solve."

Her words sound sweet and sincere, but there's really no way to ensure what she's saying is true.

The world is too unpredictable for that.

"He's miserable, Olive."

"He didn't look miserable last night."

Because I'm a glutton for punishment, I might have convinced Annie that I was feeling much better and gotten her to give me back access to my Instagram account.

I then spent the entire night watching the photos roll in from Jude's latest red-carpet event, hence the crabbiness over the 6:00 a.m. wake-up call.

Jude didn't look miserable. He was smiling and laughing. He looked like he was having the time of his life.

Dylan points a long red fingernail at me. "That's a lie and we both know it. He looked miserable."

I guess if I'm being completely honest, something did look off with him last night.

Sure, he was smiling, but that smile never reached his eyes.

Yeah, he was laughing in interviews, but it sounded wrong. Forced.

And yes, while it might have looked like he was having the time of his life, I'm almost certain that's because he had Cait and Jasper there, cutting the tension and getting him to loosen up.

"He misses you," Dylan says, her voice much softer this time. "I've never seen him like this before, and I don't like it. I want the old Jude back."

I want the old Jude back too.

"He loves you, you know."

Maybe I've not had enough caffeine yet, because there is no way she said what I think she did.

"He loves you, Olive."

Oh god. She did.

"And if my intuition is as good as I believe it to be, then you love him too."

"She does." Annie steps into the small kitchen, her eyes still puffy from sleep. "She loves him too."

"Annie!" I hiss, but she doesn't seem to care.

"She's been awful these last two weeks. Barely getting off the couch, avoiding her job. She's not even been drinking wine, and she *loves* wine. She's heartbroken because she's too damn stubborn to admit that she was wrong to push Jude away. That while she's terrified of his fame, she's still in love with him."

"Annie . . ." I say again, but the bite in my words is gone.

Everything she's said is true.

I am miserable, and I am in love with Jude.

But mostly, I am being stubborn.

Can I truly be blamed? After everything that's happened, is it really that irrational for me to fear his fame? Or his reach? I had two brands drop out of contracts because they were worried about future scandal.

That's my business. My livelihood. Sure, one of the companies that dropped, I wasn't even *that* excited about working with. And yeah, my followers are going down, but I'm okay with that too. I'd rather be followed for my actual work, not because I'm making headlines.

Maybe I'm just being stubborn because this thing with Jude scares me. Not just his fame—though that is terrifying in its own right—but also the way he makes me feel. The way my heart races when he's around. The way I *like* that it races.

I never want to have my heart broken like it was when my father died, and Jude has the power to do that.

And I am absolutely terrified of that possibility.

"Listen, Olive," Dylan says, dropping her shoulders and losing the edge that always seems to be in her voice, "I'm not trying to tell you what to do. You're not my client, so I can't." She laughs lightly. "But if you want my unsolicited opinion on it, as someone who has known Jude for a long time, he wants this. He'll fight tooth and nail to make sure you're safe and taken care of, no matter the cost. So if you're scared, don't be. When a Rafferty loves, he loves for life, and he'll do anything to protect that love." She shrugs. "Think about it, okay?"

I nod, unsure of what to say to her right now.

She basically told me the man I love loves me back and that I should push aside every single doubt and fear running through me and put my faith into him.

She sends me a smile, then grabs the oversize purse she walked in with, slinging it back over her shoulder. She gives Annie a small smile and sends Remi a wave before making her way to the door.

The familiar creak echoes through the apartment as she pulls it open; then I hear, "Oh, and Olive? He'll be at Cait's bakery this morning. You know, just in case you wanted to go looking for him."

With that, she leaves, her words still echoing in my head.

When a Rafferty loves, he loves for life, and he'll do anything to protect that love.

◆ ◆ ◆

With a steadying breath, I tug open the door to Cait's Confectionery, the scent of warm sugar hitting my nose almost instantly.

But that's not what makes me smile.

No. It's the man sitting in the middle of the busy bakery, his head dropped low as he stares at a laptop.

Jude.

He's right where Dylan said he'd be, a coffee and piece of fudge beside him on the table. The mere sight of him after two weeks apart is enough to steal the breath from my lungs.

He looks the same yet different. A little worn and defeated—the same two things I see in the mirror every morning.

It took me all of ten seconds after Dylan left to decide she was right. Annie and Mrs. Hammish too.

I can't let this pass me up because I'm scared.

I've been scared before. Many times. Like when my dad passed away. Or when I moved to New York City on my own at eighteen, fresh out of high school. When I applied to Uma's agency. When I went to my first shoot, not having a clue what I was doing. Hell, I still get scared when I post certain outfits to my Instagram.

But this? Love? Trust?

I can't be scared of that.

It's too big. Too important. Too damn real. I can't keep pushing those things from my life just because I'm scared they'll bite me in the ass.

If there's anything I've learned, it's that life's too short not to forgive. And really too damn short not to love.

A low murmur moves through the crowd when people realize I've walked in, heads turning my way. I'm still not used to being stared at and talked about, but I guess it's something I'd better get accustomed to—and fast.

A gasp travels across the room to grab my attention, and I find Cait standing behind the sweets counter, her eyes wide and her smile even wider. Her belly is finally starting to poke out, and I already know she's going to be one of those pretty pregnant people, thanks to those damn Rafferty genes.

Jude doesn't miss the sound, either, his head shooting up, turning to check on his sister.

He follows her line of sight, turning back around, searching, searching, searching . . .

Me.

For the first time in two weeks, our eyes collide, and just like that, everything feels right in my world again.

Then he smiles, and I realize I was wrong.

Now everything feels right.

My feet move on their own, dragging me through the bakery and right to Jude.

He stands in a rush, pushing aside his laptop and clumsily knocking his knees against the table, almost sending his coffee falling to the floor. He catches it just in time, setting it back down on the table, then looks up at me with a crooked smile.

"Hi."

I laugh. "Hi."

He clears his throat, then lifts his hand, running it through his hair like I've seen him do so many times before, his biceps flexing with the movement.

"Uh, do you want some fudge?"

I tuck my lips together. "*That's* what you have to say to me? Two weeks pass, and you ask me if I want some fudge?"

He chuckles, tucking his hands into his front pockets, the tightness of his plain gray T-shirt apparent as it stretches over his chest. "In my defense, it's really good fudge."

"Is that so?"

He rocks back on his heels, looking extra cute. "Yep."

I grab the back of the chair. "Can I?"

"Yes!" The volume of the word startles even him. He coughs. "I mean, yeah. Yeah. Sure."

I pull the chair out, sitting down slowly, and Jude matches my pace, dropping back into the chair opposite mine.

We sit in silence for several minutes, staring at one another.

Me, because I can't believe I'm seeing him again.

Him, because . . . well, I don't know. But I guess the goofy grin on his face means it's for a good reason.

The crowd in Cait's Confectionery slowly turns their attention back to their own tables and conversations, scraping their forks against their plates, ignoring us like good New Yorkers.

Jude rests his arms against the small table, leaning closer, just enough for me to get hit with a wave of what's quickly become my favorite scent—pine.

"Hi."

I laugh. "You said that already."

"I did?" He shrugs. "Guess I'm nervous."

"Why?"

He shoots me a look. "You know why, Sunshine."

Sunshine.

The single word sends a blanket of warmth through me. I didn't realize how much I missed it until now.

"I didn't think I'd see you again," he tells me.

"I didn't think I'd see you again either."

"I hoped."

"Me too," I confess, because it's true. I *did* hope I'd see him again, even if it was just running into him at JT's. "Dylan told me you'd be here."

"You're stalking me through my publicist now?"

"You stalked me through my best friend, so I guess we're fair."

"Technically, I stalked you through your nurse."

I roll my eyes.

"That's a good one, by the way. The eye roll. Is it weird I missed that?"

"Yes."

"Well, then I guess I'm weird because I missed that almost as much as I missed you." He inches closer, dropping his voice. "And I really, really missed you, Sunshine."

I sigh. "Say that again."

"I missed you."

"I missed you too." The words fall out effortlessly. "So much, Jude. I'm so—"

"Don't," he cuts me off. "Don't you dare apologize. You don't need to. *I'm* the one who should apologize. I should have . . . Fuck, Olive. I should have been more careful. Should have eased you into this world slower. I grew up in this. I'm used to the cutthroat aspects of it. You're not. That wasn't fair of me to drop you into this and expect you to be okay with it. I'm so sorry."

His eyes—those gorgeous green ones I missed so damn much—shine with emotion, and I know without a doubt he means what he says.

"And to make up for that, I'm going to do something equally embarrassing."

He grabs the laptop, pulling it back in front of him.

Eyes scanning the screen, he taps the keyboard, concentrating hard.

He exhales heavily, then forcibly presses the Enter key.

"There. Done."

"Done? What's done?"

He grins over at me. "We're even now."

"Even now . . . ?" I shake my head. "What do you . . ."

Phones start going off at random tables in the bakery; then the stares return. People dart their attention between their phones and us, their eyes widening as they take in whatever is splashed across their screens. They lean together, whispering, their murmurs growing louder by the second.

Did he . . . ?

Oh no.

No, no, no.

I snatch the laptop off the table, pulling it over to my side.

My eyes search the screen, confirming my worst fear.

It's his Instagram profile, and each little square looks like a piece of paper, all of them containing several lines of writing that all start the same way.

> Hey Journal,
>
> It's Jude. Today, Jasper broke Mom's Tiffany vase. Yeah, we're in our twenties and shouldn't really worry about getting in trouble with our parents anymore, but my dad is scary as hell. Of course I'm going to worry!
>
> I wouldn't admit this to anyone else but . . . it was my fault. I shoved him.
>
> But I'm still letting him take the blame.

I grin, knowing that story well from Joel Rafferty himself. It's even better now, knowing it was really Jude instead of Jasper who broke it.

> Hey Journal,
>
> It's Jude. I met someone today at that coffee truck I love going to.
>
> She called me an Asshat.
>
> Can you believe it? ME!

Is it wrong if I found it kind of hot?

Probably.

Hey Journal,

It's Jude. I had a meeting with Larry Brickey today. We did a video call and I farted. Like LOUDLY. In my very empty, echo-y apartment. It was embarrassing as hell, but I think I played it off well enough.

At least, I hope.

Can you be kicked out of a movie you've already filmed? I'm the star, so I don't think it's possible, but who knows with technology these days.

Note to self: No farting on video calls.

Hey Journal,

It's Jude. I popped a boner in the park today because Olive was grinding on my lap.

I really, really, really, REALLY hope that paparazzi didn't get a picture of it. Yeah, I'm proud of what I'm packing, but I don't need the entire world to see my underwear and my boner all within one year, you know?

Hey Journal,

It's Jude. I took my sister to a movie premiere today. I'll totally never tell her this, but I actually had fun.

Fuck, I can't wait to be an uncle. I'm going to be the best uncle ever. Way better than Jasper, that's for certain.

Jasper, if you somehow find this and read this like you used to do back in high school, I'M UNCLE NUMBER ONE, YOU FUCKER.

I peek over the screen at him, torn between the horror and hilarity of what I'm seeing. "Jude, tell me you didn't."

"I did."

"Why?"

"All your secrets were shared with the world, so I figured it was only fair all of mine were shared too." He shrugs like this is no big deal. Like he, Jude Rafferty, didn't just post his journal to his Instagram for the whole internet to pick apart.

And they will. I know from experience.

They'll dissect every single word and create their own stories from it.

He's in for a world of hurt.

My shoulders sag. "Jude . . ."

"No. No *Jude*. I had to do this, Olive. You shouldn't have had to endure all that alone, and now you won't have to."

I shake my head at him. "You're nuts."

"Maybe. Maybe not."

"You are."

"That remains to be seen."

I point at the laptop. "Oh, it's *seen* all right. And it's about to *seen* by millions."

"That's fine. Let them read it. I just really, really hope they read all of it, especially the last page." He grins slyly . . . suggestively.

The last page?

I drag my finger over the trackpad, scrolling past every post that contains all Jude's secrets that I want to read, but I'm not going to. I'll wait for him to tell me about them himself.

Except for the last page. I have to know what that says.

After fifty posts, I finally find it.

I lean forward, reading each line carefully.

> So, journal, that's it. That's everything. That's all of me. Everything you'd ever need to know about.
>
> Except one thing . . . One little, tiny thing I haven't told anyone yet.
>
> I'm in love.
>
> Like madly in love. Stupidly, if posting this is any indication.
>
> I'm in love with Olive O'Brien, and I want the whole world to know.
>
> And I guess they do now, huh?
>
> Until next time . . .
>
> XOXO
>
> Jude Rafferty

I can't help it. I laugh. Hard. So hard I snort.

"Hey!" He chuckles himself. "Are you laughing at my love confession?"

"No, no. I'm laughing at . . ." I exhale sharply, trying to get it under control. When I finally do, I say, "Why did you sign off like you're Gossip Girl?"

He lifts his shoulders. "Kind of felt fitting, you know? I mean, I did spread a ton of gossip about myself."

I grin, shaking my head at the man sitting before me.

The man I'm madly and stupidly in love with.

"You know, there's probably going to be some other Olive O'Brien out there who will be *very* happy with this confession."

"I'm really only worried about what one particular Olive O'Brien thinks of it."

"Yeah? Do you have her number to check in with her?"

He narrows his eyes, trying to play along, but I see it—the worry in his gaze.

He's scared I don't feel the same.

"Hey, Jude?"

"Yeah, Sunshine?"

"I love you too."

His breath catches in his throat; then he exhales slowly. "Say that again."

"I love you."

"I love you, too, Olive. And if you decide to give this another shot, I promise you, I'll do everything I can to protect you, even if that means giving all of this up."

"Jude . . . no."

"I would," he continues. "I'd do it right now if that's what you wanted. The movies, the TV shows, the fame and glitz and glam . . . I'd give it all up if it meant spending another day with you. You know that, right?"

I can't even find the words.

I don't want him to give up his dreams. I want him to be happy. And I want to be happy with him, just like he is.

So I don't say anything at all.

I lean over the table and press my lips against his like I've been dying to do since the second he came home from London.

He's stricken for only a moment before he's returning the kiss with equal eagerness, his hand slipping to the back of my neck, holding me to him like he never wants to let go.

I don't want to let go either.

Not now and not ever.

Because this thing with Jude? It's real, and it's everything I've ever wanted.

He's everything I ever wanted.

And I can't imagine giving him up now.

The crowd bursts into cheers and applause. A few people even let out loud whistles. It's enough to break us from our spell, our kisses slowing until our lips are barely brushing together.

When I pull away and peel my eyes open, Jude's smiling like a loon.

"You look crazy," I tell him.

"Only for you."

I roll my eyes, and his grin grows wider.

"I missed that."

"What? Me rolling my eyes at you?"

"Yep. The good ones and the bad ones."

I shake my head, doing a poor job at trying to tame the grin that's threatening my lips. "You're so annoying."

"I know. But you love me anyway."

"I do, Jude. I really, really do."

Loving Jude is going to be scary. I know that.

But this time? I'm facing my fears.

Because loving Jude is worth it all and more.

ACKNOWLEDGMENTS

I've been writing since I was young. I spent a lot of time penning horrible fan fiction that will never, ever see the light of day. But it wasn't until 2014, after my husband went off to follow his dream of joining the military, that I finally sat down to write my very first novel. If he was chasing something he'd always wanted, why couldn't I?

I never, ever thought that years later, I'd be here, publishing my first novel with a publisher.

But, reader, that's what you just read.

Can you believe it? Because I sure can't.

None of this would be possible without a team of people behind me, and I'd be the worst person ever if I didn't take a moment to recognize them.

So here goes . . .

Henry, my husband and partner and the man who keeps me fed and reminds me to shower so I don't look like a bridge troll . . . I can't thank you enough for the endless support. You let me fall away from the world for weeks at a time, even though you know I'm going to act like a total fool when I go "into the out" again. Thank you for being my person. Thank you for being my everything. Thank you for letting me follow my dreams. I love you always. And forever.

My mom, who has always, always, always told me I'm capable of great things, even when I didn't believe them myself. I guess you were right, huh?

My father, who keeps track of every book I publish and always reminds me of it when I'm feeling down, pointing out to me that if I wrote all those other books, I can write the next one too.

My sisters. They don't totally understand what I do for a living, but damn, are they proud of me.

Aimee Ashcraft, my amazing agent, and the rest of Brower Literary. You took a chance on me. You gave me room to grow. You fought for me. *This* is all you. Thank you.

Laurie Darter, friend first and PA second. I'd be lost without your encouragement and kick in the ass. Thanks for being my sounding board. Feelings are super gross, but I love you.

Alison Dasho for championing for me. Krista Stroever for whipping this into shape.

Nina, Kim, Meagan, and the rest of Valentine PR. I was feeling so lost in my career, and then you happened. You came in and gave me direction while allowing me to be myself. *Thank you* really doesn't feel like enough for everything that's happened since I found you ladies.

Grandma Pat. You aren't here to see this, but I have no doubt you'd be proud as hell. You always were. I miss you terribly.

Every single Bookstagram post, book blog, and BookTok account that has taken a chance on me. It will never, ever cease to amaze me that you not only read my books but promote them too. Your power in this community is unmatched. Thank you for loving authors the way you do.

My Tidbits, my favorite place to hang out on the internet.

And finally, younger me. We fucking did it. And damn, does it feel good.

ABOUT THE AUTHOR

Photo © 2019 Perrywinkle Photography

Teagan Hunter writes steamy romantic comedies with lots of sarcasm and a side of heart. She loves pizza, hockey, and romance novels, though not in that order. When she's not writing, you can find her watching entirely too many hours of *Supernatural*, *One Tree Hill*, or *New Girl*. She's mildly obsessed with Halloween and prefers cooler weather. She married her high school sweetheart, and they currently live in the PNW. For more, visit www.teaganhunterwrites.com.